The Orion Affair

A Joseph Michael Barber Thriller

THE ORION AFFAIR -- SUMMARY

In the wake of a catastrophic terrorist attack on a beloved American icon, Walt Disney World, the President vows "never again". A new covert government anti-terrorist group is established, buried deep inside the National Security Agency. Its mission – stop the next terrorist attack before it happens. Their remit is to do whatever it takes, and there are no rules. Frightening new technologies are leveraged to spy on terrorists and everyday citizens alike in pursuit of public safety. And the government deploys a new and deadly offensive weapon against terrorists operating on U.S. soil -- a domestic strike drone disguised as a civilian aircraft to mask its mission.

Joseph Michael Barber, the CEO of his own security firm, Orion Bellicus, is drawn into the government's web of deceit and incompetence when he is asked to investigate the deaths of a dear friend's wife and children during a botched terrorist attack near Detroit, Michigan. Barber, the son of a Vietnam-era Navy sniper and a former special forces operator himself, will draw on all of his skills, training and the enormous smarts of the people working for him at Orion Bellicus to untangle the web. What he finds is astonishing and beyond his worst fears.

Mistakes are made, innocent people are murdered, and the constitution gets shredded as the new government agency becomes more focused on plausible deniability and self-preservation than protecting the American people.

From the distant mirror of the Vietnam delta to the Middle East; from South America to San Francisco; and from mainland China to Washington D.C., *The Orion Affair* delivers heart-pounding action ripped from today's headlines.

"Those who would give up essential liberty, to purchase a little temporary safety, deserve neither liberty nor safety"

Benjamin Franklin

"Men occasionally stumble over the truth, but most of them pick themselves up and hurry off as if nothing happened."

Winston Churchill

For Edith Tosh, without whose love and support this book would not have been written,

For Billy Machen – you gave the last full measure of your devotion long ago, but you are not forgotten, and your legacy lives in all who have earned the Trident while walking in your long shadow,

For Joey B and Donny B – you made my working life such a pleasure, and this book is my small way of saying "thank you",

For all who serve – you have made us proud and have created a debt we cannot repay.

Greater love hath no man than this, that a man lay down his life for his friends.

John 15:13

This book is a work of fiction. Any resemblance to actual persons, living or dead, or actual events, is purely coincidence.

Dennis A Tosh

Like I said, this book is purely a work of fiction.........or is it?

Acknowledgements

Many people have contributed to the successful completion of this manuscript. First and foremost, I wish to thank my wife Edith K. Tosh, without who's love, support and patience this effort would not have been possible.

Very special credit is due to my three editors. Sandy Horning, long-time friend and crack legal secretary, did great service in reading and editing the manuscript as it was being written, then completing the entire process again once I had finished. In particular, her contemporaneous feedback during the writing process empowered me to up my game as the manuscript progressed. Loretta Hitchcock, my cousin and retired English teacher, also read and edited the entire manuscript, as did James Owen Keefer, my long-time boss at Ford Motor Company. All three did great service in quelling my excessive and errant use of commas, too many adjectives, and miscellaneous grammar errors, and provided valuable insight on weaknesses in the storyline. Any errors that remain are entirely mine.

Finally, this project was undertaken after I completed a nearly 42-year career in Finance and Treasury at the Ford

Motor Company. I would be remiss if I didn't also acknowledge Alan Mulally, our (retired) Chief Executive Officer and a once in a generation leader. He put the shine back on the Blue Oval, revived an American Icon, and thereby ensured a comfortable future for so many of my generation and others, including me. It was a privilege to serve under his leadership. Oh, that leaders of his metal were not so exceedingly rare

The Cast of Characters

The Antecedents:

- **Albert Francis Barber (AFB):** Father of Joseph Michael Barber, Navy SEAL deployed as a sniper during the Vietnam War, life saved by his OIC (Officer in Charge), Lt. JG Walt Maxwell

- **Lt. JG Walter Maxwell:** AFB's commanding officer (OIC) deployed with AFB in Vietnam during the prologue engagement

- **Warren (Max) Day:** Navy SEAL deployed in Vietnam during the prologue engagement as AFB's spotter

The Principals:

- **Joseph Michael Barber (JMB):** Protagonist, son of AFB, former SEAL sniper & CIA Special Activities Division, presently CEO of his own corporate intelligence and protection firm, Orion Bellicus

- **Marcus Day:** Chief Operating Officer of Orion Bellicus, son of Warren Day, and best friend of JMB

- **Charles Westbourne Reynolds III ("Westy"):** Antagonist, CEO of private equity firm PrinSafe, progenitor of Progressive Dawn Advocacy Group, visionary behind Big Data Mining, the Sparrow Program, and Domestic Strike Drone

- **Ryan Jennings:** Special Agent in Charge, Intelligence Directorate, National Security Agency Department of Special Activities (NDSA), Special Agent in Charge, Project Sparrow

The Supporting Cast:

- **Jennifer Adams:** 27 year old executive assistant to Joseph Michael Barber

- **Allison Belinda:** Deputy Chief of Staff to the President of the United States

- **Donald R. Benson:** Executive Assistant Director for Intelligence, FBI

- **Jorge Bisongno:** Director, CIA Intelligence and Analysis Directorate

- **Dr. Lauren Cartwright:** Director of Forensics, Orion Bellicus (PhD in forensic science, Cal Tech, PhD in applied physics, University of Michigan)

- **Dr. Emma Clark:** CEO of QuarkSpin, direct report to Westy Reynolds

- **Dr. Trae Collins:** Director, NDSA

- **Sara Einhorn:** President of the United States

- **Admiral George Erby:** President's National Security Advisor, member of ExComm (NDSA Executive Oversight Committee)

- **David Ericson:** Director of National Intelligence

- **Brian Falzone:** NDSA digital Forensics Analyst

- **Emit Fields:** Director of the FBI

- **William Fitzpatrick:** Chief of Staff to the President of the United States

- **Amanda Green:** Assistant Special Agent in Charge, Intelligence Directorate, NDSA

- **Dr. Adam Johnson:** Director, National Security Agency, Chairman Excomm

- **Gerhard Krause** Deputy Director, National Clandestine Service, CIA

- **Eric Longstreet:** National Security Correspondent for the Washington Post

- **Walt Maxwell:** Son of Lt. JG Walter Maxwell, who saved the life of Albert Francis Barber, and fraternity brother of Joseph Michael Barber

- **Veronica Maxwell:** Wife of Walt Maxwell Jr., killed in the Troy, Michigan domestic drone strike

- **Emilee Magnesson:** Contract assassin, tasked with killing JMB

- **Sandra McConnell:** Executive Assistant Director, National Security Branch, FBI

- **Lt. Col. Julia Richardson:** Deputy Commander, Special Ops, NDSA

- **Edwin Rodgers:** NDSA digital Forensics Analyst

- **Dr. Margaret Schevenko:** Director of the CIA

- **Col. Jeffery Taylor:** Commander, Special Ops, NDSA, Directorate, Special Activities Division, National Security Agency

- **Allen Wellesly**: Homeland Security

- **Jonathon Wellington III:** Attorney General of the United States

The Orion Affair

Prologue

(Mekong Delta, Vietnam, October 27, 1967)

The damn insects were murder. Nothing breeds enormous bugs with nasty bites like the hot, humid environment of a tropical delta. Petty Officer First Class Albert Frances Barber remained quiet and prone in his sniper position, buried in the rotting vegetation of the jungle floor as a swarm of loud and hungry insects attacked him from every angle. He could have sworn that several of the flying variety buzzing about his face were so big they had the name of the helicopter company, "Sikorsky", on their abdomens. And, of course there were the lovely creatures crawling about the ground. Legions of those critters managed to crawl up into his fatigues and feast on what felt like every square inch of his body as if he was lying there naked. Thank God for the training. In spite of the misery he lay there silently and stoically completely focused on the mission as if the insects weren't even there.

The air was thick with humidity and his fatigues were soaked with perspiration as he lay there, hot and miserable. He didn't have to like it; he just had to do it. That mental reminder was a very powerful phrase that helped him survive many a miserable experience during the long months of training that brought him to this point. He chuckled a little under his breath, more mentally than audibly as he remembered how miserable he felt so many times during that training. That misery seemed like a picnic compared to the real thing, laying here. His instructors had told him as much. Not that he believed them. More Navy bullshit he told himself at the time. He believed them now. And he replayed that phrase over and over again in his head. He most certainly didn't like it. But he would do it. He would do it because that's what his new breed of warrior did. He would do it for his spotter lying next to him. He would do it for the Army Rangers he needed to protect with the badass sniper rifle he was holding. Oddly, he thought, he would do it for his wife back in New York and his young son, Albert Junior, who was 3. He realized that telling himself he would do it for his family was a bit odd given this was a job for which he volunteered. But he also knew that doing it well would mean there was a better chance he would see them again and not die in this God-forsaken place. And maybe that was true because his focus and skills would help keep him alive. Or maybe that was true because that God up there the Priests and the nuns of his childhood kept telling him about really did exist and cared about an Irishman like him. Or maybe it was some measure of both. Or maybe he just did it because that was the way he was wired. A man has to be whatever he is, and Albert Francis Barber was just not capable of giving anything his second best. Whatever the reasons he was here, he was focused, and he would do it well.

Petty Officer First Class Barber was a Navy SEAL, a new animal created by executive order of John F. Kennedy in 1962. They were born of the proud tradition of frogmen and UDTs of World War 2 who cleared the beaches at Normandy and so many other God forsaken rocks in the Pacific. He was an unconventional warrior for a different kind of warfare. And this most certainly was a different kind of war. Not that the ticket-punching morons up the chain of command understood that. There were many officers he respected, and he loved his OIC, Lt. J.G. Walter Maxwell, Annapolis class of 1965. That man was a natural born leader who cared for his troops and didn't suffer fools gladly. He knew how to get things done. Maxwell would be accompanying the Rangers on this mission as an observer. That was a joke, Barber told himself, because Maxwell's wiring didn't allow him to be just an observer of anything. Taking the observer slot was just his way of leading from the front instead of watching the action from an air-conditioned trailer somewhere in the rear. But the officer ranks were filled with far too many who had visions of stars on their shoulders. It seemed like the entire system was geared to them. Six months on the line, six months in the rear, then off to staff school or some other worthless endeavor when they were really needed downrange. It seemed as if the Maxwells of the world either died young doing their job or left the service because they couldn't cope. Oh they could cope with the combat, the harsh conditions, the heartbreak of losing men they loved, the need to order yet even more into the breach of a firefight and maybe their deaths, that's what leaders do; they just couldn't cope with the epic political bullshit, or especially the subservience to lesser men. He wouldn't do this for the morons up the chain of command. But he would certainly do it for Lt. J.G. Maxwell.

The Swift boat had inserted Barber and his spotter into Indian country about 48 hours ago. Their mission was to make their way towards a suspected enemy camp where an NVA General was believed to be getting ready to launch some kind of major operation. The fact that this guy was actually NVA made the wizards in military intelligence believe the possibility of something much bigger than a local operation was about to be launched. And boy wasn't "military intelligence" so often a contradiction of terms, Once there, Barber was to confirm the General's presence, then provide sniper cover for a small team of Army Rangers from the 101st Air Cav that would be inserted with the mission to capture and extract the General. The guy would be a treasure trove of information about the NVA and VC's operational plans. Some of the lads back at MACV possessed some very effective skills for eliciting "cooperation" out of high-value Intel assets like the NVA General, and they were anxious to find out what this man knew.

Barber's spotter, Petty Officer First Class Warren Max Day, lay next to him peering through his Bell & Howell M19 binoculars at the campsite.

"Ain't this living the dream, Big Al? I thought that nightfall might break this humidity a bit, but if anything it feels even more oppressive," Day whispered.

"No shit," Barber replied, "At least this should be coming to a conclusion shortly. According to my watch the Rangers should be on the ground about now and making their way towards this party."

Barber squirmed a bit in his soaked fatigues as he positioned himself to better peer through the scope of his Remington 700 sniper rifle. It was chambered with a 300 magnum to guarantee the flattest trajectory possible for the lethal package it would deliver. Most of the day the scene had been crawling with what looked like NVA regulars. They had spotted the General at least twice 5 or 6 hours ago, a valuable piece of intel they immediately reported back to MACV. Things had gone quiet in the last couple of hours after nightfall, but security continued to look disciplined and tight.

About 2 clicks to the west, a pair of helicopters hovered low as the small team of 12 special operators fast-roped into a small clearing. Along for the ride was Barber's OIC, Lt. Maxwell. Maxwell didn't have command responsibility on this op, that was the Army's job, but this was a rare exercise in inter-service cooperation ordered by the Man himself. The brass hoped the experience would help create better support of these types of ops in the future. Army Lt. Walt Hunter, the Ranger commanding the mission, knew full well that Maxwell wouldn't just observe, and he was happy to have another shooter along.

Lt. Maxwell keyed his mike and said in a low voice, "Hey Big Al, we are on the ground now and making our way towards the camp. Give me a SITREP."

Barber replied, also in a low voice, "Hey skipper, good to hear your voice. Everything looks quiet. Haven't seen the primary target since nightfall. We see six guards at this edge of the camp. They are obviously NVA regulars

– very alert, but don't appear to be apprehensive or expecting anything. Armed with AK47s and side arms. We don't see any heavier firepower, at least nothing that is obviously deployed and ready for use, but I suspect it's in there somewhere."

"Affirm. We estimate about an hour and a half to two hours to get into position. Any evidence they have sent out patrols?"

"No," Barber replied, "nobody's left the camp, at least that we've seen."

"Good," Maxwell replied. "Let's keep this net quiet unless you guys detect a threat. Under no circumstances are you to make contact with the enemy short of needing to call an abort. I'll contact you when we are close, then once again when we are in position and ready to launch. Each time I'll give you two clicks of the mike. Respond with one click. Also, under no circumstances short of an abort are you to use voice communication. One exception, I will ask for a final voice SITREP about 5-10 mikes before we launch the raid. Keep it brief – you know the drill. Stay alert. I'll be honest with you; I've got a bad feeling about this."

"Got it," Barber replied. In spite of the oppressive heat and humidity, "Big Al" Barber felt a chill at those words. Day looked at him and mouthed the silent words, "Oh shit." They had never heard Maxwell make such a comment before, and it was really out of character. Maxwell never showed bravado, but was careful to always appear upbeat. It was a measure of his leadership. For a man like this to be nervous was very unsettling.

The team of Rangers moved quickly and quietly through the thick jungle. The plan was simple – simple plans usually worked the best. Hide a couple hundred yards back from the forward sniper position and wait until about 1 or 2 A.M. to launch the raid. Somewhere between 1 and 2 A.M. eight of the 12 Rangers, along with Maxwell, would quietly push into the camp and attempt to neutralize the NVA regulars providing perimeter security. The other four Rangers, including the Army Lt., would extract the General. Once out of the camp and well on their way to the LZ and two exfil helicopters, Barber would call in an air strike and the two Air Force F104 Starfighters would NAPALM the camp and everyone left in it. Given its remote location in the middle of thick jungle, they believed the security would be relatively light. They were wrong.

Towards the middle of the camp, NVA Colonel Ho Le Chit sat at a simple table surrounded by other members of his command. "We have received confirmation that the General is now safely on his way to the alternate site. The Americans are monitoring the progress of their Ranger team from MACV headquarters. Our asset inside MACV has been able to convey real-time intelligence about the mission's progress. It would appear as though the Rangers are now in position and about to launch the raid," he said. "Our perimeter recon teams have the Americans in site, and we also have eyes on a sniper team about 50 yards west of the camp and are ready to take them out on your command."

"Very well," the Colonel replied. "I want to wait until they commit and are all within range so we can take out as many as possible. If an extra minute or two of waiting requires the sacrifice of a few perimeter guards so be it. It's important that we capture prisoners, and especially the two officers. It is imperative we capture the officers alive. They are the priority. Under no circumstances are they to be killed. I don't really care about the rest. Kill as many of the others as you can, but once they are in retreat do not pursue. I don't want our forces divided. Send a small patrol around their flank and follow them to the LZ but that's it."

It was now about 1:30 A.M. and the night sky was brightly lit with a full moon. Maxwell keyed his mike twice and whispered to Barber, "We're a go, final SITREP."

Barber keyed the switch on his radio and whispered in a low voice as he replied, "All quiet. No change. We have your six." At the conclusion of those words Maxwell flashed a thumbs up to Lt. Hunter who then motioned a couple of hand signals to initiate the advance on the camp. Eight Rangers fanned out and began approaching the camp from different directions. Barber and Day watched the Rangers' progress through their scope and binoculars as the team crouched low towards the guards at the edge of the camp.

"I'm starting to get that really bad feeling myself," Barber said, as things continued to look quiet. "It's almost too quiet here." Just then Barber looked through his scope and saw a Ranger use his K-bar to cut the throat of a guard, as Day saw another guard about 5 meters away drop from a K-bar in the back. As one of the Rangers took out a third guard by quickly twisting and snapping his neck, Barber and Day saw the team of 4 Rangers, including Hunter, slip into the interior of the camp to go after the General.

"I've got the same ugly feeling," Day replied, "this is looking too easy." At that very moment they heard gunfire start to erupt from outside the camp on both their flanks. Three of the Rangers dropped, mortally wounded. Another turned and took two steps towards the relative safety of the brush and was dropped in his tracks as 7.62 X 39mm rounds stitched across his chest.

"Holy shit!" Barber exclaimed. "That gunfire isn't coming from inside the camp, it's coming from outside! They are deployed on our flanks. This is a freaking ambush!"

Day responded, "Muzzle flashes from your 10 o'clock! Can't be our guys! Sounds like AK47 fire!" which he knew was very distinctive. "Fire towards your 10 o'clock and see if we can take him out!" Before he could sight in his rifle, they heard another AK47 report from a different direction, and Petty Officer First Class Barber felt a sharp pain in his shoulder, then another one in his side. He looked to his left at his spotter, Warren, and saw that a large chunk of his head was missing. Petty Officer Day was dead.

Lt. J.G Maxwell did not have command responsibility on this mission, but leaders lead, especially when things turn ugly. "Abort abort abort!" Maxwell screamed into his radio, "This is a trap! Fire is coming from the perimeter, repeat, the perimeter. They were waiting for us! I have command of team Alpha. Exfil to the LZ immediately!" There was no need to communicate with Hunter and team Bravo. Maxwell knew they were on their own, given how far they had likely progressed into the interior of the camp as soon as the first three guards were taken out. He was not optimistic about how this would end for them.

"Barber, you can't help us here. You and Day Exfil NOW!" Maxwell yelled. He knew unless he ordered them to leave that Barber and Day would stay put until all of the Rangers were out of the immediate fight.

"I'm hit sir," Barber replied, "and Warren is dead."

"Can you move?" Maxwell asked.

"Negative," Barber responded. "I've taken at least a couple of rounds. Get out of here. I can't stand, but I can still pull a trigger. I'll do my best to cover your exfil."

"Negative Albert," Maxwell replied, "I'm coming to get you. Try and cover my approach as best you can." With that, Maxwell turned to the senior Ranger NCO and shouted, "You've got command! Get your men out of here! We'll meet you at the LZ. If it's hot, then get the hell out of there and don't wait for us. Got it?"

"Yes sir," the Sergeant replied.

Fortunately for Barber, Lt. Maxwell had seen the report of Barber's rifle just before he was hit and knew exactly where he was. Within minutes, he arrived at the sniper's position and helped Barber to a crouching position. Lucky for them, the NVA troops did not seem to be following the Ranger's retreat and the gunfire had slowed. As they crawled away from the edge of the camp they encountered thicker jungle, which provided better cover. Maxwell pulled Barber up, slung one of the wounded SEAL's arms around his shoulder, put his free arm around Barber's waist and proceeded as quickly as he could.

"I know you're losing blood, Al, but you've got to stay with me and give this all you have. We have to move as quickly as possible. I know it hurts, but just do it. I'm going to get you – us – out of here."

"Why aren't we taking fire?" Barber asked.

"Shut up and preserve your strength, Al. No talking," Maxwell replied. "I suspect they have gotten their hands on Team Bravo and have lost interest in us, at least for now."

"I don't have to like it," Barber quietly whispered. "I just have to do it." He thought about his wife and son as he took each painful step through the jungle, and take those steps he did.

A very painful 2 hours later Maxwell and Barber emerged out of the jungle into the LZ, and to their amazement they saw a single helicopter quietly waiting for them. Barber had lost a lot of blood and was almost unconscious. At the side of the chopper's open door stood the Ranger that Sergeant Maxwell had put in command.

"I got four guys out on the first bird, sir," the Sergeant said. "The Chief Warrant Officer and I thought we'd stand here and enjoy the view for a bit and see if the two of you showed up."

"Anybody make it out from Bravo?" Maxwell asked.

"No sir," the Sergeant's face turned grim. "Haven't heard from them either. We waited a bit because we knew at least the two of you were alive and on your way, but frankly I was only going to give it a few more minutes."

As the three of them started to walk towards the chopper, the bird's turbine started to whine as the engine came to life. When they were about two meters from the door, gunfire rang out from the edge of the clearing.

"LZ is hot!" screamed the Sergeant as he literally leaped into the doorway and prepared to help Maxwell lift Barber in. Barber was now almost unconscious from the loss of blood and incapable of standing. Maxwell picked him up and draped him over his shoulder like a sack of potatoes and muscled him the last few feet to the door. As the Lieutenant made a strained heave of Barber's body to lift him onto the chopper floor, an AK47 round penetrated Maxwell's lower back. The round blasted his spine, and the explosion of bone fragments tore a large hole in his abdominal aorta. For a moment he was still standing and conscious, but for all practical purposes he was already dead. As Maxwell started to drop, the Ranger Sergeant lunged forward, grabbed Barber and pulled him into the helicopter's hold. He then jumped out, grabbed

Maxwell, and pushed his lifeless form onto the platform where he had just been crouching. As he jumped back into the chopper, he too was hit with an AK47 round in this left shoulder, but not before he managed to get most of his mass back inside the bird and scream at the pilot to get out of Dodge.

* * * * *

OIC Lt. Walter Maxwell would receive the Navy Cross, posthumously, for saving Barber's life, as well as a Purple Heart. He also would leave behind a young son. First Sergeant Eric Johnson would receive a Silver Star and a Purple Heart and go on to serve another 15 years in the 101st Airborne. 1st Lt. Walt Hunter, 101st=
Airborne, would spend 5 years in an NVA POW camp north of Hanoi before dying in captivity from his interrogations. He would reveal no important secrets.

Petty Officer First Class Albert Francis Barber's physical scars would heal, although many emotional scars would remain. He would leave the Navy after his physical rehab, go back to New Jersey, start a construction company and raise his family. A second son, Joseph Michael, or "Joe-Joe" as his mother would call him, was born in 1973. By a remarkable turn of fate, the paths of the Barbers and the Maxwells would cross again, in another life, in a manner that neither of the principals could have imagined.

Walt Disney World, Orlando Florida – 45 Years Later

The carnage was unimaginable. At 12:05 PM the Cessna Skylane began a rapid descent towards Cinderella's castle in the middle of the Magic Kingdom theme park. A pair of F15 Eagles from the 125st fighter wing of the Florida Air National Guard was scrambled out of Jacksonville as soon as the

28

Cessna entered the restricted airspace and refused to answer warnings from air traffic control. It would be all over before the jets arrived on station. The Skylane's descent morphed into a sharp dive as the castle came into the pilot's view, and just over a minute later it crashed into the heart of the crowded attraction detonating 200 pounds of plastic explosives that were strapped into the right-hand seat. At the moment of impact the explosion itself, besides its primary destructive effect, also was a signal to numerous other martyrs spread throughout the theme park to detonate the smaller explosive packages in their backpacks. Each of them had strategically positioned themselves in crowded areas and key attractions to ensure maximum effect in terms of both human casualties and symbolic destruction. This den of iniquity was an affront to Allah, and it had to be destroyed. September 11, 2011 would see almost as much death as the attack a decade earlier, and coming at a time when the World Trade Center carnage had become a distant memory and people felt largely safe. It scarred the American psyche in a deeply profound manner. Images of dead children and young families tended to do that. Al-Qaeda immediately claimed credit, and warned the West that the attacks had just begun. Oddly, a second group, that referred to itself as The Islamic State, also claimed credit. Little was known about the second group at the time of the attack, and their claims were largely dismissed as those of a rival, and much lesser faction vying for power.

The public response was beyond measure. People of all persuasions demanded action. There were even discussions about a nuclear attack against Al-Qaeda strongholds in the Middle East. Fortunately calmer heads prevailed. But people still demanded action. The Republican administration was widely blamed for a lack of diligence, and both the President and Vice President were swiftly impeached and convicted in what almost appeared as a Congressional mob action.

Ironically, the Democratic Speaker of the House was sworn in as President, given that position's place in the Constitutional Succession Plan. Newly elevated President Sara Einhorn found herself in a position to which she had never aspired. As the most powerful Speaker of the House in several generations, she reveled in the role of being a thorn in the side of the Administration. But she was now the "side" and no longer the "thorn". Others would take the mantle of her former role with her now the target, and she didn't relish the prospect. The daughter of a Hispanic mother and a German Jewish father, she had married the son of an Orthodox Czech Jew. But neither she nor her husband ever showed the slightest interest in anything remotely religious, much to the consternation of his family who was never enamored of the marriage to begin with. Elected to the House from a safe, highly progressive district in Northern California, she could say and do almost anything she wanted. Nobody could touch her. And she had powerful friends in high places and access to vast campaign funding that made her a force to be feared and reckoned with. Her grip on the Speakership had been iron clad, as the corpses of many a ruined political career could attest. All of that was gone now. Now she would have to appeal to a much broader constituency, much of which she actually detested. Fate can play cruel tricks, she told herself, and that realization made her already mercurial personality and volcanic temper even more dangerous to anyone attempting to cross her.

The new President was under enormous pressure to do something. A military response was not in her nature, and she had spent most of the last ten years criticizing previous administrations' military adventures, as she called them. But she was smart enough to know that doing nothing was not an option. She had a profound mistrust of most of the military and intelligence establishment, but she had a special relationship with her Chief of Staff, William Fitzpatrick, whom she trusted completely. He told her he had a plan. He needed her to sign a Presidential Finding to authorize it, and mentioned that for the plan to work, it had to be kept the most closely guarded of secrets, need to know only. And, he emphasized the point that nobody in the Congress had a need to know, at least not at this point. She had been one of the most powerful Speakers of the House in decades, but in reality she held most of her colleagues in utter contempt. They were her "lessers", and to be tolerated only in so far as it was necessary to accomplish results. She could charm a colleague with the almost narcotic effect of a Siren if she needed something, or could verbally disembowel anyone who crossed her. She was not respected as much as she was feared. She liked to feign a sense of humor, and kept a sign on her desk that read, "If you have them by the balls, their hearts and minds will soon follow". But people knew it was no idle joke. She coveted the Presidency, but knew her personality and public persona would keep it out of reach. At her best, she couldn't appear on television without coming across as the nun that was about to wrap your knuckles. At her worst, she was the Wicked Witch of the West. But fate had handed her the Presidency, and though even she was greatly saddened by the reasons, she would exploit present circumstances to the maximum advantage. What she craved was a legacy like none other, and she would do anything – anything to accomplish it. She therefore embraced the secrecy of the plan completely, especially the part that kept most of the details from her. Plausible deniability was a wonderful thing. And so was having a Chief of Staff who would fall on his sword for her. So a plan was hatched. And what a plan it   was.

Chapter 1 – The Terrible Swift Sword

Present Day – Undisclosed Location

Forty-two-year old United States Air Force bird Colonel Jeffery Taylor stood ramrod straight in the CNC of his new command, Operations Directorate, Special Activities Division, National Security Agency. His six-foot four-inch frame was dressed in an impeccably tailored Brooks Brothers navy blue suit, with a rep tie and a no-iron, cotton white French-cuffed dress shirt that retained the appearance of being freshly pressed regardless of whether he removed his suit jacket, which wasn't often. His secondment from the Air Force to the National Intelligence Service brought the expectation that in most circumstances he would be dressed in civilian attire and not the uniform of an active duty Air Force Officer. There are times appearing low key can be an advantage. The suit jacket was tailored with a bit of extra room at about 4 o'clock on the right-hand side of his waist, to accommodate a Glock 43, a compact 9 mm pistol loaded with specialized 43 grain jacketed hollow point ammunition for increased stopping power over standard ammunition. His command required him to be armed at all times, not for fear of falling victim to some random street crime but because his responsibilities made him a high value target to many enemies of the State, both foreign and domestic. Considerable practice enabled him to draw and fire the weapon in slightly less than a second, and he could put an entire magazine in a two-inch group at 10 yards. Third in his class at the Air Force Academy, Colonel Taylor, who came by that title via an early promotion "below the zone", was a combat veteran who flew F16s in Desert Storm and Kosovo, transitioned to F117A stealth fighters and flew in Operation Iraqi Freedom. He was a distinguished graduate of the National War College and completed an MBA at the Harvard Business School, second in his class. He had checked the most impressive list of tactical, command and education assignments of any officer his age, short of a Ph.D., and had excelled at every one of them. If ever an officer was destined for two, three, or even four stars, it was Colonel Taylor, and he had the reasonable expectation that a successful completion of this assignment would likely bring his first.

There was another attribute Colonel Taylor possessed, however, that was even more important than his intellect, combat experience, or command presence. He had an iron will and a commitment to the mission that would motivate him to drive through any conceivable obstacle and endure any conceivable hardship to complete it. This was once again confirmed as he passed the most arduous vetting process for this assignment that any U.S. military officer had ever experienced. During the "enhanced" portion of his vetting, he was water boarded and subjected to other forms of enhanced interrogation techniques that had yet to make it into the press. His "final exam" was an evolution designed to trick him into thinking a mistake had been made and that his life was in real jeopardy. He had passed. It was clear that this man was prepared to die and even to sacrifice members of his family before giving up a secret. It is said that every man has his breaking point, and Colonel Taylor no doubt had his. But the best and brightest in the business had done everything short of actually disabling or killing him, and they couldn't find it. And during the entire process he had no idea what assignment he was being evaluated for, which made his responses all the more impressive. The term "above reproach" was often used and seldom deserved, but Colonel Taylor exemplified it. That is what brought him to this particular place at this particular moment in time. That attribute had implications, however, that later would prove, well, interesting to say the least.

His command had gone operational two months ago. Today was the first time he was called upon to execute an actual mission. This was not an exercise; this was real, and its new Commander was determined it would be flawless. Colonel Taylor, call sign "Westwood One", stood in front of a board

34

with a series of displays designed to provide a comprehensive situational awareness of the mission. Half a dozen individuals sat at consoles directly in front of and slightly below the Commander's station. It actually looked a bit like a scaled down version of NASA's Mission Control. Taylor wore a Bose noise cancelling tactical headset, with a single earpiece similar to what was worn by an NFL head coach on the sidelines, and a small boom mike that wrapped around the right-hand side. This configuration allowed him to communicate with his assets in the field as well as have an open ear to communicate informally with others in the CNC, or "off-net", as it was called. In the center of the board were two 81-inch high definition displays mounted side by side. Both were labeled "AIRCRAFT", with the one on the left also labeled "PILOT VIEW" and the one on the right labeled "TARGET VIEW". The PILOT VIEW screen showed an aerial view of what appeared to be a four-lane road with light traffic. Although the GPS coordinates appeared at the bottom of the screen and would be captured in the digital recording, it was impossible to tell where the road was from the view itself. It did appear, however, to be in a reasonably developed area, which at least ruled out Third World. Colonel Taylor, of course, knew exactly where the road was. And that troubled him somewhat. The "TARGET VIEW" display on the right was a tightly zoomed view of a black SUV of some sort that was progressing down the road. The vehicle filled up most of the display, and there was a red cross hair in the middle of the vehicle's roof. Two hours ago Colonel Taylor had received the orders to take his command to an alert status called "cocked pistol", which, borrowed from the U.S. Strategic Forces Defense Readiness Codes, meant a terrorist attack on U.S. soil was imminent. This wasn't supposed to be, as they had received intelligence they thought would enable them to neutralize the threat at least 24 hours in advance, but here they were. The attack had obviously been accelerated, and Colonel Taylor's team was ordered to stop it.

Downtown Riyadh, Saudi Kingdom, earlier that morning

35

Aalim Mohamed walked out onto the balcony of his Riyadh high rise and surveyed the skyline of the capital city of Saudi Arabia, as was part of his normal morning routine. He loved the meaning of his first name, which in Arabic meant "religious scholar", although it was not exactly a moniker he wore by way of merit. His luxury apartment was one of the perks of being a member of the large, extended royal family, although he was not exactly in the line of succession and arguably was a lesser among equals. The fire of Islam, however, consumed his being. After a fairly self-indulgent lifestyle while mostly abroad at University, in both Germany and the United States, he fell under the spell of a charismatic Yemeni-born cleric who had radicalized him and led him to his path of righteousness. And with Aalim's financial resources, connections and influence it would not be the path of a martyr – no, far more important things were part of his destiny. He burned with anger as he absorbed the teachings of his mentor and contemplated how greatly his family had failed in their holy trust, protectors of the faithful, of Mecca and Medina, of the sacred Muslim lands. And how they had allowed their own privilege, their pride for their kingdom, and station as a royal family to dismiss what he now understood to be the true vision of Islam and the establishment of the caliphate. But this was a good day, Allah u Akbar, as he would restore at least some small measure of his family's honor. He pulled a small burn phone from his pocket, retrieved the call list, and typed a simple two-letter text, then pressed send. A simple text, "Go", appeared on a select number of cell phones thousands of miles away. With that text, six different cells, six groups of brothers, four each, with lives dedicated to Jihad, literally, were given the green light for their missions. What a glorious day. The infidel's world was about to come crashing down. Each team, working independently, completely unaware of even the existence of the other cells, was going to achieve life's highest ambition of martyrdom. Soon they would be in the arms of 72 virgins, a just reward for such a glorious endeavor, striking at the heart of the unbeliever's decadent obsession with self-indulgence, hedonism, and disrespect for Allah. These fools, these unbelievers, who listened to their music, who watched their sick movies, whose wives and daughters disgraced them with their immoral dress and uncovered heads, who drank alcohol and ate the flesh of unclean animals, would pay the price for their wickedness and their desecration of Muslim lands. How little these fools understood, their naive belief that Islam was a religion of peace. The attack would help them understand Islam was really a religion of submission – complete, immediate and unquestioned submission to Allah in every aspect of one's life. Submission is what is required, complete submission is the only road to Paradise, the only behavior that Allah respects, demands, the only way to peace. Without complete and unquestioned submission there was only one possible and just outcome – death and eternal damnation. Death, to be delivered by the hands of the faithful, and what a glorious endeavor, what a righteous endeavor, what a joyous act to spill the blood of these infidels; to see them suffer and writhe in pain; to see the fear in their eyes as they realized the fate they were about to endure from which there was no possible escape. Submission, submission, submission; offer the choice, and let the response to the choice be swift and decisive – the embrace of a brother, or apply the terrible swift sword, figuratively or literally, in as terrifying and violent way as possible. Not only as just vengeance, but also that others may learn and come to follow the path of the Prophet. For Islam was not only a religion of submission, it was also one of conquest. It was that simple. Of course, the fact that submission was defined, determined, and compelled by bearded old men, committed in their hearts to the nomadic world of the 9th century, was one of those annoying little facts that can be so inconvenient. But such was not his worry, or the worry of the brothers in the field today. No, today was the culmination of all the training, the planning, the prayers, the achievement of their glorious mission, and the high calling of martyrdom. What a glorious day.

Downtown Riyadh, 1,500 yards away

Chief Petty Officer Eric Cassidy looked through the scope of his Heckler & Koch MR762A1 as the crosshairs were trained at center mass of a man on a balcony in flowing, traditional Arab dress. The man seemed to have something in his hand, but from that distance it was impossible to tell what it was. Petty Officer Cassidy dialed one more small adjustment for a breeze that was blowing from the west. He then took a deep breath, let it out slowly, and purposely slowed his heartbeat to the point where it was barely discernible. He became one with the high-tech sniper rifle as his finger began to apply pressure to the trigger. When the rifle spit with the report of a discharged round, it almost came as a surprise to him, which was the way it was supposed to happen. About 1,500 yards away, a large hole was blown through the chest of his target, and the man dropped from sight behind the wall of the balcony.

"Target down," Cassidy's spotter reported into the tiny microphone that was in front of his mouth on the end of a small boom that wrapped around the side of his head. "Repeat, confirm target down. We are getting out of Dodge – beginning exfil."

Unfortunately, intelligence is much more of an art than a science. The humint, or intelligence provided to the local CIA Station Chief by an informant who was also a rival to the Sheik, was wrong by about 24 hours. The mission was supposed to be prosecuted at least 24 hours before the terrorist set his wheels in motion. Unfortunately, Chief Cassidy's shot was about 3 seconds too late. Sheik Aalim had just completed his task, and the wheels were set inexorably in motion.

Present time – undisclosed location

The four brothers were loaded for bear as they headed east on a 4-lane road towards their target. It was a "soft target" as often characterized by the clueless western media. This was their only regret – the mission was almost too easy. It was astonishing to them, actually, that no one had done this before. Hundreds of unbelievers would be about their daily tasks, with little or no sense of danger and ripe for the killing. The brothers were assured, of course, that the relative ease of their task did not in the least distract from its glory; that the impact would be high, that it would strike terror in the hearts of countless more than would actually be killed. Each brother was reminded, not so subtly, that complete and unquestioned submission was also required from each of them, including submission to glorious martyrdom. All were armed with an AK 47, multiple magazines, and two 45 caliber Glock 21s as backups, just in case. In total, each man carried several hundred rounds of hollow-point ammunition. And each man planned to make every round count. They had no illusions about surviving the experience. Indeed, they had no intention of surviving it. They planned to keep shooting and shooting until every round was spent or they were shot themselves. And one of the reasons they carried so much ammunition was to ensure it was the latter, not the former outcome that occurred. This was their glorious quest, and they would be in the arms of Allah, and their 72 virgins, within a couple of hours.

* * * * *

Jason Andrews sat in an air-conditioned trailer in the middle of nowhere. He twisted his back a bit in the uncomfortable chair to relieve the tension and palmed a roller ball on the console in front of him with his left hand to slightly adjust the zoom on the high-resolution camera that had eyes on the suspected target, a non-descript Toyota Land Cruiser. With his right hand he lightly held a joystick with just his thumb and first two fingers.

Jason loved his job. He had graduated around the middle of his class at the Air Force Academy but had not made the cut for pilot training due to the impact of four years of studying on his eyesight. Flying Predator drones, however, and being a member of the "Chair Force" had been a lot of fun, especially flying these birds on station in Afghanistan, and he believed he actually made a difference in the war on terror. It was clear, however, that his skill set, as well as his class standing and good, but not great marks for leadership on his efficiency reports, meant he would never wear stars on his shoulders or likely even eagles. And besides, there was other handwriting on the wall. A new President, of a decidedly more restrained world-view, was going to wind down the action and reductions in force were coming. So as a Captain he decided to get out. And a higher paying civilian job would provide the income he would need to pursue a civilian pilot's license on his own. Then he got that call. A job offer from a civilian contractor to the Pentagon who was looking for someone with his skill set and experience – at three times his Captains salary. With that income he not only could learn to fly, he could get an instrument rating and aspire to bore holes in the sky in something a bit more ambitious than a Cessna 152. So here he sat. He wasn't even sure what kind of UAV he was flying or where it was, let alone what target he was following. It was such a secret mission that not even the pilots knew the exact details. In point of fact, it was not even entirely clear for whom he was working. Everything with his employer seemed to be need to know, and the only thing the pilots seemed to know was how to fly. But he had passed the security screening with flying colors, had consistently demonstrated a high regard for discretion, and here he was.

Though he was unaware, Andrews was actually flying the brand-new Predator model SDS, for "Stealth, Domestic, Strike". The bird circled slowly overhead at about 7,500 feet as it followed the Toyota. It was built to look exactly like a Cessna 172 and, although at about a 75% scale, from the ground it was indistinguishable from the real thing, except for the lack of manufacturer's badging. That's where the similarities with its full-sized civilian inspiration ended. The design cue clearly violated several intellectual property laws, but the powers that be weren't particularly worried about that little detail, because as far as the American public was concerned this aircraft didn't exist. Under the nose of the craft was an optical quality window, covering the underneath of the aircraft nose, and continuing with a second pane joined at an 80-degree angle up the front of the nose ending about four inches below the bottom of the engine nacelle and propeller. Behind the horizontal window sat a fully articulated high-resolution camera that could easily identify small facial features from up to 20,000 feet. The camera was used for acquiring and tracking a ground target with extreme accuracy. Behind the second window, in front of and above the target camera sat another camera, also fully articulated, which could provide up to a 270-degree view of surrounding area, effectively being the pilots eyes. The glass was flush to the airframe, with no pronounced bulges, so as not to compromise the aircraft's civilian profile. It was equipped with advanced radar-absorbing electronics capable of rendering it nearly invisible when necessary. That wasn't often needed, however, as its radar signature, as well as its transponder, would lead all but the most sophisticated of radar systems to view it as a small civilian aircraft and not a threat. That conclusion would be very wrong. In the underbelly were two doors, arranged much like the classic bomb-bay doors of military bombers, which could open to deploy the launching mechanism for a small self-propelled smart bomb about eighteen inches long. Not quite a missile, but more than just a bomb, a small rocket motor would provide a one second burst and served to deliver the ordnance to target quickly to reduce the risk of the wrong people seeing it. Behind the weapon deployment doors was a port that would open to allow a laser to paint the target. The system was extremely accurate and could deliver the package to within a three-centimeter tolerance from 20,000 feet. The bomb was tipped today with a one-pound Semtex warhead, and if the occasion warranted, it could carry a two or three-pound warhead as well. Anything over one pound would be gross overkill for today's mission, however. A magazine system that sat just underneath the fake pilot figure carried five more smart bombs to facilitate multiple shots if deemed necessary by CNC. An advanced Lycoming engine with over 300 horsepower powered the drone, and the airframe was titanium and engineered to withstand significantly higher aerodynamic stress than the civilian counterpart. As a result, this beast could fly over 250 knots and had a service ceiling that, although classified, was substantially higher than a real Cessna 172. Onboard was a sophisticated computer that controlled all of the systems and the autopilot. Once a target was acquired, the operation could engage full automation and the drone would continue to track and paint a target until the weapon was fired or the operation disengaged. As this marvel of engineering flew along its course, former Captain Jason Andrews, call sign "Westwood Two", disengaged system automation and the onboard computer and took active control of the PSDS flight systems. At this point Andrews applied his full focus on the weapons system. To actually fire the weapon would require two things – an electronic release code that would take the weapon "hot", and the execute order itself.

On the ground, a late-model, non-descript Honda Civic, call sign "Westwood Three", was sitting at a traffic light at an intersection that was in the path of the Land Cruiser. Two field agents of the NSA Directorate of Special Activities, or NSADSA, sat in the front seat and watched the Land Cruiser as it continued toward its target. Their job was to ensure positive identification and to provide a real time battle damage assessment. For many missions similar to this, in many parts of the world, this type of eyes on the ground presence would not be practical or even possible. Present circumstances, however, facilitated it. Just before the light turned green, the Toyota drove through the intersection, directly in front of the two agents who were stopped at the light.

The comnet came to life as two field agents on the ground began to do their job. "This is Westwood Three. Suspect vehicle just passed right in front of us. Four dark-skinned males with beards are in the vehicle. The two on the driver's side match the description of the suspects. We can't see the two in the back, but we can confirm the Toyota has a rented plate as suspected. Positive confirmation on the target."

In the CNC, Colonel Taylor fixated his attention on the "Target View" screen and watched the vehicle pass through the intersection. He was irritated. Rules of engagement required the field team to provide a positive ID on the target vehicle license plate before approval of a kinetic action. With the irritation dripping from his voice, he asked the obvious follow up question: "Westwood Three this is Westwood One, can you corroborate plate number?"

Jason Andrews pressed his com button before Westwood Three could respond. "This is Westwood Two. Aircraft confirms the correct plate number. Repeat, positive identification of plate number from aircraft. Tape is now rolling – image captured."

"Westwood Two this is Westwood One, thank you," Taylor said, with a tone in his voice that, unmistakably, was designed to reinforce his irritation at the oversight. "All assets report traffic density and risk of collateral damage."

"This is Westwood Three. Traffic light to moderate, but good target separation at the moment from other vehicles. Risk of collateral damage is small but non-zero. Our judgment is that this is about as good as it's going to get."

"This is Westwood Two. Confirm on the ground conditions. Requesting permission to go weapons hot."

"This is Westwood One. Westwood Two is cleared for weapons hot. Repeat, Westwood Two is cleared for weapons hot." With this comment, Colonel Taylor turned a key on his console that transmitted a 3 digit code from the Permissive Action Link, or "PAL", that allowed the pilot to arm the weapons systems.

"This is Westwood Two. I confirm weapons are hot. Target is painted. Requesting CRM114 clear code. Do I have permission to fire?"

The onboard targeting system of the aircraft was designated CRM114 – someone at the Agency obviously had a sense of humor. Before the operator could actually release the weapon, Command and Control, or CNC, had to transmit a go code to unlock the permissive action link of the weapon, or PAL.

"This is Westwood Two, be advised we are coming up on an intersection and I would really like to take this shot before the target gets there. There are several vehicles at the traffic light on both sides of the road and collateral risk goes way up if I can't get this shot off within seconds."

The comm net was silent for what seemed to be an eternity, and Andrews thought to himself, "can't these morons make a decision?" Then his headphones came to life.

"Release code transmitted. Weapons hot. Execute execute execute!"

Simultaneously with the transmission, a green light illuminated on the PSDS pilot console, and Andrews depressed a trigger on the control stick, very much like playing one of those flight simulator games on PC he had as a kid. Just after doing so, he called out the verbal confirmation, "Rifle rifle rifle, 20 seconds to impact." Within milliseconds, the warhead was falling quickly towards its target, guided by the aircraft's laser system. Fifteen seconds later, a one-second burst of very highly compressed air pressure provided a thrust that accelerated the small projectile towards its target and made it a blur. Unfortunately, a moment of hesitation by Colonel Taylor had allowed time for a Chrysler minivan with a mother and three children to make a right hand turn on red into the lane of traffic just about 5 or 6 feet in front of the Land Cruiser. The one-pound Semtex warhead hit the roof of the target between the front and back seats, and the vehicle was instantly incinerated. Shards of molten hot steel were hurled in several directions, including through the back of the minivan. The hot shrapnel cut through the backside of the van into the passenger compartment and instantly killed the two children strapped in their child seats. A chunk of molten steel also collided with the underside of the van and penetrated the fuel tank. With that, the entire van exploded and was rendered in a condition not much different from that of the Toyota.

"Oh SHIT!!" Andrews said. "Where the hell did that minivan come from? Westwood Three, do you have eyes on?"

"Yes. Female driver, likely mid-30s to early 40s. At least one child in the front passenger seat. Could not see in the back as the windows were darkened. The thing was obliterated. None of the occupants could have possibly survived that. Primary target completely destroyed, but oh my God, Colonel Taylor, that entire family must have been killed!"

"This is Westwood One. Everybody quiet, now! Maintain operational discipline. This comnet is not a damn chatroom. Mission critical comments only. Westwood Three, do you confirm target destroyed? Yes or no?"

"This is Westwood Three. Yes, confirm target destroyed. Yes, repeat, confirm target destroyed."

"Westwood Three this is Westwood One. Thank you for following my abundantly clear instructions about answering yes or no. Exfil immediately."

"This is Westwood Two. Aircraft returning to base. No civilian chatter reflecting aircraft involvement in the incident." The aircraft operator's control panel had a full complement of aviation communication radios that allowed Andrews to listen to, and if necessary, communicate with civilian air traffic control to keep up the ruse.

Minimizing collateral damage was one of the mission rules of engagement. The term minimize, however, could be broadly interpreted in the context of the importance of the mission. After extensive debate on this topic, a very simple and antiseptic cost-benefit assessment was to be applied in real-time to all command decisions. Everybody understood that killing terrorists and stopping their missions saved lives. But nobody was naive. Everyone recognized there was a risk of collateral damage in every situation. In-theater experience in places like Iraq and Afghanistan made that abundantly clear. Mission Commanders were expected to exercise their best judgment. And all were promised the organization and its secrecy would guarantee management had their backs.

The four Jihaddis never saw it coming and never knew what happened. The Toyota Land Cruiser and its occupants were obliterated in an instant. Collateral damage was unfortunate, but many lives were saved that day by stopping the attack. The Jihaddis would not be firing their weapons, they would not find themselves in Paradise, and at the moment they were likely as far away from 72 virgins as one could be.

Nobody on the ground had a clue what happened, let alone that a drone had just taken out the SUV with a missile. The SDS banked slowly in a partly cloudy summer sky over Troy, Michigan and headed back towards its home. Nobody was going to die at Somerset Mall that day. Unfortunately, there were five other teams, undiscovered, and their intended victims were not   so   lucky.

Chapter 2 – The Sparrow

Big data was the new frontier in intelligence work, and it was being collected from more sources than the public could imagine. Everyone knew the Government listened to and recorded phone calls. The press had hammered on that for years, initially to satiate their hatred for "W", as they called him, or President George W. Bush, and his "Mini Me", Dick Chaney. The two were the progenitors of the despised neo Patriot Act that, among some, was viewed as the beginning of a descent into a police state. In the political climate that was becoming increasingly polarized, neither side seemed to lack in hyperbole. Ah, but when the "W's" second term came to an end and the "Chosen One" was elected, the fourth estate discovered that "W's" successor not only continued the practice but did so with a zeal previously unimagined. The press became overwhelmed with cognitive dissonance. It simply could not be. From reporters to editors to publishers, almost every one of them had voted for the guy. And while on one hand they found it difficult to restrain their unbounded fawning for him, on the other hand their progressive instincts led them to hate such a remarkable expansion of the "Surveillance State". In the end their adoration won out, and they chose to largely ignore it. It proved remarkably easy to do, because most of the public gladly accepted the prospect of Government spooks modestly invading their privacy as the necessary price to pay for keeping them safe. Far too many of the public simply didn't care. And besides, most people believed the Feds were listening to other people's phone calls and certainly not theirs. An uninformed and ambivalent citizenry was a far greater threat to democracy than rogue politicians. Neither a skeptical press nor a handful of libertarian politicians could get any traction from the issue. And no one, of course, had any idea of exactly how big the collection of big data had become, how pervasive, or how sophisticated those spooks were at mining it, and most importantly, how it would be used.

And my, did the government ever up their game. Not just phone calls, but emails, then text messages. It was the text messages that the wizards of Lord Moldevort, AKA The Director of National Intelligence, believed held the treasure trove of potential terrorist intelligence. And their instincts were correct. But there was the problem of that damn Apple encryption. Terrorists found the iPhone and iMessage to be an extraordinarily effective and secure method of communication, and the U.S. Government could never convince Apple, let alone a skeptical public, to give up their security. There is of course, a solution to every problem, especially if one is creative enough and not encumbered by the desire to play nice. The NSADSA considered two alternatives. The first potential track was the old fashioned way – throw a bunch of math Ph.D.s at the problem and break the encryption code. And that they did, but the problem was the science had advanced just a bit from the days of Joe Rochefort breaking the Japanese naval code before Midway, and the technology was growing at a geometric rate. Encryption science wasn't exactly sitting still while the government was trying to engineer the digital key to unlock it. And there was the problem of time. Even though they had high confidence in their ability to eventually crack the code they believed they were racing against the clock of a major attack and had little faith the encryption could be broken in time to stop it. But for once the government had actually been far-sighted, even before the establishment of the new Special Activities Division of NSA. Four years prior, the NSA had launched a program they called "Son of Deep Throat", where some very bright software engineers were planted in several high-profile tech companies, including Apple, as deep cover with a mission to feed their industrial secrets to the NSA. This broke a whole host of Federal Laws, but that of course was nothing new to the several U.S. alphabet-soup intelligence agencies. It was all done of course, in the name of national security, and to protect the public. The program's original intent was twofold – first to ensure the NSA stayed abreast of new technology, because after all if we could invent it some other country could as well, and potentially use it against us. Second and most importantly, they wanted to ensure nobody had a better tool bag than they did. The Feds hadn't foreseen the Apple encryption problem when the program was launched, but the timing was fortunate, and the contribution of "Son of Deep Throat" towards solving this particular problem was beyond their wildest dreams. There were three deep plants at Apple, and one of them, a real genius at code, had risen quickly in the software division and now had responsibility for the encryption software. Problem solved. Of course, the NSA, Homeland Security, and other agencies and officials manufactured a public ruse about how the Apple encryption was compromising national security, etc., all to keep the cover. But they did so while quietly reading and cataloging encrypted text messages at will.

As impressive as all of this was, it paled in comparison to Operation Sparrow. It gave birth to a remarkable device, named the Sparrow, designed to facilitate a remarkable objective. What if you didn't have to depend on a phone call to retrieve a conversation? Traditional listening devices, or "bugs", were largely useless at this because they were so easy to detect. But there were over 6 billion cell phone subscriptions active in the world and almost as many actual cell phones as people. What if every one of them potentially could be turned into a listening device? The technology already existed and had been used for years in more conventional settings like U.S. embassies. Diplomats ushered into the offices of senior diplomats were routinely asked to surrender their cell phones beforehand, and the devices would be locked in a radio-proof safe. This was to ensure the phones were not turned into passive listening devices. But while this was very effective in localized situations, it was difficult to accomplish on any kind of scale. Enter the Sparrow, developed under the supervision of the NSDSA by a Silicon Valley company called QuarkSpin, it was a nano-drone only 75 microns in diameter, thinner than a human hair, and barely visible even to a very sharp naked eye. It would turn any cell phone within a 50-foot radius into a listening device capable of being monitored by the NSDSA over the phone's cellular network. It was cheap, manufactured en masse, and drew so little power it would last for up to three years, Delivery to the unwitting recipient would be via U.S. mail in an envelope labeled "Important I.R.S. document" to maximize the chances of being opened. Once the envelope was opened, the device would activate, become airborne, and was programmed to imbed itself just beneath the skin of a human by targeting the heat signature of the body, usually the side of the neck. The device was coated with a small amount of anesthetic to minimize any potential sensation and would burrow deep enough to avoid being accidently removed by the host. It was waterproof and would continuously recharge itself with body heat. So, every time the host was within 50 feet of any cell phone, the NSDSA was capable of listening to everything said within earshot of the person. The real beauty of the effectiveness of the program was the result of an artifact of modern human behavior. People were addicted to their smart phones. These things now rarely left their owner's side. They would typically be the first thing picked up in the morning on getting out of bed, would be carried into the bathroom, and would rarely leave their side until placed on the nightstand at the end of the day. This behavior actually made the 50-foot effective range gross overkill, and the intelligence value was incalculable. The amount of data being collected was almost beyond comprehension, which led to a problem as daunting as anything the intelligence community had yet faced. How do you make sense of it and extract actionable intelligence? Moore's Law and a very talented team of NSA software wizards solved this problem.

Moore's Law is the observation that the number of transistors packed into one square inch of an integrated circuit has doubled every year since the invention of the transistor. More importantly, it postulates that this trend will continue into the foreseeable future. Transistor count is a proxy, of course, for computer processing power. Stated more simply, Moore's Law is the observation that computer-processing power is growing at a geometric rate. Since the transistor was invented in 1947, that growth curve is now almost vertical. The state of the art of computer processing power is astonishing compared to even 10 years ago, let alone to 1947. The processing power of a device as small as the iPhone possesses a large multiple of all the computer processing power used by NASA to go to the moon. All of this meant the NSA was now in possession of supercomputers that could stand up to the task of analyzing such monumental amounts of data.

Of course, all of that processing power would be useless without the software to harness it. Developing the software required solving two separate problems. First, how do you sort and catalogue massive amounts of data from phone conversations, texts, emails, and other forms of electronic information in a manner that allows it to be efficiently retrieved? That breakthrough came from, of all things, advances in library science. It was a pretty safe bet that nobody would ever suspect the NSA of acquiring a state-of-the-art capability in that discipline. The second problem was how to effectively mine it for actionable intelligence when the search is actually far more daunting than the old analogy of looking for a needle in a haystack. For over two years a team of the brightest software engineers on the planet labored deep inside the bowels of the NSA to develop software algorithms and filters that could plumb the depths of the data library and find things no mortal could have uncovered after years of detective work. The program focused on key words, then patterns of key words, then conversations that came from the patterns. Sources of the data were tagged, and the person most likely engaged in the conversation was identified from cross-referencing cell phone and email accounts. Part of what the Sparrow retrieved was the complete contact list from the person of interest's cell phone, and every name on the list would receive a mailing that contained the Sparrow in it. Additional conversations would be mined, evaluated, and the intelligence would continue to be refined until it was read for review for potential action. The fusion of state-of-the-art hardware and software gave birth to an artificial intelligence capability second to none. And the results were breathtaking. So they thought.

* * * * *

It was a bright and sunny day as the mail truck pulled up in front of the residence of a Washington Post reporter. The driver retrieved several envelopes and a variety of advertisements addressed to "occupant" and placed them into the resident's mailbox. Included among the collection of letters and other assorted debris was a letter marked "Internal Revenue Service, Official Business". The Postman had no idea of the forces he had just unleashed, and the impact it would have on the individual quietly enjoying his coffee   and   toast   before   leaving   for   work.

Chapter 3 – His Father's Son

1997, Lashkar Gah District, Helmand Province Afghanistan

It was bloody cold in this place, he thought to himself, and the cold was unexpected. Joseph Michael Barber lay prone, nestled in a crevice that gave him a good view of a house about 600 yards away and at least a hundred yards lower than his overwatch. He shivered a bit as he peered through the Carl Zeiss scope on his Blaser R93 tactical German sniper rifle, chambered in 300 Winchester mag. This kind of involuntary movement was not a good thing for a man with the job of pulling off two precision shots from such a long distance. Those Germans knew how to make a quality firearm, he thought to himself as he gently cradled the weapon, but unsteady hands could quickly negate that quality advantage. He reached for his go bag and pulled out a thermal blanket and covered himself with it. The blanket would retain his body heat, and in a few minutes he would be back in his sniper's Zen.

He silently chuckled to himself as he reflected on the extremes of weather this job had exposed him to. A few years ago, he was sweating away a dangerous amount of his body's hydration in the middle of the Iraqi desert during the noonday sun as he took out a General from the Revolutionary Guard. The General had been, shall we say, less than cooperative with coalition occupation forces. He was still in the Teams back then, although most of his missions had come from the C.I.A. He quickly learned that almost everything from the CIA had been off the books. After a stint in the Agency's Special Activities Division, he now worked on a contract basis, code name Orion. It was a much better gig. Working as a contractor meant the pay was vastly better, and also gave him lots of downtime between missions. He loved the fellowship of the Teams but hated a lot of the Navy bullshit. Before his father passed away he had warned Joe-Joe about that. He wondered why some things never changed, generation to generation. He had quickly concluded the Agency wasn't much better, especially given that SAD was manned with largely ex-military types.   Working as a contractor provided much more favorable terms of employment, but he had to admit the missions were becoming increasingly more troubling to him. The Agency's motive for using contractors was obvious.   The missions he was given were the kind where the government needed plausible deniability. If captured or killed, the Feds would disavow any knowledge of Barber. Barber, code name Orion, was a non-person and completely expendable. That's why they paid him so well. To assuage his conscience, he insisted not only on knowing the who, but also the why.   He wanted to satisfy himself that his targets deserved the fate he was about to present to them. Problem was his comfort level seemed to be diminishing with each mission.   It wasn't any one thing.   Sometimes the targets themselves seemed questionable, although he was never presented with a target that just looked wrong. It was subtler than that. Sometimes it was the way the mission was presented. Too little detail, or even too much. There were even times when he questioned whether his case officer was telling him the truth. Loss of trust could be a deadly thing in his business, and he admitted to himself he was coming dangerously close to it. Maybe it was time to get out. There were lots of opportunities for a man with his particular set of skills, and the compensation rose exponentially the more he was willing to work in the shadows. But that kind of work would hardly be the best route to assuage his conscience.   He wasn't just a trigger or a door kicker, he told himself. He was smart. Maybe he could use his smarts and experience to provide a security service. He still knew lots of people, both potential partners and potential clients who could be interested. His best friend had told him he would regret the day he took this job. That day was getting close.

His mind snapped back to this particular mission.   There was something about this mission that really bothered him. Normally he would receive very specific intel about his targets.   The intelligence would include details about what the person did, why he or she was in his crosshairs, and why they deserved the particular fate he would dole out. Most importantly, he was given pictures of his targets. He was given lots of pictures. The rules of engagement required him to positively identify the target before he could pull the trigger. But this mission was different. They had relaxed the ROEs. He was to identify the targets only by proximity to the house and by their general mode of dress – "Afghan & Pakistani casual" as his handler joked. This meant if the two males were in the right place at the right time and wearing the right dress, he was to put them down. He could abort only if there was something that positively identified them as not the target, like one of them being a blond-haired Westerner in a suit. He didn't like it. It was sloppy and undisciplined. He also thought it odd that the mission came with a 50% bonus over his normal fee. He voiced all of these concerns to his case officer who repeatedly assured Joe that the mission was on the level, and to stop belly aching and get on with it. He was only told that one of the targets was reportedly a former Afghan warlord who was now a rising star in the newly ascendant Taliban. The other was his Pakistani ISI handler. The two were responsible for a reign of terror over the locals as the Taliban broadened its grip on the area. This was their safe house, if there could ever be such a thing in Helmand Province, and the Agency had the highest quality humint, or human intelligence, that positively identified the time and place of the meeting and confirmed that these two bad guys would be there. Joe was told that was all he needed to know. So here he lay in this crevice waiting for these two clowns to appear.

There was still no sign of his targets as daylight quietly faded into dusk. Joe hated to shoot at night, because the muzzle flash from his rifle could betray his position and make the exfil measurably more dangerous. It was colder too, and he was thankful he had pulled out that thermal blanket and covered himself. The blanket would also mask his heat signature. That would be very useful if anyone was using infrared imaging as part of the security protocols for the meeting. It was frankly the reason he brought the blanket in the first place. As he continued to peer through the scope, he began to hear a faint sound in the distance. The volume of the sound slowly grew as he picked up a pair of binoculars and focused in its direction. An automobile was traveling up the road towards the house, and in less than a minute he could make out a Range Rover. The make of the car was another piece of the target confirmation intel. Look for a Range Rover they had told him. As the vehicle stopped in front of the house, its back doors opened and a single man emerged. A second man walked out of the house, also by himself, to greet the Rover. The man from the house was attired in Khet partug with Parahun wa turban with a Peshawari cap, the traditional loose-fitting linen clothing worn by Afghan men. The second man, from the vehicle, was dressed in a Shalwaar Kameez and a Sarakaiki turban, traditional Pakistani dress. The attire was spot on. These men were his targets. Both faces were non-descript. As he surveyed his targets there was something that really bothered Joe. He could understand the difficulty in getting photos of an Afghan warlord, although it still seemed odd for a guy who was supposedly becoming such a big deal that he had to be put down. But a Pakistani ISI officer? How in the world could the wizards at the Farm not have a picture of him? It was an obvious question, and Joe was mad at himself for not asking it during the mission brief. But he hadn't asked it, and these two were clear matches to the mission profiles. So, Joseph Michael Barber put the thought out of his mind, and like his father before him took a deep breath to slow his heart beat and became one with his rifle as he zeroed the scope on the man on the right. Within a second or two he was almost surprised as the rifle spit its 220-grain round at almost 2,900 feet per second towards the target, blowing an almost softball sized hole through the man's center mass. A quick cycle of the bolt and the process was repeated on the second target with a similar result. Head shots made for great theater in movies, but the percentage shot at that distance was always a target's center mass. As both men dropped within a second or two of each other, the driver apparently slammed on the accelerator in a desperate but hopeless attempt to get out of harm's way. Fortunately for Barber the Rover had a rather large windshield, and before the SUV could develop much momentum a third shot sent the vehicle careening off to the right under control of the slumped and very dead driver until it hit a tree and came to a stop. Joe continued to survey the area through his scope for several seconds to see if anyone else would emerge from the house. They didn't. He guessed whoever was in the house was likely cowering under the furniture. Good opportunity to get out of Dodge, so he quickly broke down his rifle, packed his go bag, and started to leave the area and head to his exfil point. He still wasn't happy about the loose nature of the ROEs, but the 50% bump in his stipend would help, and it would provide the means to decompress somewhere with warm sunshine and cold beer. What was done was done

72 Hours Later, Doha Hotel, Marriot Marquis City Center, Qatar

Ever since the first Gulf War, the nation of Qatar was the unofficial host of Coalition Forces military commands, largely American. This meant the city center and major hotels were teeming with MAMs, or "military-aged males", largely of Western appearance. As such, seeing so many that fit that description didn't raise any particular alarms as Barber proceeded on his morning run. A quick eight miles at a seven-and-a-half minute pace was a good way, he thought, to get his blood pumping before heading to the Embassy for the mission debrief. Joe decided to pick up the pace a bit as he passed the Sheraton Grand on Diplomat Street and approached Al Funduq for his turn to the West. He had planned out a route that led him along the Gulf, then inland just a bit to a turn north on Majillis Al Taawon Street, and then a large loop all the way back to Diplomat Street before turning onto Conference Center Drive and back to the hotel. There were a lot of runners out on this bright and sunny morning. He had to admit that while he found the culture of the country stifling, it was hard to match the scenery and the beauty of the azure waters of the Gulf.

If there was one thing his training in the Teams and his work for the Agency had taught him, it was the importance of remaining constantly vigilant.

It was a behavior that kept people alive, especially in this part of the world, and especially in his line of work. He always ran with an erect posture and head facing forward, surveying the scene ahead of him and scanning for potential threats. That's what caused him to notice a man, Western in appearance, about five yards ahead of him. The man had just put his hand in his pocket. Strange behavior for a runner, Joe reflected as his first instinct. He also noticed the runner wasn't wearing earphones of any kind. Almost everyone out running that morning was wearing earphones, likely listening to music or an audio book. That's what runners do. It provided a distraction to the monotony and often helped a runner to push a bit harder. That is what most runners did, of course, except for Joe. Why was this guy not wearing earphones, and given that he wasn't, what possible reason could he have for placing his hand in his jacket pocket. He obviously didn't need to adjust the volume of whatever it was he wasn't playing. There was a well-defined progression wired into the threat assessment portion of Joe's brain. Level one was simply an anomaly. Level two was threat confirmation. Level three was escape from the threat and failing that, Level four, neutralize the threat. Successful operators always did their best to avoid Level four. At level one, an anomaly was an observation of something that seemed out of place or in some other manner incorrect. It was something that didn't belong. The difference between the people in Joe's line of work who survived compared to those who met an early demise was the ability to quickly spot an anomaly. That's why a lot of traditional "door-kickers" were good at the situations that required primarily violence, but terrible at operating independently in the field and coming home alive to tell the tale. Spotting anomalies required a brain wired for subtlety and nuance and not just the possession of out-sized athletic and combat skills. It also was important to follow a disciplined progression and not to overreact. Too quick a response to an irregularity could betray the wrong conclusion, tip one's hand, bring about unwarranted attention, and often greatly narrow the tactical options. Too quick a reaction is often what drove failure instead of success. And in Joe's line of work, failure usually meant death. His instinct was to remove the suspicion about a potential threat by simply altering his route and turning down the next street he passed. If the guy didn't follow, he could safely put his concerns back in a box and get on with his day. As he came up on Al Shaat Street he decided to make a turn to the left. The street had a fairly good-sized median, so it would not be something a runner would naturally try and cross unless he or she had a specific reason. Joe kept running forward until there was a break in the traffic, then bolted across the street and ran in place in the median waiting for a clearing of traffic in the other direction. The first thing he noticed was the guy starting to slow down. This was not good. The guy still had his hand in his pocket. Also not good. As the traffic cleared Joe bolted across the street again and proceeded along Al Shaat at an even faster pace. He knew he'd have final confirmation of a threat if the guy attempted to keep up with him, so he really pushed it. He turned right alongside the Aparthotel Adagio and really poured it on as he headed towards the Intercontinental Hotel just down the street and on his left. This area was not nearly as busy as the route around Diplomat Street and he was beginning to regret his turn to the West. These decisions were always a trade-off, he reminded himself, and it was not exactly like he was expecting any kind of threat that morning. He realized he had another problem. He didn't have eyes in the back of his head. There was no way he could verify if the guy was still following him and gaining ground without slowing down a bit to turn around and look. Not a good idea, he thought to himself. He concluded his best option was to get to the Intercontinental as quickly as possible and get lost in its lobby. About that time his circumstances obtained an unfortunate clarity as he heard a loud thump and the ground exploded about five feet in front of him to his left. By the sound and the physics of the impact, it was a round from a small-caliber suppressed handgun. Likely a 380, he thought. It was hard to fire such a weapon with precision after running, and Joe's fast pace added to that difficulty. The shooter would be winded and fine muscle control would be difficult, even for a professional. The man had obviously shot low and to the left, a common miss when firing either fatigued or under stressful conditions. He knew the difficulty of the shot was the principle thing he had going for him right now. The only weapon he had on his person was a knife, which would be useless at a distance from a pistol, especially since he was facing away from his assailant at the moment. Joe quickly broke left, then zigged right, and continued the process a couple of times as he raced towards the hotel. The random movements would make the shot even more difficult. He would be at the safety of the hotel in just a couple of seconds before the bad guy could discern the pattern of his movements, anticipate them, and improve the accuracy of his aim. Joe turned hard right and sprinted straight for the door. Within about 10 feet of the lobby entrance, he heard the sound of tires screeching in the street. There was the sound of a door opening, then closing again, followed by the sound of the vehicle driving away, this time more disciplined and without burning rubber. He walked into the lobby, bent over and placed his hands on his knees to catch his breath. For the moment, and fortunate for him, he looked like any other jogger returning after a brisk morning run. He pulled the phone out of his pocket and immediately called his case officer, who answered the phone on the first ring.

"Ident," the case officer said without the slightest emotion in his voice.

"Orion," Barber responded.

"Challenge phrase?" the case officer asked.

"The eagle has landed," Barber replied.

"Identity confirmed," the case agent responded. "What is your status?"

"What the hell is going on here?" Joe barked into the phone, but with a tempered volume so as not to attract attention. "Somebody just took a shot at me while I was out for my morning run. Who would want to do that?"

"Where are you Orion, and are you injured?" the voice on the other end of the phone asked.

"Lobby of the Intercon. I ducked in here for safety after the shot. And, no, the bad guy missed."

"Stay put," the voice responded. "I am sending a car for you right now. Don't go back to your hotel. We'll pick you up right in front of the lobby. It will be a red Lexus LS 500. There are some people here really pissed right now."

"What are you talking about? About what? Why?" Joe asked, almost angry now. "It was a successful mission and a routine extract. By the way, who the hell is this?" he asked. "You're not Evan."

"Never mind who I am and just wait for the car. You shot the wrong two men," the voice responded.

Two Hours Later, Mission De-brief, CIA. Station, U.S. Embassy, Qatar

Barber sat in a secured briefing room at the American Embassy in Qatar and waited, alone. The solitude was unsettling. He felt more like the subject of a rendition than an operator who had just returned from a successful mission. About the only thing missing were the restraints. He had been sitting there for the better part of half an hour when four men walked into the conference room and all sat across the table from him, reinforcing the impression this was going to be more of an interrogation than a debrief.

There were three suits and a guy in khakis and a polo shirt. This was not going to be good, he thought to himself.

One of the suits was the first to speak. "Mr. Barber, my name is Greg McMasters, and I'm the Agency Associate Counsel assigned to Qatar Station. You're in a lot of trouble."

Great, Barber thought to himself. After my morning, the first thing I get presented with is a smart-assed lawyer. He gave the man a steely stare as to convey the truth, actually, that he could squeeze the life out of this pencil-neck without breaking a sweat. After a pause for effect, Barber responded with a low, calm and measured voice: "I disagree. I have the mission brief back in my hotel room including all of the ROEs. I didn't like them and made that known during the pre-mission brief. I thought they were too lax, but after reassurance from an analyst," he said, with a distinct emphasis on a literal pronunciation of the words first syllable, "I followed them to the precise letter. If anybody is in trouble, it's one of your clowns who didn't do his job. By the way, who is Mr. Casual here?" he said, looking at the one man not in a suit. "You're not my case officer."

"I'll be asking the questions, Mr. Barber," the lawyer responded. "John Clark is no longer with the Agency."

"Who the hell is John Clark?" Joe asked. "That's not the name of my case officer. Is this name somebody's idea of a joke?" he questioned, in reference to the fictional figure in many a Tom Clancy novel with the same *nom de guerre*.

"Not important," the suit continued. "While you were being picked up we sent another team to your hotel room to retrieve our classified documents," he said, pushing a folder across the table towards Joe. "As you can clearly see from the contents, your description of the mission brief is not accurate. There are several pictures and a complete written description of

64

each of your subjects. They bear no resemblance whatsoever to the two men you assassinated three days ago."

Joe almost came out of the chair in response to the lawyer's comment, but his desire to throttle the guy lost out to his curiosity about what was in the file that had just been pushed in front of him. He opened the folder, started looking at the contents, and immediately was filled with an overwhelming sense of dread. There in front of him, just like this smart-ass lawyer claimed, were several pictures of both a guy purported to be a rising Taliban General and a Pakistani ISI officer. It felt like a thousand thoughts were firing through his brain simultaneously. He tossed the pictures out of the way and started to read the profiles of each of the targets. The profiles were detailed and precise. The profiles were exactly like the ones given him on most previous missions. His emotions were a mix of near explosive anger and dread. Somehow, he had been played. "This is the first time I have laid eyes on these materials. I have no idea where this folder came from, and it is not the mission brief that was given to me. You gentlemen must know perfectly well my case officer's name is Evan McMullen, not John Clark which, by the way is a pretty pathetic attempt at a joke. Where is he and why is he not part of this debriefing? And if these two were the real targets, who did I put down?"

"The two men you assassinated…..," the suit said, only to be quickly interrupted by Joe.

"Don't use that word! "Joe barked. "I didn't assassinate anyone, and you know that word is not to be used at any time in these discussions. That's not what we do. We don't assassinate. We put down the bad guys!"

The suit continued in a quiet and measured voice. The lawyer's demeanor, which was dripping with authority and confidence, was another thing that was really starting to piss Joe off. He had to keep reminding himself that when you lose control of yourself, you lose control of everything, so he took another deep breath and let the suit talk.

"A distinction without a difference, I would say, but that's beside the point. The two men who found themselves on the business end of your particular set of skills…," the lawyer continued, with another effort at sarcasm, "were very high ups in the Afghan opium trade. The Afghan was responsible for most of the heroin coming out of Helmand Province, and the Pakistani was a mid-level intelligence officer in the army who helped facilitate the transportation. Nobody is shedding any tears about their untimely demise, but it begs a couple of very big questions as to how the Agency got involved in this, and who ordered it."

"I have no idea, and again this was not the mission brief I was given," Barber responded. "You should be talking to Evan, not to me. I'm just the trigger."

"We would if we could find him, but he seems to have vanished into thin air. The two men you put down have been engaged in a bitter and violent turf war with another drug faction further north. We believe the war has interrupted, or at least complicated the transport of the product back to the States. Getting these two out of the way solved that problem. We suspect the client in the States is some mystery man on the West Coast. We know very little about him, but the working theory is that McMullen was on his payroll and arranged the hit. We don't take kindly to Agency assets freelancing on behalf of some domestic drug lord. Mr. McMullan is, as we say, placed beyond salvage."

Those words sent a chill up Joe's spine. "Beyond salvage" was agency speak for putting down one of the Agency's own. Joe was furious, as things actually started to make sense. "I was played. As I said a minute ago, I didn't like the ambiguous nature of the brief, and I can tell you it's not the first time I've had that feeling. And I get it – we have to go through this dance here to see what I know. I don't know anything. Find McMullen and I suspect you'll get your answers."

"Mr. McMullen's usefulness to his client, or clients, is essentially non-existent now. If they don't already know that, they will soon. We suspect they already know it. We suspect the mystery client was the one behind the botched attempt on you this morning. If they are after you as a loose end, they are most certainly after him. I doubt he's going to be able to tell us much of anything."

Barber just sat there and stared at the lawyer. The suit continued. "And there's one more little fact that we need to discuss with you. Facts can be such inconvenient things, don't you agree?" the lawyer said, his voice dripping again with sarcasm and smugness.

The urge to reach across the conference table and throttle this guy was almost overwhelming, and for a brief moment Joe almost thought the consequences would be worth it. "Take a breath big guy," he said to himself.

The lawyer continued. "We checked your bank account. Yes, we have all of the numbers and know where each account resides. We are, after all Mr. Barber, in the intelligence business, aren't we? We took particular interest in your last two deposits. There was an Agency deposit to your Swiss account that represented 150% of your normal fee. That's very interesting, wouldn't you think? Why the bonus? We don't do bonuses. And then there is that deposit made yesterday to one of your Cayman Islands accounts, which was double your agency fee. Exactly double, to the dollar. And that deposit was not from the Agency. It was a deposit from a private source that we have been unable to trace, as of yet. Was it payment for some off the books work, perhaps? From our West coast mystery man? That's our working theory, at least." The lawyer betrayed a slight smile as he concluded his comments.

Joe's head was now spinning as he struggled to maintain his composure. Fortunately, his years of training had inculcated in him a capability that allowed discipline to triumph over emotion. He started to speak. "The Agency deposit was per my agreement with McMullen. I thought it a bit odd and questioned him as to why this mission was worth more. He told me it was because of the nebulous nature of the intel, which they believed created a higher personal risk to me. It was odd, but still a credible explanation. And I'm not in the business of normally turning down a 50% raise. I have no idea where the second deposit came from, and can only conclude I am being set up. I checked the Swiss account day before yesterday when I got here. It's where all the Agency payments are made. I had no idea there was a large deposit in the other account, and I had no reason to check it."

There was a long pregnant pause as he waited for a response. Nobody spoke.

"So where do we go from here?" Joe finally asked. "Am I beyond salvage as well? Is that what that shooter really was about? If so, I might observe you guys are a little off your game. That was pretty sloppy work. Of course, I suspect he wasn't in your employ. I think you are right. Evan was one of those loose ends, and I am the other. I also suspect that they got to my room before you did to plant that second mission brief and pull the one that I was actually given."

The station chief now spoke up. He was the senior guy in the room, and it was pretty clear from the body language that when he decided to talk the smart assed lawyer was to keep his mouth shut. "We haven't decided exactly what to do with you yet Joe, but let's just say the optimistic end of the options entail a private room at Fort Leavenworth. It kind of depends on how cooperative you are."

By now Joe was expecting as much. What he wasn't sure of yet was whether the threats were real or just another part of the game intended to scare him into telling the truth or in some twisted way prove his innocence. The next step was a polygraph, no doubt, although those were of limited utility in a case like his. The disciplines necessary for an operator to perform successfully in the field made it pretty easy to trick a machine. One thing he was now sure of, it was time to get out. He had no use for these types and would no longer do their bidding. He had been thinking about that for a while now, as the missions he was assigned made him more and more uncomfortable. It was now time to play a little card of his own with these clowns.

"Gentlemen, I think I prefer to take what's behind door number two," Joe said.

The four men on the other side of the table now looked a bit confused. The station chief was the one to respond. "I'm sorry, but I don't quite follow. You don't have your own choices here, other than what you earn by being cooperative."

"I'm hurt," Joe responded. Now his own voice was the one dripping with sarcasm. "The Agency obviously has a lower opinion of me than I thought. I actually walked through door number two before I even entered this room, or the building for that matter. I activated my O.I.P."

Now they all looked even more confused. This time the lawyer spoke up. "What the hell is an O.I.P.?"

Joe smiled. "Operator's Insurance Policy. We all have them, in case some rogue element of Agency management regards our services as no longer necessary and expresses that opinion with extreme prejudice. It entails two things. First, a copy of every one of my mission briefs is stored on both paper and encrypted electronic form in numerous places. Redundancy is the first tenet of a successful insurance policy, wouldn't you agree?" sarcasm continuing. "Multiple D.C. law firms have been engaged to ensure the contents go to The New York Times, The Washington Post, the three major networks along with CNN and Fox News. Oh, yeah, and the Justice Department and the Speaker's Office. It will make fascinating reading, don't you think? This happens, of course, if I should come to an early demise of any kind. Those instructions were dormant and non-operative until about 90 minutes ago. Second, and this is the really interesting part. I have three separate, unrelated freelancers on retainer. They are not Agency contractors, of course. If anything happens to me, and I can assure you they are highly skilled at judging whether an early demise is the result of Agency actions, they are under contract to put down two people of my choosing." Joe now looked directly at the Station Chief, and then the lawyer, as he said, "I choose you, and I choose you." He couldn't help betray a slight smile as the lawyer went pale. Joe thought the guy was going to wet himself. Smugness gone. The second part was a lie, of course, but he delivered it with such conviction that it was likely to leave an element of doubt even long after they concluded it probably wasn't a real threat. It would certainly buy him a little time. "I think you guys are smart enough to know that if I was really part of a rogue operation here I wouldn't have called the Agency for help and certainly wouldn't have come in. This was all part of some twisted act to figure out if I really knew something. And you can be sure that I am smart enough to know that my professional engagement with the Agency is over, at least as an operator, so I'm out of here. I want my retirement to be healthy and happy, but also, shall we say, amicable. If there is anyone higher up in your chain of command who doesn't have his head up his ass and would like my counsel, I'm always happy to talk. I suspect you know how to contact me," he said, sarcasm in full bloom now. "My only advice is to do it carefully. It's going to be a long time before I ever trust any of you clowns again, if ever. Oh, and just one more thing. My insurance policy has no expiration date. If I should meet an unusual demise of any kind, even, let's say, 25 or 30 years from now, the

70

policy still pays in full. I suggest you either fully purge all records of this unpleasantness, or make sure your successors understand the long-term risk."

The CIA case officer Barber referred to as "Mr. Casual" was fidgeting in his chair, in spite of the fact he wasn't on the hit list Joe had just announced. Nobody in the room had any idea he had replaced McMullen in the employ of the mysterious "West Coast Interest". He couldn't care less about the prospect of an early demise for the Station Chief, and even allowed himself to relish a bit the thought of the lawyer finding himself on the business end of an operator. Everyone hated the guy, although he was admittedly pretty good at what he did. Everything would come crashing down, however, if those files that were part of Barber's insurance policy ever saw the light of day. He suspected his new client would be inclined to quickly finish the job McMullen had screwed up. He had to stop that from happening. The case officer was pretty certain the West Coast client could be compromised by the release of those files with a little detective work and connecting a few dots. Joe Barber would be allowed to live. In the grand scheme of things, Barber now had a lot to hide as well, and would render his own insurance policy useless if he ever released those files as some sort of whistleblower exercise. No, Barber was far too much a survivor to do something like that. The case officer had to make a phone call, as soon as he could possibly get out of this room. He looked at his watch and tried to figure out what time it was in California.

Don Julio Parrilla Restaurant, Buenos Aires, Argentina

Evan McMullen sat at an outdoor table at the restaurant and took a long sip from his glass of Malbec. He had already consumed more of the wine than he was accustomed to during an entire meal, and the appetizer hadn't even arrived yet. He was not accustomed to being on the run. But being on the run with means, however, considerable means, he reflected, was something he could probably get used to. His West Coast client was certainly not the first person he engaged as an unofficial customer of Agency services, and he had managed to build up quite a nest egg over the years. He liked to think of himself as an "off balance sheet" Agency entrepreneur. Before heading to the restaurant, the telephone number he kept dialing from his room just rang and rang and rang with no answer. That was about the worst sign he could imagine. The call was supposed to confirm his plan to tie up loose ends had been successfully concluded. The plan was to frame Barber with planted evidence in his Qatar hotel room and ensure his early demise before he could be interrogated. But no answer meant there was no confirmation. No confirmation could only mean the mission failed. And McMullen was a realist. He understood that failure meant too many loose ends and as far as his employment with the Agency was concerned, he was toast. That was ok, he thought to himself. The smart entrepreneur needs to know when to retire, and he reminded himself that was the benefit of a great run.

McMullen looked at his watch. He figured he had officially been on the run for an hour and 10 minutes at this point, the amount of time that had transpired since he hung up the phone in his hotel room before walking out to become invisible in the crowd and find a place to eat. Argentina seemed like a good waypoint. The original plan was to go to the Embassy there, check in and do a little official fact finding business, or whatever else he could come up with as a way to cover his sudden presence there. That was not going to happen now. The last thing he wanted was exposure to U.S. Governmental personnel of any kind, let alone Agency types. So the restaurant seemed to be a good place to enjoy a meal and think about where he needed to go to stay off the radar screen. Rio, he thought. Yes, that would be a great place to hide during a cooling off period. It was a place where it was easy to become invisible, and it had lots of very pleasant distractions. He had thought about San Paulo, but that place sucked. It was dirty, too crime ridden, and was void of serious beaches like farther north. There was a little voice in his head that kept suggesting he was drinking too much great wine right now, and that might not be the best idea given his predicament. But he was over eight thousand miles from the danger zone. Even though the agency had assets all over the world and certainly in a prominent city like Buenos Aires, nobody expected him here and it would take at least several days to figure out even what direction he had flown. By that time he would be long gone again.

Through the fog of the wine, however, he didn't realize he was thinking Agency. He wasn't thinking about his client. And he was completely unaware of the resources the client would commit to ensure they knew his exact whereabouts at all times. McMullen had become unreliable. He was making mistakes, acts of carelessness. He was leaving loose ends, either by oversight or by sloppiness in his work. Failure to take out Barber was sloppiness, but it was not an isolated incident. An isolated incident could be forgiven. It was another in a growing string of behaviors that fit that moniker. McMullen was obviously enjoying the fruits of his labor a bit too much and had become less vigilant, even careless. Those were unpardonable sins. He had become a liability. And as any good businessman knows, a liability must be offset with an asset. And the asset, so to speak, had been dispatched.

A cool breeze wafted through the eating area and made the experience all the more pleasurable, thereby driving the concerns of the moment even further from Evan McMullen's mind. Yes, he was going to really enjoy Rio, he thought to himself. He gazed at the locals, as well as a few obvious tourists who walked by the restaurant as he waited for his appetizer to arrive. He was actually getting somewhat hungry now, and frankly a little impatient with the service. A tall, dark-skinned man dressed in an impeccably tailored suit and carrying an expensive looking briefcase walked past his table, and McMullen barely had time to process the thought that it would be great to buy a suit like that, when the man turned slightly, as if to make way for another person to pass, and said disculpe, or "excuse me" in Spanish. As he did so, he gently placed his hand on McMullen's shoulder then walked away, lost in the crowd. It was an innocent gesture, but one that was somewhat out of place. McMullen had been momentarily disoriented by the man's liberal use of cologne, which delayed for just a second or two the realization that he had just felt a brief pin prick on his shoulder where the man had touched him. The disorientation, of course, was intentional and part of the mystery man's tradecraft. Overload the sense of smell for just a second or two. It bought just enough time to allow the mystery man to fade into the crowd before McMullen's senses could shift focus to being poked, and then to process what was actually happening. At that point it would be too late. Next came the sensation of an explosive pounding in McMullen's chest, and before he could utter an expletive in response to realizing what had just happened, he went face down into the empty plate in front of him and was dead, just as the waiter arrived with his appetizer.

Conference Room, CIA. Station, U.S. Embassy, Qatar

Barber's face betrayed the slightest of smiles as he watched his interrogator's response to his comments. He then said, "I think we are done here." With that, he stood and started to walk out of the conference room. He was not surprised that nobody tried to stop him. He had presented them with a very credible threat, and they knew it. The only thing he wasn't sure about was whether these clowns could call off or neutralize the hit on him before a potential second attempt. If it was the C.I.A. that made the attempt earlier this morning he likely would be safe. If it was some independent actor, like this "West Coast interest" well, that was another story. He was going to have to do something about that. And he was going to have to be very careful.

Offices of Orion Bellicus, Rye, New York, Present Day

74

Joseph Michael Barber sat in his office on the third floor of the Rye International Corporate Center, in the heart of the city of Rye, New York. A bright sun poured into the floor to ceiling window, which forced Joe to squint as he looked out over the manicured landscape. It had been years since he had left the CIA and started his security firm, Orion Bellicus, which loosely translated, means fierce and warlike hunter. The name fit his concept for his company perfectly and was an apt description of how he and his employees served their clients. Security wasn't a passive business, and there was a word that described people who approached it that way – dead. His approach to providing security or intelligence for his clients was to attack the problem with the same intensity he applied to his work as a covert operations officer for the CIA, and his earlier career in the Teams. He had a plaque at the front of his desk with the inscription, "The best defense isn't a good offense; the best defense is complete annihilation". To the lower right of the phrase was the attribution, simply stated as "anonymous", but the statement was his, and his clients knew it.

As a child Joe was a scrapping, skinny kid who was constantly getting into trouble with the nuns at his Catholic school until he learned to channel that energy into something more constructive. He managed somehow to get into Holy Cross College and graduate with a degree in economics and followed in his father's footsteps by joining the Navy and becoming a SEAL. The training was brutal, and there were many times he wanted to just give up, but he kept remembering what his father told him the night before he left – "You're going to have to do a lot of miserable shit to get through this, you are going to learn to hate your instructors and there will be times you will swear to yourself that signing up for this was the stupidest thing you've ever done. But I want one thing burned into your memory as you step off that bus in San Diego – "Barbers don't quit; you don't have to like it, but you sure as hell have to do it." Those words kept coming back to haunt him at many a dark moment during his training, but in the end, they served him as well as they served his father and Joe emerged not only as a SEAL, but as a sniper as well, just like his dad. Initially offered a commission because of his degree from Holy Cross, he opted instead for the enlisted billet. It made his mother mad. It made his father proud. Joe was smart enough to figure out that the real work, the heavy lifting, was done by the non-coms, and they had a much longer tenure doing that work. The officer core tended to have a short tour as actual operators before going on to the command billets that were the lifeblood of anyone aspiring to responsibility beyond that of a senior Lieutenant. And hearing the occasional mutterings under his father's breath, often while watching the news, about "those ticket-punching assholes" was something that really stuck. His father never talked about it, but Joe was a very perceptive child, and understood completely.

Orion Bellicus hired three types of individuals. Operators were all ex-special forces, and Joe was not biased towards just the Navy. Army Rangers, Marine Force Recon, and others were welcome. Nor was he biased towards only men. Several of the operators were women, all ex-military, and all capable of dropping men much larger than themselves, provided the man didn't have their training. There was actually a joke among the women of the firm that the big guys made the easiest mark, because they were all so full of a false self-confidence based on nothing other than an accident of birth. And the physical standards for everyone, men and women alike, were very high. Joe had hired one of his BUDS instructors as the firm's Chief Training Officer, and he was responsible for vetting potential employees and keeping the teams in peak condition. Despite his age, late 40s, the guy was a genuine bad-ass who jealously guarded the firm's standards. And making it in the door of Orion Bellicus was just the first step. Every operator had to pass a PT test each year, as well as demonstrate extraordinary marksmanship and tactical skills and those who couldn't were politely shown the door. That almost never happened.

The second type of employee comprised the investigative staff, and they were recruited from the ranks of the FBI, Treasury and CIA. They were also subject to a strict PT regimen, although the bar wasn't quite as high as that for the operators. The most valuable assets were combinations of both elite operators and investigators. These individuals not only had the experience and successful records of their careers in the FBI, Treasury, or CIA, but also could meet the highest physical conditioning and self defense standards of the operators. There was no special designation for these employees, but everyone knew who they were, and many of them were women. And they could be extraordinarily "versatile" as well. And if you were an adversary of one of OB's clients, you didn't want to know what the term "versatile" meant.

And last there was the support staff. What an understated title. These people were hired for their sheer brainpower, with Ph.D.s in math, physics and computer science, and provided the firm with both physical and cyber forensics capabilities that rivaled those of any organization on earth. The mission of Orion Bellicus encompassed a wide remit, and it provided a variety of services to its clients that ranged from routine security and executive protection, to industrial intelligence, to things that were, well, a bit "off the books" as they say. Nobody on the planet was better than one of OB's operators in keeping somebody safe. It was rumored that the Secret Service had an "off the books" consulting contract with them around principal protection. The Secret Service, of course, was having a few issues these days and could use the help. The investigative staff was in high demand on matters of industrial intelligence, and the outcome of their work resulted in more than one senior executive being shown the door. But their best work resulted from the harmonic convergence of skills across the different teams. Officially they would pierce the veils of the deepest and most obscure penumbras, extract critical intelligence and uncover a problem. Unofficially they would fix it. This, the fix, was their *"piece de resistance"*, and many of these efforts were off the books and pushed the envelope of what was legal. But Joe was a fiercely loyal boss who ensured there was a failsafe plan for every operator. The employees of OB were family, his family, and each of them knew it. And he had a secret weapon, their General Counsel, Diana Barber. Columbia Law School and former partner, Covington and Burling, Diana was not only a brilliant legal mind but had the killer instinct, in legal terms, of a Navy SEAL herself. She had a charming air, which could easily disarm an opponent before going for the kill. And her work at C & B gave her contacts across the globe that were priceless. Diana was also possessed with a grit born of her blue-collar upbringing in suburban Detroit, and this gave her the same perspective towards a good defense as Joe's. Many an OB client foe would try and cross her, and they would all pay a high price. She had the OB family's six, and they all knew it. And when her work occasionally turned dangerous, she knew they had hers.

As Joe turned back from the window his eyes quickly caught the framed picture of his family, and it became another one of those moments when he reflected on just how blessed he was. He had become wealthy doing a type of work he loved, and something that really made a difference to his clients. His résumé brought instant credibility when he had started out, along with a rapidly expanding client list. In all aspects of the operation, the firm's success and Joe's personal reputation enabled him to hire the very best in every field, and he paid them well. The impressive results he consistently achieved had allowed him to build the firm he led today as Chief Executive Officer.

As his mind continued to wander, the sharp ring of the phone on his desk startled him momentarily and broke the self-reflective mood. He reached across the desk and picked up the receiver on the third ring. Joe was a guy who preferred to answer his phone calls himself. He regarded every resource in the firm a treasure, and used each to its fullest potential. His administrative assistant was much more than a secretary, and he could answer his own phone. As he lifted the phone to his ear to take the call, Marcus Day walked into his office. Marcus was his Chief Operating Officer, a former Marine Captain who stood about six foot four and weighed every bit of 245 pounds. He looked directly at Joe and in his deep baritone voice simply said. "Put the phone down."

Joe looked up at Marcus and appeared a bit irritated as he replied, "I'll be with you in a minute, Marc." Day walked a couple of steps closer to the desk and in a voice many would have found menacing said, "Put the damn phone down right now Joe. It's about Walt and Veronica." Barber simply uttered the words, "I'll get back to you," into the receiver as he placed it back in its cradle. The conversation that was about to ensue would set off a series of events that, at that moment, neither of them could even begin to imagine.

Chapter 4 – Mistaken Identity

National Security Council Department of Special Activities, McLean, VA.

It was a very special place. It occupied about two thirds of the fourth floor of 1517 Westbranch Drive, and the glass façade that stood as the entrance to the office space was emblazoned with the moniker of New Generation Investments, LLC. Just below the firm's name were the words, "By Appointment Only", which served as a distracter to the curious. The French style doors were secured via card access, not that a person could actually get in that way. Anyone walking by the faux entrance could see a long reception desk, occupied by a non-descript middle-aged woman. Looks could be deceiving. She was actually a senior non-com in the Army Rangers, and beneath the desk there was an impressive variety of firepower at her disposal. Behind the reception desk on either side was a pair of doors that appeared to be the gateways to several inner offices. Also evident was a beautiful lobby, decorated with impressive art work and leather furniture that would be fitting for the reception area of a high-end investment management firm. The entrance itself was positioned in a location on the floor that made casual traffic a relatively rare thing. A web search of the firm's name would reveal nothing. Routine access to the space for its everyday occupants was accomplished by entering a building across the street. The building was owned by the National Security Agency, although nobody would know it by looking at the place. Inside the adjacent building there was a card access elevator that would take the employees down two floors to a tunnel. One would then walk through the tunnel, past two stations of Marine guards, crossing under the street to arrive at a second card-access elevator at 1517 Westbranch itself. That elevator had only one stop – the fourth floor and the special place itself. The reality of what occupied the space supposedly belonging to New Generations, LLC, was very different from what the name would imply. It was a very special place with an extraordinary mission. Behind the wall was a working environment that was enclosed in a womb of security rivaling any place on earth. It was a cocoon, completely shut off from the outside world by a special, energized wire mesh that lined the floor, the ceiling, and all of the inner walls. The mesh prevented any radio signal from getting into or out of the secured area. As a redundant security measure, all of the inner walls were also lined with several inches of foam to absorb sound that could potentially be picked up by passive listening devices. Around the exterior of the area and facing the outside wall of the building itself were a series of offices that would be occupied by the seniors. This would help maintain a normal appearance to anyone looking at the building from the outside and would also allow select individuals to communicate with the outside world as necessary. Such communication would not be done by standard telephonic land-lines. The facility was equipped with a specialized satellite communication system protected with state-of-the-art encryption. And even the perimeter offices had a highly translucent mesh applied to the inside of the windows to block electronic intercept of conversations. The mesh looked like the kind of film appliqué used on commercial buildings to make them more energy efficient. In the center of the space was a womb within a womb, another secured area that completely replicated every aspect of the outer area's security. As part of the strict security protocol, there were no electronic means of communication between this area and even the outer security area, let alone the outside world. No electronic devices of any kind were allowed inside, other than the flat panel display on the wall and the digital media player that fed it. Multiple, redundant detection devices were employed to ensure this rule was never broken. It was simply referred to as "The Room". Equipped with a long conference table, it was a special meeting area for a select group of individuals granted security clearance above SAP, or Special Access Program, and designed to facilitate conversations of an unimaginable sensitivity. New Generation Investments, LLC, was the front for the National Security Agency Department of Special Activities, or NDSA., and the "Room" was the meeting place of its Executive Council, or "ExComm" as it was called. Much debate had gone into the location for the new organization. Some felt it should be housed in the NSA facility itself in Fort Meade, Maryland. But its mission was so sensitive that the principals, or more accurately its progenitors, believed that even senior NSA staff, without the need to know, should not be allowed to be aware of its existence. The only way to guarantee complete anonymity, especially among a team of professionals who by the very nature of their wiring were highly curious, was to make the location of NDSA and its activities as remote and non-descript as possible.

Special Agent in Charge, Intelligence Directorate, Ryan Jennings sat upright in his chair and stared at the morning intelligence brief that was sitting on his desk. He felt a cold chill, more like a foreboding, as he reflected on what it said. Jennings had graduated in the second quartile of his class at Georgetown Law – not good enough to land a high-profile judicial clerkship, but good enough to get him a well-paying job as an associate, partner track, at one of the countless law firms inside the beltway. But he had quickly grown weary from the treadmill of billable hours and being relegated to legal research that seemed like little more than a dive into a grinding minutia that was terribly unfulfilling. On the heels of the 9/11 attacks his luck changed. The attacks had revealed two very obvious deficiencies in the U.S. Government's ability to protect the homeland. First, and most obvious, was the lack of quality intelligence about potential terrorist threats. But this wasn't the most glaring deficiency, however. There was a failure that was even subtler and more pernicious, and it was the utter lack of quality analysis of that intelligence. There had been much criticism about how various Federal Agencies wouldn't talk to each other. The result was that nobody could connect the dots. The reality had been that too often they didn't talk to each other because they didn't properly understand what they had. They couldn't connect the dots because they couldn't see them, even though the dots were before their very eyes. As a result, almost every lettered intelligence agency in the Executive Branch looked to aggressively up their game. They aggressively recruited and developed a cadre of analysts to address the weakness. Two years out of law school a headhunter called a frustrated Jennings about a job with the NSA. He was told he would be doing work that would save lives, and he leapt at the opportunity to escape the drudgery of the legal associate treadmill. He finally was being offered the chance to do something that sounded meaningful.

So here he sat, after almost 12 years, as the newly appointed Special Agent in Charge, Project Sparrow. He had been selected for the assignment about 2 years ago and was read into the vision for the NDSA as well as Project Sparrow itself as part of the on boarding process. The scope of the project, and the sheer volume of communications the Agency planned to mine and evaluate, left him almost breathless. He understood how civil liberties lawyers could become apoplectic about this, to say nothing of the press, if details of the program ever became public. Its scope was almost unimaginable. How could such a program ever stand up to the scrutiny of the Constitutional guarantees of privacy and unreasonable search and seizure? There was no analogy to the F.I.S.A. courts, or any other independent body that would vet the collection or use of the data or otherwise supervise the overall effort. The mission was entirely self-contained as a matter of design, to ensure its security. Yet as a lawyer, Jennings also understood the concept of exigent circumstances. Bureaucratic oversight would greatly slow the process down and likely prevent action in time to actually save lives. These were dangerous times.

The public was demanding the government do something, and people increasingly didn't mind paying the price in terms of their privacy. And besides, Jennings five-year-old niece was at The Magic Kingdom the day of the attack and actually saw Cinderella's Palace explode. She was ok physically but terribly scarred emotionally.   She suffered recurrent nightmares and acute separation anxiety every time his sister, the girl's mother, would even attempt to leave the room. This should not be the plight of a five-year-old little girl, he kept telling himself, and Jennings was resolved to do anything he could to prevent it from happening to another child.   Law school had taught him to think in terms of nuance and shades of grey, of subtleties and gradations. It was a process that reflected the need to build, refine, challenge, and iterate to find the truth. Over the last twelve years these skills had gradually atrophied as he increasingly viewed his world, and his work, in shades of black and white. He hadn't even realized the changes in his thinking, of how it was becoming more binary.   These changes were masked by the growing strength of his convictions, and this trait itself made him increasingly resistant to challenge, less open to the possibility that his conclusions could be wrong. He didn't consciously acknowledge it, but the changes in his thinking ideally suited him for his new assignment. Dismissal of other views became to him the admirable character trait of not suffering fools gladly – essential, so he thought, to a man in his position.

He looked down again at the intelligence brief on his desk and reread the conclusions and recommendations section. The crazies were about to launch another terrorist attack – that was as certain as the imperfect art of intelligence could guarantee. And his team had uncovered the plot in time to stop it. He almost felt a sense of pride as he rose from his desk to head towards the meeting. This was indeed meaningful work, he thought to himself. He was about to save lives.

Agent Jennings and Colonel Taylor walked side by side through the long hallway towards the Room. Each man was buried in his thoughts and said nothing to the other. As they silently walked the hall, Taylor was unsettled as he contemplated the first agenda item with ExComm.   Jennings' team of computer wizards running the Sparrow threat detection protocol had uncovered another terrorist threat and submitted it to ExComm for decision a couple of hours ago. The ExComm decision process was designed to be nimble and ensure that timely decisions were made in the face of a clear and present danger. Nobody wasted their time by preparing formal presentations or fancy PowerPoint decks. They all knew the cost of bureaucratic drag in this business would be measured in terms of lives. Condensing the time between threat detection and action was a high priority. The NDSA decision process actually was a rare example of government efficiency, motivated by a recognition of the extraordinarily high stakes. The raw intelligence, analysis, and recommendations had been quickly packaged in a standard template and sent to the ExComm members hours before the meeting. Taylor knew that the likely outcome of the meeting would be a decision to clear his team for action to neutralize the threat. ExComm had probably already arrived at that decision, he thought to himself. Within 48 hours of their first actual mission, they would be sent back into the breach. Another high-end shopping mall in suburban Washington D.C., called Tyson's Corner, was believed to be the target this time. Although this threat appeared to be largely unrelated to the recent incidents, the M.O. was exactly the same. Isolated terrorist cells operating independently seemed to be the method now favored by Al Qaeda and its growing number of copycats. Several months ago the Sparrow software began flagging conversations that brought together pieces of a new puzzle. It slowly started coming together as Jennings' team worked their magic. Several Pakistani college students at Mary Washington University, about an hour and a half south of D.C., were repeatedly using words such as "blast" and "bomb" in cell-phone conversations between themselves and a Pakistani expat working at the college IT department. This resulted in each individual being targeted for a Sparrow implant. The passive listening capacity uncovered numerous similar conversations among them at their local mosque. Routine investigation of the IT employee, who seemed to be acting as a mentor to the group and encouraging the conversations, revealed that 15 years ago he had ties with a suspected terrorist organization while traveling through Afghanistan.   This brought it to Jennings' attention and ultimately elevated it to what they called a "Level 1 Threat", similar to the threat assessments for the terrorist cells that had struck yesterday.   Level 1 was attack imminent, over 98% confidence level. A "Level 1" status was necessary to clear into action the Spec Ops team commanded by Colonel Taylor.

Those responsible for developing the Sparrow Protocols had debated extensively whether or not it was better to send local or Federal law enforcement to arrest the terrorist suspects before they could do their damage. Problem was, there were several inconvenient legal complications about how the threat detection process worked, and the confidential nature of the process itself made it very difficult to take action against suspects in a conventional law-enforcement manner. First, sharing the intelligence with the local police or FBI would hopelessly compromise the program's security and could render it useless against subsequent threats. It likely would be a "one and done". If there was one thing Federal Agencies were good at it was self-preservation. Once given birth, an arm of the Federal Government became all but immortal. Second, nothing about the intelligence itself would stand up in a court of law, or even make it to a court of law for that matter. There wasn't a first-year law student who would regard evidence collected under Sparrow as admissible in court. Stopping the terrorists by arresting them, therefore, wasn't an option. And nothing about Operation Sparrow contained anything that even remotely resembled due process. Colonel Taylor's mission was designed to fill this gap.   The more polite and conventional law enforcement process seemed too often to come into play only after the fact. Why not just hunt the terrorists down and shoot them? The obvious choice of neutralizing terrorists well before they acted, or more bluntly, assassinating them, was another option hotly debated. Taylor certainly had a team that could accomplish that if necessary. But that was messy business and left too many loose ends. It would also bring in local, even Federal law enforcement to investigate. Nobody knew about the NDSA but the NDSA itself and a handful of seniors.   Targeted takedowns had been used overseas where the Feds faced far less risk of legal scrutiny. It was a special expertise of the CIA. Special Activities Division, or SAD, and they did it well.   Doing it on U.S. soil, however, was another matter altogether. It had never been done domestically, at least so far as anyone was willing to admit.   Well, at least not yet.   So the progenitors, NDSA and Sparrow, were convinced the most effective deterrent was to stop the attacks in route and, if necessary, feed the cover story of bumbling terrorists prematurely detonating their bomb as cover.   It was blatantly unconstitutional, but the President regarded terrorism as an undeniable threat and believed with every fiber of her being it was justified on National Security grounds. Talk a good game in public but do whatever was necessary in secret. It was essential for the survival of the nation, and most definitely essential for her survival politically. And she wasn't the only true believer in the Administration, even among those not read in. And everyone knew that most of the public would gladly accept a little more surveillance for the perceived lesser threat from a terrorist act. And if it allowed the feds to kill a few bad guys in the process, all the better. So ,Taylor's team would once again be ordered into the breach.   They had missed three other attacks yesterday. They would not miss this one.

The second item on the agenda was the post mortem on yesterday's mission, simply called "The Brief". "Brief" was a non-descript term intended to keep judgment and emotion out of the after actions review. But people are people, and one can no more extract judgment and emotion out of human failure or success any more than one can stop a dog from barking.   Such things are deeply seated human instincts inexorably embedded in the first level of Maslow's hierarchy survival and are permanent and immutable. The powers that be could call the meeting anything they wanted, but both men knew hell was about to be paid. By most metrics the mission had been a complete success – at least the attack in Michigan had been stopped and countless lives were saved. And the cover story of the SUV exploding from the premature detonation of the terrorist's bomb was bought hook, line and sinker by the press, largely because it simply made sense. Nobody had come forward to report that a civilian aircraft crossing the summer sky had apparently fired a missile, and nobody reported seeing anything hit the vehicle. The missiles compressed air propulsion burst had done its job admirably and the spectacular explosion had instantly drawn and locked everybody's attention, rendering the likelihood of seeing the missile, let alone connecting it with the aircraft, very remote. Short of somebody actually filming the event, the risk of detection was regarded as minimal. Nevertheless, there was that damn minivan that, as a quirk of fate, would make an ill-timed turn at an extraordinarily ill-timed moment resulting in the death of a young woman and her three children. As both men walked towards the entrance to the Room, Taylor was sick to his stomach about it. He knew the risks, and the virtual certainty of something like this eventually happening was recognized by everyone in the program, yet it happened on his watch, and it happened on his first mission. He was the one who asked for the final assessment of collateral risk, he was the one who judged it to be within "acceptable parameters", a tradecraft phrase that now sickened him, and he was the one who gave the order to execute. Every aspect of the mission was strictly by the book, and every decision he made was defendable in the heat of the moment, and many lives were very much saved that day. Yet still he felt sick, and he knew that he would have to carry that feeling for the rest of his life. Agent Jennings, however, was not nearly so circumspect. Oh, he wasn't happy about the loss of innocent life, but his mind kept coming back to two points – his job was analysis and threat detection, and he did that job quite well, at least with respect to the attack in Michigan. Second, he wasn't the one who pulled the trigger, so his hands were clean. Of course, there were three other successful mall attacks that day that NDSA and Jennings had failed to uncover. He would no doubt suffer some manner of criticism for that. But his defense was solid – this was a new program, it was the first Op, and at least he detected one of the four terrorist cells. Without the program nothing would have been detected. As the program progressed, he could easily argue, their threat detection capability would mature, become much more effective, and countless more lives would be saved. It's simply not rational to expect perfection the first time out, but the program clearly worked. Perfect, he thought, as he walked down the hall with a bit more spring in his step than Taylor.

The two men approached the door of the Room, where two Marine guards stood at attention with automatic weapons in their hands. They were both dressed in civilian clothes, as was the protocol for every military person stationed at 1517 Westbranch Drive. The presence of uniformed personnel at the facility didn't exactly support the cover story of an investment management firm. But that didn't prevent the military from more creative ways of ensuring everyone knew the pecking order. Non-coms wore dark grey windowpane suits, junior officers wore Navy pinstripe, and senior officers, bird colonels and higher, wore solid navy suits, all from Brooks Brothers. The Marine guards on either side of the door into the Room were dressed in windowpane. Jennings and Taylor in succession stepped up to a security device and were required to perform three separate actions to gain access. First, they would swipe their card, and this would activate a fingerprint verification device much like the device used to unlock an iPhone. After verification of their fingerprint, which was the second step, a retinal scanner would activate to provide the final confirmation of authorization for entry. If any of the steps failed, the Marine guards would drop the men to the floor and zip-tie them. At random intervals a Red Team would test all measures of facility security to verify its integrity and to insure the military guards would follow their orders. Of course none of the individuals wearing either windowpane or pinstripe suits had any idea what went on where they worked. They just knew it was an NSA satellite where some highly sensitive national security work was done. Spook stuff. Any military person, however, wearing one of those Brooks Brothers solid navy-blue suits, like Colonel Taylor, was fully read in. Both Taylor and Jennings received green lights as they performed the security steps, which allowed the outer door to the Room to open. This granted them access to a small waiting area just outside the Room itself, nicknamed "The Holding Tank", where they would sit and wait until called for by the principals.

The NDSA principals, or Executive Council, sat around the long conference table in The Room. In the background was a distinct low volume humming, a white noise designed to further mask conversations. At the head of the table sat the Chairman of ExComm, Dr. Adam Johnson, whose day job was Director, National Security Agency. To his right sat the Director, NDSA itself, Trae Collins, Ph.D. in forensic economics, Massachusetts Institute of Technology, and career employee of the NSA. To the left was Vice Admiral George Erby, the President's National Security Advisor. Also present was the President's Chief of Staff, William Fitzpatrick. Fitzpatrick had no formal role in the organization, but everyone knew he was the real force in the room.

Johnson began the conversation. "Ok this meeting is called to order. To be clear, consistent with the Presidential Finding that governs this program, there are to be no minutes taken of this meeting. And let me remind everyone that nobody is to take notes. We walk into this room with only what is in our heads, and we walk out of the room the same way. Deviations from this directive represent a violation of the National Security Act, and will result in criminal prosecution, etc., etc., etc. Everybody clear on these directions?"

"Spare us the drama, Adam," Admiral Erby replied. "There isn't a prosecutor anywhere in the federal service with the security clearance sufficient to bring criminal charges, so to speak, so let's dispense with the theatrics and get on with this. Or are you referring to the term prosecution in the more creative sense?" he asked with a thinly veiled note of sarcasm. "I fully buy into the remit of this organization, and continue to believe it has great potential to protect the American people, but there is no getting around the fact that forces of the United States Government 24 hours ago engaged in an activity, on U.S. soil I might add, that ended the lives of four of our citizens, and regardless of the mission's otherwise success, is a fact that is deeply disturbing."

"We all understood the risks of collateral damage going into this, and we all signed off on it," Johnson shot back. "The loss of innocent life at some point was inevitable, and the cold hard fact is that without the execute order yesterday many more people would be dead. That family's death, however tragic, served a greater good, period."

"I understand that, Adam," Erby replied with evident and growing irritation, "but it wasn't supposed to happen on the very first mission and let me remind you the very first mission only neutralized one out of four terrorist cells. When I look at the early loss of innocent lives from an otherwise justified mission, and our 25% hit rate in light of the extraordinarily invasive nature of the program, I can't help but question whether we have a proper assessment of the cost versus the benefits, and this is one thing we promised the President would guide our actions."

"I agree, George," Johnson fired back, struggling himself to hold back a growing sense of irritation. "But the program is just starting, and now is not the time to go wobbly. We have to give this a chance to work."

"Alright, gentlemen," Bill Fitzpatrick now interjected. "I think we all need to take it down a notch. A big notch. George, I understand your very valid concerns and I too am disappointed about things gone wrong here. That's the very reason for this meeting and the whole purpose of designing post-mortem process. We need to trust the process right now and see it through. It's preposterous to do anything else at this stage; we've recruited the very best people," he said, "so let's see how this plays out."

Erby sat there with a look on his face that was a cross between irritation and resignation but nodded as he looked up to Fitzpatrick and said, "Got it. I agree." It was an odd thing, actually, that the President's National Security Advisor was part of the executive council instead of, say, the Secretary of Homeland Security, whose remit was much more closely linked to the work of NDSA. The reason was simple. Everyone knew that the Homeland Security cabinet position was a political appointment that put the person in charge of a large, sprawling and completely disjointed Federal bureaucracy. Creating the cabinet position was largely for show, so the political class could claim they had actually done something, when in reality they had done nothing at all. The Homeland Security Secretary could accomplish little in his or her position, and as a result it usually went to a political hack. Translation, none of the seniors, let alone the President, trusted the person. A seasoned Flag Officer was a much better choice. Such a person could be relied on to be a real sanity check on operations and to understand the importance of security. But most importantly, of course, at the end of the day the person would salute sharply and do what he or she was told, or at least the chances of that were much better than with some political opportunist.

Director Johnson looked around the room and spoke up to regain control of the conversation. "Let's get Taylor and Jennings in here and get this thing started," he said. "I think we can dispense with the first agenda item quickly. We've all seen the intel on the threat and it appears rock solid. And I'm sure none of us wants to miss another attack so quickly. The Nation has been deeply traumatized by what happened yesterday and we can't afford another failure on its heels. If the cell makes a move tomorrow, as suspected, I want Taylor's team cleared to neutralize it. Any objections? Alright, so ordered. Now let's get them in here." With that, he pressed a button just to his right on the top of the conference table, and on the wall in the Tank a light that was glowing red switched to green, the signal for the two men to enter the conference room.

Taylor and Jennings walked into the room and sat down next to each other on the side of the table to Johnson's right. Both men appeared outwardly calm as they waited for the proceedings to start. The outward calm was a sign of their professionalism, but on the inside both men were unsettled. This Brief was supposed to be a celebration of the very best outcomes that intelligence work and efforts to protect the American people could produce. It was to be a confirmation that taking an aggressive approach to threat detection and prevention would yield results previously unimagined. Instead they were sitting here about to discuss things gone wrong, terribly wrong, and both men felt a silent dread about what was about to transpire.

Johnson broke the momentary silence. "To remind everyone, nothing that is discussed in this room is to leave it, other than discussions among the principals, or in direct conversation between any of the principals and POTUS. Nothing will be recorded in any manner, and nobody is to summarize the proceedings from memory in any written form after leaving this room. Violating these rules of engagement will result in immediate dismissal, with prejudice. We are all intelligent people here, and I'm sure everyone can figure out what "with prejudice" means. This is to be an open and direct conversation with only one rule – one person speaks at a time. I will exercise the prerogatives of the Chair to enforce this rule or to keep the discussion going in a constructive manner. OK, any questions before we start?" Nobody spoke. "Good. Let's get directly to the two primary subjects of this Brief."

"First," Johnson said, "ExComm approves action against the Tyson's Corner threat with extreme prejudice." The words, "with extreme prejudice" provided Taylor's SpecOps team the clearance necessary for lethal force and authorized the use of the drone. "The threat is to be neutralized. Any significant movement of the targets today?" he asked.

"No sir," Jennings replied. "Several of the targets appear to be spending the morning at a local soccer field, and their handler is at his place of employment. Sparrow intel continues to corroborate early afternoon tomorrow as the most likely time for the strike. We'll have GPS confirmation of the cell assembling when it happens and agents on the ground to confirm." One of the fringe benefits of the Sparrow program was the GPS chips included in most modern smart phones. Not only could NDSA listen to the conversations, they could track the whereabouts of suspects as well.

"Great," Johnson replied. "It is imperative that we stop this attack," he continued. "We cannot afford another miss within 48 hours of yesterday's attack, and neither can the nation. The psychological impact would be devastating, to say nothing about the very real risk that POTUS would regard us and this program as nothing other than a paper tiger."

Johnson turned his gaze towards Taylor. "OK, on to the mission debrief. Colonel Taylor," Johnson said in an even voice, "at what point did your team realize the minivan was in the kill zone?"

Taylor took a deep breath, let half of it out, and then started to speak in an equally even and non-emotive voice. "Sir, both the aircraft and the agents on the ground confirmed what was believed to be a reasonable separation from other vehicles. The minivan was sitting at the traffic light on the road perpendicular to the direction of the target." Taylor picked up a clicker, pointed it towards a large flat panel display on the wall, pressed the button and activated the video feed. He continued. "As you can see sir, the Target appeared to slow down slightly – we have no idea why. At the point it slows down, you can see the minivan dart into the oncoming traffic just ahead of the target. The target actually appears to step on its brakes to avoid a rear-end collision, which allowed the van to start to pull away. Unfortunately, insufficient separation was achieved before the ordnance hit. We believe the van turning in front of the target and its continued proximity is what created the secondary explosion. In doing so, the van effectively exposed its gasoline tank to hot shrapnel projected forward from the explosion. If the van had stayed at the light, even if the target had been hit in the intersection, or if it had turned quickly behind the target and not directly exposing the gas tank, its damage likely would have been minimal, and certainly the risk of collateral fatalities would have been much lower. We gave the execute order based on the conditions on the ground just before the van darted into traffic. The ordnance was released from the aircraft the same instant the van moved, rendering it impossible to abort. There is no way the action sequencing software could have known that van was going to make an abrupt turn. Digital Forensics has tasked the software engineers with programming "what if" scenarios, like the van rapidly turning, as a support function to the tactical assessment. I'm afraid the reality, however, is the risk assessment can't be relayed to the decision maker fast enough to matter. We don't see any way it could have changed the outcome. We have also looked at whether any type of abort function is possible after launch. While it's certainly feasible from a technical standpoint, it's just not practical. Aborting the ordnance after it is fired from the aircraft would be an event highly visible to anyone in the area, which would almost certainly compromise the program. It would also leave unexploded ordnance on site for local law enforcement to retrieve. This was a tragic sequence of events, but one that nobody could have foreseen or reacted to in time to make any difference. As grieved as I am over the loss of innocent life, this was unavoidable, and as we all know many lives were likely saved as a result of stopping the target." Taylor sucked in another deep breath and slowly let it out. He hated what had happened but was satisfied with himself that he had answered the question effectively. "In addition, sir," he continued, "after a couple of news cycles there is still no evidence the program has in any way been compromised. As we all know, this is still being reported as a premature detonation of the terrorist bomb, and the investigative slant seems almost exclusively focused on who the terrorists were and where they came from. Not a single mention from any source about this being anything other than a terrible tragedy for that family."

Director Johnson turned his attention to Special Agent Jennings. "Any Sparrow intel from the press suggesting anyone is thinking differently, Jennings?"

"No sir," Jennings replied. "None whatsoever. And we have fairly extensive Sparrow coverage in Southeastern Michigan given the large Muslim population in Dearborn. Close to 100% of every major news organization employee in the area has active Sparrow implants, and our coverage of East Dearborn in particular is north of 60% and growing. Our digital forensics team has been combing the data since shortly after the mission, and we have not uncovered a single conversation that suggests suspicion of anything other than a premature detonation of a bomb."

"Good," Johnson said. "Obviously we will continue to monitor this, especially the press, but I think it's reasonable to conclude that any potential fallout is likely to be contained. Unless there are additional developments ExComm will consider this matter closed."

"Godspeed on your mission, gentlemen," Admiral Erby said. "Let's stop these bastards before they can do any more harm."

One Week Later

The Islamic Center of Fredericksburg is located a few miles west of the I95 corridor just south of Virginia Highway 3. It was nestled in an area rich with Civil War history, and East of the famous Wilderness and Chancellorsville Battlefields.

It hardly looked like a house of worship, let alone one dedicated to a faith that was starkly foreign to most of the local residents. It was crowded inside the mosque, as the local Imam said in a low voice, "To Allah we belong and to Him we shall return." It was a funeral for a father and three of his sons, who had just died en route to a soccer match in Tyson's Corner, an hour and a half north of their home. The father was a mid-level employee in the IT department of a local university hospital. He was blessed with sons who were exceptionally bright, earning each of them partial scholarships at Mary Washington University, where he worked. One of them was even an honors student enrolled in a pre-med curriculum. And each of them was a gifted soccer player, and proud to have their father as an unpaid coach of their team. The family loved to talk about how they believed they truly exemplified the American Dream, escaping the grinding poverty of the Islamabad environs to a better life in their adopted homeland, only to have it snatched from them by a senseless tragedy, the explosion of their Ford Explorer SUV en route to a soccer game. The wife and mother sat quietly sobbing as the service continued. Her life had been so full of joy and hope. She could not believe how quickly it had all evaporated. Three others had died in the accident as well. Two of them were African American, and one was the son of an Asian Indian mother and a Caucasian father. Seven people headed to a soccer game. Their lives ended as if they were merely, in the poet's words, "a vapor in the wind".

Chapter 5 – Something Very Odd

It was a bright and beautiful Spring day in Westchester County. The morning sun beamed through the windshield enveloping the cockpit in comforting warmth. A gentle breeze barely lifted the airport's windsock as the nearly cloudless sky foretold a perfect day to fly. Joseph Michael Barber sat in front of the flight deck of his new Beech King Air 90 turboprop and carefully reviewed the checklist as he started the second, or right engine. He loved to fly, and he loved that airplane. Having recently earned his multiengine rating, he had sold his single-engine Cirrus SR-22T and decided to trade up right into a turbo prop. He was amazed at how easy the transition was, and how pilot-friendly the big King Air was to fly. Piloting his own plane had become a passion and was one of the perks he could indulge himself in on the heels of his company's success. He could easily purchase a first-class airline ticket now anytime he wanted, but flying his own plane gave him both the pleasure and the flexibility he found so useful. He no longer was tied to an airline schedule. No more indignity of the TSA lines or the inconvenience of a delayed or cancelled flight. He could simply get into his plane and go. And it often allowed him to fly to smaller airports that were much closer to where he needed to be. His King Air, of course, couldn't fly at over 500 mph like an airliner, but with a cruise speed of close to 300 mph and its inherent flexibility, it often got him where he needed to be much faster than any airline could. And besides, piloting this bird was fun. Well it was usually fun. It wasn't fun today.

Joe pushed the microphone button on the left-hand side of the control yoke and spoke into the boom mike that extended from the left ear cup of his Bose Aviation headset to the front of his mouth: "Westchester ground, this is King Air two niner seven Bravo Charlie. We are at the terminal ramp with Juliet ready to taxi for departure, would like IFR clearance to Oakland Troy Michigan, identifier, Kilo Victor Lima Lima."

"King Air two niner seven Bravo Charlie, advise when ready to copy," responded the ground controller.

"Seven Bravo Charlie ready to copy," Joe responded back.

Airport ground control then transmitted Joe's IFR instructions: "Seven Bravo Charlie cleared direct to Oakland Troy. Climb and maintain seven thousand, expect eleven thousand 30 minutes after departure. Altimeter two niner niner eight, squawk four zero two seven."

"Westchester ground," Joe replied, "cleared direct to Oakland Troy, climb and maintain seven thousand, expect eleven thousand 30 minutes from departure, altimeter two niner niner eight, four zero two seven on the box."

"Read back is correct," Ground control responded.

Once cleared for takeoff, and with his navigation plan programmed into the state-of-the-art aviation GPS, Joe taxied the powerful twin-engine bird onto runway 34, lined up with the centerline, and pushed the throttles forward to begin his take off. At about 100 knots of indicated airspeed he gently pulled back on the control yoke and the plane effortlessly lifted into the sky and began its climb at a rate of almost 2,000 feet per minute. He would be at his initial cruise altitude in less than four minutes. Joe never grew tired of the experience, but the normal joy of flying was greatly diminished this morning by the nature of this particular trip. He was en route to a funeral, well, actually four funerals. The wife of a friend and his three children were killed two days before in a tragic example of being in the worst possible place at the worst possible time. The lives of Veronica Maxwell, along with Peter, Ellie and Jennifer were ended as a fireball engulfed them from behind, triggered by what was reported as the premature detonation of a bomb being transported by four terrorists. It had consumed their SUV as they were on their way to a favorite shopping mall. The press called it collateral damage. The term offended Joe. It was so impersonal. But whatever it was called,

101

the lives of four beautiful people had been abruptly ended. They were the wife and family of his fraternity brother from Holy Cross. And not just any fraternity brother, Walter Maxwell Jr. was the son of the man who had died saving the life of Joe's father. Joe sat there, alone in the cockpit, and thought about how different his life would have been if he had grown up without his dad. In the middle of the control panel was a large multifunction display, one of the wonders of modern aviation electronics. A line on the display depicted the King Air's course, and a miniature aircraft on that line depicted the bird moving ever closer to its destination. He grew angrier as he thought about these innocent lives being snuffed out. How was this attack missed? But as much as he wanted to, he couldn't blame the government. These precious lives had been snuffed out by monsters, and he realized that it was impossible to prevent every potential attack. And they were incompetent monsters at that, incapable of constructing a bomb that would go off at the right time. That's what killed Veronica and the children – terrorist incompetence. He had to agree with the media speculation that this incompetence no doubt saved many lives by preventing the attackers from reaching their actual target. He shuttered at the speculation that the target was Somerset Mall. The body count there could have been terrible. But as much as this was solace for the mind, it certainly wasn't solace for the heart.

The sun continued to shine brightly as he passed through Detroit's class bravo airspace and began his descent into Troy. He knew the route well, as he had made this trip numerous times to visit his wife, Diana's, family, and even occasionally to visit clients. Detroit's air traffic control cleared him to conclude the flight into the airport itself under the simpler visual flight rules, or VFR. Within just minutes he had the airport in sight. Joe gently banked the big King Air as he entered the downwind leg of the airport's traffic pattern at a 45-degree angle for runway 27, and began going through his pre-landing checklist. He reduced power and started to deploy the plane's wing flaps. Once below about 160 knots, he pulled a lever to lower the landing gear, and three green lights on the cockpit panel indicated all three wheels were down and locked. Within just a couple of minutes he crossed the runway's threshold, pulled power back on the two massive turboprop engines and brought them to idle. His eyes now focused on the far end of the runway to improve his depth perception, he brought the bird down then raised the nose slightly high to bleed energy. The two main gear wheels touched the pavement first as the big bird gently settled onto the pavement and slowed to a crawl. Joe taxied off the active runway and headed towards the terminal ramp where his baby would be parked for at least a couple of days while he attended to the unpleasant affairs. As he gently coaxed the bird towards the terminal, he reflected how very long those couple days were going to be.

* * * * *

The chapel at A.J. Desmond and Son's funeral home was crowded. A friend of the family had just sung the hymn "It Is Well With My Soul", as Walter Maxwell Jr. sat in the front row and quietly sobbed. The funeral director stood up in front of the collected mourners and provided instructions for passing by the casket to show last respects. The organist began playing "Amazing Grace" as people rose from their seats and began the solemn procession past four caskets, three of them child sized. Joseph Michael Barber sat about three rows behind the family and continued to be deep in thought. The night before Walt had shared with Joe a sense that something about the incident just didn't seem right, although he conceded that he couldn't put his finger on what specifically bothered him. Joe had tried to gently explain to Walt how it was normal to look for other explanations for such a senseless tragedy, especially if you are a grieving husband and father who suddenly had everything dear to you ripped from your life. Then Joe thought about how Walt must have felt when learning that his father had been killed and learning he would grow up without a dad. Nobody should have to experience such a tragedy twice in a lifetime, Joe thought, and if he owed Walt anything here

103

other than being a sympathetic friend, it was lending a sympathetic ear. He had promised Walt at the end of their conversation that he would look into the incident and see if there was anything he could find out. From the press reports things appeared pretty straightforward, and Joe was convinced he would find nothing. But helping to bring a small sense of closure to a friend was the least he could do, he thought to himself. And Walt knew Joe's professional reputation, and the reputation of his firm, Orion Bellicus. A confirmation by Joe that things were exactly as they appeared would provide that sense of closure. As he sat there, he couldn't imagine a more appropriate use of his time over the next couple of days, even though he was convinced it would produce nothing.

That evening, Joe hosted a post funeral dinner for family and close friends. Joe insisted on making the arrangements and paying the bill himself, and he chose a local Morton's Steakhouse, where he knew the food would be good and the wine would be even better. It was not an inexpensive place to buy dinner for 17 people, but whatever the cost, he didn't give it a second thought. He grew up with a father, after all, while Walt Jr. didn't. He entertained no sense of guilt over this, but rather a profound sense of gratitude. And Joe was the kind of man whose gratitude translated into behavior. Joe stood up from the table as the group began to disburse and waited for an opportunity to talk to Walt Jr. privately. After several minutes of the group hugging Walt and everyone telling him he would be in their prayers, Joe and Walt finally found themselves alone in the foyer of the restaurant. Joe then suggested they spend a few final minutes in the bar before leaving. Both men ordered a single malt Scotch, a Lagavulin 16 – one of Walt's favorites - and then began to talk.

"Hey pal," Joe said, "I promise you I'm going to look into this, and I'll use every resource of my team to turn over rocks if we get even the slightest hint of anything. I've arranged to stay an extra day or so to take a look around, and I've got a few connections back at the ranch. I'm having Marcus see what he can dig up with the Feds."

"I know you will Joey B, and I can't tell you how much I appreciate you indulging me on this," Walt Jr. replied.

"It's nothing, my friend," Joe responded, "but I want to be honest with you. I'm going to give this a reasonable look, but I honestly don't think there is anything for us to find. Most of the time the obvious explanation is the correct one and I'm pretty convinced that's the case here. And I gotta tell you, Marcus agrees with me. If that gut of yours reveals anything more specific, you know how to get in touch with me. I'm probably here until tomorrow night sometime or the next morning, and then I'm going to be taking my plane back East. I'll call you before I leave."

"Thanks Joey," Walt Jr. replied. "I know it's probably just some phantom fear or something, but this would be just a tiny bit easier if you could confirm there's nothing else there."

"Love ya pal," Joe replied, "now let me drive you home. I'll have Di's brother retrieve your car tomorrow morning and get it back to you. I don't want you driving anywhere tonight."

After dropping Walt Jr. at his house, Barber sat in the lobby of his hotel with his laptop and read the numerous press reports about the incident. One of the things unfortunate for him, but probably fortunate for Walt Jr., was the absence of any visual recording of the explosion itself. Given our ubiquitous presence of cell phones with video recording capability, there was plenty of footage shared with the press of the immediate aftermath, and the smoldering wreckage of both vehicles. The only thing these videos did, however, was confirm the obvious. That was to be expected, however. People don't take out their cell phones and start recording until after something happens. And Joe had already checked and confirmed there was no traffic camera at that intersection. In the corner of the hotel lobby was a large, flat panel TV that was tuned to the local ABC News television channel. All of the local networks, along with both Fox News and CNN had been covering the incident almost 24/7. Joe's concentration on his laptop was momentarily broken as the local reporter started discussing the extraordinarily quick response that had been made by both the FBI and D.H.S to the crime scene. Agents from both organizations had been on site within an hour of the incident. They had conducted what was reported to be a very thorough review of the scene, and then quickly sanitized it. The reporter commented on how the rapid clean up of the crime scene had no doubt helped reduce the community's trauma over the incident. At first, being drawn to the TV was nothing other than a momentary break of Joe's concentration. It made sense, he thought, that the Feds would respond to such an onerous event so quickly. But the more he thought about it, the more something started gnawing at him as well, as if he was experiencing the same doubt about the incident as his friend. He tried to dismiss the notion, telling himself the official explanations all made perfectly good sense. But something just didn't seem right. Of course, the FBI would be on the scene quickly and even an SAC, or Special Agent in Charge. They had a local field office in Detroit. There was no reason they wouldn't be on the scene as quickly as local authorities, with the obvious exception of the Troy Police themselves. And it would make sense for them to immediately take jurisdiction over the crime scene given it was likely terrorist related. So why was he having this growing feeling in the pit of his stomach that something didn't seem right? He couldn't shake it. The more he continued to go over things in his head the more he became convinced that everything fit; but his unease wouldn't relent.

Then it hit him like a pile of bricks. OK, he'd buy the FBI being there immediately, but D.H.S.? What was that about? Even if they sent agents by a government jet, there was no way they could be on the scene within an hour.

It was almost as if they had people pre-staged there. And why clean up the scene so quickly. The FBI forensics lab was, if not only extremely capable, extremely thorough. How could one sanitize a scene like that in just a matter of a couple of days and not somehow lose evidence in the process. His unease was now starting to turn into a bad feeling. He kept going over and over in his mind what motivation on the part of the Feds could possibly be explained by these facts. Then that pile of bricks hit him again. What if the Feds had suspected, or even uncovered the terrorist plot? What if they had positioned agents on site to try and stop it? And what if they had likely kept local law enforcement in the dark as a way of protecting their sources or their methods. If that was the case, their efforts clearly failed. You couldn't even argue they partially succeeded, because by all reports the attack was thwarted by the terrorist's poor bomb making skills. What if the Feds had engineered some sort of cover up to mask their failures? As he thought about it, Joe doubted this was anything that would provide the slightest bit of relief or closure for his friend. It would only make him angry and increase his pain. It was making Joe angry. For now he chose to keep these thoughts to himself. Except, of course, for that conversation he was about to have with Marcus. The thought of a cover-up really angered him. If true, such behavior on the part of the government was terrible. And it also demonstrated a failure of the most fundamental obligation of the government, that of keeping its citizens safe.

"Let's not jump to conclusions, JB," Joe quietly muttered under his breath. "Think with your mind, not with your glands." At that point, the television got his attention again. Somebody had changed the channel to CNN, and the screen was filled with the image of another vehicle engulfed in flames, but he could tell it was not a minivan and the surroundings were definitely not suburban Detroit. What was this, he asked himself. As he looked at the screen, a man in a suit was holding a microphone and discussing how a Ford Explorer had just exploded with seven male passengers en route to a soccer game in suburban Washington D.C. Early speculation was that

107

something had gone terribly wrong and caused an explosion of the vehicle's gas tank. A complete investigation was to be ordered by the National Transportation Safety Board, and the stock of the vehicle's manufacturer was down sharply in aftermarket trading. The reporter was talking about how the incident was reminiscent of the old side-saddle gas tank problem of General Motors and their pickup trucks, and also similar to the problem decades ago with the Ford Pinto. There was one big difference, however. The truck and Pinto gas tank problems exploded on impact. This very popular SUV seemed to spontaneously erupt. There was no collision, and no other vehicle involved in any way. And there had been no reports of problems with the Explorer since the Firestone tire problem over a decade ago. Early speculation centered on a faulty electrical system or fuel pump. The scene on television transitioned to an interview with a man in a white coat from the National Automobile Safety Lab, who promised a quick and thorough investigation. With a transition back to the reporter, the reporter emphasized that this was the only report of such an incident and the public should not as yet be unduly alarmed. Joe could not help but notice an eerie similarity between the video of the terrorists' Toyota Land Cruiser he had recently watched on his laptop, and the appearance of the burning Ford Explorer on the hotel lobby's flat panel television. "Get a hold of yourself, Barber," he said once again under his breath. "You're starting to let your imagination go wild; remember, mind, not glands," he thought again. "Let's try and collect, then analyze the facts." He reminded himself that Marcus was going to call in a few chips with the Feds and see what he could find out. That likely would put to bed his recent affection with conspiracy theories. There had to be a reasonable explanation as to why DHS was so quickly on the scene, and the more he thought about it, the more sense it made that the Feds would want to clean up the scene as quickly as possible. His next steps, however, were very clear. At first light tomorrow morning he was going to drive to the area of the incident and take a good look around the newly sanitized scene. Even very smart and thorough people make mistakes when in a hurry, he thought to himself. Maybe, just maybe, he would find something. Problem was, Joseph Michael Barber was a man who simply did not believe in coincidences, and his gut was far from settled.

Chapter 6 – No Accountability

NDSA Headquarters, McLean, VA

Colonel Jeffrey Taylor sat in his office along the outside wall of the fourth floor of 1517 Westbranch Drive. It was another beautiful Virginia Spring day, and he could see a few cherry trees in full blossom as he looked out over the neatly manicured yard. The beauty of the scene, however, sharply contrasted with his mood. He had commanded two missions in as many days. The first was a partial success, but with catastrophic collateral damage. The second was a complete failure. Not only had the wizards of Project Sparrow failed to correctly identify the Tyson's Corner threat, the clowns had delivered him a false positive. Now for the second time in less than a week innocent lives had been snuffed out by his hand. And there was no writing this one off as tragic collateral damage. The innocents were actually the targets. Seven young soccer players and their coach were simply headed to a game. The Sparrow threat algorithm had focused on the suspects repeated use of key words, such as bomb and blast and headshot. The potential threat had continued to rise through the various software filters as the target words were used over a period of weeks in multiple locations, including college dorm rooms, the home of the coach, the practice field and their mosque. The progressive timeline of the discussion, along with the escalating combative tone of the suspects and the specificity of the date of attack drove the conversations ever higher through the threat detection process. Throw in the ethnicity and religion of the suspects, and the software was all too happy to flag the thread of conversations as a high-probability threat. This is what brought it ultimately to Jennings' attention. The human factor was supposed to be the failsafe. The threat detection software was only supposed to identify the potential of a threat. Jennings and his team were supposed to vet it with quality analysis. But that took time, and it was

111

becoming increasingly apparent to Taylor that time was the program's Achilles heel. The attacks of 24 hours ago had created an extreme sense of urgency, and the failure to detect two out of the four attacks had rendered the entire team obsessed with the desire not to repeat the mistake. Under these circumstances a short-circuiting of the vetting process was a foregone conclusion. As Special Agent in Charge, Jennings was the one responsible for the analysis and the final conclusions and recommendations. He was the one who recommended a green light on the op and was determined not to make the same mistake twice. Taylor consoled himself ever so slightly over the fact that, as the Spec Ops Commander, he did not have a voice in which threats to attack. That was Jennings' job. Just as Jennings had no voice or operational control over the actions of the Spec Ops team itself. It was the principle of separation of duties, a fundamental tenet of operational control. He kept telling himself it was a valid mission order and the intelligence failure was not his. But he was the one who pulled the trigger, with the result that seven innocent people were now dead. The Sparrow algorithm had failed to parse the subtle difference between words uttered as a terrorist threat and words uttered simply as soccer slang. It had no way of detecting that the date of a potential threat might be nothing more than the date of an important soccer match. The inescapable truth was that there was no such thing as completely objective software code, let alone one that was foolproof. People wrote the code, and people were inescapably biased and fallible. And those biased and fallible people had validated the threat. Taylor had hoped this would now be painfully obvious to ExComm. He would be wrong.

Taylor had just returned from the ExComm Brief. He had walked into the Room expecting to watch Jennings get eviscerated for a colossal screw up. But that hadn't happened. The ExComm members, and even the President's Chief of Staff, all seemed to be in survival mode and completely dismissive of the staggering magnitude of the failure. And Taylor found it quite unsettling how antiseptically they had discussed their options. ExComm's response painfully validated the prime directive of any government agency – survival. Jennings was all too happy to feed this process and, to Taylor's utter astonishment, had seemed to emerge from the discussion completely unscathed. Taylor simply couldn't believe it. Even more incredible, nobody seemed to have the slightest of second thoughts about the program, let alone the inclination to kill it. They seemed to be as concerned with maintaining viability as they were with providing themselves with plausible deniability.

There was something even more unsettling about how the conversation in the Room played out. Taylor replayed the conversation over again in his mind. He was astonished when Chief of Staff Fitzpatrick looked at him and asked, "Colonel Taylor, what is the mental state of your team right now?" Fitzpatrick then had followed up with a question that made the hair on the back of Taylor's neck stand on end when he asked, "Are we going to have a problem with that drone operator, or anybody else?"

Taylor had replied, in an even voice that masked his deep level of concern, "Define problem, sir."

Fitzpatrick straightened his back slightly as he sat in his chair, and in a firm tone fired back, "Colonel, you know perfectly well what I mean by problem. I want your assurances that whatever measure of understandable regret or pain of conscience your trigger-man or anyone else on your team feels for the unfortunate manner in which events of the last several hours have unfolded, they will remember their oath, and more importantly remember to keep their mouths shut. I want everyone in this room to understand that these events, while regrettable, even tragic, were nevertheless the result of an unfortunate mistake. ExComm is committed to seeing that mistake fixed. I don't want anyone entertaining the notion of leaking anything here to the press, or even their priest for that matter." Fitzpatrick's tone seemed to become increasingly authoritarian, almost threatening as he concluded his remarks.

Taylor responded, "My team, sir, while clearly unhappy about the way things unfolded...," he looked at Jennings while as he said these words, then turned back to Fitzpatrick to complete his response, "... are professionals and will do nothing to compromise the program."

"Good," Fitzpatrick fired back, and then turned to Jennings. "Agent Jennings, that goes for your team as well."

"My team is rock solid," Jennings replied, as he briefly glanced at Taylor in response to Taylor's previous glare at him.

Taylor ignored the implied snub by Jennings. He then directed his attention away from the President's Chief of Staff and turned towards the two individuals who actually had responsibility for the program, Drs. Collins and Johnson. "Director Johnson," he said, "I have complete confidence in the integrity of our extended team and our ability to maintain program integrity," a clever term, he thought to himself as he said it. What was really meant by that was everyone keeping their mouths shut. He continued, "But one thing I believe is very clear and we have to acknowledge as a team, and that is we cannot afford another mistake." Taylor continued looking at Johnson and avoided the temptation to glance again at Jennings. "I believe ExComm should at least consider the possibility of us all standing down until we jointly develop more robust mission rules. I acknowledge we have saved lives in the last several days, but the cost was too high. I am convinced we can and must to do better."

Fitzpatrick spoke up quickly before Director Johnson could reply. "Thank you, Colonel. That's a fair point and we'll take it under advisement. Adam," the Chief of Staff continued, "I think this meeting is over."

Taylor went to his office and continued to think about the conversation. Just exactly who was running this show, he thought to himself. As a military officer he fully understood and accepted the precept of civilian control of the military. But that was Johnson's and Collins' job, not the job of the President's Chief of Staff. He was extremely uncomfortable with the high profile of Fitzpatrick's involvement. That wasn't civilian control, he told himself, it was outright political control, driven by political motivation. And Jennings? Taylor's interaction with the man up to this point had been entirely cordial and professional. Each man knew the other had gone through an extraordinarily difficult vetting process to be where he was, and this drove a mutual respect, up until the last several days, anyway. Taylor, however, was becoming increasingly wary of the guy. He was supposed to get along with him, to work with him, even to trust and respect him as partner in the NDSA efforts to protect the American people. But the shortcomings, the cut corners and the outright carelessness in Jennings' work were now starting to fill Taylor with borderline contempt instead of trust. And Jennings was beginning to reveal himself as far too political for Taylor's liking as well. Taylor resigned himself to the fact that for the time being there was really nothing he could do about any of that, and his energy was best focused on ensuring he did his job exceptionally well. He would take the initiative to try and craft better mission rules. But after the recent meeting he wondered how the bosses would respond to them. And more importantly, he thought about how he would, or should, react to the next mission order if there weren't meaningful changes to the process. He reminded himself of his commissioning oath, then thought about the phrase "lawful orders". That phrase seemed to take on much increased significance in light of the events of the last several days. He wondered what he would do. He didn't know anymore.

* * * * *

Dr. Trae Collins sat behind his desk in his corner office. He pushed a key on his laptop to wake it up, entered his password, then pulled up the Drudge Report to scan the news, praying he wouldn't find some conspiracy theory about the Explorer's explosion. After a few moments of scanning the

115

headlines the site revealed nothing, to his great relief. His concentration was broken as his office intercom buzzed. At the same time his door opened and Bill Fitzpatrick walked in. He hated how the guy just went anywhere he wanted, unannounced. But he was the President's Chief of Staff and Collins knew there was little he could do about it.

Fitzpatrick walked up to Collins's desk and said, "Whose idiotic idea was it to float the cover story of the explosion being the result of a faulty vehicle?"

"The suggestion came from Jennings' team, but ExComm signed off on it," Collins answered. "It seemed like the only viable explanation to float in such a short period of time."

"It was an epically stupid idea, Trae," Fitzpatrick snapped back. "You floated a story that pulled in another Federal Agency, NTSB, and they are up in arms about not getting immediate access to the wreckage. Furthermore, the manufacturer is screaming bloody hell and the story won't stand up under scrutiny."

"As to the wreckage," Collins replied, "we were fortunate that the vehicle had almost a full gas tank. There isn't much of the SUV left. It's just a melted, burned out shell. I have been assured that there is no forensic evidence of the ordnance. Our people were on the scene quickly to ensure that. As to the manufacturer, given there are no other reports of incidents, the story will quickly drop from the news cycle, the NTSB won't find anything, and life will go on."

"It bloody hell better," Fitzpatrick snapped again. "And keep a careful eye on Taylor," he continued. "I don't trust that guy. I'm becoming afraid we have a Boy Scout on our hands who is about to go wobbly."

"Taylor will be fine, sir," Collins replied. "But of course we will keep close tabs on his mental state. And you will recall that as part of the program security protocol, one of his operators actually reports directly to me as an inside pair of eyes."

"Good," Fitzpatrick replied. "And I also recall that we have a failsafe contingency for this, correct?" the Chief of Staff asked.

"Yes sir, we do, for every person in the program with Level 1 clearance," he answered. "I am confident, however, that we will not need to use it."

"Let's hope not," Fitzpatrick replied. "Keep me advised of any developments, Mr. Director," the Chief of Staff said with his back to Collins as he walked out the door.

"What an arrogant ass," Collins whispered under his breath as the door closed. "I'd like to have a contingency for you," he muttered in a barely audible   voice.

Chapter 7 –- The Trouble with Curiosity

It was a fortunate thing for Joe that his time in the Teams had taught him to be a very careful observer. This was a skill especially drilled into him during his sniper training. In that line of work it wasn't simply a matter of doing ones job well, it was a matter of survival. The ability to see, and more importantly to be curious enough to properly consider and evaluate details that others completely missed could make the difference between mission success and failure; it also could make the difference between life and death. He initially drove through the intersection several times where the explosions had taken place. As he had feared, this was an unsatisfying exercise that revealed nothing in particular. His curiosity, however, wouldn't let go. He decided to park the car and examine the area on foot and take several pictures. He retrieved the Nikon D810 camera from the seat next to him and mounted a Carl Zeiss Otus 85 mm F1.4 short telephoto lens, exited the vehicle and began walking towards the intersection. The camera body and lens together cost almost $10,000, but there was no combination of digital sensor and glass that could deliver anything near the same sharpness and resolution of fine details. Shooting the pictures in raw format captured every detail in files that could exceed 75 megabites or more of data. Processing those files with software like Lightroom, where he could play with exposures, remove shadows, increase contrast and digitally zoom into the picture could reveal things the human eye easily missed. Digital photography had become another passion of his as well as an essential tool of his tradecraft. Joe stood on the side of the road 75 feet from where the explosions had occurred and again looked for anything that might reveal something the authorities had missed. But there was nothing. Other than some residual scorch marks on the pavement from the fires, which could have easily been mistaken for dirt, there wasn't a single bit of forensic evidence that suggested anything had happened here at all. But in that nothing, he gleaned the germ of a meaningful observation. It was really odd, Joe thought to himself, how clean the area was, and how extraordinary the care the Feds had taken to sanitize it. Was his imagination getting the best of him? Joe took several pictures, which he would have reviewed at the forensics lab back at Orion Bellicus.

Joe couldn't decide if he was disappointed or relieved at finding nothing as he walked back to the car. He carefully placed the expensive camera rig on the seat next to him and decided to drive around the adjacent neighborhood just in case he might stumble across something else. He had little hope of finding anything at this point but being thorough was something encoded in his DNA and there was that curiosity again. Besides, he felt he owed Walt Jr. something more than just a drive by of the scene itself. Joe drove up and down several streets on each side of the road where the tragedy had occurred in a systematic pattern to ensure a disciplined and exhaustive survey. He carefully scanned the yards, facades, and roofs of each building for anything that seemed potentially out of place. Then about 4 streets away from the main road, something caught his eye. He pulled the car to the side of the road, retrieved a pair of Nikon binoculars and squinted slightly as he peered through the glass and looked at the roof of the commercial building in front of him. Resting there appeared to be an object that looked like a small piece of metal, partially covered in blue paint, with part of the paint obscured by what looked like soot or some kind of burn marks. He then remembered the description of the terrorist's SUV. It was blue. He redirected the focus of the binoculars to the front of the building and then to the yard to see if there was anything else. He was slightly startled when a man suddenly completely filled his field of vision. Quickly recovering from this surprise, he became even more curious when he noticed the man seemed to be carrying something in his left hand. It appeared to be another piece of something metallic, with the same blue paint and scorch marks. He noticed the man was dressed in blue jeans and a polo shirt and wasn't wearing the official windbreaker of the FBI or any other Federal Agency. Maybe he was a detective, Joe thought. But a detective would likely be dressed in a suit. He had to get a look at what the man was carrying. He sat the binoculars down, opened the car door, and started walking towards him.

"Good morning," Joe said as he approached the stranger holding the object of considerable interest.

The man hadn't noticed Joe get out of the car and start walking towards him, and as a result he appeared to be momentarily startled. He gave Joe a bit of a wary, even defensive look, and then returned the greeting. "Good morning," he said.

"Sorry if I startled you," Joe said, "but I'm curious about what you've found there."

The man's wary look seemed to intensify, but he stood his ground. "And why is that?" he asked.

Joe knew from extensive professional and personal experience that the best way to put someone at ease was a smile, a friendly countenance, and a non-threatening conversational voice. He could think of no reason why this person would represent a threat, and he was convinced the two pieces of metal he had just noticed could be significant. Joe decided to be completely transparent. "My name is Joe Barber, and I'm a close personal friend of the husband and father of the Maxwell family that was killed in the terrorist incident a few days ago. I own a corporate security firm back east and was here for the funeral. I promised my friend I'd look around a bit just in case the authorities missed something."

The man's appearance immediately relaxed with these words, and his next comments were far more relaxed. "I'm Jack," he replied, "Jack Foster, and I'm a reporter for the Detroit Free Press. Thought I'd do a little looking around myself."

"Mind if I take a look at what you've got there?" Joe asked, as he continued to walk towards the man.

"You mind if I look at your driver's license first?" the reporter replied.

"Not at all," Joe said, as he retrieved his wallet and handed his New York license to the man.

The reporter took the license from Joe and glanced at it. He put the piece of metal in his back pocket, retrieved his cell phone, and took a picture of Joe's license. "Just being cautious," the reporter said.

Joe was actually impressed by this. "No problem," he replied. "So, what drives your curiosity in all of this? Official explanation looks pretty straight forward."

"I agree," the reporter replied, retrieving the piece of metal from his pocket and handing it to Joe. "But it seems a bit too neat. I'm no forensics expert, but I find it very odd that there is debris that suspiciously looks like it came from the explosion four streets away. Notice that the metal looks a lot like a piece of automobile sheet metal, and it's painted blue."

"Interesting that you say that, because the moment I saw a similar piece on that roof over there I thought exactly the same thing," he responded, pointing towards the roof.

"There's a piece on the roof?" the reporter asked.

"Yep," Joe replied, "right up there," as he pointed his finger again.

"Well I'll be damned," the reported replied.

"Hey," Joe continued. "You mentioned that you're no forensics expert, and I'm not really one either; however, it just so happens that my firm has a state-of-the-art forensics lab back in New York, and I'd love to make a deal with you. How about letting me borrow that piece of metal and have my team evaluate it? I'll give you the results before they go to anyone else, and besides I just pointed out that other piece on the roof that I'm sure a resourceful reporter could get his hands on."

The reporter once again adopted a wary eye, which Joe picked up immediately. "That's a great offer man," Joe emphasized. "You and I both know that if that turns out to be material evidence it's going to have to be turned over to the FBI, and besides, what are you going to do with it other than speculate?" Joe asked. "At least my team can verify what it is, and quickly I might add. I'm flying back home this afternoon, and I can have the lab report to you by mid afternoon tomorrow. You'll have your story. You can quote me as an anonymous expert. And besides, you've got a copy of my driver's license. Here's one of my business cards to go along with it."

The reporter stared at Joe for several seconds as if not knowing what to make of him. Finally he spoke. "OK, deal," the reporter said, as he put Joe's card in his pocket. "I'll be looking to hear from you tomorrow afternoon sometime."

"You will," Joe replied. "Believe me, you most certainly will."

* * * * *

Joe sat in the cockpit of the King Air, engines running, and taxied it up to the active runway for his return trip home. He cycled the props one final time, then turned onto the active, pushed the throttle to take off power and within seconds the bird was airborne. As he climbed towards cruising altitude he kept thinking about the last couple of days. When he left he had told Walt Jr. that there were a couple of loose ends to follow up on, but that he had found nothing so far that would contradict the official explanation of events. No need to trouble his friend with speculation. At the moment, speculation, borne of his outsized curiosity, was all he had. Yet he was still troubled that the official explanation might not be entirely true. He had to find a way to shake these doubts. Finding that piece of metal and talking to the reporter certainly hadn't helped with that. He hadn't shared those details with his friend. But there were two things he knew he needed to do. First, he would have his lab do a complete work up on that piece of metal. Second, he decided that just maybe he needed to poke around a bit in Tyson's Corner, Virginia as well where that Explorer had exploded. He wasn't sure what he could possibly find there and was fairly certain he would find nothing. But Joseph Michael Barber was a man who could become very curious, and troubled, by coincidences. In his world they were rare. In his world, as a matter of fact, what appeared to be coincidences more often than not represented   a   threat.

Chapter 8 – An Immeasurable Heart of Darkness

Palo Alto, California

Human intelligence is a fascinating thing. Across the broad range of its normal distribution, or "Bell Curve", its presence is highly correlated with success, and its absence is equally correlated with failure. Of course, the fact that really smart people are often very successful is no great revelation. But some very interesting things start to happen when you begin to reach the boundaries of true genius and beyond. The correlation actually starts to break down.

Needless to say, there are many examples of brilliant people who were not only successful, but also relatively normal. Albert Einstein comes to mind, along with more contemporary examples such as Professor of Mathematics Terrance Tao of UCLA, scary smart at an IQ believed to be north of 225. But history is also littered with examples of individuals whose genius was a double-edged sword. Leonardo Di Vince, IQ estimated at 190, was a man of historic accomplishments but more of a sociopath in his interpersonal relations. And the man widely believed to have the highest IQ ever recorded, William James Sidis, IQ estimated to be well above 250, immeasurable really, was socially incompetent, mired in legal problems for much of his life, and died at the age of 46 from a cerebral hemorrhage having left no lasting legacy. It was almost as if such individuals lacked the emotional intelligence to cope with their cognitive brilliance. Things such as the capacity for self-awareness, emotional maturity and knowing how to relate to other people are the essential tools necessary to constructively channel an outsized brain. Without them, such gifts as logic, problem solving, abstract thought and creativity can consume their owner with self-destructive frustration and doom, the gifts themselves to become things of little lasting consequence. But find the person who is gifted with both, and you find someone rare indeed. The problem, of course, is there is no guarantee that such a person will necessarily focus on the greater good.

Charles Westbourne Reynolds III, or "Westy" to his friends, was a remarkable man. A child prodigy, he could speak and read Spanish, German and French by the time he was 6 years old. He had mastered calculus at age 7. His brilliance, however, made for a difficult childhood. He shared little in common with other children his age and had little to do with them. This wasn't borne out of childhood arrogance. He simply had no interest in social interaction with children whose brains were so less capable than his own. It wasn't even a conscious decision on his part; it was simply the way he was wired. His contemporaries reciprocated, not just with neglect but with contempt. He was often picked on and even bullied. Bullied, that is, until his growth spurt and natural athletic abilities began to blossom in full at about seven or eight years of age. Fortunately for him, this short-circuited any risk of earlier experiences causing a long-term lack of self-confidence. He even became popular among some of his contemporaries. He went from being the last kid picked for playground sports to the starting quarterback of a junior league travel football team. He had a real problem, however, with public school sports programs. By the time he was 11 years old, he was a senior in high school. But for a normal brain, it would have been easy to envision him quarterbacking a college team in the Rose Bowl or even playing in the NFL.

Admitted to the California Institute of Technology at the age of twelve, he earned a Ph.D. in theoretical physics by his eighteenth birthday, publishing a thesis that did groundbreaking work on String Theory. He was offered a position on the faculty of M.I.T. where he spent the next several years teaching graduate courses in quantum mechanics on a tenure track. It was an endeavor he found woefully unsatisfying. M.I.T., however, also happened to have one of the top economics departments in the world. He was introduced to the field by one of his bridge partners who happened to be a Nobel Laureate in the discipline and was soon smitten by a passion for the "dismal science". He read everything about the topic he could get his hands on, and after four years he had earned a Ph.D. in econometrics as well.

Along the way, he began to understand the possibilities of a different kind of success and a different kind of life. A life of immense wealth could not only provide comfort and security, it could provide the potential for immense influence and power. As his interests morphed from theoretical physics to economics he became intoxicated by the prospects. It was his study of economics that led him to understand the potential of enormous wealth. It wasn't the luxury, the toys, or the security that intoxicated him. What he lusted for most of all was the power it could bring.

Westy Reynolds' gifts were not limited to his enormous intellectual prowess. He now stood six foot four with an athletic build. He no longer had time for team sports, but after several years of lifting weights in the faculty gym as a way to clear his mind, he had acquired an imposing presence. He took up golf as a way to network with faculty and others he considered important to his success, a term he was still defining for himself, and within two years he was an 8 handicap. A year after that he dropped to a 2. Add to that an uncanny ability to read and play people, Charles Westbourne Reynolds III was a man brimming with charisma. People instinctively liked him, and in spite of his outsized intelligence, he could conduct a conversation in a way that never showed it off and immediately set a person at ease. He could draw a person into a conversation that made them believe they were almost equally as smart as he. Of course, he didn't believe that for a minute. What he knew to an absolute moral certainty was that he was without the slightest doubt always the smartest person in the room. And he could quickly dispatch anyone who tried to seriously challenge him. Even in his mid-20s he knew he was destined for greatness.

Westy Reynolds sat in his office at 135 University Avenue, nestled in Palo Alto, California, close enough to the Stanford University campus to give the area a college vibe but far enough away to ensure at least a decent amount of privacy. He loved the central coast of California - its wine, its sunshine, and the mountains that framed the background of his drives along so many pastoral roads that connected countless vineyards. And the weather! How he loved the weather – the sunshine, the moderate temperatures and the cool evening breezes that would roll off the ocean. No matter how busy or whatever the crisis, every mid afternoon he would walk to a small wine café a few blocks from his office and sit outside listening to Bach or Mozart or some other composer and enjoy a glass of cabernet and just think. It would invigorate him for the rest of the day's endeavors that could run late into the night. Winston Churchill had his naps. Westy Reynolds had his afternoon dose of sunshine.

The office building was non-descript, a fact that he appreciated, given his penchant for privacy. It suited his needs perfectly. And while the exterior of the building was certainly nothing that would cause a passerby to give it a second glance, the inside, well, that was another story altogether. A bright morning sun had made its dramatic appearance just above the horizon as he sat at his desk about 6:30 A.M. Pacific time and read the New York Times on his iPad. It was part of his morning routine. He diligently read seven newspapers each morning – the Times, the Wall Street Journal, The Washington Post, the F.T., as well as Le Monde, Süddeutsche Zeitung, and Pravda. And, of course, he read the German, French and Russian papers in their native language. He could complete the entire exercise in a little over an hour. Knowledge was power, and he had an insatiable appetite for it.

The last twenty years had been extraordinarily good to him. As Chief Executive Officer of the private equity firm PrinSafe, he had built an estimated fortune of over twenty billion dollars. He had eventually left M.I.T. for a

128

position at Pacific Investment Management Company, or PIMCO. He was a Managing Director in three years, and became modestly wealthy in the process, but he also found the investment advisor business to be tedious and unfulfilling.

It was private equity that ultimately became his passion. He loved the scale. He was no longer simply picking stocks or bonds. He was picking companies. And it was hands on. He would tear them down and put them back together again as far more successful enterprises, becoming even wealthier in the process. It was holistic, and he could focus on the things that really interested him instead of being the slave of some investment committee or meddlesome client.

Rejecting the high profiles of such financial titans as George Soros or Warren Buffet, he preferred to do his work quietly, anonymously. He had built and run his firm in a manner that deliberately kept it under the radar screen. He wanted power, not notoriety. True power was its own reward, and notoriety in his opinion was the balm of the marginally gifted, essential to maintaining a sense of worth that was constantly under assault from self-doubt. Reynolds suffered no such doubt. Consequently, he never sought the role of a talking head on the "hair on fire" business cable channels like CNBC or Fox Business and turned down enough invitations that producers stopped asking. The praise of lesser men he regarded as properly suited for, well, lesser men. But his anonymity was not just a character trait born from a lofty self-esteem that needed no external validation. It also had a purpose. It gave him access to the corridors of power because his low profile made him a person whom the powerful trusted. Anonymity gave him an outsized reputation for discretion. Presidents, both past and present, leading members of Congress, retired Generals and Admirals, and even a couple of Justices of the Supreme Court were investors in PrinSafe, along with an assortment of high net worth individuals who craved privacy in their financial matters almost as much as Westy Reynolds did. And he stroked them.

The PrinSafe client investment contract contained three immutable covenants. First, absolute control was ceded to the CEO, Reynolds himself. He and his team made the calls, period. Second, there was a five-year lockout period – funds could not be withdrawn for a period of five years from signing. This gave him the freedom to take the long view. His clients understood this, and it was exactly what they wanted. Third, and most important to both PrinSafe and clients alike, was the complete anonymity of investors. His clients did not know each other's identity; the contract included a non-disclosure clause to ensure their relationship with PrinSafe was kept secret. The contract also included a provision that would assess a one million dollar fine if anyone ever discussed his or her involvement with anyone other than the IRS. And it had an ingenious enforcement mechanism. Anyone caught had the fine assessed against his or her equity position in the Fund. And it didn't go to Reynolds – it went to the client who turned in the offender – anonymously. Reynolds could demand these terms because he delivered the goods. Returns were consistently spectacular, and even more important, they were spectacular in all market conditions. He made himself and his clients very wealthy.

The PrinSafe portfolio of companies had an overreaching strategy that focused on three legs. First was the traditional private equity focus on companies that were in desperate need of fixing, undervalued as a result, and provided the private equity investor with enormous profit potential. Reynolds and his team oversaw a number of such companies which were periodically IPO'd to the delight of PrinSafe investors and, in the process, continued to fuel Reynolds' wealth.

Second, there were companies that provided unique and highly valuable, often top secret, products and services to the Federal Government.

He focused only on products and services that were so unique and valuable that it guaranteed the ultimate decision makers were at the very top of the pyramid. The purpose for owning these companies was to ensure access to the corridors of power. These companies often didn't even make money, but Reynolds didn't care. The losses were regarded as investments in access, for through these companies Reynolds bought a direct line to high-ranking military officers, the White House and the President herself. Oversight of this leg of his strategic triad was restricted to Reynolds and a small cohort of his most trusted Lieutenants. Two companies in particular fit the bill. His crown jewel was QuarkSpin, a high-tech firm staffed with scientists and engineers put through a vetting process that included an interview with Reynolds himself. He wanted to ensure the company employed the brightest people money could buy. QuarkSpin had three focuses – nanotechnology, advanced software and encryption engineering, and digital forensics. The firm had developed the Sparrow device and the software for its threat detection protocols. PrinSafe's second crown jewel was the non-descript General Aviation Services. An aircraft manufacturer, it produced a couple of models of a high power, single engine turboprop private aircraft capable of flying wealthy owner-pilots over 350 knots coast to coast. This business, while highly profitable, was largely a cover. In the middle of the Nevada Desert was a facility that was responsible for the design and production of the domestic strike drone. Security around the facility and the program itself was tighter than what protected the SR-72 Blackbird. Both of these companies, and their products, were the brainchildren of Reynolds himself.

The third leg of his strategic triad was the most forward looking. Access to power in and of itself was not enough. He recognized that to achieve his true potential, access to power was something that had to be sustained. He could not allow it to be simply the artifact of luck or clever dealing in the moment. Sustainability had to be carefully crafted and nurtured. This was accomplished by assuring the right politicians were elected to office, especially at the national level. But this was not restricted to politicians who agreed with him, or even ones who supported him, although these things were obviously important. He had to ensure the election of people who owed him their jobs and even more importantly owed him their power. There was one nearly fail-safe way to ensure that would happen. Give them money, and lots of it, to fund their elections. So, he created the super PAC, Progressive Dawn, and funded it with whatever it took. The manifesto of Progressive Dawn sent a thrill up the leg of left-leaning politicians everywhere. And numerous celebrities were all too happy to lend it their names and faces in pursuit of its mission. It offered the progressive paradise – a collection of free everything, with countless other causes larded on from national gun confiscation to draconian legislation on climate change and everything in between. And it offered to pay for its vision of social justice by gutting the rich. Its populist appeal was enormous, and resonated deeply with a large segment of the population that was both restive and resentful.

Charles Westbourne Reynolds III of course couldn't have cared less about making life fairer and more equitable for the masses. Point in fact, he would be perfectly happy to see a third of the global population euthanized provided he could pick the third.   What he cared about was power and wealth, mostly power.   Progressive Dawn helped ensure that he acquired and held on to both. And he wasn't the least bit worried about being gutted as one of the rich, for the entire thesis of Progressive Dawn was built on a particularly cynical but quite accurate theory of human behavior he called "The Progressive Quandary". It was a theory he shared only with his most trusted Lieutenants and never discussed publicly. Growing disparities in the distribution of income and wealth created a restive and resentful population. The greater the disparity, the more the populist message resonated with those who felt the system was stacked against them. Part of the beauty was with the advent of globalization; it now seemed to impact voters on both the left and the right. The growth of electronic media and the internet only increased the speed at which all of this happened. The restive could see life's unfairness paraded before them every day. These concepts, of course, were hardly novel. Indeed, they were the antecedents to countless revolutions throughout history. But there were two additional precepts that gave the Progressive Quandary its life. First, you didn't actually have to deliver on the promises other than in some token way. People by their very nature were prone to confuse motion with progress, particularly the uneducated and uninformed. Just a little bit of progress or something symbolic often was quite enough. In fact, delivery on the promise was actually counterproductive. Sustaining a measure of resentment was necessary. It's what elected the politicians Reynolds wanted. It was a balancing act – keep the resentment high enough to get the necessary votes but not so high as to create the risk of an actual revolution or other substantive change. And this is where the second precept comes into play. It was an evident reality that life in the United States was actually quite grand for many people, and vastly better for everyone compared to 50 or 100 years ago. This meant a large portion of the voting population would be relatively happy with the status quo, or at worst, only tolerate modest changes to it. It provided the perfect check and balance against populist resentment pushing change too far. The prospect for real change was simply an illusion, nothing more. Reynolds and his billions were perfectly safe. A slightly higher tax rate and a few tax loopholes closed here and there were nothing to him other than the cost of an insurance policy that helped underwrite his grand designs. If the cost of energy rose on the altar of climate change legislation, it would not impact his lifestyle in any noticeable way. As for all the social causes that were part of the manifesto, he wasn't as much a progressive as he was utterly indifferent. Those things, in his mind's eye, were the balm of lesser people, and they couldn't have interested him less.

So, Charles Westbourne Reynolds III established the super PAC, Progressive Dawn, dedicated to furthering the progressive cause and electing politicians who would run on its promise. And those politicians, a lesser breed if ever there was one, would be very grateful to Charles Westbourne Reynolds III. He cared nothing about the promise or the masses that craved it. It was simply a tool to sustain his power, and he would infuse it with billions of dollars. And access to the powerful would most definitely be his.

Reynolds' concentration on his iPad was momentarily interrupted by a buzz from the intercom on his desk. He laid the iPad down and reached across the desk to press the button that would open the line. His secretary's voice announced in an even tone, "Bill Fitzpatrick is on line one, sir."

"Thank you, Michelle," he responded. "I'll take the call."

Reynolds actually respected the President's Chief of Staff, frankly more so than he respected the President. The position itself was little understood by the average American, but Reynolds knew that Fitzpatrick served as the President's gatekeeper. Controlling access to the highest office in the land made him a real player with great power. In many ways the office served as a kind of Deputy President, even acting President, and never more so with Fitzpatrick occupying it. And besides, Fitzpatrick was an accomplished person in his own right, having served as Chief Executive Officer of the Boeing Corporation before being asked by the President to serve in his present role. Reynolds touched the icon on his call director to open the line, leaned back in his chair, swiveled it around and gazed outside his office window as he began the conversation. "Good morning, Bill, rough couple of days I would guess," he said.

"You can't even begin to imagine," Fitzpatrick replied. "We are in full damage control right now. The President is still committed to the program, but frankly she's become unnerved as a result of these screw ups," Fitzpatrick continued. "I've got to tell you Westy, she's now questioning the entire program. I don't think her support will endure another mistake, certainly not a mistake of the magnitude we've seen over the last few days. Where the hell is your team on scrubbing the software algorithms?"

"I've got the brightest minds on the planet working on it right now, Bill. The issue is in the threat detection probability assessment. It clearly shouldn't have been as high as 98%. We believe that can be fixed with two things. On the software side, I've got a team of linguists building a more extensive data library of colloquialisms and examining correlations. This should greatly improve the effectiveness of the filters. Frankly, nobody thought about the correlation between a game of soccer and obvious threat markers like blast or bomb. But the weaker link in our minds is with the subsequent analytical assessment and threat confirmation process performed by Jennings' team. The threat assessment clearly shouldn't have been as high as it was, but Jennings' team is supposed to be the failsafe."

"Well I certainly don't disagree that Jennings screwed up here," Fitzpatrick replied, "but the reality on the ground was we were facing a massive time constraint and had to act quickly. I don't know if Jennings had had more time he would have rejected the Sparrow's conclusion, but bottom line is those software geniuses of yours have to be the real failsafe point. And remember, this entire program was founded on the principle, and frankly sold to the President, of taking the human factor largely out of the equation."

"I know," Reynolds replied. "Like I said, we have the best software engineers on the planet working on this, and we'll plug this hole. You have my word."

"Good," Fitzpatrick replied.

"Now I've got one for you, Bill," Reynolds said, with irritation in his voice. "What's with your cover story on that Explorer having some kind of safety issue? In all candor that was colossally stupid. First, it pulls in a bunch of the National Transportation Safety people who are going to give it a lot of

135

visibility and ask a lot of questions we don't want asked. Second, the manufacturer is going to scream bloody hell and want to send its own people in."

"Relax, Westy," Fitzpatrick said, "is it a perfect cover story? Of course not. But we had to respond quickly. And besides, you're overstating the risk. Fortunately for us the vehicle had a full tank of gas and only a burnt-out shell remains. There is no way anyone is going to find anything. Yes, there will be an investigation, which would have happened anyway. But far better that it be handled by the DOT than the FBI. The FBI has better forensic skills. Besides, our people quickly reviewed the scene and frankly there wasn't much to sanitize given the fire completely consumed the vehicle. After a few news cycles on this it will fade from the public eye and the investigation will turn up nothing, which will get the manufacturer off the hook. Net result – all interested parties will stop asking questions."

"All right," Reynolds replied, "so we may get lucky here, but understand this. I don't like relying on luck, and what really bothers me here is your team seems to have been unprepared. Making up a cover story on the fly is fraught with risk."

"Fully understood and agreed, I've already put resources on it. Let's both do everything we can to ensure this is something that will not need to be discussed again," Fitzpatrick said as a not so veiled reference to a software problem.

Fitzpatrick continued, "Now another point of concern. I am starting to become just a bit nervous about this Taylor guy in all of this, the Ops Commander. Nothing specific, but his tone and demeanor during the briefs suggests to me that he is starting to feel real remorse over what has happened and may even be in the early phases of having second thoughts over his actions, maybe even his involvement. Your psych vetting process scored him as high as Jennings, but I am seeing two distinctly different sorts of behavior. Jennings is approaching the whole situation with complete analytical detachment, almost to the point of it being creepy. It's almost as if the guy doesn't even care about the loss of innocent lives as long as the good guy/bad guy arithmetic remains net positive. Taylor, by contrast, seems torn by it. How confident are you in REHAB?" he asked. REHAB stood for the acronym REHB, or Reliability Evaluation, Human Behavior. It was a psychological testing process developed by QuarkSpin, and used extensively by the U.S. Government, the military and industry. It was the ultimate test of a person's reliability under a variety of highly stressful scenarios. It was joked about as being a real-life Kobayashi Maru, the infamous test from Star Trek that was impossible to beat, with the exception, of course, of one Captain James T. Kirk. A specialized version of it was developed to vet people who would become part of Project Sparrow.

"Bill, you know the quality of the people involved in REHB. The best in their field: neuroscience, psychiatry, psychology, and behavioral economics, every one of them. I would take a deep breath and resist the temptation of getting overly concerned," he added, as a mild rebuke. Reynolds liked Fitzpatrick but was starting to become a bit annoyed by his hand wringing. "And besides, there is a contingency for every problem, right? I firmly believe we will never have to use it, but that base is covered, my friend."

"That is correct," Fitzgerald responded. "I certainly hope your confidence is well placed, because that is a road I never want to go down."

"Me either," Reynolds replied, "but remember that road was built by careful planners for a purpose, and it's there if we need it."

"Agreed," the Chief of Staff said. "Please get back to me by the end of the day on where your team stands. Frankly I don't think ExComm will approve another action until this mistake is resolved."

"Understood, and by the way, tell the President that Progressive Dawn has made an initial commitment of fifty million dollars to educate voters on her suitability for the office of President," Reynolds said with obvious sarcasm dripping off the word educate. "Hopefully that will placate her volcanic temper somewhat."

"That's great to hear, Westy, you know how much the President appreciates your support. I am sure this will help calm her a bit. Talk to you later, my friend," Fitzpatrick concluded, as the line went dead.

Reynolds spun his chair around, faced forward again and pushed a different icon for the direct line to Dr. Emma Clark, CEO of QuarkSpin. Reynolds regarded this as the second most important job in his organization, second only to his. Clark was his closest friend, most trusted Lieutenant and, well, sometimes a little bit more. After only one ring, she picked up the line.

"What's up Westy?" she asked.

Reynolds replied with a question, "What's the status of Hawk?" he asked.

"On target to go operational in 72 hours," Clark replied.

"Good," Reynolds said. With that, he reached across the desk and hit the button to disconnect the call

Chapter 9 – Growing Seeds of Doubt

Washington D.C. Area, 24 hours later

The big Beechcraft King Air 90 leveled off at 1,200 feet, the traffic pattern altitude for Stafford Regional Airport. The airport was about 45 minutes south of Tyson's Corner, Virginia and just off the I-95 corridor. It was small, but plenty big enough to handle even private jets, and more importantly was vastly friendlier to general aviation aircraft than Reagan National. The security procedures at Reagan for a twin-engine private plane like Joe's were a nightmare. Avoiding them for the relative obscurity of a regional airport like Stafford more than compensated for the slightly longer drive time to his destination, even in the horrible traffic that was typical for I-95 in Northern Virginia. Joe disengaged the plane's autopilot and banked the bird into a left downwind pattern leg for runway 15. The late afternoon sun poured through the cockpit window and made several of the instruments difficult to read. He continued his descent and at last found some relief from the sun's intense glare when he turned the aircraft into its final approach to the runway, which was on a southeasterly heading with the sun at his back. In less than 90 seconds the airplane was on the ground and taxiing to the terminal ramp in front of the fixed based operator where he would refuel and park for the night. After securing the plane, he retrieved the rental car he had reserved and began his drive north towards Washington D.C.

Eric Longstreet was an investigative national security correspondent for the Washington Post and also an acquaintance of Joe's. It was probably too much to call them friends, but they had a cordial relationship built on mutual interests in security matters and their mutual need for information. Eric had originally reached out to Joe after hearing him speak at a security conference. He would often ask Joe for insight into some particular type of threat or threat detection technology. Joe was all too happy to answer Eric's questions, which he would admit became increasingly more sophisticated as their relationship progressed. He regarded this as evidence of both Eric's intelligence and his professionalism, attributes that gained Joe's respect. Eric would in turn occasionally brief Joe on the status of some particularly interesting investigation he was working on, or something unique he had heard from his many contacts at DHS & the FBI. Eric thought he had the better end of the deal, but Joe knew the opposite was true. What Joe gave to Eric was largely technical insights that were part of the standard tradecraft. What Eric gave Joe was usually something quite unique.

If there was one thing Joe was good at, it was nurturing useful relationships. Eric had a weakness for fine cuisine and regarded himself as a bit of an oenophile, two interests that were difficult to exploit to the fullest on his reporter's salary. Joe was all too happy to oblige by filling in the gaps. In point of truth they were both great interests of Joe's as well, as his light middle-aged paunch would attest, and he frankly was quite happy to find someone who was professionally useful with the same interests. It made wining and dining, as they say, an act of pleasure instead of a tedious professional obligation. Joe had planned a dinner that night at one of his favorite restaurant's in D.C., Founding Farmers. It was exceptional without being pretentious, and focused on local ingredients, something which Eric found trendy and intriguing.

The restaurant was crowded and noisy, something Joe thought useful for keeping attention away from the conversations they were about to have. They were ushered towards a booth in the middle of the dining room. Eric carried a medium sized paper bag in his right hand which he laid down on the seat next to where he would sit, and then they both scooted into the booth. After the normal introductions by the waiter, Joe asked for the wine list. He ordered a bottle of Opus One, one of his favorite cabs, or near-cab blends more accurately, from a California vineyard that was a joint venture by the Mondovi family and Baron Philippe de Rothschild. It was exquisite and had a price tag that reflected its extraordinary character. Regardless of its lofty price of almost $300 per bottle retail and easily twice that in a restaurant, it was his go to wine for important clients, friends and family. And what good was his commercial success, he would tell himself, if he couldn't indulge himself and his friends. Within a few minutes the waiter brought the wine. After having Joe taste it, he asked if Joe would like the wine decanted for a bit before serving. Joe responded by saying that decanting the bottle would be a fine idea, but it was so good that he couldn't wait and asked the waiter if he would please pour both of them a glass. The waiter happily obliged. It wasn't often a customer ordered a bottle priced at $650 and the waiter very much hoped Joe would include its price in calculating the tip.

The conversation between them began with the usual small talk with Eric asking Joe about Diana and, given Eric lived alone, Joe somewhat sarcastically asking Eric about his cat. Eric asked Joe about the flight down from Rye and reminded Joe again he had promised to give him a ride in his new King Air. Joe responded by telling Eric he would be happy to, but it would have to wait until after he was finished with this present work for his friend. That immediately brought the conversation to the point of the dinner.

"So, look," Joe said, "as I mentioned over the phone, it was the family of a friend of mine that was killed in that aborted terrorist attack in Michigan. He seems to have some kind of funny feeling that the story doesn't totally hang, which frankly is understandable given the magnitude of the tragedy for him."

"No kidding," Longstreet replied. "I can't imagine losing your wife and three small children in something like that."

"I can't either," Joe replied, "and also there is some pretty significant history between our families that makes me feel compelled to do everything I can to run this to ground. I've read everything I can find on the Michigan incident, and gave the scene a pretty thorough going over yesterday. I have to say, other than a few odd things about the scene and some similarities with the incident in Tyson's Corner, I just can't put my finger on anything other than it is what it appears to be. Having said that," Joe continued, "frankly I can't seem to shake a feeling of skepticism myself."

"So, what are the odd things you are referring to about the scene?" Longstreet asked.

"Well, first," Joe replied, "I'm a bit surprised about how sanitized the scene looked so shortly after the incident. It was almost as if somebody was waiting there to do it. I did the mental math, and I don't know how the Feds could have gotten to the scene that quickly, let alone cleaned it up, unless they were pre-staged."

"But the FBI has a Detroit field office," Longstreet replied, playing Devil's advocate.

"I know," Joe responded. "But it wasn't the FBI that was first on the scene. I'm still trying to verify who, but it's almost as if I'm being stonewalled on this. Although I'll admit the Feds probably have better things to do with their time than answer questions from a skeptical private citizen like me."

"I would have thought your reputation and rumored connections would have made them a bit more cooperative," Longstreet replied.

"My connections are at a pretty senior level, and primarily with the FBI, as I suspect you know," Joe continued, "and that can actually be counterproductive in a conversation with field agents, who typically don't like the meddling. I almost never play that card unless I really need to, which is one of the ways I hang onto it. And besides, I'm not sure what I'd tell my friend in high places if I called him."

"Which is of course why you are talking to me," Longstreet smiled as he made the comment.

"To be clear, I'm talking to you because you're a smart guy who digs up things I occasionally miss," Joe replied.

"Flattery will get you nowhere, Joey B, but the Opus One, now that's a highly effective lubricant!" Longstreet replied, as they both chuckled and clinked their wine glasses. "So what other odd things did you find at the scene?" he asked.

"Well, I found some debris several blocks away from the scene of the explosion. I actually ran into a reporter from the Detroit Free Press who was nosing around as well. I spotted something on a rooftop, and the reporter found something on the ground next to the house. They were chunks of metal that were only melted along the edges. It's almost as if they had arced several blocks through the air before hitting their resting place. The explosion itself could certainly have sent some shrapnel flying, but they would have to have arced fairly high to travel that far and it seems unlikely to me that the explosion itself could have done that. It was almost as if the vehicle was initially hit from above," he said. "I know I'm probably starting to sound like a conspiracy theorist but, finding those pieces of shrapnel is one of the main reasons I can't fully come to peace with the official explanation and is what is giving me the same sense of unease my friend has. I flew back to Rye before coming down here so that I could leave the evidence with my forensics lab. Doubt they are going to find anything, but I felt at least I had to run it to ground. The Free Press reporter wouldn't loan me the fragments he found unless I agreed to tell him the results of our lab analysis. If we turn up anything you may have some competition on the story."

Longstreet's attention seemed to sharpen as Joe talked. By the time Joe finished his comments, the reporter's expression was serious. In point of fact, the hair on the back of Longstreet's neck was standing on end, and he was hardly breathing. He reached to the side, retrieved the bag he had brought into the restaurant, and placed it on the table.

"I was wondering what that was," Joe said in a curious tone, not having fully grasped the change in Longstreet's countenance.

Longstreet instinctively looked back and forth in the restaurant as if to see if anyone was watching them. He leaned forward a bit over the table and looked Barber directly in the eyes. "I suggest you take this back to your lab as well and have them give it the same look they are giving the pieces from Michigan."

Barber now caught Longstreet's change in mood. "What is it?" he asked.

"A piece of metal found four blocks from the scene of the Tyson's Corner explosion. Looks like a piece of sheet metal to me, probably from the vehicle's roof. Don't open it and look here, but it still has some paint on it. It's the same color as the Explorer carrying those soccer players. Given it still has paint on it, my guess is it went flying just a nanosecond or so before the gas tank exploded, and I find that theory hard to explain," he said. "And by the way, I also thought the scene was sanitized very quickly, especially given the fact DOT was called in. Those folks tend to be very slow and methodical."

Joe sat back in his seat as his expression suddenly became very sober as well. He picked the bag up and placed it next to him. They had both lost their appetites. "I think I have some business to attend to, so if you don't mind I think I'll go wheels up and get my ass back to Rye," he said. "Enjoy the rest of the wine. It's yours. I'll be in touch."

145

"Thanks," Longstreet replied.

Chapter 10 – Revelations & Contingencies

Forensics Lab, Offices of Orion Bellicus, Rye, New York

Dr. Lauren Cartwright was a very bright woman who loved being a student. As a matter of fact, she had spent most of her adult life being one. She held twin Ph.D.s, first in applied physics from the University of Michigan, then in Forensic Science from Cal Tech. The life of a graduate student was a bit subsistence living, but it allowed her to pursue her passions without the restraints of the more plebian endeavors in life such as making a living. By the time she was in her early 30s, however, she started thinking more and more about the perks of a higher income, such as a nice place to live, the ability to travel and, well, even toys. Her father had owned a series of Mustang GT convertibles, and she had been totally smitten by the more recent version decked out in a bright yellow with black leather interior. So, recognizing that her education and skills were actually worth something to any number of potential employers, she finally set out to leave the world of post-doctoral fellowships and find, as her mother called it, a real job.

Fortunately for Lauren, Joseph Michael Barber and Orion Bellicus were looking for bright young forensic scientists for their state-of-the-art lab, and Lauren fit the bill perfectly. Not only was she bright, she had an outgoing personality and was a natural leader. She was also, as both her male and female colleagues would say, easy on the eyes and had a self-confidence that made her comfortable with that observation. To be plain looking, or even frumpy for that matter, was just fine with her. She never judged an individual based on their looks. And she loved the culture of her new employer. The people were all incredibly smart, just like her, and it wasn't the stuffy corporate environment she had feared. People were given the freedom to do their jobs, and most responded to the freedom by doing them exceptionally well. Those who didn't wouldn't last. Results, and getting those results in a manner that relied on teamwork were what mattered. Everyone said the culture reflected the CEO and the rest of the senior leadership team. That was obvious to her. She could walk into anyone's office anytime with a question or idea and nobody stood on corporate protocol. That was true from the first day she walked through the front door. This even included Joe Barber himself. She thrived in the environment and quickly secured a reputation as someone who consistently delivered impressive results. Within three years she was appointed Director of Forensics and was running the lab. Her predecessor had taken a job with the FBI as a senior forensics scientist, GS 15, and Joe was delighted for him. It not only gave Joe the opportunity to promote and retain a person of Lauren's caliber, it was also nice to have friends in high places. And for Lauren there was one absolutely delightful consequence of her promotion and the higher salary that went along with it – a 2016 Mustang GT convertible, yellow with black leather interior, was sitting in her garage at the end of the day.

Barber walked into Lauren's office, a non-descript work space in the corner of the forensics lab. Proximity was important. The office was functional and unpretentious, with two walls of glass that gave Lauren a full view of the floor. When she was appointed to the position, she immediately had the office door removed. It was a personal statement, and her team loved it. As Joe walked through the opening he noticed a very quizzical look on her face. She was so engrossed in studying the lab report in front of her that she didn't even notice her boss entering the room.

"So, Abby," Joe said, to get her attention. Occasionally calling her Abby was a running joke between the two of them. It was a reference to the character Abby Sciuto from one of the only TV shows the two of them regularly watched, N.C.I.S., although there were few similarities between Lauren and the fictional character. She looked up at Joe and didn't smile, which struck him as odd. Lauren always smiled when beginning a conversation. "You called me, remember?" he asked. "I've been anxious to see if you found anything from those chunks of shrapnel."

"I'm afraid I did, and I'm afraid it's not something that is going to put your feeling of unease at rest," she said.

"Somehow I suspected you were going to tell me that," Joe replied, as he walked closer to where Lauren was standing.

"First," she replied, "let's talk about the metals."

"Metals, as in plural?" Joe asked, with a puzzled look on his face.

"Yes, most definitely plural," she replied, "plural, and frankly quite distinctive. Fragments from both of the scenes are two very different types of metals. The first is a steel compound, of chemistry clearly consistent of the automotive industry. Obviously, there's no surprise there. The presence of a second metal is no surprise either. Automobile manufacturers use aluminum, copper, lead, zinc, and all sorts of things in cars these days. It was the particular strain, or type of second metal that surprised me. Titanium. It's just small amounts, but it's unmistakable. I had my people do some basic Google research and we couldn't find any evidence of titanium being used in the fabrication of an automobile. It had to be foreign to the vehicles themselves."

Joe stepped back from the forensics report in front of Lauren, which he couldn't read anyway, and looked at her with a puzzled expression. "So how did those two pieces of metal come into proximity with each other in a way that suggests they were both engulfed in the explosions?" he asked. "What's your theory, and is it possible the titanium was part of the terrorist's bomb, or other ordnance?"

"I don't have a theory right now, and it's unlikely it would have been part of a homemade bomb. It's far too hard to get and I'm not sure what

150

kind of purpose it would serve compared to more conventional metals," she replied. "As to some other kind of ordnance, that's an interesting theory, Joe; I'll think about it. Problem is it is not the finding of titanium itself that's most interesting, it's what's on it."

"OK, you're killing me, girl," Joe replied, "let's cut to the chase."

"On the titanium found at both scenes, both Michigan and Tyson's Corner," she said, "we found significant traces of Pentaerythritol tetranitrate, cyclotrimethylenetrinitramine, and styrene-butadiene, along with traces of at least two or three other things we can't identify."

"Plain English, please," Joe replied

"They are all components of Semtex," she said.

"Semtex?" Joe responded, with disbelief in his voice. "Are you absolutely sure about that?" he asked. "Hey, I'm sorry", he continued, "dumb question, of course you are. I'm pretty sure the manufacturer doesn't use that in their SUVs."

"Well that isn't even the most interesting part, Joe," Lauren continued. "These chemicals have very distinct markers, and I'm pretty sure the trace elements are exactly the same."

"What are you telling me, Lauren?" Joe asked.

"What I am telling you, Joseph, is that I am ninety-nine and forty-four one hundredths percent certain that the Semtex came from the same place," she said. "I'm a scientist, and I don't like to speculate, but if I did speculate I'd say the presence of both titanium and Semtex suggests some kind of similar ordnance, likely from the same source. And if it struck from above, that could explain a high arc and how the shrapnel was found several blocks away. Just a theory, but the explosion could have sent the materials flying a couple of nanoseconds before the fuel tank explosions consumed everything."

"Wow!" he responded. "So not only does this suggest both explosions were the result of an overt act, they were both likely coordinated as part of the same plot. So much for the lone wolf theory."

"Exactly," she said.

"Also, so much for erasing my sense of unease," Joe said. "But what I don't get is the why. If we are looking at some new kind of terrorist capability here, why attack their own team in Michigan before the terrorists were able to strike? The loss of life in that intersection paled in comparison to what it would have been had that car reached the mall. That just doesn't make sense. And how would they have done it, especially if the strike came from above?"

"I don't know," Lauren replied. "None of it makes sense. The attack in Tyson's Corner wasn't even aimed at terrorists. My business is fact, yours is theory. I can give you the dots, but you're going to have to connect them."

"Don't define your job so narrowly, Lauren," Joe retorted. "You're one of the smartest people in this building and I want one hundred percent of your brain on this."

"You've got it, Joe," she replied, "as always. All I'm really saying is that I can't think of any theory right now that squares with these facts. You're going to have to bring me, bring us, a whole lot more of those dots to connect to crack this one. You may want to think about bringing in the Feds at this point. Finding the pieces and testing them is fine. You had no credible evidence other than a hunch that the shrapnel in any way related to the two explosions. But what you are sitting on now my friend is likely material evidence of criminal, even terrorist activity. Holding onto that without telling the authorities could get you, make that us, in a whole peck of trouble."

"You're right," Joe answered, "and you sound like Diana, now, counselor. Out of fairness I need to call Longstreet and let him know what we've found, and then I think I need to have a conversation with my friend Donny Benson at FBI. Don will serve as our first contact with law enforcement. I totally agree we can't sit on this."

Joe sat in his office a few minutes later and thought about his conversation with Dr. Cartwright. He had thought his trip to Detroit would bring closure and enable him to set his friend's mind at ease, yet the opposite had occurred. It frankly didn't change things a lot for his friend. Regardless of what his forensics lab had found, it didn't change the overwhelming evidence that his friend's family died at the hands of terrorists. What really happened might be very different from what the authorities tried to spin, but the essence of what happened to his friend's family was not changed at all. Joe now found himself being sucked into a vortex he hadn't envisioned. He picked up his phone and placed a call to Eric Longstreet.

"Longstreet," the reporter spoke into the phone.

"What's the matter, Eric, your caller ID not working?" Joe asked.

"Sorry Joe, I didn't look at the face of the phone before I answered. What did you find?"

"Are you in your office now, Eric?" Joe enquired.

"Yep," Longstreet replied. "Don't worry I'm in the Washington Post's cone of silence right now."

"This is actually pretty serious, Eric. The shrapnel we evaluated was two different metals from both locations. Steel and titanium. I have no good way to explain the titanium."

"Could it be unrelated to the incident, Joe? Are we over-analyzing this?" he asked.

"I'd buy that, Eric, if it were true for just one of the locations. But both? That's too much of a coincidence, especially for such a unique metal. And besides, I'm afraid there's something much more ominous."

"Ok, you've certainly got my attention now," Longstreet replied. "What?"

"Before I go on, Eric, we've got to be clear on the rules of engagement here," Joe instructed. "I need to have your word that what I am about to tell you stays between the two of us for now. I can't be reading any speculation in the Post, not yet anyway. Are we agreed?"

"For how long?" Longstreet asked.

"Not sure yet," Joe replied. "At a minimum I need first to have a conversation with a friend of mine who's a senior at the FBI. And given the nature of what I am about to tell you, if you agree to my terms, I might have to turn the pieces over to him. Sorry. Let's say my best guess is 48 hours, but I'm going to need to include an option to extend, depending on how my conversation with the Bureau goes."

"That's a pretty big ask, Joe," Longstreet replied, with not so subtle skepticism in his voice. "And you're going to Benson with this?" a reference to Joe's friend, Donald R. Benson, Executive Assistant Director for Intelligence, FBI.

"Who's Benson?" Joe asked, with modest irritation. "I don't know anyone named Benson."

"OK, yeah, whatever, Benson who?" Longstreet said in a mocking tone. "You know you guys are not the only ones who do background research on people, Joe, and you're not the only one who likes to know with whom he is talking."

Joe was a little annoyed but impressed. He knew Longstreet was both thorough and resourceful but was still surprised the guy had uncovered Joe's connection to Don Benson, a former fraternity brother of Joe's and graduate of Chicago Law School.

Longstreet continued, "Here's what I can offer. I'll sit on it for 48 hours. You know we won't go with a story with just one source. If I get confirmation of what you are about to tell me elsewhere, there's no option to extend. Sorry. If I can't corroborate, your option is a moot point. Agreed?"

"Agreed," Joe said.

"By the way," Longstreet continued, "what about that Free Press reporter? Is he under the same rules of engagement?"

"I don't know the guy, so I don't trust the guy. I haven't told him anything, at least not yet."

"So, a promise isn't a promise, Joe?"

"Don't bust my balls, my friend. I promised the guy I'd share some details. I didn't promise when."

"Ok," Longstreet replied, "what did you find out?"

"Our forensics lab found traces of Semtex on both pieces of titanium. And not only that, the chemical composition suggests that the Semtex on both pieces came from the same place."

"Holy Shit!" Longstreet exclaimed. "Ordnance of some sort? Are we looking at a more sophisticated terrorist capability here?"

"That's our best guess, at least for the moment. Nothing else seems to make sense. But I've got to tell you we can't even begin to figure out the motive for the attacks. Hitting a terrorist cell en route to an attack and then killing a van full of soccer players doesn't make any sense. It could be the foreign terrorist variant of conducting some sort of test, or maybe some domestic militia types taking things into their own hands. But frankly I regard both of these guesses as really weak. We're grasping at straws. My personal view is we don't have a clue."

"So, what I don't get is why the story about a fuel tank safety problem with the vehicle in Tyson's Corner?" Longstreet asked. "Could the government be trying to cover up something?"

"Well, it certainly wouldn't be the first time they tried to spin something that didn't conform to their preferred narrative," Joe said. "That theory occurred to me, but it's a real leap of faith based on what we have right now."

"Right," Longstreet replied.

"Agreed," Joe responded. "But that theory also could explain why both scenes seemed to be sanitized so quickly."

"You're right," Longstreet said. "But I've got to tell you Joe, we're both starting to sound like a couple of conspiracy theorists from a really bad B-movie. I'm not sure I want to go down that road right now."

"I don't either," Joe replied.

"Ok," Longstreet continued, "You go talk to your non-existent friend, Director Benson, and I'll go plum a few contacts I have in high places as well. I can guarantee nobody's going to tell me anything. but gauging how they react to my questions might be interesting. How about we circle back with each other in 24 hours and compare notes. I think that's a fair trade for me agreeing to keep my mouth shut for the next two days."

"Agreed," Joe said. "I'll call you sometime tomorrow afternoon."

"Good," Longstreet confirmed.

Joe reached across his desk and hit the icon on the touch screen to kill the call. The unsettled feeling that gnawed at him was becoming increasingly worse.

*　*　*　*　*

Eric Longstreet had carefully nurtured a number of important relationships over the years. It was reminiscent of his hero and role model, Bob Woodward. He had also built a reputation of extraordinary integrity and discretion, the discretion part bolstered by not one, but two tours in a D.C. jail for refusing to reveal his sources. The second tour gained particular notoriety when the D.C. Federal Circuit Court vacated contempt charges against him. These things made him a man people trusted. He was skilled at eviscerating the powerful with his pen, or keyboard more accurately, when they abused that power or broke the law. People's reaction to him as a reporter was binary – he was either trusted explicitly or feared. His reputation had one particular downside, however. As a reporter known for breaking difficult stories, he became an early center of attention, and target, for Project Sparrow. There was only a handful of individuals targeted for continuous monitoring. He was one of them, and of course he didn't have a clue.

Within 15 minutes of Longstreet and Barber's conversation the previous evening at Founding Farmers, a senior intelligence analyst was in Ryan Jennings' office. They were very worried. The initial cover story on the Explorer explosion had seemed to play well and had fallen out of the news cycle after only two days. It was a colossal understatement to say it was worrisome to have a man like Longstreet looking into it. They needed to know whatever was discussed in that follow up call planned for the next day, and they needed to know it immediately. Arrangements were made to have a human asset monitor Longstreet's phone in real time to intercept the call the next day from the mystery man, Joe. Fortunately for Joe, he was not, at least as of yet, a direct subject of Sparrow and was not being monitored. At this point they only had his first name, and his city of residence, Rye, New York. His reference to owning a King Air during the conversation, however, gave them hope they could trace him down, but that was likely to take several days. Jennings didn't think he had that much time, particularly with a guy like Longstreet nosing around. When the follow up call came, the analyst immediately called Jennings and had the conversation piped into his office, real time. At the end of the call, they were no longer worried; they were terrified. At the end of the conversation, and without hesitation, Jennings called his secretary on the intercom and told her to schedule an emergency brief with ExComm. He was contemplating the unthinkable. There were contingencies for situations like this, although nobody liked to discuss them, and to this point they had not been used. But this situation might just warrant it. If he was king, Jennings thought, the wheels would already be in motion. But he was not king, and he had to make the case to the small group of very powerful men who would soon meet. First, of course, he had to convince himself. That took about ten seconds. Lives were at stake. Program viability had to be maintained.

In government, as well as in business, it is the meeting before the meeting where real decisions often get made. Jennings didn't want to walk into the ExComm brief and hit them with this cold. He needed to brief Collins first and gage his reaction. He also needed to plant a seed that was best planted in private and not for the first time in front of a group of people. As he sat at his desk and thought about it for a minute, he got up and walked to his outer office where his secretary sat.

"Please call the Director's office and tell them I need to see Dr. Collins right away. Tell them it's urgent and related to the ExComm meeting I just called," he said.

"Yes sir," the secretary said in a polite tone.

Jennings walked back into his office and closed the door. It was going to be a long afternoon. And an important one.

* * * * *

It was a remarkable chemical compound, and the outcome of a great deal of hard work by a handful of talented chemical engineers. Its lethality was breathtaking. It was a thousand times more lethal per volume than cyanide. And it left virtually no trace, unless one had access to some very expensive diagnostic equipment. And even then, most physicians would hardly expect anything nefarious without knowing exactly what to look for. A puzzled cause of death, or COD, of nonspecific natural causes would likely be the conclusion, or maybe a myocardial infarction. Delivery was ingenious. A tiny dose was encapsulated in a microscopic sphere of a specialized plastic compound designed to melt at 95 degrees Fahrenheit. The tiny sphere was itself enclosed in the W-variant of the second gen micro drone with a small portion of the sphere protruding from the drone's underside. Also protruding from the underside of the drone was a tiny needle, coated in wasp venom; not enough to really cause the pain normally associated with a wasp sting, as the device was way too small to carry sufficient venom for that. But it was enough to leave a trace, which would be good cover if a curious medical examiner happened to notice a small red mark on the victim's hand. Instead of being designed to burrow under the victim's skin like the Sparrow, it was designed to give a glancing blow. It was smaller than the Sparrow, for Moore's law seemed to apply to miniaturization as well as computer processor speed. But there was a trade-off for the smaller size, and that was a more limited range, but the range was sufficient to do the job. The victim would open a familiar looking package, an envelope with the standard zip tab. Pulling the zip tab would activate a microburst radio signal that would launch the drone. It was equipped with a heat-seeking sensor that would likely target the hand or forearm or whatever was the closest. After a quick glancing blow to the nearest exposed skin, the melted plastic would disable the device and it would fall to the ground and to oblivion. It had a total flight time of only 3 seconds. This was another limiting factor resulting from its small size but was also regarded as a safety measure. It minimized the risk of the device floating around for too long and hitting the wrong target. This characteristic, however, was more the outcome of a desire for accuracy and effectiveness, than it was the product of some latent morality.

The Sparrow had been weaponized. The new variant was The Hawk.

* * * * *

Eric Longstreet parked his Tesla Model S in front of his fashionable Alexandria, Virginia townhouse, opened the driver's side door and stepped out. It was still warm and humid, as was typical of the D.C. area from early Summer to Fall. Thank heavens the days of wool suits and starched shirts were long behind him, he thought as he momentarily reflected on the comfort of the polo shirt and khakis he was wearing. As he rounded the front of the vehicle and started to walk towards his front door, he noticed a thick yellow envelope leaning against the side of the building, just under his address numbers. On reaching the front of the townhouse, he leaned over to pick up the envelope, retrieved the other mail from his mailbox, then proceeded to unlock the front door and walk in, leaving the door slightly open, which was his normal habit in the Summertime. His cat met him immediately and began rubbing up against his leg and purring. His senses almost felt like his body had given him a hit of endorphins as he encountered the blast of cool and dry air-conditioning upon passing through the front door. He set his keys and the mail on the table in his foyer, retrieved his cell phone from his pocket and set it down as well, then leaned down to pet his cat as a reward for such an affectionate greeting. Longstreet walked into his kitchen, poured himself a glass of red wine, a Groth cab, 2005, which he had opened the previous night. He then turned to his refrigerator, opened the door and retrieved a vacuum-sealed package of 4 steaks, filets, tore off three and set them on the counter. He was having a couple of friends over for dinner in a few hours and the steaks would grill much better if he let them come to room temperature before putting them on the grill, so the experts said. He placed the spare steak back in the refrigerator, walked back into the foyer and retrieved his mail, which he then began sorting as he took the first sip of his wine. After flipping through several normal-sized envelopes, mostly bills along with the normal assorted junk mail, he came to the larger envelope from Amazon delivered by UPS. Odd, he thought. He hadn't ordered anything. Of course, he reflected on the fact it wouldn't be the first time he had forgotten his use of the one-click function on their website only to remember what he had purchased upon opening the package. It was a standard UPS envelope used for delivery of smaller items not requiring a box. He pulled the zip tab to open it, retrieved another envelop from inside with simply his name on it, which he proceeded to open. Inside was an Amazon gift card for $100, but nothing else. No note, no clue about who it was from. He had no idea, he thought to himself, but he would take it. He had been meaning to read the 3-volume biography of Winston Churchill by William Manchester, recently republished, and this card would more than cover it. As a newspaper man, he preferred real books, hardcovers actually, and couldn't bring himself to transition to a Kindle. For the briefest of moments, he thought he saw a gnat hovering over his left hand. He hated the things, as they seemed to share his taste for wine, and he would all too often find one of the annoying insects floating in his evening glass of cabernet. He set the wine down, then swatted the top of his left hand with his right palm, all the while careful to hold onto the gift card. He turned to walk back towards the kitchen where his laptop awaited him on his kitchen

161

counter, the gift card still in his hand. As he did so, his left leg suddenly buckled slightly. All of a sudden, he felt very ill. The cat had been sitting on the kitchen counter looking out the window. It heard a loud thump as Eric Longstreet dropped to the floor. The cat jumped off the counter and ran up to its owner who was now lying on the floor very still. The cat sensed something was not right and began meowing loudly. Eric Longstreet continued to lie there, motionless. He was dead, and his friends would be in for an unpleasant surprise in a couple of hours.

Chapter 11 – The Dark Side of the Force

NDSA Headquarters, McLean, VA, The Room, 2 hours later

Colonel Taylor and SAC Jennings walked into the ExComm meeting and took their respective places at the conference table. They both immediately noticed that Fitzpatrick was sitting next to Admiral Erby. Fitzpatrick's presence at the meetings really annoyed Taylor, who was increasingly uncomfortable with the routine presence of such a political operative. It was, in his opinion, no place for such a senior Administration official and Taylor didn't like its implications. Jennings' reaction was a little different. It was part curiosity, but also part opportunistic, as he knew that getting on the guys good side could be enormously helpful. But frankly it was also part fear. Jennings was smart enough to realize that the attention of such a powerful man could be a double-edged sword. The guy had the capacity to turn direction and impale him just as quickly as he could propel him. A guy like Fitzpatrick wouldn't give a second thought to throwing a career bureaucrat like Jennings under the bus for even the slightest of political motives. But they were both equally puzzled by the presence of another person in the room whom neither of them recognized. It was a woman who appeared to be in her late 40s, impeccably tailored and exuding that characteristic called presence. As was becoming the norm at these meetings, Fitzpatrick was again the first to speak.

"Before we get started," Fitzpatrick said, "I'd like to introduce Sandra McConnell. Ms. McConnell is with the FBI. She's the Executive Assistant Director for the National Security Branch. Ms. McConnell serves as an advisor to the NDSA, and has been read in on its mission and scope from the beginning. Given the nature of what you are about to share with us, Agent Jennings, we thought her professional remit could be particularly useful."

Admiral Erby interjected. "Pardon me, Bill, but if Assistant Director McConnell is an advisor to NDSA, how is it that this is the first time I have met her?"

"Ms. McConnell is more accurately an advisor to me regarding all matters related to the NDSA," Fitzpatrick responded. "I decided her input would be useful, given the exigent nature of present circumstances."

Erby didn't respond to the comment, but Taylor saw the man's jaw muscles flex a couple of times. The Three Star was clearly irritated.

"Nice to meet you ma'am," Jennings replied, hiding his astonishment that such a senior person in the FBI was not only aware of the program, but de facto a part of it.

Taylor said nothing. He was astonished. How could a senior member of the FBI be read into the NDSA's remit and mission? He frankly couldn't decide what to make of it. This woman was a lawyer. Wasn't she aware of the Posse Comitatus Act? She had to be. It expressly forbade exactly what this entire organization was doing – deploying forces of the U.S. Military on domestic soil in a law enforcement capacity. Sure, there was a legal opinion in a safe somewhere and a Presidential Finding that provided legal cover for everyone commissioned in the NDSA and its oversight in light of the exigent circumstances of the terrorist attacks; but how could that cover possibly apply to a senior executive of the FBI acting as an informal advisor and not part of the organization itself? He was struggling to come up with a positive interpretation of this new revelation.

Fitzpatrick continued. "Everyone is to understand that Director McConnell's relationship with the program, and her presence here, are highly confidential. Her role is strictly advisory, not operational, and no one else in the FBI is aware of her involvement, including the Director. These facts are to stay in this room," he said. "Adam, your meeting."

So much for a positive interpretation, Colonel Taylor thought. The Posse Comitatus Act required the legal opinion to be given by the Attorney General. How could it be that the FBI Director was clueless, but sandwiched between the AG and an AD who were in the know? More importantly, he thought to himself, why was the FBI Director clueless but not one of his Lieutenants? It smelled. Taylor had regarded the previous mistakes in the program as just that – mistakes. They made him sick, but he understood the reality that the minute a battle begins the plan goes out the window. And he understood that the Nation was indeed in a battle, and innocent lives were at stake. His job was to protect those lives. These things helped him push past any sense of self-doubt and do his duty as an officer. He would sit there and listen to how all of this played out, but he now had a sinking feeling in the pit of his stomach. He was especially annoyed, almost angry from his observation that he seemed to be the only guy in the room who didn't have a clue what this meeting was about. For the first time in his military career he began to think about what constituted a legal order on the part of his superiors. He was willing to define that legality in a moral sense, the greater good, and not just strictly the letter of the law. But for the first time since the vetting for this assignment had taken place he began to wonder what he had gotten himself into. His mind's progression began to wander a bit, probably as a defensive mechanism, to his early days of flight training and flying the F15 Falcon. He was brought back to the present when Johnson began to speak.

"Ok, Agent Jennings, please give ExComm a summary what you told me earlier today."

"Yes sir," Jennings replied. "As you are all aware, Sparrow now targets extensive coverage of the news outlets in large metropolitan areas. Coverage of the metro desks of the New York Times and Washington Post is essentially 100%. The investigative expertise of these organizations, and especially their contact with suspected terrorist organizations, provides a treasure trove of humint, and often provides the corroboration of other sources that is necessary to approve action under our rules of engagement. We have found the conversations of one reporter particularly useful in this regard, and that is Eric Longstreet of the Washington Post. His conversations are directly monitored in loop separate from the normal data-base that is monitored by the Sparrow threat detection software. Less than 48 hours ago, we picked up a series of conversations related to the incident in Tyson's Corner. Of particular concern is a conversation he had at a local D.C. restaurant with our mystery person, whom we only know by his first name, Joe. Evidently Joe is connected somehow with the unfortunate collateral damage incurred in Michigan and is investigating it. Joe seems to believe there is some connection between the two events, and apparently has a relationship with Longstreet and called him to arrange a meeting to discuss the recent events."

"Define relationship," Executive Assistant McConnell asked, to almost everyone's surprise. Evidently her involvement in this meeting was going to be something more than just an observer.

"We're not sure ma'am," Jennings replied, "but it appears to be casual, likely professional of some sort, and doesn't appear to rise to the level of friendship. The conversations don't reveal much about that. Our best guess is they find it useful to share information from time to time. Nothing out of the ordinary for a reporter."

"What do we know about this person, Joe?" Fitzpatrick asked.

"Not much, at least not as yet. We have gathered a few useful bits of information that should help us identify him, but I'm afraid it's going to take some time. He lives in Rye, New York and seems to have some kind of business that has a lab of some sort. He talked as if it was a forensics lab. He also is a pilot and owns a Beechcraft King Air. With those facts I believe we can trace him down, although as I said, it's going to take some time, likely at least a few days," Jennings continued. "That kind of research is not normally part of our remit, so we're going to have to be a bit resourceful."

Both Jennings and Taylor noticed that Director McConnell was taking notes while Jennings was speaking. She looked up at Jennings and said, "I'll have his name and address for you by mid-morning tomorrow."

Both Jennings and Taylor were a bit taken aback from the unexpected offer of help, although Taylor was far more unsettled by it than impressed. "Thank you ma'am," Jennings replied.

"Keep going, Agent Jennings," Johnson said.

"Yes sir," Jennings replied. "During the early stages of their dinner meeting, our mystery man, Joe, commented that he had found pieces of shrapnel several blocks away from the Michigan incident and intended to have his lab evaluate it. Longstreet then told Joe that he had found the same thing. Longstreet had evidently brought a bag to their dinner that contained what he had found, the shrapnel that is, which he proceeded to give to this Joe. Then it gets a whole lot worse. The next afternoon Joe calls Longstreet's cell phone and tells him his lab had found traces of Semtex on the samples from both places. Then it gets epically worse. Our mystery man, Joe, is evidently friends with Don Benson, the FBI's Executive Assistant Director for the Intelligence Branch, and Joe tells Longstreet he plans to meet with him."

"Is this Benson read into the program?" Admiral Erby asked.

"Absolutely not," Fitzpatrick responded. "Sandra is the only one and was handpicked and read in by me personally. Nobody else in the FBI is aware of Sparrows existence."

"What is Director Benson's reaction likely to be, Ms. McConnell?" Erby asked.

"Hard to know," she responded. "He's a straight shooter, a Boy Scout. If he actually became aware of the program I have no doubt he would go to the Director, and even the AG. I believe his first instinct would be to bring it down. But I also believe at this point we have two things working in our favor. First, he's a natural skeptic, and certainly not a man prone to conspiracy theories."

Interesting choice of words, conspiracy theory, Taylor thought. As he continued to listen his sense of discomfort grew.

McConnell continued, "This Joe character would certainly get his attention, but I believe it would be difficult to convince Don of anything. If anything, he would be inclined to continue to believe the terrorist angle. And from what you've said so far Agent Jennings, it appears that our mystery man, Joe, still regards that as the most likely explanation himself."

Wow, Jennings thought to himself. He actually hadn't said that yet in this ExComm meeting. He had only told Collins that portion of the conversation just a few hours ago. Obviously, he concluded, this woman has been thoroughly briefed.

McConnell continued again. "Second, being a straight shooter means he will not go rogue, at least certainly not without a whole lot more clear evidence than this. It would be a mistake to conclude Don is an actual threat to the program, at least at this point."

"What about our mystery man, Joe?" Director Johnson asked

Nice of you to finally ask something in your meeting, Taylor thought to himself.

"At this point I don't know, sir," Jennings replied. We'll have a much better idea about that once Director McConnell provides his identity."

"OK, I'm going to throw the moose head on the table," Collins said, in reference to the thing that was obvious to all of them and the thing that all were reluctant to talk about. "We all know we have contingencies for this sort of thing, the indisputable threat, that is.   You're not suggesting we contemplate that sort of action now, are you Agent Jennings?"

"No sir," he said.   Of course, getting a decision to take out this troublesome reporter was precisely his plan as he walked into the Room, but Jennings was a realist. It was obvious he was not going to get approval based on what he had at the moment, and frankly the unexpected presence of an Executive Assistant Director from the FBI made him extra cautious. Her offer of help in identifying this Joe character was great, but she was still a new variable in the equation, and if Jennings was anything, he was cautious. It was a survival skill. He also was highly adaptive and decided to quickly change tactics and settle for the notion of just planting the seed. "We don't have anywhere near the evidence right now for that," he continued, wanting to appear to be the voice of reason, and not the alarmist. "We'll know a lot more in 24 hours or so, but I think it's healthy that we all remind ourselves we have planned contingencies for a reason and that we each think about the criteria we need to implement."

"Agreed," Johnson replied.

"We now have an asset dedicated to monitoring every word coming from Longstreet's mouth," Jennings said. "And we'll do the same with our mystery man Joe, as soon as we identify him."

"Good," Dr. Johnson replied. "If there's nothing else left to discuss at the moment, I suggest we meet again in 24-48 hours when we have more information on this Joe character, and hopefully a little better insight into what Longstreet has and what he may plan to do with it. If both of these clowns buy into the terrorist theory and lead Director Benson in the same direction, this could work in our favor."

"Except for the fact that discovering of the Semtex completely blows our cover about a vehicle safety issue and disclosing the presence of Semtex could make the accident scene investigators look foolish, as though they missed something obvious," Collins said.

"I disagree," Fitzpatrick retorted. "First, evidence that the Tyson's Corner incident was terrorist related, while not the baseline script, isn't exactly the end of the world. And the ethnicity of the victims could corroborate it. Second, NTSA doesn't exactly look for exotic explosives when investigating a scene. There would be no reason to assume the explosion was caused by anything other than a tank full of gasoline. Let's all take a deep breath on this and try and conclude this meeting on a constructive note. I want us all to deal in facts, not in speculation. Our decisions need to be data driven. That best serves the program and best serves the American people. I have no reason to believe right now that there is any threat to the program that's not manageable, so let's keep our heads and reevaluate in 24 hours when we have more solid data. I'm prepared to support whatever action ExComm deems necessary."

Colonel Taylor was stunned. He knew perfectly well what contingency meant. As a matter of fact, as Director of Operations it would fall to him to implement it. He could not believe the Chief of Staff of the President of the United States had just acknowledged his approval, under the appropriate circumstances, for the execution of a private citizen, and a member of the Washington press corps. And the whole thing had been discussed in the presence of an Executive Assistant Director of the FBI, who hadn't said a word. With every ExComm meeting, Fitzpatrick's role, meddling actually, seemed to be growing, when in reality the guy shouldn't even be here in Taylor's view. Both Johnson and Collins seemed to have no appetite for challenging the Chief of Staff, and it made Taylor angry that they weren't taking more control of these meetings. He also was becoming deeply disappointed in Admiral Erby. As a career military officer, Erby was supposed to play the role of an independent and dispassionate advisor, even a devil's advocate, to help ensure the organization made quality decisions. As a three-star, he had the chops to do it. His extensive experience in the intelligence business, as well as his most recent assignment in running Naval Intelligence, gave him the background to ensure he could speak with a voice of authority. Yet right now the guy didn't seem to have much of a voice at all. Taylor wondered if Erby was having similar thoughts to him, and perhaps just waiting for the right moment to challenge this growing insanity. Taylor desperately hoped so, because he knew that Erby was likely the only person capable at this point of derailing this insanity. As he stood up to walk out of the Room, he knew one thing for sure. There was one decision he had just made and there would be no turning back from it. Whatever Jennings' work of the next 24 hours would uncover, if that contingency was seriously discussed, he would push back and push back hard. Not only that, he realized that he had just decided if his view did not prevail and he was ordered to implement that contingency, he would refuse. As he turned towards the door, a few feet behind Jennings, he wondered what the implication of that would be. Would they then be worried about him? Was there a contingency for him? The hair stood up on the back of his neck as he thought about that and realized the likely answer. But those thoughts didn't change his decision or his resolve.

* * * * *

Amanda Green was stunned as she sat in the Sparrow operations control center and listened to the conversations being picked up from Eric Longstreet's cell phone. As the Assistant Special Agent in Charge, she had directed the intel team to alert her whenever any meaningful conversations were picked up, now that an asset was assigned to monitor Longstreet 24/7.

172

For the last several minutes she listened to a replay of the chatter from 25 minutes ago, as the analyst sitting next to her continued to monitor the conversations in real time. There was an initial expression of distress from two individuals, male, and clearly not Longstreet, who had just discussed finding Longstreet's body on the floor and apparently non-responsive. Next they had called 911. While waiting for the paramedics to arrive, they continued to discuss Longstreet's condition and were very concerned he may be dead. The analyst sitting next to Green all of a sudden snapped his head up, turned to her and said, "You've got to listen to this," with a sense of urgency. He turned a dial on his control panel that switched her audio feed to the channel that was feeding the conversation in real time. The paramedics had arrived on the scene and were working on Longstreet, and from what they could hear they were trying to revive him.

"I still can't get a pulse," one of the paramedics said, clearly indicating they had already searched for a pulse and couldn't find one.

"Any history of heart problems or other medical issues?" the paramedic asked.

"Not that I'm aware of," one of the friends said.

"Me either," the other friend responded.

"Let's try epinephrine," another voice said, evidently the other paramedic.

"Rick, these guys said he's been unresponsive since the call. And there was no respiration when we arrived. I don't think there's any bringing him back," the first paramedic said.

"Just humor me, partner. No harm in trying," the second paramedic replied.

"OK, hand me the syringe," the first paramedic asked. He injected the fluid into the IV they had started when they first arrived.

"Nothing," the first paramedic announced after administering the injection.

"Let's hook up a lead just to be sure," the second paramedic suggested.

Green and the analyst then heard a series of noises, difficult to interpret, probably related to hooking up electrocardiogram leads to Longstreet. In less than 90 seconds one of the paramedic's voices was heard again. "Nothing. OK, let's declare. Time of death, 9:47 P.M."

Green had heard enough. The analyst could monitor the rest of the conversations, but it was clear that Eric Longstreet was dead. She almost leapt out of her chair, burst out of the monitoring room and started running towards Jennings' office. When she arrived, she ran past his secretary, threw open his office door and quickly entered. Jennings was sitting at his desk and looked up the minute he heard his office door open. He looked at her and noticed she had a quizzical look on her face and appeared to be breathing a bit heavy as if she had just been running.

"What's up with you?" he asked, "and what's with the dramatic entry?"

"I just came from the station monitoring Longstreet. There's been some kind of an incident tonight. We monitored a 911 call apparently made by one of his friends who found him at his townhouse on the floor and unresponsive. We then monitored in real time the conversations of the paramedics on the scene. They attempted to revive him and failed. Eric Longstreet is dead," she said.

Jennings was stunned. His mind raced. His first thought was problem solved. He then wondered if somebody within NDSA had ordered the contingency implemented without telling him. But who? Was somebody rogue? Taylor? That certainly seemed unlikely. Was there some sort of parallel command structure he wasn't aware of? That one scared him a bit, but he quickly thought that he shouldn't get too far ahead of himself. Remember, he told himself; know the facts before drawing conclusions.

"Do we know the cause of death?" Jennings asked Green.

"The paramedics didn't speculate," she responded. "The only thing I can say definitively is nobody, neither his friends who found him nor the paramedics, said anything that would suggest foul play."

"Any way we can find out what the hospital concludes?" he asked, then followed up, "I assume we know where they are taking him?"

"Not as of the time I left. I'll ask that question when I get back to the analyst monitoring the feed. As to knowing what the hospital determines, you know that hospitals are Sparrow dead zones. We didn't think they were a useful source of intel for threat detection. And I'm highly skeptical if the guy's friends were program targets, unless they were from the Post as well. We may be out of luck. Longstreet was a fairly prominent reporter, however, so I've got to believe we are going to see this in the Post within the next 24 hours. I'll put somebody on their website right away," she said.

"Good," he replied. "And get back to me the minute you find out anything. Is Collins aware of this?" he asked.

"I doubt it," she responded. "This sort of thing would go through you unless he specifically requested it."

"OK, thanks," he said. "I'm going to call him right now. Get back there and see what else you can find out."

175

"And sir," she said, implying she had another question.

"What?" Jennings responded.

"This could really be a stroke of good luck, couldn't it?" she asked.

"Yes, it could, Agent Green. Yes, it could. Please close the door as you leave," he said, signaling their conversation was over.

As Green left his office, Jennings turned his chair around and looked out his window. The dark of night felt like a thick blanket of unease. Longstreet's unexpected demise was indeed fortuitous, but the timing was troubling. It was too convenient. He didn't believe in coincidences, and he certainly didn't believe in luck. In his business luck was the outcome of careful planning and flawless action. The likelihood of an apparently healthy middle-aged man just dropping dead, especially that particular man in this particular moment in time, well, it was like winning the lottery. Somebody, or something had to be behind this. And he needed to find out. Not just as a matter of professional responsibility, but as an act of self-preservation as well. And what about this character named Joe? What were his motives here, and how would he react to this news? He was anxious to get that report from Director McConnell in the morning. There was one thing his professional experience had taught him well. Never underestimate your adversaries. And Identify them early.

Chapter 12 – Inconsistencies

FBI Headquarters, Office of Donald R. Benson, Executive Assistant Director, Intelligence

Joe Barber emerged from the Federal Triangle Metro stop into the warm Spring sunshine and started walking towards Pennsylvania Avenue. As he arrived at the intersection of Pennsylvania and 12th Street, he couldn't help but instinctively look to his left. A few blocks down the avenue sat the White House, and in spite of his feelings towards its present occupant he could not help but feel a sense of awe every time he looked at the place. Its symbolism, its outright majesty, could almost bring a lump to his throat, if he was given to such emotions, which ordinarily he was not. After a brief look, he turned in the opposite direction and began the block and a half walk to FBI headquarters. As he did so, the nation's Capitol building loomed large on the horizon in front of him at the other end of the avenue. It also was a building that could inspire awe, at least from its architecture, if not in the least bit from what occupied it. There were some members of Congress, of course, whom he respected. There were even a few members he regarded as friends. But the place was a superb example of the whole being vastly less than the sum of its parts. He quickly dismissed such thoughts from his mind. This morning was not the time to indulge in political musings. He had vastly more important things to occupy his mind at the moment.

Joe walked up to the FBI headquarters building and after entering a door, went directly to the security checkpoint. One thing Joe hated about Washington D.C. was he could not be armed. He felt almost naked without his Sig P224 hugging his side, but the nation's capital had some of the strictest gun laws in the country, and basically only the police or very privileged people were allowed to carry a weapon. And that was on the street; even if he had a license it would be no good once he crossed the threshold of the FBI building. His pistol remained locked in a safe on his King Air, where it would stay until this trip was over. After he surrendered his driver's license and cell phone at the security desk, the officer confirmed his appointment with Director Benson and gave him a visitor badge complete with the picture they had just taken. Once he had passed through the metal detector, he was ushered to an elevator that would take him directly to the executive offices.

Donald Robert Benson sat behind a large wooden desk in a fairly ornate office as Joe walked in and greeted him. The two of them began their conversation by exchanging pleasantries and asking about each other's wives and families. Although they had remained friends since college, their relationship now was more social than close. This being the consequence of the two of them going in very different directions after graduating — Don to law school then the Bureau, Joe to the Navy and ultimately the Teams, then CIA. Once Joe left government service and started his security business, they had a common professional interest again, along with their shared passion for golf, and both of them tried to get together several times a year. Sometimes it was for fancy dinners with their wives. Sometimes it was for 18 holes. It was a relationship Joe was happy to nurture. He liked Don, of course, but it also was obvious that Don was on a fast burner at the Bureau, being one of the youngest agents to make SAC, and enjoying several plumb assignments that were obvious signs he was being groomed for big things. Joe knew it was good to keep friends in high places. But he viewed Don as more of a sounding board than a resource. The two of them loved talking shop, discussing challenges and the state of the art in the security and intelligence business, and they both learned by sharing each other's perspectives. It was a matter of a strong mutual interest and almost never as an effort to use each other for something they were working on. This meeting was a clear departure from that norm, of course, and Joe could tell Don sensed it the minute he walked into the room. Both men sensed their opening repartee was almost forced, and anything but social. It was also very short.

Joe began the business part of the discussion by describing what he was working on and why. He had shared with Don the story about his father and his friend Lt. Maxwell several times, so Joe's interest in the circumstances surrounding the terrorist attack resonated with Benson.

"You know, Joe," Benson said, "those pieces of metal from Michigan are arguably material evidence in a federal investigation. You need to get those out of your possession and into the hands of some law enforcement organization pronto."

"Given what I'm about to share with you, I realize that, Don," Joe replied. "That's one of the reasons I'm here."

Benson frowned a bit, clearly understanding the implication of Barber's comment that he, Don Benson, was likely the law enforcement individual Joe had in mind. He frankly didn't know quite what to think about that. "Where are they?" Benson asked.

"I left the bigger pieces in the plane," Barber replied. "I couldn't see myself walking into FBI headquarters with a large box of shrapnel from auto sheet metal."

"Fair point," Benson said. "But what do you mean by the larger pieces?" he asked in follow up.

"I have several smaller pieces, of a different type of metal, in my briefcase," Joe replied again. "I'd like to leave those with you as well, and more about them in a second."

"Ok I'll admit that finding pieces of metal a few blocks away from the street where the terrorist vehicle exploded appears a bit odd, but it's hardly the stuff of conspiracy theories, Joe," Benson said.

"What do you know about the SUV that exploded in Tyson's Corner?" Joe asked.

"Nothing really, other than what I read in the press. It was reported as some sort of safety issue. The manufacturer, Ford I think, is being taken to task on it. It's not FBI jurisdiction. As a matter of fact, it's not even a crime, at least in the normal sense of the term. I understand it's being investigated by DOT. Why do you ask?"

"What if I were to tell you that similar pieces of shrapnel were found several blocks away from the location of that explosion as well?" Joe asked.

"Joe, my friend, I'd tell you that you've been reading way too many Brad Thor or Vince Flynn novels. Frankly, buddy, you're surprising me a bit here," Benson said with a look of incredulity on his face. "It's unlike you to craft a theory on such thin evidence. As a matter of fact, I would argue on almost no evidence at all."

"If that was all I had, I'd agree with you, Don," Barber replied. "In spite of the fact I can't explain how a conventional blast could cause shrapnel to arc so far, I agree – if that was all I had I wouldn't be here now and we wouldn't be having this conversation."

"Ok, I'm listening," Benson replied.

"What if I told you that the smaller fragments I have in my briefcase are of a type of metal that had no business being at either scene. Titanium. Titanium isn't used in auto manufacture, at least to any measurable size. And what if I told you that my labs analysis of the pieces suggests the titanium from the two scenes was linked, that it came from the same place?"

181

"I would say that you have found titanium in the same vicinity as the vehicle shrapnel, but that you still don't have a shred of evidence the two things are in any way related," Benson replied. "What are you driving at, Joe? This is unlike you. Frankly with every comment you make I keep asking myself the "so what" question and I can't craft a meaningful answer. The only thing you've said so far that's resonated with me is a sort of confession that you are in possession of evidence related to separate and completely unrelated vehicle explosions and that you need to turn it over to the authorities. I'd love to hear your point, because so far I still don't see it."

Barber looked Benson in the eyes and paused for a couple of seconds for effect before making his next comment. He took a deep breath and then began to speak in a slightly lower voice, also for effect. "What if I were also to tell you that my lab analysis found traces of Semtex on every piece of that titanium. Titanium, remember, from both scenes that appears to have come from the same source."

Now it was Benson's turn to wait a few seconds before making his reply. And it wasn't for effect. It was to fully absorb what had just been said. "I think maybe you better give me that briefcase, Joe," Benson replied. "You understand that I will need to have my lab look at the pieces as well?"

"Of course," Joe replied. "I was hoping you would say that."

"Ordnance of some sort?" Benson asked.

"I suspect so, and that's the only theory I have right now that fits the facts," Joe said.

"I'm inclined to agree," Benson replied. "And an ordnance from above could possibly explain the higher arc of some of the vehicle metal and its travel."

"Precisely," Barber said.

"But there's still one major problem, Joe," Benson continued, "how would the ordnance have been delivered? This is the United States, not Afghanistan. There aren't exactly Predator drones circling over Southeastern Michigan, and there sure as hell aren't drones circling over Northern Virginia so close to D.C. The physical evidence may be consistent with your theory of ordnance, but the context of the evidence absolutely rules it out."

"What about some sort of private aircraft?" Joe asked. "Why couldn't somebody fire a projectile from some kind of private aircraft?"

"It's theoretically possible, but it's also an absurd stretch in my view," Benson replied. "If some terrorist organization had demonstrated that kind of capability, the government wouldn't be covering it up; it would be pulling out all the stops to find it. For Heaven's sake, Joe, we'd ground the entire general aviation fleet and every resource in DHS and the Bureau, including my people. We would be working on nothing else. It would be impossible to keep something like that under wraps."

"I agree it's a wild theory, but there's no other theory I can come up with, at least for now, that isn't less credible when looked at in context," Joe replied.

"Let me come at you from a different angle then," Benson continued. "If these two incidents are related, why the story of a vehicle safety issue then?"

"I don't have a good answer for that one, Don," Joe replied, "unless some of your colleagues over at DHS are trying to cover up some new terrorist capability, I don't know; maybe in the hopes of not creating a panic until they know more, or maybe just trying to hide something that doesn't fit with their narrative, but I really have no idea."

"Wow, I think that's really a stretch, Joe," Benson responded. "You've got my attention here, but I am still inclined to believe there has to be some kind of rational explanation. Frankly the notion of a government conspiracy to cover up not just one but two back to back attacks on civilian targets sounds preposterous. I hate to say it, but I'm more inclined to think of government incompetence. The field agents over at DOT may have actually believed there was some kind of safety issue with that vehicle. Think about it. The gas tank did actually explode, and there was no evidence whatsoever of any kind of foul play from what I've read; although I can call a colleague over at DOT and ask if they are working any other angle, but I seriously doubt it. And remember the Bureau has the domestic remit. If there was some kind of new terrorist capability we would be all over it and I've heard nothing. Nothing," he said with increased emphasis on the second pronunciation of the word. "There has to be some other explanation."

"Well if you find one I'd love to hear it," Joe fired back, "cause I sure as hell can't think of anything."

"Who else is aware of this?" Benson asked.

"Other than the folks in my lab, only two," Barber responded. "I ran into a reporter from the Detroit Free Press while I was looking around, and we sort of both found the pieces together. In exchange for taking the pieces he found, I had to promise him I'd get back with him if I turned up anything. I've probably got another day or two before the guy starts to hound me."

"Who else?" Benson asked.

"Eric Longstreet from the Post," Joe said. "The guy's actually a friend of mine. He's the one who found the pieces at Tyson's Corner, not me. I had dinner with him the other night to discuss what I thought might be similarities about the two incidents. He actually brought the pieces he found to the dinner and handed them over to me so I could do the forensics. That's how I got possession of them."

"Eric Longstreet?" Benson asked with considerable surprise in his voice.

"Yeah," Barber responded. "Why do you sound so surprised?"

"Have you seen the news this morning?" Benson asked.

"What news?" Barber responded with growing concern in his voice. "I haven't seen any news this morning. I was wheels up at oh five thirty from Rye and didn't even stop at a Starbucks after getting off the Red Line."

"It was on the TV news this morning, and it's probably on the Post's website by now," Benson replied. "Eric Longstreet was found dead in his townhouse last night. No details have been released, as yet, other than they believe it was natural causes. He was found by a couple of friends who apparently had come over to his place for dinner."

Joe Barber sat back in his chair as if he was just hit by a ton of bricks. He couldn't believe what he had just heard, and his reaction was a harmonic convergence of both shock and anger. Then fear, as the hair stood up on the back of his neck. The inconsistencies were growing.

Chapter 13 – The Hawk

McLean, VA, same morning

Colonel Jeffrey Taylor heard the news on the radio as he was driving to work. He almost missed his exit. He was stunned. True, Jennings had broached the topic of implementing a "contingency", as it was so antiseptically called, against the reporter Eric Longstreet. That, all by itself, was shocking. Even more shocking was the fact that nobody in ExComm immediately killed the idea, and some even seemed to embrace it and did so in front of an Executive Assistant Director of the FBI nonetheless. Taylor knew he had assets in his command who could carry out that order, but he always thought the mission would be to take out a terrorist, not assassinate a U.S. citizen. His mind raced as he retraced yesterday's conversation in the Room. If those assets were to be used, the orders were to be conveyed by him. That was the chain of command. Unless, of course, there existed some parallel organization that took orders directly from ExComm. That thought really troubled him. And what did Jennings know about all of this? Could he be involved in some way? The more Taylor worked with Jennings, the less he trusted him. He didn't like the guy. He had the wrong profile for this type of work. The guy was too much of an opportunist, and that was a dangerous trait in an organization like this. One thing he knew for sure – he intended to confront Jennings about the news the second he got to the office. Jennings would be his first stop. His mind connected this train of thought to his reflections yesterday on what constituted a lawful order. Killing a terrorist on U.S. soil, without due process, was something he was prepared to do. Hell, he had already done it a few days ago in Michigan. But killing a U.S. citizen who potentially knew too much, as a way of protecting the organization? No way would he do that, absolutely no way. His mind then shifted to the most sobering thought he had while sitting in that Brief. Did the contingencies they made reference to include one for him?

Taylor parked his car and within minutes was on the 4th floor and going through security. He walked past his office without stopping and proceeded to the next door in the hall, Jennings' office. Placing their two offices next to each other was management's way of fostering teamwork. At the moment teamwork was the farthest thing from Taylor's mind. He opened the door to Jennings' office and briskly asked Jennings' executive assistant if he was in yet. She nodded, then without breaking stride he opened the door and entered. Jennings was sitting at his desk and looked up the moment the door opened. He immediately noticed Taylor's elevated energy. It was unsettling, almost primal, which projected the raw aggression of a warrior about to engage an enemy.

"What do you know about Longstreet?" Taylor asked, his voice elevated and projecting an accusing tone.

"Slow down, Jeff," Jennings responded. "I heard about it last night and know nothing about the circumstances other than what I've read and heard on the news. My people were monitoring Longstreet's Sparrow intel. We have on tape the commotion as his friends found him unresponsive in his townhouse, but there's nothing from the moment he walked in to his residence to the moment he was found unresponsive that would suggest foul play. We have the conversations from the first responders who tried to revive him as well as their confirmation that the guy didn't make it. His cell phone was apparently not on his person because shortly after he was taken from the scene for transport to the hospital we lost all transmission. As you know we have no assets inside of hospitals."

"Were you behind this?" Taylor asked, with an almost menacing tone.

"Slow down! Of course not!" Jennings almost shouted back. "I was going to ask you that," he said with equal parts anger and fear. "And I went to Collins with this last night right after we heard. His response seemed to be one of genuine surprise. I can read the guy and I don't think he was feigning it."

"This is too much of a coincidence, Ryan," Taylor said, slightly more even now and less agitated, "especially in terms of the timing."

"I can't disagree with that," Jennings said. "But sometimes the most obvious answer is the correct one. Maybe he did have some sort of a health condition. And sometimes you just get lucky."

"The death of Eric Longstreet isn't luck, you bastard," Taylor snapped back, anger rising again.

"All right, all right. Agreed, and sorry," Jennings responded, conveying more of a desire to placate than real sincerity. He then continued. "Collins has called an ExComm meeting this morning. It starts in about 10 minutes. Apparently, Director McConnell has some information on this Joe character, but I'm sure we'll talk about Longstreet's demise as well."

"Good," Taylor snapped back. "And I intend to find out if anyone in this organization is responsible for what happened last night," he said with an ominous tone.

Jennings initially had been thrown back on his heels in the conversation by Taylor's abrupt entry and menacing tone, but he was in the process of regaining his footing. He took a breath and responded more authoritatively. "I'd be careful not to get too overreaching with this Jeff, until and unless you have some evidence that's more compelling than the timing of recent events. Throwing accusations around is not going to sit well. Whatever conclusions we come to and whatever we do about them, it has to be based on the forensic evidence, the facts, full stop."

"I don't make accusations without facts," Taylor replied. "But one way you gather facts is by asking questions and I'm going to start asking a lot of questions that could make some people uncomfortable."

"Right, but just remember some questions, especially with an inappropriate tone, can be viewed as accusations, as you so eloquently have demonstrated over the last several minutes," Jennings said. "Gather your facts carefully, Jeff, lest you leave the wrong impression."

"Is that a threat, Ryan?" Taylor asked with a tad of sarcasm born of thinly veiled contempt.

"No, Jeff, it's not a threat," Jennings replied. "It's a fact, and just a little friendly advice."

* * * * *

Taylor and Jennings were seated at their usual positions at the Room's conference table, as were the ExComm members Collins, Johnson and Erby. Chief of Staff Fitzpatrick, Sandra McConnell and Director Collins walked in and sat down almost directly across from them. Collins called the meeting to order, as Taylor reflected favorably on the fact that for the first time in his experience the ExComm Chair was the first person to speak at an ExComm meeting. He also took some small sense of comfort as Collins immediately turned to the subject of Longstreet.

"As we are all now aware and frankly shocked, Agent Jennings team followed in real time the unfortunate and untimely demise of Eric Longstreet. I also understand that we have no information, as yet, on cause of death; is that correct, Ryan?"

189

"Yes sir," Jennings replied. "As I mentioned last night, we have few Sparrow assets in hospitals. They just aren't viewed as likely sources for threat detection, and, in spite of the events of last night, I still believe that is the proper perspective."

Fitzpatrick cleared his throat a bit then began to speak, somewhat unexpectedly. "I think I can help with that," he said. "I know the Executive Editor of the Post socially and called him before this meeting to offer my condolences and to see if he knew anything about what happened. That phone call is why Sandra and I are a few minutes late. I pumped him a bit on cause of death. It turns out that Longstreet was being treated for a mild cardiac arrhythmia and had been seeing a cardiologist about it for a couple of years. He was taking a beta blocker of some kind and seemed to have it under control, or so they thought. The physicians at Virginia Hospital Center's emergency room think the most likely cause was some sort of arrhythmia event. It's unlikely there will be anything more definitive than that. Given his medical history and the circumstances of his death, there is no reason to do an autopsy, and the family is proceeding with funeral plans. That's about all I know."

"Ok I know the timing of this will appear a little odd to the people in this room, especially in light of yesterday's conversation, but I see no evidence of anything untoward here," Collins said. "It's pretty clear his investigation didn't get far enough to present a disclosure threat to this organization, so I regard this matter as closed. Any questions or follow up?"

The Room remained silent. Taylor reflected on the convenience of the explanation and was again uncomfortable with yet another example of Fitzpatrick's direct engagement in their business.

Director Collins continued, "Sandra, I understand you have some information for us on the mystery man, Joe, is that correct?"

190

"Indeed, I do," Executive Assistant Director McConnell spoke up. "It was pretty easy to figure out who this guy is. There are apparently three Joes who live in Rye and own Beechcraft King Air airplanes. Finding three surprised me initially, but Rye is a fairly wealthy community with a lot of residents owning private aircraft. We looked up the tail numbers on the three birds. An ophthalmic surgeon owns one and an investment banker owns one. Based on a review of pilot-filed FAA flight plans, neither of these two are likely our Joe. The surgeon's plane is undergoing an overhaul and the I-banker's plane hasn't left the ground for six weeks. One however, tail number N3544B, has made recent trips to both Michigan and Northern Virginia, including the morning of the dinner meeting with this Joe and Longstreet. And it turns out this Joe, full name of Joseph Michael Barber, happens to own a private security business called Orion Bellicus. He is also ex-special forces, a former Navy SEAL, and former CIA covert ops. This is our guy. Here's his home and business address," she said as she slid a file folder across the table.

"What do we know about this outfit Orion Bellicus?" Collins asked.

"Didn't do much research on them," McConnell replied. "I'm sure you folks can handle that task. But a quick Google search suggested, as I said, that they are in the private security and corporate intelligence business. I don't have any particulars beyond that, and frankly that's about as far as I am comfortable going with using FBI assets," she said.

"Thanks, Director McConnell," Collins said, sliding the folder across the table towards Jennings. "We can take it from here. Agent Jennings, I want Sparrow assets on this guy ASAP. Let's target the senior leadership of the firm as well."

"Yes sir," Jennings replied. "To expedite I'll have agents deliver the packages within the next few hours, as soon as we can get people on the scene. We don't have the luxury of using the normal U.S. Postal routine, and

191

we have packages pre-staged in this building for just such a contingency," he said, referring to Sparrow devices already placed in envelopes designed to look like U.S. mail but pre-prepped to enable direct delivery by hand.

"Good," Collins replied. "Use the Citation we have at Reagan. Colonel Taylor, have your people alert the crew to have it standing by."

"Yes sir," Taylor replied. It would be an understatement to say he was concerned about what ExComm might decide to do with the intelligence they collected on this Joe Barber guy, but for now the regarded this as a legitimate order and would comply. He also decided this was not the time, at least not yet, to start asking those uncomfortable questions. At least he had a little bit more time, he thought to himself, and this gave him a modest sense of relief as he stood up to leave the Room. As he walked through the door, however, he did not expect that sense of relief to last.

* * * * *

As William Fitzpatrick got into his limousine, he told his driver to drop him by his townhouse and plan on waiting outside for about 30 minutes. He mentioned he had something he needed to quickly take care of before returning to the White House. It was a beautiful cloudless day, and the late morning sun was high in the sky and hot as the Chief of Staff emerged from the vehicle parked in front of his home. As per the normal procedure, a Secret Service agent walked up to the front door first, entered a security code on a pad next to the front door and walked into the townhouse while Fitzpatrick waited on the front porch. After a quick walk through the house and confirming it was safe, the agent walked back outside and uttered the words, "It's clear, sir," which was Fitzpatrick's cue that it was now safe to go inside. The agent then took his position on the front porch, hands folded in front of him and standing almost at attention. The agent's eyes slowly and carefully scanned the area in front of the house through a pair of Ray Ban aviator sunglasses, the almost perfect stereotype of how a member of the Secret Service was supposed to look and act. Sometimes being conspicuous was a good thing, like the security system decals on the front doors of almost every townhouse in the neighborhood.

Fitzpatrick walked through the foyer to a staircase that was just outside his kitchen and that led to the basement. At the bottom of the stairs to the right was a steel door similar to the kind that would be used for a safe room. The room was a private office. It was not nearly as large and ornate as the two-story study just across from his living room, and not lined with about 3,400 plus books like his study contained, but it was arguably the place he did his most important work. It was actually more like a vault than an office, and contained a large and relatively plain but functional desk with several computer screens including a Bloomberg financial and news terminal, which allowed him to stay on top of events and provided him with an extraordinary research capability. Among the more interesting features of the workspace were the two small computer towers that sat in the corner. One of them housed dual Apple CPUs, and the other contained a stack of solid-state hard drives that provided storage and back-up for up to 12 terabytes of data. Together they represented a private email server. He never used it for official business and certainly never used it to communicate with the President or any other senior official in government. He knew that to be fool's errand and he wouldn't make the same mistake as that egomaniacal woman from State. But it provided him a highly secure and encrypted method of communicating with only a handful of his closest confidants. Another interesting feature of the place was the electronic shield that lined the floor, ceiling, and all four walls. That shield, along with the encrypted phone system that sat on the desk, rendered the phone calls and conversations that emanated from the office fully Sparrow-proof. He regarded the risk of himself being a target of Sparrow as pretty low, not only because the consequences for the people at NDSA would be well, unpleasant to say the least, but also because he knew what to

193

look for. Bottom line: the security in this office allowed him to conduct the more interesting parts of his business in complete anonymity. He closed the door, which automatically activated the electronic security screen. The phone system on his desk was actually a call director, similar to the ones used by Wall Street trading houses. With one push of a button he was directly connected with his contact on the West Coast via a dedicated line.

"Good morning, Bill," the familiar voice on the other end of the phone said, "if it's still morning there, that is. It's certainly still morning here."

"Good morning," Fitzpatrick responded. "The Hawk obviously landed last night, and it would appear as though its mission was a complete success."

"Agreed," the voice replied. "I expected nothing less. We beta tested it on several large dogs, and after success with that the team engineered a clever way to test it on a vagrant who fit the profile of an illegal immigrant, a low risk target. We wanted to make sure it was equally effective on a human and would not just make them sick. Complete success there as well, so I was highly confident it would perform as designed. Looks like the delivery mechanism also worked flawlessly, although that was arguably the weakest link in the process and the piece that made me the most nervous."

"I was pretty nervous about that also," Fitzpatrick said, "and I still believe it's important to design some kind of failsafe into the thing in the event it doesn't get its intended target. I'm not comfortable with the notion of those things just falling to the ground."

"Agreed," the voice replied. "The team is working on it, but I still think it's a remarkable achievement. What do you know about this character, Joe?"

"McConnell came through in spades on that one," the President's Chief of Staff responded. "We've got the guy's name and address, and the

194

name and address of his business. NDSA is delivering Sparrow assets to both places as we speak. We should have the intel up and running by tomorrow sometime. I'll keep you posted on what we find."

"It could save you a lot of time and trouble if we simply had the Hawk pay him a visit," the voice observed, more as a test of Fitzpatrick's reaction than a real suggestion.

"That's way too premature," Fitzpatrick replied, with a distinct tone of concern in his voice. "I'm still concerned we acted prematurely with the reporter. There's no way Johnson or Collins are going to buy another fortuitous coincidence, let alone Erby. The Hawk needs to be kept in its cage and not released unless I explicitly authorize it. Are we clear on that?" he asked authoritatively. "And one other thing," he continued, "if it is necessary to implement a contingency on this Joe person I want to use more conventional means. It's important to keep ExComm and the team believing they are in control and have effective methods at their disposal. Those contingencies were developed by people who had no knowledge that the Hawk was under development, and there is no way we can keep this thing under wraps if our problems all of sudden just start disappearing by mysterious means."

It was exactly the response the voice on the other end of the conversation was looking for. Restraint. There was nothing more dangerous to his long-term goals than an overzealous bureaucrat, especially one with a new and lethal tool in his hands. "Got, it Fitz," the voice responded, "and don't worry about that reporter. I tend to agree that it wasn't necessary to act so quickly, but it was important to field test Hawk, including the delivery mechanism. And it worked splendidly. The bird will stay in its cage until and unless you authorize release. Let's see what Sparrow turns up on this other character."

"Good," Fitzpatrick replied. "I expect the feed to be up and running by the end of today, and we should know a lot more within 24-48 hours. And remember, Sparrow exists to protect the American people and that's where the bulk of our resources need to be directed. If that means it takes a little longer to figure out what this Joe Barber is up to, so be it."

"Fully agree, Fitz," the voice responded, in a sympathetic tone that was the result of considerable self-restraint. "But let's touch base tomorrow sometime."

"Not to worry," Fitzpatrick responded, "but it will have to be tomorrow night. You know I'm not about to make that kind of call from the West Wing, and we've got a full schedule tomorrow. There's nothing in the evening, but I still won't be home till after eight o'clock, so don't expect a call before nine."

"No problem," the voice on the other end of the line replied. "Just get back to me as soon as you can."

William Fitzpatrick pushed the release button on his call director and terminated the conversation. At the same time Westy Reynolds sat back in his chair about three thousand miles away and smiled. He would go through the charade of asking for Sparrow updates, but it was largely for appearances sake. In reality he had a fully functioning network of assets monitoring Sparrow intelligence himself, located in a vaulted room at QuarkSpin. The focus wasn't so much on threat detection. He frankly didn't really care much about that, unless the threat was close to home. It focused mostly on business intelligence which proved invaluable in his private equity work. Knowing the plans of the people sitting across from you in a business negotiation proved highly lucrative on a number of occasions subsequent to Sparrow going live. It was based on a slightly altered device that would not play to the NDSA's intercepts and was focused on a much smaller group of targets, but it delivered a gold mine of information. The QuarkSpin team, however, did have the ability to monitor the NDSA's frequencies if they chose to, and they would certainly be listening to the intelligence coming from Joe Barber at the same time as Agent Jennings. Protecting the program's anonymity and viability were one of his highest priorities, and he would do anything necessary to ensure it. Outside of his own organization, Fitzpatrick was the only person aware of project Hawk. Several operational Hawks had been prepped for delivery should the need arise, and one of them had been used on Longstreet. Most others sat in their cages as Reynolds was fond of saying, awaiting a joint decision from him and Fitzpatrick prior to their use. One, however, was very special, and sat in a very special cage, to use the metaphor again. It sat on top of a wine cork just underneath the foil on a bottle of Opus One, vintage 1983. The bottle and its contents were real, but the original foil had been removed and replaced after planting the Hawk. The ruse was flawless. The bottle was in a UPS overnight shipping box, with return address of Charles Westbourne Reynolds. There was something exquisite about hiding such a threat in plain sight. Reynolds knew Fitzpatrick to be a compulsive oenophile who relished the process of carefully cutting and removing a bottle's foil and that Opus One was his favorite. They had a standing tradition between them that each time either one of them experienced exceptionally notable success, Reynolds would ship Fitzpatrick a bottle of his favorite cult cabernet with a note that they were each to open their respective bottles at a predetermined time and enjoy a virtual toast while on the phone. The package, which was actually a deadly weapon, sat in the safe in Reynolds office. He hoped he wouldn't have to use it. He liked Fitzpatrick despite their differences and his regard for him as somewhat of a lesser man. He wouldn't lose any sleep if he had to, however. Business was business, and it was outcomes that mattered, not sentimentality. Sentimentality was the balm of lesser men.

Chapter 14 – Mysterious Connections from the Past

Joseph Michael Barber was seething with anger as he pushed the throttle of the King Air forward and began his takeoff roll. He couldn't have cared less what Benson had said about not jumping to conclusions or getting so upset. There was absolutely no way Eric Longstreet's death was a coincidence, and if it was the last thing he did he would get to the bottom of it. He now had two mysteries to solve and potentially avenge. He would summon every resource of his firm and his past to find out what had happened, and those resources were considerable. He would find the individuals responsible, and they would pay a price they couldn't imagine. On the exterior he was a successful business executive who ran a profitable security and corporate intelligence firm. He was a husband and father. But on the inside at the core of his being, he was a product of his past. Years in the Teams followed by his work as a field officer at the CIA had infused him with a work ethic and commitment to results that were unrelenting. It also gave him the necessary skills. And it gave him a network of connections that he didn't often call upon, but when he did those connections could be extraordinarily helpful. Oddly, the experiences of his past could bring out in him a great compassion. Many a time he had seen the darker side of life and the result of evil in the world. But it also made him a man who, if properly motivated, could be ruthless and an adversary's worst nightmare. He had done things in his past that he regretted. But he didn't beat himself up over them. He learned from them. He learned from his faith that absolution for the sins of his past was complete. And as he put that principle into practice, he learned something even more important – that forgiving himself for his past could be a powerful force multiplier in the present. The older he got the more he tried to put the ruthlessness behind him, mostly by doing his best not to place himself in circumstances that could summon the darker angels of a previous life. But occasionally those circumstances would find him. Eric Longstreet was not a close friend, but he was somebody who had trusted Joe, and had gone out of his way to help him. Joe simply could not abide that such a trust had resulted in Longstreet's death, and he was convinced it had.

The King Air clawed its way toward flight level 20, or 20,000 feet above sea level, in a blue azure sky. Barber pulled a cell phone out of his flight bag and turned it on. It was a special phone equipped with an encryption algorithm developed by Lauren Cartwright herself. It was harder to break than Apple's. He pressed the number 3 on the keypad and waited. The sound of the phone starting to ring was loud and clear in his Bose noise cancelling aviation headphones over the sound of the twin jet-prop King Air engines. After several seconds Joe became worried he would be sent to voicemail, but after the sixth ring a voice on the other end simply answered by saying, "Ident please."

Joe responded, "Echo Romeo Hotel one niner niner."

"Identification confirmed," the disembodied voice replied. "Stand by."

In a few seconds a familiar voice came on the line. "Good morning Joe. To what do I owe this unexpected pleasure?" the voice said.

"I've got a situation," Joe replied, then proceeded to quickly summarize the events of the last several days. "This looks like some kind of new terrorist capability, and frankly I'm not sure what brand – could even be domestic for all I know. My instincts also tell me that someone in the government is trying to cover it up. Not sure why, but there are too many things that don't make sense. Longstreet must have been on top of a whole lot more than what he let on to me, which frankly wouldn't be a surprise. It's his signature M.O. Then the guy suddenly succumbs to an all too convenient premature demise."

"I saw it on the news, but it looks pretty straightforward. The guy apparently was being treated for some kind of cardiac arrhythmia," the voice replied, and then asked, "what do you want?"

"I want to know if you have anything on the threat boards that could be connected," Joe said. "I've talked to Benson from FBI, and he actually has most of the titanium fragments I found. He is running them through F.B.I. labs to confirm and see if they yield anything more. If they find something else I could get the Bureau interested, but right now Don is a skeptic. He tells me the Bureau isn't even looking into the incident in Tyson's Corner. It's being investigated by the DOT."

"DOT? They couldn't identify a terrorist if the guy was standing in front of them with an AK47 screaming Allah whatever," he said with sarcasm. "I have to say, though, I understand why Don's a skeptic. Think of the dots you'd have to connect. First, Longstreet is on to more than he told you; ok I'd buy that. The terrorists are aware that Longstreet is on to them. How? That seems like a real stretch. Second, why would they pay any attention to a reporter? I doubt they would even know who the guy is, let alone suspect he knows something that could compromise them. Third, the terrorists decide to kill Longstreet to keep their identity or means under wraps. You have to validate the dots one and two to connect the third. But ok, let's say we do. Why, then, kill him by some mysterious means that looked like natural causes. If these bad dudes wanted him dead, Joe, wouldn't they just bomb his house or his car? Or shoot him? Isn't that what terrorists do? I just don't get the high-tech subterfuge."

"I'll admit the motive for the method is the most difficult part of my theory," Joe responded. "But the timing of his death is just too damn convenient. No way it was natural causes."

"I'll admit the timing is hard to explain away. But frankly, pal, it's easier to explain than the other questions I raised."

"Humor me, please," Joe said to the disembodied voice. "All I'm asking for here is that you take a look at what is already on your threat boards. I'm not asking you to initiate something."

"Ok, I'll see what I can dig up. Maybe at least we can rule out either domestic or foreign, which should be a big help. But don't get your hopes up. Call me back later today, after twenty-three hundred zulu. If I can't turn up anything by then, I'm afraid there's not much we can add."

"Thanks, John," Joe responded. "I owe you one."

"Yes you do, Joseph, yes you do," the voice said. "And don't worry, we'll collect."

"I have no doubt about that," Joe said. He then pushed the end button and disconnected the call. It would be a relatively short flight back to Rye. Not much time to think, but think he would.

* * * * *

The home was nestled well into the interior of a beautiful neighborhood. The houses that lined the street were huge by the standard of middle-class America, but not particularly large by the standards of the residents. All of them were large colonials and each had exterior features that conveyed great attention to detail, to say nothing of expense. Most families occupying these homes, mansions actually, were of considerable means. One of the primary things that separated them, however, from their truly wealthy neighbors to the East in places like the Hamptons or Central Park is that the people occupying these homes derived their means from professional success and not inherited wealth. These were the homes of the partners in large law firms, neurosurgeons, corporate executives and Wall Street bankers. And

201

the particular home in question, nestled among numerous majestic oak trees, was the residence of Joseph Michael Barber. At the end of a long circular drive rested a mailbox. A BMW M5, not particularly unique for this neighborhood, casually pulled up to the mailbox. An arm extended from the passenger side, then opened the mailbox door and pushed several large envelopes then closed it. About an hour earlier the same BMW had delivered a series of similar packages to the offices of Orion Bellicus addressed to a variety of employees of varying stature within the firm. This would serve to maximize the potential for effective coverage. As those packages were opened the Sparrows would come to life. A listening net inside the Barber's household and Orion Bellicus' offices would slowly but surely materialize. The Sparrow's ears would monitor and record almost everything said, certainly anything important. And the National Security Agency's Department of Special Activities would not be the only ones listening.

Chapter 15 – Sudden Disappearances

Offices of Orion Bellicus, the next morning

Joe Barber and Marcus Day sat in the conference room two doors down from Joe's office. Joe regarded his office as a place to work by himself, not a place to conduct meetings or work in groups larger than one. It wasn't neutral territory, and no matter how senior the employee, Joe was smart enough to realize that having a conversation in his space gave him an advantage. It was a mark of his leadership that he didn't want that advantage; it was something he learned in the Teams by watching his best OICs. When you were in the boss's space, even the strongest individual had to fight the subliminal tendency to hold back, and Joe knew that wasn't the way the best decisions were made. Marcus Day was no wallflower, to say the least. And there was that little matter that both Joe and Marcus knew that Marcus could kick Joe's ass without even breaking a sweat. But even a bad ass like Marcus needed neutral ground to give Joe his best, and Joe desperately needed Marcus' best.

"I talked to John last night," Joe said, "They had been watching an ISIS domestic group and he believes there's a high probability they were responsible for the attack in Michigan. The chatter they collected clearly supports that, and it's what tipped off the Bureau and DHS to the threat."

"Did Benson confirm that as well?" Marcus asked.

"No," Joe replied. "He's not involved. Benson runs the Intelligence Branch. The National Security Branch would handle this sort of thing. I think some woman named McConnell runs it. Don't know her."

"Ok, so all you have is the obvious," Day replied.

"Not exactly," Joe said. "Oddly enough the Feds have zero chatter connected with the Tyson's Corner attack, in spite of the similar forensics."

"That doesn't surprise me, Joe," Day replied. "It's pretty clear that the occupants of the vehicle that exploded in Tyson's Corner were not terrorists. There's certainly no reason for the Feds to hide it if they were, especially in light of what happened in Michigan. So why would someone, the same someone, hit two separate vehicles, one with terrorists in it and one not, with some type of mysterious ordnance? You realize how loose this all sounds?" Marcus continued, "If we can't connect the two events, then I think there's nothing here. You've got a legitimate right to feel bad about Longstreet, but without something more from those forensics I think your theory is a bust."

"Well I'm working on a derivative theory," Barber said.

"What's that?" Day replied with a skeptical look on his face.

"What if we are dealing with two separate terrorist organizations here?"

"What would be the point of that, Joe?" Day asked. "They all hate us far more than they hate each other. Their hatred for us is one of the few things that actually unites them. Why on earth would a second terrorist organization try to attack another on U.S. soil? That just doesn't make any sense."

"What if it's not a second foreign terrorist organization?" Joe replied. "What if it's some sort of domestic organization, maybe a militia group or something that has taken the law into its own hands and gone after the terrorists itself?"

"Hmmm. That's interesting, but my first reaction is there are several major problems with that," Day fired back. "First, how is some domestic militia group going to identify the threat in the first place? It's not some high-tech arm of the FBI or NSA with a tech capability that would likely cost hundreds of millions. It would most likely be a group of local wing-nuts playing army. OK, you get the occasional spec ops type that join up, but think about it – even the best of these groups don't have the kind of operational capability you are describing. And how would they deliver the ordnance, especially from above?"

"A general aviation aircraft of some kind?" Joe asked, testing Day's reaction.

"That's crazy, pal," Day responded. "This isn't Afghanistan. People don't go flying around Northern Virginia shooting at vehicles from the air."

"That's exactly what Benson said to me," Joe replied.

"And besides," Day continued, "why make it so complicated? If they wanted to take the bastards out, why not just hunt them down and shoot them before the perps saddled up. Even if they had the capability, seems to me there is far too great a risk of getting caught, especially in this neck of the woods where Air Traffic Control has eyes on everything. Far too great a risk of mission failure, especially when compared with the alternative of just shooting the bastards before the fact."

Their conversation was interrupted by the abrupt ring of the telephone sitting between them on the conference table.

"I really hope that's Benson," Joe said as he reached over and touched the button that activated the speaker phone. "What's up, Jennifer?" Joe responded to Jennifer Adams, his administrative assistant.

"Director Benson from the FBI is on line two, Joe," she replied.

205

"Thanks, Jenn. Put him through."

"Good morning, Don," Joe answered as the line clicked revealing an open connection to the incoming call. "I've got Marcus here with me. He also thinks I'm seeing alligators under my bed. Did you guys turn up anything else on those fragments?"

"Not exactly," Benson replied.

"What does that mean?" Joe asked with a puzzled expression on his face as he looked at Day.

"As of this morning I still hadn't heard anything, so I called about 30 minutes ago to check on the status."

"And....?" Joe replied.

"And there's no report. The lab evidently never officially logged the fragments. They appear to have gone missing."

"Don, the FBI does not lose case evidence," Joe responded, incredulity in his voice.

"No, it doesn't," Benson replied. "No, it certainly doesn't."

Chapter 16 – The Next Target

Palo Alto, California

Dr. Emma Clark sat in an electronically shielded vault in the basement of QuarkSpin. As the Chief Executive Officer of the company, she had overseen the development of every one of QuarkSpin's projects over the last five years. Sparrow was her most prized accomplishment. But she not only led the development of the device itself, it was her idea to engineer a variant that operated on a different frequency and develop a monitoring capability parallel to the NDSA's. When she pitched the idea to Westy Reynolds he loved it. It had a very different mission. Reynolds and Clark both knew there were two distinct types of organizations interested in collecting "big" data. They were hunters and gatherers. The NSA and its covert arm, the Department of Special Activities, was a gatherer. The NDSA collected massive amounts of communications without really knowing specifically what they were looking for. They used sophisticated software programs to sift through it and identify threats. But Reynolds and Clark knew exactly what they were looking for. They were looking for commercial intelligence – the ability to listen to the conversations of their business adversaries, people and organizations on the other side of the negotiating table. It would give PrinSafe a monumental competitive edge. This part of their plan was so successful and profitable that they actually had to scale back a bit on how much of the information they used. They usually didn't sit across the table from fools, and creating suspicion among their competitors or the authorities, especially the Securities and Exchange Commission, was the last thing they needed. Present circumstances, however, had given them a new and unexpected objective – protecting the program. Sloppy analysis by NDSA and tactical errors in the early pursuit of terrorist threats had created an unacceptable risk of disclosing the Sparrow and its capabilities. So Reynolds had directed Dr. Clark to set up and monitor a parallel net of NDSA's Sparrow intel to flag any potential threat of program disclosure. He had also directed her to develop an insurance policy, which led to one of her most impressive engineering feats to date – the Hawk. On its very first deployment, it had worked flawlessly.

As Dr. Clark sat in QuarkSpin's digital forensics lab, she removed her headphones, set them on the desk in front of her and rubbed her temples. She then placed them back on, adjusted the small boom microphone so it was close to her mouth, pressed a button on the call director in front of her and spoke. "I assume you got all that?"

"I did," Westy Reynolds replied, while sitting at the desk in his office several miles away. There was a scrambled phone line between the QuarkSpin vault and Reynolds' office that allowed him to listen to Sparrow conversations in real time. Clark's analyst had been monitoring Joe Barber's conversations that morning and knew that shortly there was likely to be a conference call with Benson. As soon as he picked up the conversation between Barber and Day in their conference room, he immediately summoned Clark and asked her to begin listening in. QuarkSpin's parallel Sparrow net was relaying the conversation. It was using Barber's cell phone as a passive listening device, even though he wasn't even speaking on it. After listening for less than a minute, she pressed another button on her call director, which flashed a red light in Reynolds' office. He had then picked up the phone as the audio feed played. Over the conversation, he heard Clark's voice say, "You've got to listen to this." As he did so, he was stunned. Barber had obviously connected several important dots without much information other than his gut. He had correctly concluded the incidents in Michigan and Tyson's Corner were related; he had correctly concluded there had been some type of high-tech ordnance used, and he was pondering a theory that there was some sort of domestic militia group responsible for its delivery, and worst of all was speculating about a potential government cover up. Reynolds was almost shaken by how close to the truth all of this actually was, and how somebody could come to those conclusions so quickly. And worst of all, Barber was in direct contact with a senior executive of the FBI

Reynolds didn't know Benson personally, but he certainly knew him by reputation. Fortunately, Benson appeared to be a skeptic and up to this point was pushing back. Intercept of the physical evidence, however, could be a game changer and really light a fire with Benson. It was an incredibly stupid move, he thought. Besides, Barber was likely to have held some of the fragments back, so in the end what did it even accomplish other than likely drawing the FBI into the investigation? The disappearing evidence would add to a growing list of unexplainable coincidences. Worse, it could provide further evidence of the potential government involvement. That was one of the problems of the government – to many actors, each with their own agenda. To Reynolds they represented potential fail points, to say nothing about being royal pains in the ass.

Both Reynolds and Clark listened to the conversation between Barber, Day and Benson until it ended. She then headed to her office to call Reynolds on her private line. She didn't waste words. "I don't see any conclusion here other than this Joe Barber represents a genuine threat to the program. He seems to have gotten his hands on a lot of information rapidly and has drawn some preliminary conclusions that are remarkably close to home," she said. "He's a little too smart for his own good."

"I agree," Reynolds replied.

"Further," Clark continued, "there seems to have been one countervailing force, Benson's skepticism, but I fear that some idiot has blown that by intercepting whatever physical evidence Barber had given to Benson. We're obviously going to have to adjust our program simulation algorithms to crank up the moron factor, but that's a different conversation for a different time. Bottom line, I don't see any solution here short of neutralizing Barber."

"Are you suggesting we launch the second Hawk?" Reynolds asked.

"Yes," Clark responded crisply.

"Can we get our hands on any information about Barber's health first, just to see if there is some rational explanation for what happens to him?" Reynolds asked. "We got lucky with Longstreet given his pre-existing conditions. It would be nice to know if we had the same kind of similar cover for Barber."

"I've already done that," Clark responded. "As soon as we determined his identity we hacked into the data base of his primary care physician. The guy's got a few relatively minor issues but nothing serious enough to provide a natural explanation for his early demise. There will no doubt be a lot of questions from the people who are close to him, but there will be no answers. The kill-agent leaves no trace unless you know exactly what you are looking for and specifically test for it. They'll find nothing. The calculus here is one of relative risk. It's far riskier to ignore him given what he could potentially come up with. Another convenient death will likely make the NDSA people all nervous and paranoid, but nobody there is going to investigate it. They will be forced to look the other way. Of course, you should certainly be prepared to answer questions from Fitzpatrick."

"I can handle Fitzpatrick," Reynolds said. "I'll tell him we had nothing to do with it with a wink and a nod of course. He won't like it, but he'll keep his mouth shut. I led him to believe he was part of the decision to take out Longstreet, which makes him up to his neck himself. He'll wring his hands a bit, then keep his mouth shut. What about Benson?" Reynolds asked.

"Are you asking about his reaction to Barber's death or whether he should also be a target?" she asked.

"Both," Reynolds replied.

"On the first point, no doubt it will not set well with him, and he'll investigate, but he'll find nothing," she said. "As to the second point, no, we should leave well enough alone. It would be reckless to go after someone so senior without a whole lot more. Relative risk balance would be way out of our favor."

"Agreed, highly asymmetric," Reynolds said. "Launch the Hawk against Barber."

"Roger that, boss," Clark replied. "You're making the right decision. We'll pick up confirmation of success from the chatter Sparrow receives off his cell phone. We have a device pre-staged in the East Coast. We can have the package delivered within about two hours, directly to his office."

"I don't need the details Emma, please."

"Sorry boss, got it," she replied. "I'll message you as soon as we confirm."

"Thank you," Reynolds replied, as he pushed the button to end the call, unlocked his iPad, and began reading the digital version of the FT.

Chapter 17 – The Best Laid Plans

Two hours later, offices of Orion Bellicus

A UPS truck pulled up in front of the International Corporate Center in Rye, New York, and an ordinary looking deliveryman stepped out of the truck with a small package. It was another warm and humid day as he walked towards the building, pushed his way through the revolving door and went inside. He left the package at the front security desk, turned around and left. Of course, it wasn't a real UPS truck, and it wasn't a real UPS driver, but it was important to maintain proper appearances so as not to cause suspicion or appear in even the least manner out of the ordinary. A currier took the package and made her way to the elevator bank and after a short ride arrived at the offices of Orion Bellicus. She handed the package to the receptionist at the security counter then left. About 20 minutes later, the package arrived on the desk of Barber's administrative assistant. She pulled the zip opener on the outer envelope, which was marked "overnight express", retrieved the inner envelope and immediately noticed two things. First, it was marked "to be opened by recipient only". Second, the return address said it was from E.W. Longstreet. These markings were designed to ensure that Joe himself would open the package and do it quickly. It was a clever ruse, except for one fatal flaw. Joe Barber trusted his administrative assistant completely, and she had routine access to all of his correspondence that wasn't regarded as classified, including his permission to open packages that were marked "to be opened by recipient only". Joe would not be the person to open the package – she would. She opened the inner envelope and started retrieving the contents. She pulled out several clippings from the Washington Post that contained recent stories on the terrorist attack in Michigan and the vehicle explosion in Tyson's Corner. As she stood up to walk into Barber's office she thought it odd two unrelated news clippings would be sent overnight express. It was something that could have easily been emailed as PDFs or even the links to the stories on the Post's website. The odd nature of the contents caused her to hesitate a moment to contemplate why Longstreet would go to so much trouble on something so obvious. The moment's hesitation was exactly the reaction the sender hoped for; but from Barber and not from her. As she walked into Joe's office with the clippings in one hand and the inner envelope in the other, she commented, "You're going to find this odd, uh," but then appeared not to complete the sentence. Barber was sitting at his desk and had looked up as she started to talk. He noticed her sudden silence, and then saw her leg buckle a bit just before she dropped to the floor. He almost leapt around his desk to see if she was ok. After shaking her a bit to try and wake her up, he noticed she wasn't breathing. He felt for a pulse and was stunned when he didn't find one. He yelled into the corridor for someone to call 911 as he proceeded to perform CPR. As the paramedics arrived, he continued the CPR as one of the first responders attempted to insert an IV while the other started to attach EKG leads. The first IV needle apparently had a flawed seal and a modest amount of her blood squirted onto the carpet as Joe continued to compress her heart. The paramedic quickly switched it out and attached a saline bag. The second paramedic opened a portable EKG machine, turned it on and began to read the feed. Nothing.

"How long have you been doing CPR, sir," one of the paramedics asked.

"I would say at least 15 minutes," replied Barber.

"I'm afraid she's gone, sir," the paramedic replied.

"I'm not giving up yet," Barber snapped.

The three of them moved her quickly to the gurney. Joe was still performing CPR as they carried her to the ambulance. He yelled out to Marcus Day who had run into Joe's office as soon as he heard the commotion, along with what seemed half the employees on the floor. "Tell Lauren to retrieve that blood from my carpet and put it throw everything she's got at it."

"Got it boss," Day replied.

Joe rode in the ambulance and continued to perform CPR all the way to the emergency room. Shortly after they arrived, Jennifer Adams, 27 years old, was pronounced dead. Joe was stunned. She was an ardent marathoner and had even placed in the top 100 in her age group in the New York. She spent her weekends and occasionally her evenings instructing Cross Fit. To Joe's knowledge she had never had as much as a cold, and certainly never missed a day of work while in his employ. He didn't want to believe in more involved conspiracy theories, but this was troubling, and it wasn't lost on him that the package was addressed to him. He would at least have Lauren Cartwright summon every one of her tricks to see if the blood analysis would provide any clues.

* * * * *

Offices of QuarkSpin, several minutes later

Dr. Emma Clark sat in her office reviewing the coming weeks production plans for the Sparrow. Her concentration was broken by a buzz from the call director on her desk. She looked up and noticed it was the line from the forensics lab where she knew an analyst was continuously monitoring the conversations from the Sparrow assets targeted on Joe Barber, his wife Diana, and others at Orion Bellicus. She was expecting the call, hoping to provide Reynolds with a report of success as quickly as possible. She put down the report, picked up the phone and pushed the button on the call director that connected her directly with the lab. "Do you have confirmation?" she asked, before even allowing the analyst on the line to say anything.

"We do," he replied, "but it's not what you think, and you're not going to like it."

"What?" she fired back with the crisp one-word question.

"The Hawk landed and delivered its package, but it appears to have hit the wrong person," he responded.

"What do you mean it hit the wrong person?" she asked, voice now elevated and with evident concern.

"The package was marked to be opened by addressee only, but apparently Barber's secretary opened it before attempting to walk it into his office."

"Attempting to walk it into his office?" Clark fired back, now standing and almost shouting into the phone.

"Correct – attempting," he replied. "She evidently dropped shortly after she passed through his office door. The Hawk did its job but on the wrong person. We monitored the entire chatter: Barber's response, the paramedics arriving, the transport to the hospital, and Barber's conversations with the ER physicians. He accompanied her in the ambulance and into the hospital, so we were receiving Sparrow data the entire time. They pronounced her dead shortly after she arrived at the ER."

"So, the target is alive and well, and we took out a secretary?" she asked, now sounding more angry than concerned.

"That's right, but that's not all," he replied.

"Whiskey Tango Foxtrot does that mean, pal," she snapped back, angry again.

"From the conversations, we believe the paramedics initially tried to insert an IV that had some kind of defect and it resulted in a blood splatter of unknown quantity," he replied.

"So what?" she snapped back.

"As Barber was walking out with her he yelled to someone to have a person named Lauren retrieve the blood, send it to some kind of lab and quote, "summon every one of her tricks to see if the blood analysis would provide any clues", end quote."

"CRAP!" she screamed into the phone, then took a breath before continuing. "Is there any way they can identify the agent?" she asked.

"It's very unlikely," he said, "but it depends on their capability and exactly what those tricks are that he referred to. If that lab he referred to includes a skilled chemist and they get creative in their search, it's not impossible, but that's got to be a very low risk."

"We need to find out what kind of threat we are dealing with here. I'm not going to be a bystander and just see what happens. I'll call Reynolds now and brief him on this screw up and see if we can do some quick field work on what kind of forensics capability we are dealing with here and exactly who this Lauren character is. Keep monitoring the Sparrow net and report back to me on anything you deem important. And when in doubt call, is that clear?"

"Got it," the analyst responded.

Clark reached across the desk again and hit the button to disconnect the call. As she did so, she recalled, almost as an epiphany, an important object lesson she had picked up while learning to land an airplane. You make a small mistake, like flaring too high, and try to correct it by pushing the nose down to bring you closer to the runway. But instead of fixing the problem, it causes you to land nose first, which makes the plane bounce up and gain even more altitude. You do it again, with the same result, such that each effort to correct a mistake actually makes your situation worse, not better. It's called negative stability, and in mathematical terms is referred to as increasing the amplitude of the sine wave instead of diminishing it. Things don't get better, they get worse. By trying to be pre-emptive and eliminate their risks too early they weren't solving their problems, they were compounding them. And worse yet, she had been largely responsible. She thought about how Reynolds was likely to react. They had crafted the best laid plans, yet they had failed. Reynolds was the smartest man she had ever known. But then she remembered a trait of human behavior she regarded as almost axiomatic. Intelligence and judgment often aren't positively correlated. As a matter of fact, the correlation all too often is negative. She had just proved that herself. This was going to be a very unpleasant phone call.

Chapter 18 – Mounting Coincidences

NDSA offices, the following morning

Special Agent in Charge Ryan Jennings sat in his office and took a careful sip from the cup of Starbucks Coffee he had bought on the way into work. It was always a bit too hot and a bit too strong, but it had the necessary kick and there were no convenient alternatives along his route. As he logged in to the Washington Post web site and started scanning the morning news stories, his phone rang. He looked at the button illuminated on his call director and noticed it was from the NDSA's digital forensics lab. "Jennings," he said crisply as he answered the phone.

"Ryan, this is Amanda," responded Amanda Green, his second in command, "I've been down here for the last couple of hours reviewing the Sparrow chatter from the net we created yesterday with Joe Barber and several of his associates."

"You are up early," Jennings replied.

"Yeah," she said, "I got a call last night about some dramatic traffic on the net. I got here right away to review it. Evidently Barber's secretary dropped dead mid-step sometime yesterday afternoon, and it was while she was walking into his office to deliver the contents of a letter or something. It gets even more interesting. His secretary told him the package was from Eric Longstreet. The reporter must have sent him something just before he died. We don't know anything about the contents, other than it was a couple of newspaper articles."

"That doesn't sound out of context of the recent conversations between the two of them. But why mail newspaper clippings? That doesn't make any sense. Longstreet could have just emailed Barber the links or

218

picked up the phone and called the guy. And my guess is Barber had read those articles as soon as they were posted. Was his secretary old?" Jennings asked. "Sounds like you are suspecting something other than natural causes."

"Well, that's just the thing," Green replied, we did a quick social media scan on her, and she has an extensive Facebook page. It turns out this woman was in her late 20's and was an accomplished marathoner. Doesn't fit the profile of someone who just suddenly drops dead."

"What are you suggesting Amanda?" Jennings asked.

"I'm not suggesting anything, at least not yet, other than it doesn't add up. Two people connected to this Joe Barber character, two people also connected in some way to his investigation of recent events are suddenly deceased. Seems like an unusual coincidence, doesn't it?" she asked.

"Yes, but it's a real stretch to connect the two deaths at this point. I'm not sure I buy the likelihood of anything nefarious without a whole lot more than that she was young and healthy," Jennings replied.

"Ok, I get that," she replied, "but think about this – she was within a few feet of Barber when it happened. What if, and just what if, there was something more sinister here? What if this was a targeted killing, and he was the intended target and not her? What if she was just in the wrong place at the wrong time and got in the way?"

"Wow, by whom?" he asked. "What motive?"

"No answers for those, but I don't like coincidences and they seem to be growing," she replied. "There's one more thing that could be helpful, Ryan, either way," she replied

"What's that?" Jennings asked.

"As they were moving the woman out of Barber's office he barked out an order to some of his people who were on the scene. Apparently. there was some blood splatter from her on the carpeting in his office. We don't know the cause. But as she was being carried out he yelled at someone to have the blood retrieved and taken to their forensics lab and analyzed. When he gets the report we will likely be able to determine what they found, either by the person briefing him or his reaction," she said.

"Ok. I'm not going to elevate this now. I don't think we have enough yet. I don't want to appear as though I'm looking under my bed for things but let me know as soon as you have something more substantial," Jennings said.

"Got it, boss, will do," Green replied.

Jennings reached across his desk to disconnect the phone call, then turned his attention again to the Washington Post's web page. Reviewing the morning's news stories had suddenly become an important part of his job.

* * * * *

Offices of Orion Bellicus

Joe arrived at his office about 7:30 A.M. It had been an exhausting night. Losing someone he interacted with on such a routine basis and a person in the prime of life to boot, was mentally exhausting. As he walked through his office door towards his desk, he could see the section of the carpet that had been cut up to retrieve the blood samples, and he was expecting an early morning brief on what, if anything, they had found. He was not disappointed. Before he could even sit down his phone rang and he saw it was a call from Dr. Cartwright.

"Did you find anything, Lauren?" he asked, skipping any semblance towards small talk and getting directly to the point.

"I think we may have, Joe, and it's a little unsettling," she replied.

The word, unsettling, caught him off guard and he felt his stomach churn as he braced himself for what "unsettling" could possibly mean. "What did you find?" he asked.

"I had the lab drill through every tox screen we could think of," she replied, "and it was difficult, given we didn't have a very good sample to work with."

"Go on," Joe said.

"Well, there's nothing terribly specific, certainly not in the sense of a smoking gun, but we found a couple of things that shouldn't have been in a blood sample - sodium hydroxide and potassium hydroxide. Sodium hydroxide can be used to extract potassium hydroxide by reacting it with pure potassium. Potassium hydroxide has a lot of industrial applications and a few niche applications as well. That in and of itself doesn't strike me as ominous, just unexplainable. But one of the niche applications is a bit disturbing. Potassium hydroxide is used to extract potassium cyanide from hydrogen cyanide."

"What?" Joe exclaimed, coming out of his chair at what he had just heard. "You found cyanide in that sample?" he yelled into the phone.

"No, we did not, Joe! Take a breath," she said. "To be clear, we didn't find any lethal agent in the blood that would explain what happened. But, and I want to be careful how I say this, if I was given to conspiracy theories I would be very suspicious that we found trace evidence of its manufacturer."

Joe pulled the phone away from his mouth for a minute, looked down, and squeezed his eyes tightly as he took a deep breath. He then raised the phone back to his ear as he let out his breath to continue the conversation.

"Are you still there?" Cartwright asked.

"Yes," Joe replied. "Keep going."

"I need to emphasize; it's just a theory," she said, "and a pretty weak one at that. And frankly I'm not sure where we even take it from here, but I can tell you that those two chemicals should certainly not have been in the blood sample of an exceptionally healthy young woman like Jennifer."

"That's great work, Lauren," Joe finally replied, having settled down a bit. "I talked to the attending in the ER late last night and he told me there was no clear explanation for her sudden death. They listed cardiac arrest caused by ventricular fibrillation on her death certificate, but the physician admitted it was only an educated guess. He also told me sometimes endurance athletes develop arrhythmias from overtraining, but the post-mortem echocardiogram suggested a normal-sized heart so bottom line is there's no good explanation. They just don't know. And you're telling me those two chemicals themselves are not lethal?"

"No, they are not," she replied.

"And you found nothing else unusual?" he asked.

"Nothing," she confirmed. "So what are you thinking, boss?" she asked.

"I'm thinking there are too many coincidences here," Joe replied. "I am also thinking that the event occurred immediately after she opened a package addressed to me, and that she died within about ten feet from my desk shortly thereafter. I can't help but wonder if somehow the two events are related. And if that's so, if it was deliberate and I was the real target, I'm wondering just what I may have stumbled onto here. I have no idea, but I can guarantee one thing – I certainly intend to find out."

Chapter 19 – Insubordination

NDSA Offices, McLean, Virginia

Colonel Jeffery Taylor seethed with anger as he sat in the ExComm conference room and looked around at his colleagues. Two innocent people were dead. Both were U.S. citizens, the very people he was sworn to defend. One was a reporter. The other was the secretary of the reporter's friend, Joe Barber. He suspected the secretary was not the intended victim, but rather her boss, Joe himself. And not only was she dead, if his theory was correct she was dead because of a screw up. He initially had come to terms with the explanation given for the reporter's untimely demise. The guy evidently had a pre-existing heart condition of some sort. But a young, healthy woman suddenly experiencing cardiac arrest for no apparent reason – that was too much to swallow, and taken together, the two deaths represented far too much of a coincidence for his disciplined mind to accept. He couldn't think of anyone not presently sitting in this room who could possibly have a motive for such a thing. But who? He had overall operational responsibility, and if a decision was made to execute a "contingency", or so they called it, it would fall to him. He wondered if maybe Jennings had a wider remit than he was led to believe. He wouldn't put it past the guy. The more he dealt with Jennings the less he liked him, and the more he worried that the guy was capable of things that were way beyond his definition of a "lawful order". He hoped this meeting would provide some answers. He would be wrong.

Fitzpatrick was the first to speak. Not a good start, he thought, and frankly a really bad sign. "So, all we know is that a second person somehow loosely connected to all of this is now dead. Is that correct, Agent Jennings?"

"Yes sir," Jennings replied. "I can assure you that nobody in this organization was behind this woman's death, but it's troubling. We suspect that this Joe Barber character was the target, but we have no idea by whom or how anybody outside of this organization would even be aware of his interest in all this."

"What a crock," Taylor thought to himself. He was beginning to believe this was all an act.

"We need to deal in facts here," Admiral Erby interjected. "What exactly do we know?"

"We know nothing about the circumstances of this woman's death," Jennings replied. "And we know nothing about who, if anyone, is responsible for it. I agree that the coincidences here are beginning to breach a credibility threshold, but I want to repeat that we don't have one bit of hard evidence that her death is anything other than what it appears to be on the surface – the result of natural causes. But there is one thing we now know for certain. Subsequent Sparrow intel confirms that Joe Barber is convinced there was a hit on him and that she stepped into the middle of it. The results of his forensics lab analysis of her blood sample, while inconclusive, have got him highly agitated. It's clear from his professional background that he's a resourceful man. I believe he has become a real disclosure risk to the program."

"Are you suggesting it has risen to the level to justify considering we do something about it, the exercise of a contingency?" Director Collins asked.

"No Sir," Jennings replied, "I am not suggesting it has risen to the level of consideration; I am declaring that it has risen to the level of action, a contingency, and frankly I am prepared to recommend it."

Taylor couldn't believe what he was hearing, and actually started to squirm in his seat in response to his discomfort.

"Wait a minute!" Admiral Erby spoke up, almost shouting. "This man is a veteran, a former Navy SEAL, and decorated to boot, and has broken no laws. We can't seriously be contemplating -- I'll use the word -- assassinating, a U.S. citizen based on nothing other than his resourcefulness and outsized curiosity, are we? Because I tell you I will not support this, and frankly I am willing to go to the President personally to keep that from happening." His voice had morphed from a shout to cold fury as he concluded his remarks.

Everybody sat in stunned silence for a moment as Erby's tirade hung in the air. Finally a voice of reason, Taylor thought.

Chief of Staff Bill Fitzpatrick was the next to speak. "Let's all take a breath here," Fitzpatrick said, with a voice that was three parts soothing, one part condescending, and all parts political. "Ryan, you raise a legitimate concern, but I'm inclined to agree with the Admiral at the moment, at least in the sense that we don't have a lawful case under the Presidential Finding to act now. We obviously need to monitor this Joe Barber character closely, and if he uncovers any credible evidence of what has happened, we can revisit, but for now we are in an intelligence gathering mode and nothing more."

Fitzpatrick's words did little to mollify Taylor, who still couldn't believe the President's Chief of Staff was playing such a prominent role in all of this. Why wasn't Director Collins doing the talking here? Why did the push back have to come from Erby and not from Collins? Who was running this place? This isn't what he had signed up for and he would have no part of it, he told himself.

"And to make things clear," Fitzpatrick continued, "there is a hard wall of separation between the President and the operational details of this organization, and that wall exists for very good reasons. If anyone is going to go to the President about any of this," he said with growing authority in his voice, "it will be me and me alone. Is that clear?" he asked with finality.

226

Erby's posture became somewhat more erect in his chair as he locked eyes with the Chief of Staff. He began to talk in low, calm, and measured tones, projecting the authority that could only be summoned by a battle-hardened warrior for whom a lifetime of experience had brought him to the top of his game. "Well let **me** make something clear, you son of a bitch. In my capacity as a member of this oversight committee, I don't work for you, and you will not tell me when I may or may not go directly to the President. I am personally growing increasingly uncomfortable with the prominent role you are taking in these discussions, and I suggest you tone it down. As a matter of fact, I just might discuss THAT with the President, you pompous ass."

Once again, the room sat in stunned silence. Fitzpatrick audibly swallowed hard as an involuntary reaction to the almost primal challenge to his authority and was the first to break eye contact with Erby, who was an imposing figure and had at least 50 pounds on the obviously portly and out of shape Chief of Staff.

"OK, I think Bill is right," Dr. Adam Johnson finally said to break the silence. "We all need to take a breath here."

Finally Collins spoke up. "Agreed. Agent Jennings, I'll be a little more direct. I think you're getting way over your head. Exercising a contingency is one of the most serious actions this Committee can take, and from now on nobody, I repeat, **nobody** makes such a recommendation to ExComm without going through me first. Is that understood?"

"Yes sir," Jennings replied.

"But I want to remind everyone," Collins continued, "the use of contingencies was envisioned for a reason, and we all need to take the long view here. What we do saves lives, and we have to keep focused on that. We all knew what we were signing up for."

"Bullshit," Taylor thought to himself. Contingencies were envisioned to handle a clear and present danger, not to simply shut somebody up; and never against a U.S. citizen. At least Erby had some balls, he reflected.

Collins continued, "Although we are a ways away from any potential action, we need to rehearse the op plan to be ready. Colonel Taylor, the operational responsibility will obviously fall to you. I'd like you to prep the contingency plan and be ready to brief ExComm if it becomes necessary. Do a dry run against a dummy target. I suggest you pick someone in this organization. To be clear again, at this point we are only trying to confirm the art of the possible."

Taylor continued to sit there in silence. He looked at Admiral Erby whose eyes were already locked on him. He then looked back at Director Collins but remained silent.

"Colonel Taylor," Collins said, "did you hear me?"

"Yes sir, I did," he said.

"Then you will prepare the operational plans for the contingency and be ready to brief ExComm, right?" Collins stated as a question but delivered more like an order.

"No sir, I will not," Taylor replied, in a calm and even voice. He then rose from his chair, put several papers in his briefing folder, picked it up and walked out of the room.

Everybody sat once again in stunned silence. "Well, I'd say that's a problem," Fitzpatrick commented.

"I'll talk to him," Collins replied. "He's a good man, and I'm sure he'll be fine."

Admiral Erby just sat there and broke into an ever so slight smile. He's a good man indeed, Erby thought, and he therefore most certainly will not be fine, and neither will I. Erby wondered if they had a "contingency" for him. He would never have thought so before this meeting, but now? No doubt, he reflected.

It was now Dr. Adam Johnson, erstwhile Director of the National Security Agency, who began to have a very bad feeling about things. "This thing started as a good idea but seems about to spiral out of control," he thought to himself. "This is not what I signed up for. How did I ever get into this mess? Good people are capable of bad things," he thought. It seemed like the cumulative effects of a lot of small compromises were the antecedents to the bad decisions. He thought about how present circumstances were likely to play out and wondered to himself where he had personally crossed his own line of no return.

* * * * *

Jeffrey Taylor stood on his deck and looked out over his backyard as the cool evening breeze enveloped him. Under other circumstances this would be almost a blissful moment, the beautiful Virginia summer evening and the reflection on his new command and all that it could bring; but bliss was about the furthest thing from what he was experiencing at the moment. He had come to a difficult decision on his drive home, and he knew the consequences would put an abrupt end to an otherwise promising career and any hopes for wearing a star someday. He had lost faith in his superiors and more importantly the process that was supposed to govern them. The fact they had actually asked him to practice executing an assassination of a U.S. citizen was something he could not abide. This whole business seemed to be getting messier by the day, and the team seemed to be more focused on self-preservation than protecting the homeland. The problem was, he had no evidence that anyone in ExComm was behind the deaths of Longstreet and

Barber's secretary. Yet he knew the deaths were far too much of a coincidence and far too convenient, and he couldn't shake the sense that the organization he served was somehow involved. Yet without evidence he was limited in what he could do. Accusing ExComm of complicity in those deaths at this point would be reckless. Yet he also knew he could no longer accept their orders, and his act of insubordination as he walked out of the last meeting pretty much sealed his fate. So he would resign. He would go to Director Johnson first thing the next morning to do so. He would acknowledge his full intent to honor the terms of his 99-year disclosure agreement, but he would let them know he was done. The only question left for him was whether he would also have to resign his commission as well. That would be up to the Air Force to decide, but he was fairly certain of the answer.

As he walked back into his house he couldn't shake the feeling that just maybe the powers that be had a contingency for him as well. That was a scary thought. He didn't want to believe it, but if they were capable of assassinating a member of the press and a private citizen for nothing other than their outsized curiosity, there was no telling what they were capable of. He decided to do something he had never done before – write down a detailed record of the events of the last several days and his suspicions. He would do it as an insurance policy and would place a copy in his safety deposit box and give one to his attorney with instructions to release it to the press if anything happened to him. He decided not to disclose its existence, at least not until he gauged Johnson's reaction to his resignation. He could be wrong about all of this, and to disclose it up front would not only be considered a threat, it could lead to serious legal consequences if his fears turned out to be misplaced. Better just to have it at the ready. He would only play that card on two conditions – if he was able to confirm somehow that his colleagues were behind the deaths, and if he perceived any kind of overt threat against himself. Unlikely, he thought. He was not about to investigate the first, and he doubted the second.

Fourteen hours later Taylor sat in Director Collins office and felt an overwhelming sense of relief. Collins had actually taken the news fairly well. Collins told him he understood, trusted his discretion, and he would be happy to let the record reflect that Colonel Jeffrey Taylor had requested reassignment for personal reasons. And because the National Security Agency's Department of Special Activities was a top-secret organization the Air Force would remain unaware of the nature of his reasons. He was free to continue his active duty career with no blowback. Taylor actually doubted that was really true and was convinced he would now retire as a bird colonel and never wear stars, but that was a trade he would gladly take for the impression that his darker fears were unfounded. Collins had only one more thing he wanted him to do. There was another Bird Colonel at CENTCOM in Orlando who had gone through the vetting program with him and been flagged as Taylor's potential successor. He wanted Taylor to fly down there tonight to have an informal conversation with him. Collins told Taylor that giving him this task should be taken as a gesture of good faith on their part, and his willingness would be regarded as the same. He silently wondered what the response would have been if he refused, but it seemed like a small price to pay to walk away on almost good terms, so he agreed. Collins even told him he would arrange an F16 to be made available for him to fly down to Orlando, and that a little stick time might help him clear his head. He had to admit he looked forward to strapping in as a pilot again, even if for only a couple of hours.

He was unaware, however, of the existence of a keystroke recorder on the laptop in his study. Every word he had written as part of that insurance policy the previous evening had been monitored. A complete transcript of it had been encrypted and emailed to Bill Fitzpatrick before Taylor had even gone to bed. The next morning Collins had called both Fitzpatrick and Johnson to give them a heads up on Taylor's resignation and the succession plans. After receiving the heads up, Fitzpatrick made a couple

231

of phone calls himself and was able to obtain the tail number of the F16 Taylor would be flying to Orlando. His next call would be to the west coast.

* * * * *

Bill Fitzpatrick sat in his West Wing office behind a large ornate desk as the sun poured through the bulletproof glass and bathed him in a sensation of warmth. He always arrived early to get a jump on his day before the endless schedule of meetings took control. He was royally annoyed when the phone rang and he saw the name Collins appear on the caller ID window. He was even more annoyed as he sat there and listened. Another Boy Scout. Would no one rid him of these troublesome Boy Scouts, he wondered. As he disconnected the call he had just taken from Collins, he pulled out his cell phone and dialed a familiar number. A familiar voice answered the phone, but there was no small talk this time.

"I need to order that package we discussed. I also need priority shipping and delivery no later than mid-morning tomorrow," Fitzpatrick said. "I will iMessage you the address in about an hour." The "address" was the tail number of the F16 that Colonel Taylor would be flying to Orlando the next morning.

"Got it," the voice on the other end of the phone replied.

"Your people are confident in the reliability of the package?" Fitzpatrick asked.

"I won't dignify that question with an answer," the voice said. "This conversation is over."

Bill Fitzpatrick heard the line go dead.

Almost three thousand miles away Westy Reynolds pushed another button on his call director to open a second line. The line was answered immediately. "We are a go, as discussed," Reynolds said.

"Understood, we are a go," the voice responded. "The package will be delivered on time."

Chapter 20 – Nurturing an Alliance

Joe Barber sat at a table next to the window at Farmers Fishers Bakers Restaurant in Washington D.C. and looked out over the Potomac. The bright sunshine danced off the surface of the water and shimmered into an impressive light show. The scene was beautiful, but it did little to subdue a growing sense of fury as he thought about the events of the last several days. He had always prided himself on being a left-brain kind of guy, driven by a cold, rational evaluation of the facts. It's what sustained him in the Teams and made him such an effective CIA case officer. It's also what made him so successful in his business. But as his fury grew, the right side of his brain was beginning to swell and take over. Two people he knew had died since he had started looking into the incident that had taken the wife and children of his friend. Both deaths occurred under highly suspicious circumstances, and both obviously connected to his investigation of the explosions in Michigan and Northern Virginia. If he had any doubts about the nefarious nature of circumstances surrounding Eric Longstreet's death they were erased after losing his secretary Jenn. He was certain that he was the intended target of whatever took her life. Why, by whom and how, he kept asking himself. He kept going over the facts in his mind as he waited for Benson to show up. The more he thought about it, the angrier he became and the more resolved he was on getting to the bottom of it. This was no longer just a favor for a friend – it had become deeply personal, and he had become obsessed. His thoughts were temporarily interrupted as a waiter asked for his drink order. "I'll have an iced tea, please," he said, wanting to ensure his senses would not be the least bit dulled from his normal lunchtime glass of wine. He felt his iPhone buzz as a text came through. It was from Benson, informing him he had just parked his car and was about a 3-minute walk from the restaurant. Joe looked out the window again. What a beautiful day, he thought. What a sharp contrast to his present state of mind.

FBI Executive Assistant Director Donald R. Benson walked up to the table and sat down across from Barber just as the waiter delivered a glass of iced tea to the table. Benson looked at the waiter and said, "I'll have the same." Benson looked out the window and said, "Nothing in the world compares to a Springtime day in D.C. I hate the August heat and humidity, but I'll take all the days like this I can get. I'm so sorry to hear about your secretary, Joe. Have you come up with any insight into cause of death? I presume that's at least in part why you wanted to meet today?" he asked.

"Thanks, Don," Joe replied. "You might say. I had our forensics lab do a thorough work up on a blood sample she left on the carpet in my office. We found no smoking gun, per se, but my chief scientist found traces of chemicals that should not have been in her bloodstream. In and of themselves, they don't really tell us much, as they weren't toxic, at least in the quantities we uncovered. But one of the traces found is used in the manufacture of some sort of cyanide derivative. We didn't find any evidence of cyanide in her bloodstream, but it's another coincidence that, when taken with the others, is impossible to ignore. She had just opened an envelope marked for my eyes only with Longstreet's return address. My theory is there was some sort of agent in that package that was responsible for her death and that it was more than likely meant for me."

"Joe, I understand you are upset, but aren't you overreacting here?"

"My God, Don, over the last several days I'm starting to hate that phrase."

"OK, fair enough, but you have no evidence that your secretary's death was anything other than the result of natural causes, though, correct?" Benson replied.

235

"That's right," Barber responded, "but she was an exceptionally healthy woman in her late-twenties who was a superb runner to boot."

"At least based on appearances," Benson replied. "And why would she have opened something marked for your eyes only?" he asked.

"She had the authority, Don. I don't hire anybody I don't fully trust, and we put her through a security review that's frankly better than what you guys use for granting Top Secret government clearance. And I think using Longstreet's return address was a ploy to ensure the package was opened quickly. Let's cut through the crap. I respect the Bureau's procedures and standards of evidence, but you know perfectly well you can't sit there and look me in the eye and tell me these were just coincidences."

There was a long pregnant pause as Barber and Benson locked eyes, then Benson blinked. "You're right, Joe," he responded.

"Damn right, pal," Joe said.

"OK, but who would do this?" Benson asked. "I agree with you that there are a lot of coincidences here, but I also think it's harder to connect the dots than you want to believe. First, I agree the disappearing evidence from our labs adds considerable credibility to your theory of a government cover-up of some sort. I'll certainly grant you that. I'll have to tread on that evidence trail very lightly though, given the high likelihood that someone in the Bureau is involved. And I also agree that your secretary's death makes me very suspicious that Longstreet's was not from natural causes. I also agree it makes sense that you were the target and not your secretary. But I see no way to connect the two deaths to the missing evidence. The notion that someone in government would kill two U.S. citizens as part of a cover-up strikes me as the stuff of Tom Clancy novels. What's your theory?"

"Let's start by summarizing what we know," Barber said. "First, we know there is forensic evidence from both the explosions in Southeastern Michigan and Northern Virginia that connects them to each other. That's irrefutable. We also know that a nosey reporter suddenly turns up dead. OK, the guy had a pre-existing condition, but it was diagnosed, it was being treated, and those two facts mean it should not have been fatal. His death was too convenient. We also know that a person very close to me, Jennifer, also died suddenly with no rational explanation, and that her death happened within seconds of opening a package that was clearly meant for me. We also know that the FBI Forensics lab unexplainably lost samples from both crime scenes that I turned over to you. Let that one soak in for a minute Don – lost by one of the most disciplined and secure operations on the planet. There is no rational explanation for that, and you know it. Each incident individually can be explained away, but taken together, believing they are all just unfortunate coincidences would require a leap of faith that's just not reasonable."

"So I'll ask again, what's your theory?" Benson responded.

"OK, I'll admit I'm still working on that," Barber replied. "I'm not sure we have to connect the deaths and the missing evidence directly. I think the most rational explanation for the deaths is we have some sort of new terrorist cell, or cells, operating within the country that are far more sophisticated and capable than any other we have faced. That has to be the case if those two explosions were the result of ordnance delivered from above somehow, which is what the forensics suggest. Think about that. If that's true, I'm almost convinced this can't be an Al-Qaeda or ISIS related group but something being directed by a hostile foreign government. I'm also convinced both Longstreet's and Jennifer's deaths were the result of some sort of sophisticated agent delivered in a sophisticated manner. Neither Al-Qaeda nor ISIS would likely have that kind of capability, at least not on foreign soil.

Maybe Iran. I wouldn't even rule out China. And worst of all, I'm also becoming convinced that there are forces in the U.S. Government that are aware of it and are trying to cover it up. Pick your motive: maybe to avoid panic, maybe to avoid political fallout, but I don't know how else to rationalize the extraordinary rapid sanitization of both crime scenes, and especially that epically bogus cover story about the Northern Virginia explosion being the result of some sort of vehicle problem. Those people were taken out, full stop. By whom, I don't know."

They both sat there in silence for several uncomfortable seconds after Joe had finished answering Don's question. Benson cleared his throat and cocked his head slightly to the right as a frown and a raised left eyebrow almost betrayed his skepticism before he began to speak. "Whew, Joe. A minute ago I said I thought you were getting a bit "over your skis" on this, but if you are actually suggesting someone in government is behind those deaths, I think you've actually flown off the side of the mountain."

"I'm open to a better explanation, Don, if you or anyone can offer one up. But understand this, I intend to get to the bottom of this, if it's the last thing I ever do, to quote an overused phrase," Barber replied.

"Be careful my friend. Based on what's happened so far that may not be an idle risk. What do you want from me?" Benson decided to go with the opened ended question as a friend to see what Barber may be up to before he was compelled to put on his FBI hat and give Joe the necessary warnings.

"I'm not sure I know at this point, Don," Barber replied. "I guess, for sure, I would like to know if you turn anything up on that lost evidence. I presume you are following that one pretty seriously, as it raises a lot of questions about the FBI's internal security risk and a potential breach. Also, to be transparent, I know you have to wear your FBI hat in these discussions, but

I would like you not to open any investigation on what I might be doing, at least not yet. Can you give me some slack on that?" Barber asked.

"Yes, I can give you some maneuvering room for a while. But you need to understand that our investigation is going to tangentially touch you, given what happened to that evidence. As a senior executive I cannot call off the dogs if they pick up a scent that involves you. Not only would I be breaking the law, it wouldn't work. Our field agents and our SACs wouldn't tolerate my interference in an active investigation," Benson warned.

"Can you at least give me an informal heads up if I get "scooped up" in any meaningful way?" Joe asked.

Benson frowned again, belaying his answer. "I'm going to have to give that one some thought, my friend," he said as a diplomatic answer, although Joe knew exactly what it meant. If Joseph Michael Barber became part of an active FBI investigation, it would play out however it would play out. "I know this goes without saying, Joe, but the best thing you can do to ensure there aren't any problems is to stay within the law."

"I get that, Don," Barber said, silently wishing himself good luck with that. He then tried to reassure Benson. "I'm not so concerned with legal trouble as I am with being slowed down or compromised. If I get called in or asked about what I've found, and you've got some kind of mole who was responsible for that evidence disappearing it could spell bad news for me."

"I understand, Joe, but again I am going to have to let this play out the way it plays out. The safest thing for you to do is to take a breath and let us handle it. I know that's hard, but I don't want the next obituary I read to be yours."

"The same goes for you," Barber responded. "I'm afraid you may find yourself in somebody's crosshairs as well".

Benson's facial expressions softened a bit as he regarded Barber's comments. "I hardly think anyone is going to have the balls to take on a senior exec at the Bureau, Joe," he said with a smile in an effort to reassure. "Besides, remember I carry a gun," Benson said with another slight smile and distinct look of confidence.

Barber sat there for a few seconds and didn't say anything. As he looked at his friend, he thought to himself, "So do I, and a fat lot of good it did Jenn, who dropped dead just a few feet in front of me. And a fat lot of good my Glock would have done me if I was the one who opened that envelop."

The waiter appeared at the table and asked them if they were ready to order. "I'm starving, we might as well make good use of this place while we're here. I'll have the tilapia, Shanghai style," Benson replied.

"Sounds like a plan," Barber responded. "I'll have the same."

* * * * *

The early afternoon sun was extremely hot as Joe walked from the restaurant to his rental car, a Porsche 911, parked in the structure across the street from the mall. Renting a Porsche while on business was one of the indulgences he allowed himself, and his Hertz Gold membership at least kept the cost to absurd instead of obscene. As he pushed the button on the key fob, the vehicle rendered the familiar flash of the headlights and location beeps. By the time he slid into the comfortable black leather seats, his anger had slipped into the background of his consciousness and was replaced by a cold, calculating resolve. One thing he knew for certain, he would do whatever it took to find the people responsible for the deaths of Longstreet and Jennifer. He fired up the Porsche and pulled out of the parking structure to begin his drive back to the airport and the flight home. The early afternoon D.C. traffic was pleasantly light as he pulled his phone out of his jacket pocket and hit Marcus Day's number in his favorites list. Day answered on the second ring. "Hey pal, how'd it go with Benson?" Day asked.

"As I expected, he could clearly sense I was not going to let this go or leave it up to the authorities, and he cautioned me to keep my coloring within the lines," Barber replied.

"Yeah," Day responded, "Benson's about as straight a shooter as they come. And I think the guy's put a firewall between the left side of his brain and his job. He approaches things like he's the FBI's Mr. Spock, albeit the Vulcan with a personality."

"Right, but I've definitely got his attention now. We'll see what our friends at the FBI can turn up."

"Exactly," Day replied.

"You know Marc," Barber continued, "this is going to take me off line for a bit. You've got the helm while I'm downrange. Jennifer's death was a blow to everyone at the firm, but we can't have both of us distracted. I need you driving the ship."

"This conversation isn't even necessary," Day replied. "Find these bastards and use your 'particular set of skills' to terminate their efforts with "extreme prejudice", as they say. We'll provide whatever resources on this you need, so stay in touch. And be safe."

"Thanks, Marc. I'll be in contact as soon as I can uncover anything or need help."

"Do you have any idea as to your next move?" Day asked.

"No, but the drive back to the airport should help clear my head. Talk to you soon." With that Barber terminated the call and ground out the Porsche in second gear while carefully glancing in the rear-view mirror for

Metro Police. What an irony that would be, he thought to himself, if his first brush with the law on this matter was a speeding ticket after leaving a lunch with an Executive Assistant Director of the FBI .

* * * * *

About 10 miles to the Northeast, in McLean Virginia, a digital forensics analyst with the NDSA pushed back from his chair and took his headphones off for a minute. He had just completed listening to and taping every word of the conversations between Joe Barber and Don Benson at the restaurant and between Barber and Marcus Day shortly thereafter.   He looked down a bit, rubbed his temples, then put the headphones back on and pushed a button on his call director that connected him with Special Agent Amanda Green. A crisp, no nonsense voice came on the line with a simple, "What's up?"

"We've got a problem," the analyst replied. "I just emailed you an audio file. I suggest you listen to it right away. I didn't send it to Jennings yet because I didn't want to immediately go over your head, but you are probably going to want to do that as soon as you listen to it."

"Let me guess," she replied. "This Barber character is not going to let go."

"That's right," the analyst answered. "But it's worse, much worse."

Chapter 21 – Another Untimely Death

Andrews Air Force Base

Colonel Jeffrey Taylor stood on the flight line and stared at the F16, canopy open and prepped and waiting for him. Despite accumulating over 6,000 hours of flying time, mostly in high-performance aircraft, he never ceased to feel a sense of awe at how majestic these birds looked and the extraordinary feats of engineering they represented. He approached the airplane and, as always, proceeded to give a thorough pre-flight examination. This was part of the discipline, and regardless of how many hours he accumulated he never cut corners. He knew the maintenance crew had done same, but he also knew that as pilot in command it was his responsibility to ensure the bird was airworthy. Colonel Taylor was a man who took responsibility very seriously. He was looking forward to this flight. It was more than just a way to clear his head of the events of the last several days. It was almost a gift. Director Collins knew just exactly which of his buttons to push to recalibrate his perspective, he thought to himself as he began to climb the ladder into the cockpit. As he swung his leg over the side and burrowed into the tight space, he couldn't help but wonder if this would be the last time he would ever do this, which subdued his otherwise almost euphoric mood.

Taylor efficiently went through his checklist, fired up the powerful General Electric F110-GE-132 turbofan, capable of producing almost 32,000 pounds of thrust, and received clearance to taxi to the active runway. He was particularly excited that he had been given clearance to do a short stint at supersonic speed, although it would require him to initially take an Easterly course out over the Atlantic to stay clear of sonic boom restrictions. The course diversion would require a few minutes longer ride and take him out over more boring scenery, but it was a small price to pay, he thought to himself.

Modern high-performance fighter jets were indeed a marvel of engineering, but their design came with a challenge. Such aircraft had what was called negative stability, which meant, unlike more mundane aircraft, like a Cessna 172 for example, they would not simply cruise through the air in a stable fashion. High performance jets required constant small adjustments to their control surfaces to even stay in the air, let alone maintain stable flight. Fortunately, innovations in software and computer controlled, or fly by wire onboard flight control systems, facilitated the countless small changes to the flaperons, elevons, and rudder that were necessary to give the aircraft stable flight characteristics. The engineers liked to call it an aircraft wrapped around a computer. Although this phrase contained a large measure of truth, pilots generally didn't like it, preferring to think the real smarts resided within the cockpit itself. The truth probably lay somewhere in between, with the flight control system providing the stability that allowed the pilot to make the aircraft do what it really needed to do. One unalterable truth, however, was the bird needed the robust software code to stay in the air.

Colonel Taylor lined up the plane on runway 19R and pushed the throttle to the fire-wall. It literally felt as though the bird jumped into the air. He then made a left turn to a heading of about 120 degrees magnetic and began his climb to a cruise altitude of 38,000 feet over the Atlantic. The bright sun bathed the cockpit as he went "feet wet" over the ocean in what felt like no time at all. At 38,000 feet he leveled the aircraft off and turned due south, to a heading of 185 degrees magnetic towards the East coast of Florida and began his pre-supersonic checklist. If his Air Force career was about to come to a close, he thought to himself, this wasn't a bad way to end it.

Taylor then pushed the throttle forward to engage the afterburner, its extra thrust necessary to muscle the aircraft forward into supersonic flight.

He sat in quiet contemplation as he watched the mach meter rise past 1.0. The sensation of flight, and its speed, was always a wonder to him. A pilot could feed the G-forces as the aircraft accelerated or executed a tight turn, but there was no sensation of going fast, per se. One of the wonders of physics, he thought to himself.

As the aircraft sped past mach 1.0 an accelerometer sent a signal to the flight stability software that caused it to shut down. A highly sophisticated virus had been uploaded to the systems of this particular F16. It was the work of a very smart hacker and was undetectable. At first the impact of the software falling offline was almost imperceptible. Taylor found himself having to make some unexpected adjustments with the control stick mounted on the right-hand side of the cockpit. But as the necessary adjustments started to get bigger and were required more often, he started to become slightly concerned. "What's going on?" he asked himself out loud as the aircraft began a series of small pitch and yaw movements that seemed to be increasing in their severity. First order of business he told himself was to slow the thing down, so he pulled the throttle back to sub-sonic and targeted a speed of about 400 knots, actually a bit slow for this plane. But as he did so, the unintended movements didn't subside; they became worse, with the aircraft now rolling as well. "Work the problem," he said to himself, "remember the training". He briefly thought about ejecting, but then told himself this had to be recoverable and he was not going to end his career by losing an airplane. Suddenly the adverse movements became distinctively more severe, and the aircraft went nose up, forward momentum slowed dramatically, and airflow over the control surfaces became disrupted and essentially nonexistent. The aircraft, still vertical, rolled to its left, layed over on its side and entered a vicious flat spin. Taylor's fleeting thought was it felt almost as though the control surfaces were being deliberately manipulated in a manner to place the F16 in an unrecoverable situation. Unfortunately, that thought took a couple of precious seconds before he concluded that ejection was the only survivable option at this point, and the delay was long enough to allow the flat spin to accelerate. He reached for the ejection rings above his head and pulled them down sharply. Nothing happened. He yanked again, with much more difficulty now as the accelerating g-forces made his arms feel like they weighed a ton each. His peripheral vision started to grey, and he soon felt like he was staring into a tunnel. His arms became almost impossible to move. Finally, the accelerating g-forces crossed the threshold where there was no longer enough blood being pumped to his brain to sustain consciousness.

Jeffrey Taylor, 42 years old, sat unconscious in his airplane as it quickly depleted its 38,000 feet of altitude and crashed into the Atlantic several miles beyond the continental shelf, ensuring a deep, watery grave. Several hours later, a call came into the West Wing of the White House to the office of William Fitzpatrick, Chief of Staff to the President of the United States. But it was to his private cell phone, and not his office phone. His office calls were logged and that just wouldn't do. A familiar voice was on the other end of the phone. "On your instructions the package was successfully delivered and accomplished the desired effect," the voice said. "Congratulations, Bill," the voice concluded.

Fitzpatrick touched the red icon on his iPhone without uttering any reply. About 3000 miles away, Westy Reynolds sat back in his office and smiled slightly. It was a quality piece of work, he thought to himself. Amazing what one can accomplish by being the master of 1s and 0s. Not only was a pesky problem solved in a highly discrete manner, he now completely owned the Chief of Staff of the President of the United States. And that, at least for the next couple of years or so, could prove a very valuable asset.

Chapter 22 – New Threats

San Francisco, California, about 10 miles south of the Golden Gate Bridge

Abu bakr Muhammad stood inside the gutted rear of a brand new Ford Transit passenger van that was parked in the open warehouse space at 1100 Thomas Avenue, San Francisco, California. The back two rows of seats had been removed to prepare it for delivery of a very special cargo. This particular vehicle had been selected and purchased by the brothers to ensure that the delivery of their package, as they called it, was done in as low a profile manner as possible. The vehicle said tourist and did so in a very discrete way. The exterior was drab silver and the interior had black cloth seats which had all been removed except for the two up front. The only things even slightly odd about the appearance of the van were the darkened windows along the vehicle sides, except, of course, for the two windows adjacent to the driver and the front passenger, which were clear. By all external appearances it was a perfect family vehicle and was even fitted with fake Oregon plates to announce that the occupants were vacationers. When the brothers had purchased the van, they had brought a sister and four of her small children so as to appear as a family and complete the ruse. America's politically correct culture, especially in a place like San Francisco, had very much worked to their advantage. The salesman at the Ford dealership could not have been nicer and even worked hard to secure for them a low-interest rate loan that they were hardly qualified for. Of course, the brothers had no intention of making even the first payment on the van. By the time it was due, they would each be enjoying their respective 72 virgins in Paradise. The sister, who helped with the purchase, would be sitting in the front passenger seat playing the role of mother, and would even be wearing a hijab that, ironically enough, was the one thing that would virtually guarantee they would not be bothered. Abu wasn't quite sure what the sister's reward would be. He was not devout enough with his Koran studies to know the answer to that question, but frankly he didn't care.

Abu bakr Muhammad crouched down and carefully soldered the final wire from the detonation device to a copper post protruding from the package. The wire led to a circuit breaker mounted low on the driver's side of the vehicle's console. Closing the breaker would in effect arm the package. Releasing a dead man switch held by a brother, who would be squatted in the back just behind the driver's seat, would result in detonation. The explosive device and the manner in which it was mounted was a very clever and effective piece of engineering. Portions of the bottom of the vehicle had been removed and replaced with a thin sheet of aluminum. The device itself was comprised of a thick layer of high explosives setting on top of sixteen conical shaped charges, four rows of four, designed to be blown down hard by the layer of explosives on top and driven into the pavement below, which would result in a secondary detonation, just microseconds after the first. If Allah was willing, it would tear out a section of the Golden Gate Bridge. A steel plate was mounted across the top of the first layer of high explosives to ensure the blast was directed downward to propel the shaped charges. The whole device was meticulously engineered with the help of the North Koreans. It was an unusual, but highly effective alliance. The North Koreans had even tested a crude version of the device to ensure the basic principle would work. After a couple of false starts it had worked beautifully. The successful test was, of course, after a new North Korean engineer had been assigned to the design team as well. Abu thought about the fate that had befallen the first engineer who had failed. Rumors were that he was torn apart by a pack of hungry German Shepherds while the new engineer watched. Abu chuckled to himself as he thought about how effective the North Koreans could be at motivation. There was, of course, no practical way to actually test the device on a real bridge so, while they were reasonably confident, they knew the outcome was ultimately in Allah's hands. At the very minimum it would likely close the infidel's beloved Golden Gate Bridge for some time and send them a profound message about the infidel's impotence at stopping them.

The brothers were paranoid about their communications with each other. They knew that being caught before delivering the package would be a failure, and they knew the infidels were very skilled at intercepting cell phone communications. But one of the brothers, whose zeal greatly exceeded his discretion and his intelligence, had slipped and used his cell phone to ask another brother some technical questions about the device. He needed the answers to correctly assemble it and he was, well, impatient to say the least. He had even subsequently called Abu himself to follow up on a detail he didn't quite understand. Abu was furious and beat the brother in front of the others to drive home his point. As leader of the cell, Abu was responsible for its security. But Abu also knew the offending brother had a zeal in his heart for Allah and the project, so after meting out the punishment, he welcomed the offender back with open arms.

* * * * *

NDSA Forensics Lab, McLean, VA

The two forensic analysts, both in their mid-20s, sat next to each other at their consoles and stared at their screens. The one on the right, Edwin Rodgers, was the analyst dedicated to monitoring Joe Barber's conversations being transmitted now directly from the Sparrow systems. The one on the left, Brian Falzone, monitored incoming intel from the Sparrow threat detection software. Falzone highlighted two audio files on his screen, clicked "save", took off his headphones and nudged his colleague. "Hey Ed, if you've got a second I'd like you to listen to something."

"Sure," Rodgers replied. "This Barber guy has gone quiet since those conversations that had everyone so animated. I've had nothing but dead air for hours. What's up?" he asked.

"I have a couple of cell-phone conversations that were catapulted over all of the threat detection routines, which has, like, never happened before, at least not to me. In both of them, some guy with an Arabic accent is asking a technical question of another guy with an Arabic accent about how to secure shaped charges beneath high explosives. The guy actually uses those words. The first guy gives him direction on how much distance to place between the two of them so they deploy themselves correctly. The guy actually uses the word, deploy. The same guy then places another call to some other dude who also has an Arabic accent, and starts to ask a similar question when the second dude goes ape shit and shuts him up. Sounds like these guys are building some kind of sophisticated IED."

"Did you get a fix on them?" Rodgers asked.

"Nothing precise," Falzone replied. "These are intercepted cell phone calls. They are not from Sparrow assets. I just checked the deployment map, and we don't have any Sparrow devices operational in this particular area. Neither conversation was long enough, but the software was able to determine it was somewhere out west and likely close to the coast, although no firm fix on where."

"Were there any targets mentioned?" Rodgers asked.

"No," Falzone replied. "Only a discussion about some kind of device they called the package. But I'm afraid we are on to something real here. You seem to have Agent Green's ear right now. Could you maybe get her to take a listen to these?"

"I can ask," Rodgers said with a bit of skepticism in his voice. "Problem is the thing that has gotten me her ear, as you say, is the same thing that will make it hard to get anyone to focus on it until we have something more concrete than what you've told me. They are all so obsessed with this

Barber business that it's hard to get their attention on anything else. I think there's a powwow going on about it upstairs as we speak."

"Be careful what you say, my friend," Falzone replied, "the walls have ears."

"You've got that one right," he chuckled. "Send me those files and I'll see what I can do."

"Thanks. I know it's a bit thin, but my gut tells me there's something serious behind it, and the software seems to agree, or it wouldn't have flagged the   conversations   so   quickly."

Chapter 23 – Growing Consternation

NDSA Headquarters, the Room

Vice Admiral George Erby sat ramrod straight at the conference table and felt his jaws involuntarily clench as the meeting of ExComm was about to begin. He was seething with anger as he glanced at William Fitzpatrick sitting across the table from him. That man has no business being here, he thought to himself, and he was going to make the point, consequences be damned. He would not lend his stars and his credibility to what appeared to increasingly be an exercise in organizational self-preservation. He was also furious about the death of Colonel Taylor. Could any of these clowns be responsible for that, he asked himself. There would be an accident inquiry and he would allow that process to play out, but it appeared that the F16 went down in deep water off the continental shelf. Recovery and therefore obtaining any conclusive evidence as to the cause would be difficult. He didn't want to believe that these men could be responsible for something like that, but then again, he had sat there just a couple of days ago and listened to it being discussed.

"OK, let's call this meeting to order," Director Collins began. "As you've all been briefed, there's been some significant new intel on our person of interest, Barber. We're going to start off by having Agent Jennings brief us on what we have from recent conversation intercepts."

"Before we begin," Erby interrupted, "I need to make a point." Erby let the comment hang in the air for a couple of seconds for effect before he continued. "The President's Chief of Staff should not be in this meeting." Erby locked eyes with Fitzpatrick as he continued. "This is an oversight meeting regarding an ongoing intelligence operation and the potential review of a tactical response. We are discussing specific individuals and the details of personal conversations. It's beyond your remit, Bill. You don't have the need to know. Whatever you and the President need to know, will be included in the PDB per our normal practice. With respect, you need to leave."

The room sat in stunned silence for several seconds as Erby's words hung in the air. Everybody's eyes shifted towards Fitzpatrick waiting for his response. Fitzpatrick finally spoke up in a calm, almost quiet and distinctly non-threatening tone. "I'm here merely as an observer, George. This is a groundbreaking organization with an extraordinary mission, and I'm proud of every one of you. My role is to ensure your success. It's what I owe to each of you, and of course it's what I owe the President. In a very real way I want this team to think of my presence as evidence I have your six, as you like to say."

The guy certainly made the effort at being a good politician, Erby thought to himself. Good opening salvo - attack, but with compliments and assurances. Try and hold the high ground by throwing your adversary off guard. But Erby regarded the comments as little more than thinly veiled condescension, which simply made him angrier. What a crock, he thought to himself. "Thanks, Bill," Erby said, with heavy sarcasm in his voice, "but my view stands, you need to leave." Erby's tone changed to an almost cold fury. It was now an unambiguous challenge.

Fitzpatrick was a man not accustomed to challenges but retained his composure and calm demeanor. "What's your take on this, Adam?" he asked, trying a flanking maneuver and using Director Johnson, the ExComm Chair, as his weapon. "Are you uncomfortable with my presence?" he asked while locking eyes with Erby as his first sign of aggression.

Another few seconds of silence passed as the occupants of the room waited for either de-escalation or an eruption. Admiral Erby spoke up before Director Johnson could respond. "With respect, sir," he said with heavy emphasis on his pronunciation of the word sir, to morph it from an honorific to an insult, "it's not Director Johnson's call. You have no business being present at these meetings. As I said before, it's beyond your remit and you need to leave."

Challenge, parry, hold ground, then challenge again – the silence was deafening while everyone waited for Fitzpatrick's next response. He had tried, but Erby was really starting to piss him off. Who did this clown think he was? He finally broke the silence and spoke. "My remit, Admiral," it was Fitzpatrick's turn to emphasize the word, Admiral, and turn it from an honorific to the badge of a lesser man, "is way beyond your pay grade. My presence at this meeting is at my discretion, and we are done with this topic. And let me remind you, as National Security Advisor, you work for me." So, an eruption it was.

"I serve at the pleasure of the President," Erby fired back, "and she is entitled to either relieve me of my command or demand my resignation anytime she wishes, but I work for the American People. If there has been any ambiguity in my comments then let me clear them up. Either you leave this room and stop interfering with the deliberations of this organization, or I leave this room and excuse myself from membership in ExComm."

Fitzpatrick's face had become flush as he began to lose all semblance of cool in response to the repeated challenges. He began to speak with his voice now raised, but summoning every bit of whatever self-control he had left to avoid shouting. "Let me remind you Admiral, that by Presidential Finding, the National Security Advisor is a standing member of ExComm, full stop. Resign from this body and you have effectively resigned as National Security Advisor. And might I add that I doubt very much we would be able to find another 3-star billet for which the President would be willing to nominate you. And let me also remind you that the National Security Advisor most certainly reports to the President through the Chief of Staff."

Erby spoke again, this time to the entire room and not just to Fitzpatrick. He was boiling with fury, but unlike the Chief of Staff he had the discipline to hold his emotions in check and remain outwardly calm. "I suggest everyone here think about the nature of this group's conversations over the last couple of weeks and think about the outsized influence that's been exercised by Chief of Staff Fitzpatrick. It's not the way an organization like this is supposed to be run. All I can say to each of you is I pray your conscience and sense of duty will drive you to make the right decisions. We've gone from a team with an historic remit to protect the American people to an organization that seems to me consumed with little else than self-preservation. I won't be part of that. As for me, I'm done," he said, as he stood up, and started to leave.

"Get over yourself Admiral, and sit down," Fitzpatrick barked, with a gratifying sense that he had finally won the argument. His command to sit down was the closest thing he could muster as an olive branch to Erby, a comment designed to convey that if the Admiral would simply regain his composure, as if nothing had happened, all would be forgiven, and they could carry on. It had the opposite effect.

"Fuck you, Bill," Erby said, and then walked out of the room. In over 30 years of active service, nobody who had known or worked with the Admiral had ever heard him swear, even a little bit, let alone use the "F-word". It was part of his mystique as the ultimate straight shooter. His childhood Sunday-School teacher would be mortified, but the comment had the desired effect.

Silence fell over the room as Erby walked out. Adam Johnson, Ph.D. in theoretical physics and Director of the National Security Agency, cleared his throat as he prepared to speak. He entertained many of the same concerns as Erby and had a rapidly growing sense of discomfort at the direction the organization was taking. But he hadn't possessed the chutzpah of a three-star Admiral to express himself, at least not until now. "Bill," Johnson said with a profound sense of caution, but also a profound sense of resolve, "the Admiral is right. I am also becoming very uncomfortable with the nature of the conversations of this group. Our meetings are becoming increasingly focused on self-preservation, and I too sense they are potentially becoming too politically focused. Frankly, I'm afraid we're going to miss something unless that changes. When was the last time we had a serious discussion in here about the threat board? We've not done so since we've been focused on this person of interest, Barber. That has to change, and it has to change now. The best way for that to happen, Bill, is for you to step away from this and let the professionals do their jobs. I'll brief you personally if you wish, but I agree that your presence in these meetings is a distraction and counterproductive."

A heavy silence returned as Fitzpatrick and Johnson's eyes locked on each other and everyone waited to see what would happen next. Fitzpatrick was a smart enough politician to recognize that a temporary tactical retreat could set the stage for an ultimate strategic victory. He relaxed his glare a bit and smiled slightly, so as to diffuse the tension in the room, and began speaking again in a calm, almost reassuring voice. "I understand, Adam. As I said, my goal here has been to have your backs; not to be a distraction. I can perhaps do that from a distance for a bit. Why don't you just give me a brief after each one of these meetings. I'll let my secretary know you have 'as needed' access to me. Good luck to all of you. You have an historic mission here that few will ever be aware of. Do it well." The Chief of Staff of the President of the United States rose from his chair and calmly walked out. As Johnson watched him, recent events kept racing through his mind. He thought about the deaths of Eric Longstreet, Barber's secretary Colonel Taylor and wondered who, or what, was behind them. For some bizarre reason scenes from the TV show House of Cards flashed through his mind. He quickly dismissed them. Those were absurd caricatures that required a major league suspension of belief. But he couldn't shake the cold chill that had just overwhelmed him.

* * * * *

About 30 minutes later Special Agent Ryan Jennings walked into his office. As he passed his secretary, she gave him a message from Agent Green and told him she had said it was very urgent. Jennings sat down at this desk and reached across for the phone, but as he did so he saw someone walk into his office, looked up, and to his astonishment saw it was William Fitzpatrick. In a calm voice, but nonetheless one that exuded authority, Fitzpatrick looked at him and said, "Regardless of what just happened in that meeting, you need to understand that I speak with the authority of the President. Joseph Barber presents an undeniable threat to this organization, and as such is a threat to the safety of the American people. I need you to effectively deal with him and to do so immediately. I am holding you personally responsible. And to be clear, you never saw me in your office, and this conversation did not happen." He then adopted a more fatherly tone as he continued – first the stick, then the carrot, "I've been very impressed by you, Ryan, and I trust you. Make sure those impressions are well placed. This organization is going to need a good pipeline for future leadership, and I can't think of a better candidate for that than an intelligence whiz."

"Yes sir," Ryan said, as he sat there in stunned disbelief. What had this guy just told him to do? Fitzpatrick's carrot wasn't all that comforting. As a matter of fact, it was downright frightening. Dr. Adam Johnson wasn't the only person to succumb to a cold chill as the potential consequences of failure flashed through Jennings' mind.

NDSA Forensics Lab, later that afternoon

Ed Rodgers walked up to his console and tapped Brian Falzone on the shoulder to get his attention as he proceeded to sit down. Falzone's face was almost buried in his computer screen, and when he was in one of his concentration trances he could be oblivious to everyone and everything around him. The several empty large Starbucks cups that cluttered his work area, along with two empty 5-Hour Energy bottles betrayed his highly caffeinated state, which further fueled his intense concentration. Falzone looked up at Rodgers as he sat down, removed his headphones and turned slightly towards his colleague to engage in what was obviously a conversation the guy was about to start. "Just got down from upstairs," Rodgers proclaimed, "and I was able to get some face time with not only Green but actually Jennings as well."

"Really?" Falzone responded, with surprise in his voice.

"Yep. Good news is Agent Green seemed very interested in the conversations you flagged and actually called Jennings while I was sitting in her office. We had to wait about 20 minutes until Jennings returned from an ExComm meeting, but he agreed to see us. Given our lack of specifics on who, what or when, Jennings didn't seem that interested. Actually, he snapped at me and told me we had nothing, and not to waste his time until we had something more useful. Green actually looked a little surprised and taken aback by that."

"Just a grumpy boss?" Falzone asked.

"Yeah, and I've got to tell you he looked really distracted and almost agitated when we walked into his office. I think something must have happened in that ExComm meeting. And after he snapped at me, he was real terse with Green, and told her he wanted a real time feed on Barber's whereabouts sent to the Ops guys or, I guess more accurately, Colonel Richardson, Taylor's second. I suppose you heard Taylor went down over the Atlantic yesterday while he was flying an F16 to Orlando. She's been appointed acting Commander of Ops until they find a permanent successor."

"Yeah, it's all over the news now. Too bad – the guy had a good reputation and I understand he had several kids," Falzone replied.

"Yep," Rodgers responded. "Anyway, I think there was some crazy shit that went on in that meeting that's got Jennings rattled."

"Remember we're not supposed to think, my friend, at least about what goes on in those meetings. I don't even want to know. Our job is to gather intel, evaluate, and report," Falzone said.

"Right, I know, above our pay grade and all that nonsense," Rodgers responded. "Listen to you – I reluctantly agree to take this stuff upstairs and now you're the one telling me to cool it," he joked. "But we did at least get their attention. As we left Jennings' office, Green told me in no uncertain terms for us to stay on this and see what we can find out. She seemed to be much more convinced than Jennings that it represented something real and maybe even imminent. I reminded her I was working almost full time now on Barber, and she promised to try and divert another analyst to help us. She authorized a Sparrow delivery to that location, I think it's a warehouse, and they should have it in place and transmitting within a few hours. She also reminded me we could strengthen her hand by coming up with something more concrete."

"That's good," Falzone replied. "To be honest with you, partner, I sense the bosses are becoming a bit distracted right now, and I don't like it."

"I agree, I don't like it either," Rodgers said as he stretched his arms, then put on his headphones to continue his work. "But as they say, sometime stuff happens."

"Right, and I don't want the stuff that hits the fan to be us missing something, especially something big."

"Well then let's just do our jobs and do them well. Leave the screw-ups to the bosses."

Chapter 24 – Budding Plans

Residence Inn, Northern Virginia

The Residence Inn at 8400 Old Courthouse Road, Tyson's Corner, Virginia was plain, but comfortable and convenient. It sat adjacent to a large shopping mall, which would be a useful source for any unanticipated necessities over the next several days or so to say nothing about providing a wide variety of places to eat. A Residence Inn was not the normal sort of place that Barber was accustomed to staying when traveling on business. Indulging in the Ritz or even the Peninsula was much more to his style, and it was a luxury he shamelessly afforded himself. But his plans for the immediate future required something much more low-key, and the Peninsula was not exactly low-key. He also returned the rented Porsche, then went to one of the local budget rent-a-car places and secured a two-year old Chevy Cruz. He hated the Chevy and thought it to be a piece of junk, but it had one big advantage the Porsche did not. It would make him invisible, and the ability to fade into the nothingness of busy people going about their daily task, which was an important part of his tradecraft. Barber knew he now was a target of some very capable people. The key was to find a way to use that fact to his advantage. They would meet again soon, he told himself, but on his terms. Of course, there was still one problem of which he was unaware. He had no clue there was a Sparrow listening device imbedded just above the hairline on the back of his neck and that it transmitted every word he said directly to the attentive ears of the digital forensics lab at NDSA.

Joe walked into the small but functional two-room suite, retrieved the laptop from his backpack, placed it on the desk in the room adjacent to the bedroom and fired it up. He pulled the Sig Sauer P224 from inside the waistband holster that was tucked in at about 4 o'clock on his right hip, ejected the magazine, inspected it, smacked it back into the pistol's handle and placed the weapon back in its holster. He then retrieved both of loaded spare mags from their sleeves tucked inside his left waistband and checked the tension on the spring by pushing down on the top round a couple of times. He was unable to press the top round of either magazine more than about a sixteenth of an inch, which confirmed they were full. Satisfied, he then tucked them back into their sleeves. A Glock 19 would have been slightly lighter and easier to conceal, but Joe was partial to Sigs after his time in the Navy. He had carried the weapon so routinely that it melted into his body as though it was a part of him, despite it being slightly fatter and heavier than the Glock. He was one of the fortunate few who had obtained the very difficult to get concealed weapon permit in the State of New York, largely as a result of his business and his position as CEO. He was, of course, denied that privilege by the District of Columbia, but he didn't care. He would carry it anyway. Better to be judged by 12 than carried by 6, he told himself. Besides, at least this hotel was in Virginia, and Virginia was a much more Second Amendment friendly state.

As he sat there and stared at a blank Google search screen, he still couldn't believe Jennifer was dead, or Longstreet. Who had killed them, and how did they figure out what he was on to? Whoever they were, they obviously had capabilities and resources way beyond anything he had seen for a terrorist group. Even the highly organized ones like Al Qaeda or ISIS didn't have this kind of capability, at least not on American soil. This was no ordinary terrorist cell, he told himself. He couldn't shake the sense that there was some sort of government behind this. Iran kept coming to his mind. Maybe their Quds Force had managed to mobilize a cell, or cells, in country and was providing support to it from abroad. That would certainly go a long way in explaining his theory that the U.S. government was trying to cover something up. The Russians, he asked himself? Unlikely they would be so reckless. The Russians had far more to gain by continuing to shake things up among the former Soviet states. While they loved poking a finger in the eye of the U.S.

and using their cyber capability to foster domestic discontent with our government, deploying military assets on U.S. soil was unthinkable. Even Putin wasn't that crazy. Whoever these people were, they had great intel and were highly capable. Unfortunately, they were also highly deadly, and in a very creative way.

Joe picked up his iPhone, unlocked it with his thumbprint, touched the phone icon, then the favorites list, and touched the second number from the top, Marcus Day's. Diana's number was of course the first. After just one ring Day answered. "You settled in, buddy?" Day responded, without saying hello.

"Yes," Joe said, "this place should work just fine. Not exactly the Peninsula, but not $800 a night either, and very low key."

"Good," Day replied. "Lauren ran another blood sample through works and didn't find anything else. Our working theory is there was some kind of very sophisticated agent that was deployed when the FedEx package was opened, but we have no clue what it was. We've extensively examined the contents and drawn a complete blank as well. We can't find anything. Whatever agent was used in that package was bespoke or custom made and likely way beyond the means of anybody we've dealt with before. This is like nothing I've ever seen and absolutely had to be the product of some government effort, and not a third world one at that."

"My thoughts exactly," Joe replied. "Given the lack of a smoking gun I couldn't get Benson interested in it. He agrees the whole thing looks very suspicious, but Don's a guy who deals in fact, not conjecture. Until and unless we turn up some hard evidence he's not going to investigate Jennifer's death. To do so he would have to breach two thresholds – that it was a deliberate act and somehow qualified as a federal case. Frankly, I doubt if they would have found anything anyway. I suspect our capabilities are every bit as good as the Bureaus, if not better."

"Better," Day fired back. "So, what's your plan? To be honest with you I'm not even sure where to start."

"Well, the one thing I am fairly certain of now is they seem to be after me. I'm the target. No way the target could have been Jennifer. You're not going to like this, but my best idea is to try and use myself somehow as bait to see if we can flush anybody, or anything, out. They must know their first effort failed. And I think we can be pretty certain they will try again, and likely very soon."

"You're right, I don't like it. As a matter of fact I downright hate it, Joe. These clowns are very capable. We're not dealing with amateurs here."

"I know that, but I'm no amateur either, and like I said, I can't think of any other idea."

"You know that particular set of skills crap is for the movies, Joe, so don't kid yourself. I am very worried, so at a minimum I want to assign our two best security agents to shadow you until this whole thing is over," Day fired back.

"That's useless, Marc and you know it," Joe responded. "Whoever this is, they obviously don't want to abduct me, they want to kill me, so what would our two field agents do? And besides, I'm afraid as good as our guys are they are going to be spotted, and that would likely spook whomever we are trying to catch, or at least make it more difficult by making them more cautious. Our guys would be zero help, to say nothing of putting them in useless jeopardy. I understand your concern, but let's focus on the mission."

"Alright," Day replied, with distinct resignation. "You're the boss, and I have to agree I don't have a better idea. So just how exactly do you intend to play out this bait idea?"

"I'm working on that. Maybe I could do some high-profile snooping in the D.C. area. I could show up at the Post and ask a lot of annoying questions, or whatever. Whoever is after me can obviously be very stealthy, so the key will be knowing what to look for. I think I'll take my laptop and head to a local Starbucks for a caffeine infusion and see if I can think of something with a bit more detail. Maybe we'll even get lucky and somebody will take a run at me there," he said sarcastically.

"You and I have a very different definition of getting lucky, pal, and frankly you should be careful what you ask for," Day responded.

"Alpha predators are hard to catch, my friend. You need to flush them out. I'll check in later tonight after I melt back into this place to hide."

"OK, like I said, you're the boss. But I am at least going to keep a real-time track going of your location, so make sure you keep that phone with you and charged at all times."

"Thanks Marc and will do."

"And I still want to at least have a ready response team staged about 10 minutes away. Humor me on that," Day said.

"OK, that's sounds like a reasonable compromise," Joe responded. "But no closer than ten minutes, Marc, seriously."

"No problem. I'll have them move back a couple of miles right now," Day said, effectively confessing he already had the agents on site very close to the hotel.

"Ever the forward thinker. But unless I get in trouble, under no other circumstances are they to get closer than a couple of miles: and absolutely no contact, even by phone," Barber replied.

"Got it, boss. They will be tied directly to the emergency exfil app on your phone."

"Thanks, I'll be in touch," Barber said, as he touched the red icon towards the bottom of his iPhone to end the call.

* * * * *

Ed Rodgers sat at his console for several more seconds to see if Barber made any more phone calls or said anything, even to himself. When the feed remained quiet for a decent interval he reached across to his call director and touched the icon for Amanda Green. She answered on the first ring.

Chapter 25 – Growing Questions

"What do you have?" she said without even uttering a hello.

"We have a location fix and some intel on his near-term plans."

"Outstanding," she replied.

"He's evidently staying at a Residence Inn close to the Tyson's Corner Mall," Rodgers continued. "We can determine his location within about six feet, but I haven't been able to tie it to a room yet. Determining elevation is a bit tricky, but we can pull the floor plan for the place and hone in on it. Both he and this Marc Day individual seem convinced they are targets of some highly sophisticated terrorist cell and that it's government sponsored. Good news is they both think it foreign government sponsored. Barber apparently plans to put himself out there as bait to try and flush us out, although he doesn't seem to have a plan yet on how to do it. Said he was going to go to a local Starbucks and try and clear his head, so to speak. And there is one more very important thing. Barber's company has placed a couple of field agents close to the hotel to protect him. Barber told his guy to move them back a couple of miles so they don't spook anyone. Also, the guy on the other end of the conversation, Marc Day, made reference to an emergency exfil icon on Barber's phone. It sounded like they have a plan in place to get him out of harms way if anybody goes after him."

"Interesting, and I'm not surprised," Green responded.

"Do you want me to forward you the conversations?" Rodgers asked.

"No, that's not necessary," she said. "Let me know if you get anything more specific about how he plans to set his trap. Jennings seems really animated about getting this guy."

"Agent Green, may I ask you something?"

"Yes," she responded, with a tone that suggested Rodgers should proceed with caution.

"We seem to be throwing everything we've got at this Barber guy, but I can't hardly get Jennings' attention on the West Coast thing which feels like a real threat. That just doesn't make any sense. I don't understand the priorities."

"The priorities are way above your pay grade, Ed," she responded, as a clear admonition but a deliberate use of his first name as a way to soften the effect without compromising its substance. "Leave that problem to me."

"Got it," he responded simply.

"Good," she said, as the line went dead.

Special Agent Amanda Green leaned forward and put her left elbow on her desk and closed her eyes for a couple of seconds while she rested her forehead in her open left hand. She then looked up and focused almost a blank stare on her office door as she shifted the hand to a partially closed left fist that supported her chin, took a deep breath, and let it out slowly. Rodgers was right, she thought to herself. She rarely attended the ExComm briefs and wasn't in the most recent, but something happened there that was really getting Jennings' knickers in a major pinch. And Rodger's assessment of the strange nature of their priorities seemed spot on. If she was king, or queen more accurately, they would be aggressively pursuing this new West Coast thing and throwing lots of resources at it in the process. One thing was certain, however. Green was becoming increasingly uncomfortable about how this organization was being run, and what appeared to be a shift away from their strategic mission to an almost paranoid focus on self-preservation. Her training at the FBI Academy at Quantico certainly hadn't prepared her for this. She had been recruited from the ranks of FBI Agents in the National Security Branch after 7 years experience and a consistent string of superb

271

evaluations. The job seemed exciting, important, and came with the title of Assistant Special Agent in Charge, clearly a promotion. And powers made clear to her, the door to return the Bureau was very much open with a likely ASAC posting and a fast track to running one of the field offices. But she had to admit to herself that for the first time she was really beginning to regret her decision. It wasn't supposed to play out this way. She was startled from her thoughts by the ring of the phone on her desk. She reached across and picked up the receiver. It was Ryan Jennings.

"So, what have you heard from your people?" Jennings asked, skipping the pleasantries.

"We've got a positive fix on Barber's location. He checked into the Residence Inn in Tyson's Corner. We picked up a phone call he made to his business partner, Marcus Day. Their conversation confirmed his intent to find out what happened to his secretary and to the Post reporter Longstreet," she reported.

"Frankly I'd like to know that myself," Jennings replied. "I won't look a gift horse in the mouth, but the coincidences seem to be piling up a bit too much for me as well."

"Are you telling me that nobody in this organization had anything to do with either of those deaths?" she asked, regretting the words as soon as she heard them leave her mouth.

"Of course not," Jennings said emphatically. "At least not to my knowledge. But I'll admit I've asked myself that question more than a time or two."

"You know we are a need to know organization, Ryan. Isn't it possible the order came from Collins directly to Taylor before his accident during that flight to Florida?"

"I'd be careful where you go with that Amanda," Jennings replied with a modest rebuke in his voice. "But I don't think so. That sort of thing would require ExComm approval, so as part of the senior leadership team I can't believe I wouldn't be in the loop. All we were instructed to do, that is all that Taylor was instructed to do, was to vet a plan, not implement it. And I think Taylor's refusal of that order would have killed any hope of trying to implement something so soon after that discussion."

"Right, sorry," she replied.

"What else do you have from Barber's phone call?"

"A lot, actually," she answered. "He plans to somehow put himself out there as bait to try to flush out whoever is responsible for those deaths. Doesn't seem to have a plan yet, but it was pretty clear from the dialogue that is something that is going to go down in the next 24-48 hours at the latest. Also, there are a couple of assets from his firm watching him. Day referred to them as security officers; wanted them to shadow him as protection. Barber told Day to move them back a couple of miles to avoid spooking anyone. We've been doing some research on their firm, Orion Bellicus and their security officers, so to speak, are all ex-special forces. I think we have to assume they are armed. I think we also have to assume that Day may not follow the spirit of Barber's instructions and will likely position somebody much closer. I think we have to assume Barber is armed as well. Day also referred to them keeping track of Barber's location at all times, presumably through the GPS chip in his phone."

"You're probably right, and I'm not surprised," Jennings interjected.

"And one more very important thing," Green continued. "Barber has some sort of icon on his phone; sounds like something developed by his firm that acts like a panic button and will summon the cavalry if he believes he is in imminent jeopardy."

"Ok, useful to know. Especially since I agree with you that they are likely to have him covered closer than a couple of miles."

"So are you at liberty to tell me what the plan is?" she asked.

"We have approval from ExComm for surveillance, but surveillance only at this point. Richardson's been tasked with that as the acting, until they appoint a permanent replacement for Taylor. They made it very clear that there is to be absolutely no contact at this point. We want to know what he is up to, what he knows, and especially if he figures anything out. Your team will continue to provide Sparrow intel in support of those objectives and will also provide Richardson's team support on the surveillance. Her assets will be on site within an hour or so, and you are to communicate directly with her on this. She will be plugged into your comms and will hear any of Barber's conversations in real time."

"Got it," Green replied. "What about the West Coast risk? My people think it's real and I agree with them. I think we need to heighten our attention on this. I'm frankly having a hard time understanding the priorities here, Ryan. Our remit isn't self-preservation. Our remit is protecting the American people. Self-preservation is an accepted part of our mission only as a means to protect the ultimate end, and it's starting to feel to me and a lot of other people around here like it's becoming an end in and of itself."

Jennings bristled as he listened to the words and suppressed the urge to hammer back at Green for questioning him. Problem was he knew she was right. He also knew that missing another major terrorist attack while chasing Barber would do far more damage than just create a huge morale problem within the organization. It would create an actual threat to the organization itself, much like the Space Shuttle blowing up almost became the demise of NASA. And there would be no hero astronauts coming to their rescue. The political types would run for cover and disavow everything they had done,

274

even their existence. They'd all be left hanging out to dry, and probably be up to their necks in legal problems as well. CIA types had been crucified for far less than what they were up to, he reflected. For the time being he would softly chasten her for challenging him while conceding her larger point about misplaced priorities as a way to soften the blow. Take the high road for now, he thought to himself as he said, "Be careful where you go with that, Amanda. I'll concede the point that a few people have been a bit distracted, even me, but let's look at it solely in the context of the mission. Put more resources on the West Coast risk. Richardson has a bird staged about 50 miles from the Bay Area, and I will personally go to Collins to lift its grounding at least until we get a better sense of how real this new threat is. If you convince me it's real, I promise I'll take it to ExComm."

"Thanks boss," she replied.

"But one more thing, Agent Green," Jennings said as he decided he didn't want to let her off the hook so easily after all. "Don't ever question the motives or the integrity of this organization again. You may challenge the actions, but you may not challenge the people or their motives. Do I make myself clear?" he asked.

"Yes sir, very," she said, summoning every bit of self-control she had to ensure the tone of her response was respectful.

"Good," Jennings replied. "Call me as soon as you have anything else, on either topic."

"Yes sir," she responded, once again with an outsized effort to sound respectful.

As she continued to hold the receiver to her ear, the line went dead. She reached across her desk and almost slammed it into the cradle of her call director. "Asshole!" she muttered under her breath.

Chapter 26 – Final Preparations

San Francisco, California, about 10 miles south of the Golden Gate Bridge, 24 Hours Later

Abu bakr Muhammad sat at the small conference table in the warehouse office with two of the brothers and the sister. On the desk a few feet away was an opened Amazon.com box, which contained a $50 gift card from the warehouse management company. It was a thank you for his business, or so the enclosed note said. What an irony, he thought, as he opened the package and read the brief note accompanying the card. He would say thank you of course as well, not only to the business owner, but also to the entire city. He would deliver a very special thank you in a very special way. He didn't realize it, but the irony of the note was actually on him. "We are only a few hours away from glory, dear brothers and sister, may Allah be praised. We will strike a great symbol of the infidels, a symbol that adorns this den of iniquity. The sword of Allah will strike at their hearts and the flag of Allah will someday fly over this place." Every word he said was now being transmitted in real time by the sparrow device that had floated out of the Amazon gift card a couple of minutes ago and implanted itself in the back of Muhammad's neck.

"Allah u Akbar!" they all said, almost in unison. "We are ready!"

"You are to leave the garage at about 4:45 P.M., which should be the time of maximum bridge traffic. That should put you on the bridge between 5:00 and 5:15. As we have planned, you are to slow down and activate the device just as you pass underneath the first support columns. Our structural engineers in Riyadh have confirmed that this location will present the best opportunity for maximum damage. Praise be to Allah brothers and sister!

Within only hours now you will smite a mighty blow and then enjoy your rewards in Paradise!"

"Allah u Akbar!" they shouted again.

"Give me the honor of serving each of you tea," Abu bakr Muhammad said, "and the privilege of sharing it with you." He got up from the table and retrieved a tea service that was sitting on the desk, and then in an almost ceremonious fashion placed a cup in front of each of the two men and the woman. He then carefully filled the cups from the teapot that was also sitting on the service tray. He retrieved a cup for himself from the office desk and sat back down at the table. "I am not worthy to drink from the pot which serves martyrs, but will you allow me to join you with this humble cup I have prepared for myself?" he asked.

"Yes, brother, join us!" one of the men said. "Yes brother, please honor us!" the other two followed. The first man spoke once again, "Without your leadership this would not have been possible. May Allah provide you safety for many more operations, and may he someday reward you with martyrdom as well."

"Such is my highest ambition," Muhammad said. "And may Allah grant you peace as you follow his path today." They each then lifted their cups and proceeded to drink their tea. Muhammad insisted they empty their cups, and he poured them more. Of course, this was more than just a ritual. The tea he served them had been spiked with a combination of valium and hydrocodone, enough to relax and mellow them out but not enough to impair their function. It was a good insurance policy against second thoughts. And he had a second insurance policy as well. The van was equipped with a GPS tracking device and a remote detonator. Abu bakr Muhammad could track their location in real time, and as soon as they were passing under the first support structure he would detonate the device himself, just in case they had second thoughts. None of them were aware of this, of course, nor were they aware that their tea was spiked. That was the way it had to be. He knew the human factor in martyrdom operations was always the wild card, and he would take no chances.

NDSA Digital Forensics Lab, a Few Minutes Later

Ed Rodgers noticed a red flashing icon on his computer screen. The Sparrow software had detected a "Priority One Conversation", as it was called, and was alerting him to the need to review it. There were two things that had facilitated such a quick alert. First, Rodgers had directed the system to focus directly on any conversation coming from the warehouse in question, thus bypassing the need to filter it through the standard Sparrow threat detection algorithms. This effectively allowed the conversations to leapfrog over millions of others and go to the head of the line for a more detailed threat detection analysis. Second, he had directed the system to cross reference any new conversations with earlier phone calls they had received. If there were similarities based on either content or voice patterns, the flag would appear on the operator's screen, allowing Rodgers to listen directly to the conversations hours before they ordinarily would have been flagged. Rodgers clicked on the icon, which displayed a link to an MP3 file. The file was identified by the latitude and longitude coordinates of its origin, as well as its time stamp. There was also a blank field that allowed the operator to name it if he or she so desired. He then clicked on the MP3 file and began to listen. As he did so, his eyes started to widen. He almost felt dizzy as the words of the conversation betrayed a detailed threat. When the file concluded, he smacked Falzone on the shoulder to get his attention and said, "You've got to listen to this, and right now". He clicked on the rewind arrow and then handed his headphones to Falzone. He didn't want to take the time to copy and deliver the file to his partner. He wanted him to hear the contents as quickly as possible.

Falzone picked up Rodgers headphones, put them on, then started to listen to the audio feed. As he did so, he began to turn pale. He looked at his partner as he continued to listen and mouthed the words, "Mother of God". When he had finished he pushed Rodgers aside so as to gain access to his partner's keyboard and console and quickly highlighted then emailed the MP3 file to Amanda Green with a high priority flag. He scooted back to his console, picked up the phone, touched the icon for the direct line to Green and got her secretary. "Where is she?" he barked, without any pleasantries.

"She just stepped out for a minute. May I take a message?" she asked.

"Go get her," he said flatly.

"Brian, I think she's in the lady's room. I'll let her know you called as soon as she walks back in."

"I said go get her, and get her now!"

Chapter 27 – Complications

NDSA Headquarters, the Room, 30 minutes later

Members of ExComm sat around the conference table and listened to the audio file. The meeting had been called so quickly under the eminent threat protocol that nobody had the time or took the time to call Chief of Staff Fitzpatrick. Director Collins looked at Colonel Richardson and asked, "What assets do we have on site right now?"

"There's nobody in the field, although we do have a bird that's deployed about 45 minutes from the bridge," she said.

"Let's get it airborne right now, Colonel. It will at least give us eyes on. I'm lifting the grounding on my authority, given the eminent nature of the threat," Collins replied.

"What about ordnance, sir?" she asked.

"I don't want to waste time loading it. Besides, this is obviously planned for rush hour, and the collateral damage from firing ordnance could be horrific."

"Not as horrific as taking down a chunk of the Golden Gate Bridge," Dr. Adam Johnson said.

"Sirs," Richardson continued, "the birds are positioned with a full compliment of ordnance. We would have to remove it if you want the drone to fly clean. I agree it's likely an unacceptable risk to fire ordnance, but it doesn't hurt to have options. And I agree that destroying that van, as unfortunate as the collateral damage would be, is preferable to seeing a large chunk of the bridge fall into the Bay. That would likely cause a much larger loss of life."

"We need to be decisive here, people," Collins continued. "Table the discussion about ordnance. I want that bird airborne and eyes on as quickly as possible."

"Got it, sir," Richardson replied. She then stepped out of the room to give the order.

Admiral Erby was the next to speak. "We need to inform the FBI field office and local authorities immediately. They should raid that warehouse before that van leaves the building. It's a less populated area, and if the van is detonated there it will sure cause a lot less damage than going off on the Bridge or in heavy traffic approaching the bridge."

"Ordinarily I'd agree with you," Collins said, "but the reality is we don't have time for that now. That van is likely to be rolling in less than an hour, and even if the President of the United States called the Governor right now, I don't think they could get the message out and mobilize quickly enough. Same for the FBI, and there would be too many questions about where the hell such an order came from and under what authority. Cold hard reality is I believe we are the only ones right now who stand in between those terrorists and a lot of potential fatalities."

"Well I hope this is a lesson for us all," Erby said. "From my vantage point I can't help but conclude that the covert nature of this organization has created unacceptable complications on how the federal government manages a rapid response to this. Also, I can't help but believe if we weren't so focused on this Barber character we might have caught the threat in time to give us a few more options."

"That's not helpful now, George," Collins shot back.

"I agree," Johnson said. "There will be time enough for that discussion after this is over. For right now let's try and stay focused on preventing a disaster. We have nothing else to discuss here. Trae and I will head down to ops and see if Colonel Richardson has that bird airborne yet."

"All right," Erby responded. "But I am putting ExComm on notice that we stand down after we deal with this threat until we can get an independent assessment of this organization's tactical effectiveness, full stop. Ever since we went operational there have been nothing but screw-ups accompanied by too many unanswered questions."

NSA Director Johnson almost turned white when he heard Erby use the word, "independent", but before he could speak, Director Collins spoke up and said, "Again, there will be time enough for all of that after we deal with this threat. For now let's stay focused."

"I'll brief the President," Erby said, as he stood up and started to walk out of the Room.

"I've not said anything to Fitzpatrick yet," Adam Johnson warned. "George, I presume you'll tell him when you call him to clear the meeting with the President?"

"I have no intention of calling the Chief of Staff," Erby replied coldly.

"How do you intend to get in to see POTUS then on such short notice?" Johnson asked.

"I plan to do it the old-fashioned way, Adam. I'm going to walk into the Oval."

Chapter 28 – An Unexpected Adversary

Undisclosed Location, Shanghai China

The Third Department of the Peoples Liberation Army General Staff, known as 3PLA, is the Chinese equivalent to the U.S. National Security Agency. There is, however, one major exception. Its remit also includes cyber warfare. Some in the intelligence business would argue that putting both electronic intelligence and cyber warfare under the same umbrella provides a natural synergy, that the two functions greatly complement each other. The United States, however, never seemed to get that memo. The U.S. cyber command was imbedded in the Defense Department, and it relied on the Defense Intelligence Agency for most of its sleuth. The fragmentation of the U.S. Government intelligence community, along with the inevitable resulting turf wars, was not just inefficient, it caused the U.S. to miss things, and the administrative structure called the Directorate of Central Intelligence did little to alleviate it. It was another classic example of the U.S. Congress mistaking motion for progress.

3PLA was the beneficiary of massive investment over the last decade and recruited some of the best and brightest college graduates that China had produced. Ironically, many of them received their post-graduate training in the U.S. at places like Harvard, M.I.T., Cal Tech and Stanford, then took their skills back to their homeland. With even more irony many of them would then marshal those skills against their former host. Some of the Chinese senior intelligence officers were operating under non-official cover as visiting professors at U.S. universities, and a few even held tenured positions. The substantial investment had provided an impressive return by providing the Chinese government with a cyber warfare capability second to none.

Many novels as well as serious books had been written about the topic of cyber warfare, with most of them focusing on the drama of the cyber attack itself. Things like the risk of power grids being taken down, disruption of air traffic control systems, even taking over the operational control of an enemy's weapons systems made for fascinating reading. But the Chinese had learned an important lesson during the early days of their efforts. Taking control of something was actually relatively easy. Knowing what to do with it and how to control it to one's maximum tactical or even strategic advantage, was hard. It required stealth and patience to exploit what they learned, especially patience. It was much more difficult to lay there, undetected, in an enemy's electronic networks and systems than it was to hack into them in the first place. But the benefits of silently probing capabilities brought immeasurable dividends. The Chinese had one major cultural advantage over the Americans – they always took the long view. Americans were by their very nature impatient, and this was especially true for the American government. It was only after a great deal of patience that one could launch a cyber attack that could be breathtaking in its vision and impact.

A natural target for 3PLA was their "sister" agency in the United States. So the organization devoted considerable resources to probing NSA systems and capabilities. It was through this process that they became aware of the NSA's Department of Special Activities and its Sparrow and Drone programs. The Chinese commanding general had been highly impressed, not so much with the ability to find it; they expected no less from the bright young minds they employed and showered with privilege. He was impressed by the genius of what the Americans had done. The sheer audacity of it. They never dreamed the American culture could produce a warrior class so willing to develop and deploy a capability that seemed so diverse from the ideals they preached and were forever attempting to force upon the rest of the world. They regarded the Domestic Drone Program, in particular, as a stroke of pure genius, so much so that they were in the process of developing their own variant. Only problem, of course, was that general aviation was far less prevalent in China, so it would be difficult to make that concept of stealth work. Not to worry, though, because they didn't have a Freedom of Information Act or an inquisitive media to worry about.

They slowly and carefully penetrated the firewalls of NSA's multiple systems. Tiny electrons became their secret agents. As their secret agents penetrated deeper and deeper into the American intelligence networks the full scope of the NSA's capabilities started to become increasingly apparent. And then they hit the mother lode – the Sparrow Program and the threat detection software. Once they gained access to the software itself they began to trace the system's output to individual IP addresses and ultimately to consumers of the data. It was like a painting that began as a blank canvas, adding strokes of color in different places gradually beginning to render a complete picture, and before long they had acquired complete command and control knowledge of the entire NDSA itself. To test the quality of their stealth they executed a number of minor cyber "attacks" against NSA and NDSA, which had no malicious objectives other than to determine if the effort, or their presence, was in any way detected. The attacks were planned and executed as a progression, with each one increasingly more intrusive and bold. The Americans remained clueless. Chinese patience had paid off. They were now ready for something much bolder, and the General Staff had finally approved an action designed to openly embarrass the American Government as well as telegraph to them that they were being closely watched. They relished the thought of serving the Americans an outsized dose of humility.

First Lieutenant Danping Xu sat at her console and carefully watched the screen. It provided a live video feed from the nose cameras of the American drone aircraft. The feed had just showed a hanger door open into the bright sunlight of a late Southern California afternoon. They could then see a man attach what appeared to be an electric cart of some sort to the aircraft's nose wheel. As the man lifted a handle from the front of the cart the aircraft began to slowly move forward and emerge from the hanger and out into the open. Within a couple of minutes, the man detached the cart and pulled it out of the way and out of the camera's field of view. The aircraft's propeller started to spin slowly, then rapidly as the engine turned over. Lt. Xu looked at the left-hand side of her console and saw that the engine was turning at about 1,000 rpms. The engine oil pressure and vacuum were both in the green arc of their respective gauges. The drone's internal navigation computer showed it was oriented to a true heading of 073 degrees, slightly north of due east.   Lieutenant Xu looked down from the console again at a control panel and gently wrapped her hand around a control stick that looked more like it belonged in the cockpit of an American F16 Fighting Falcon jet than in a much smaller drone. She then moved it ever so slightly, almost imperceptively, to the left and right to test her connections. She then lightly pressed the rudder pedals with her feet to do the same. Her connections were perfect. Both of her movements of the aircraft's control surfaces were so slight that they would likely go completely unnoticed by the American pilot. At the moment both the American and the Chinese pilot had control. At the proper moment that would change.

Spec Ops Command Center, NDSA HQ

Jason Andrews sat at his console and monitored the telemetry from an aircraft that was deployed almost two and a half thousand miles away. "November three six eight one whiskey has successful engine start and is ready for programming of autopilot," he said. "Loading target coordinates: 37 degrees, 43 minutes, 31.5 seconds north, 122 degrees, 22 minutes, 54.9 seconds west. Estimated flight time 22 minutes at 160 knots. Altitude over target will be 9000 feet above mean sea level. Flight conditions VFR, or Visual Flight Rules. Clouds are scattered at 6,000 feet across the flight route. Winds aloft about 21 knots directly from the west."

"Good," Colonel Richardson replied, as she stood behind her command console and watched the video of the drone's propeller spinning. "The scattered clouds will provide a bit of cover. Plan is to hit the building. Under no circumstances is that minivan to get anywhere close to the bridge itself." Richardson then removed the chain from around her neck that held the weapons arming key, inserted the key into the console in front of her, then looked back at the screen.

Undisclosed Location, Shanghai China

Lt. Xu also sat at her console and watched the spinning propeller of the American Predator SDS. She was fluent in English, as were most of the more senior officers in her chain of command, and they fully understood the audio feed that was playing over the intercom system. She pushed the right rudder pedal again, a little more this time to not only re-test her connections but to test the American drone pilot's situational awareness. "Aircraft control re-confirmed," she announced. "Let's see if the pilot notices the rudder deflection."

Spec Ops Command Center, NDSA HQ

"Hey Colonel, I just got a random right rudder deflection," Andrews said. "Not much, but I want to run a quick systems diagnostic before we roll."

"Do it," Richardson replied.

Andrews clicked a couple of icons on his panel to activate an automated systems check, and simultaneously alternated pushing both rudder pedals to the floor to confirm they worked. "Diagnostics clean, and manual check confirms rudder function is properly responding. Don't know what that was but we are good."

"Good," Richardson replied. "Let's get this bird in the air. Our window is very tight."

"Roger that," Andrews responded. "Eight one whiskey is ready to roll. Beginning taxi."

Undisclosed Location, Shanghai China

"They noticed my rudder movement sir but dismissed it and are beginning to taxi the aircraft to its runway. No suspicions," Lt. Xu said, as she watched the aircraft begin to move. "When the aircraft is 3 minutes from target the system will trigger the kill switch and we will have sole control." The kill switch was the software program that had been downloaded to the NDSA control systems, and once triggered it would disable Andrews' ability to exercise any control over the drone leaving it solely under the control of the Chinese.

"Good," her commanding officer said. "They will be in for a nasty little surprise, won't they?"

Lt. Xu smiled ever so slightly at the comment. She continued to intensely focus on her console, all the while never releasing the light grip she maintained on the aircraft control stick positioned in front of her.

Spec Ops Command Center, NDSA HQ

It took only about two minutes for Andrews to taxi the bird to the runway. He lined up the aircraft for takeoff and then did an engine run up and another systems diagnostics check. "Control systems are green, power plant is green, navigation systems green, weapons systems green; all systems are in the green, ready for takeoff."

"Cleared for takeoff, Jason," Colonel Richardson said. "Get this bird off the ground."

"Roger that Colonel," he responded. Andrews smoothly pushed the power lever forward as the turbocharged six-cylinder engine came to life. Everybody in the ops center was focused on the nose camera feed as the picture showed the drone quickly eating up runway as it progressed through its takeoff roll. "Airspeed alive," Andrews reported. "40 knots, 45 knots, 50 knots, 55 knots, 60 knots and rotate." With that, the nose of the bird pitched up and the video feed confirmed it had just lifted off the runway. "Airborne. Maintaining full power through climb out. Climb rate 1,400 feet per minute. Commencing 360-degree circular climb." Instead of a straight out climb, which would take the aircraft over populated areas at too low an altitude to comfortably mask its true nature, the aircraft circled the small airfield as it climbed to 7,500 feet, then turned westerly heading towards its target as it completed the climb to 9,000 feet. Within 15 minutes it had traveled most of the distance between the airfield and the warehouse that still concealed the terrorists and the minivan. "We'll be on station in approximately 7 minutes."

Richardson pushed a button on her console that opened a comm link to the digital forensics I where Amanda Green and Brian Falzone were monitoring the conversations of the terrorist cells. "Richardson here. What do you have, Amanda?"

"Conversations suggest the suspects have completed their purification rites and three of the terrorists are about to enter the van and drive away. How close are you?" she asked.

"We are about five to six minutes out at this point."

"I'm not sure you have that much time, Colonel. I will alert you the minute Sparrow confirms the terrorists have boarded the vehicle."

"Andrews, where the hell are we?" Richardson barked.

"Three and a half minutes to station," he announced. "I've gone to full power and we are pushing about 190 knots right now, which is 5 knots below the aircraft's maximum maneuverable speed, or Vne. Engine temp is still in the green but it's definitely climbing. I don't want to stay here more than a couple of minutes."

"Back it off a little bit," she responded. "That bird will do us no good if the engine blows."

"I wouldn't let that happen, Colonel, but I'll slow it down to 180 to improve the margin for error. Reducing power to 90%; 3 minutes 5 seconds to station."

Undisclosed Location, Shanghai China

"Five seconds to kill switch," Lt. Xu announced. "Three, two, one, system confirms the program executed. We have lone control, although the Americans don't realize it yet."

"Slow the aircraft to 160 knots, Lieutenant, and turn it about 5 degrees to the left of its present heading. Let's see if we can give one or two of our American friends a heart attack."

"Reducing power to 75%, trimming for true airspeed of 160 knots," she announced. The ever so slight smile returned to her face.

Chapter 29 – Fail Safe, or Not

Spec Ops Command Center, NDSA HQ

"What the......?" Andrews exclaimed, loud enough for Richardson to hear him.

"What is it, Jason?" she asked.

"I just set power and trim for 180 knots, but the bird just slowed to 160. Wait a minute – it just altered course 5 degrees to the left of what we programmed! I'm going to try and correct both and run systems diagnostics at the same time."

"What's going on Andrews? Do we have a systems malfunction?" she asked.

"I don't know Colonel. Let's hang on a second for the diagnostics. Diagnostics are clean, but the bird is not responding to my commands. I'm going to disengage the autopilot and reset it while I try to correct things manually."

Undisclosed Location, Shanghai China

"Let's begin the ops plan now, Lieutenant. Turn the drone back towards the intended target, but descend to about 2,500 feet, and do it quickly with a forward slip."

"Disengaging autopilot. Turning back to course two seven zero, reducing power to idle, nose down, full left rudder, 20 degrees right aileron, commencing slip."

"This should get their attention," he smiled.

"Ok this is looking better now," Andrews announced. "I've been able to correct course back to two seven zero." It all happened in a heartbeat, but it felt almost like slow motion to him. He was focused on the nose camera feed when he noticed the nose dip slightly. He then glanced down at the engine gauges and noticed, to his horror, that the engine rpms had dropped to about 1,000, effectively engine idle. Before he could even process that fact, his attention was drawn back to the nose camera feed by a perception of movement in his peripheral vision. He looked up and observed the nose of the aircraft had just yawed sharply to the left. He then saw it pitch sharply down. He looked at the artificial horizon gauge and saw the aircraft was nose down in a slight right bank with a full rudder deflection to the left.

Before he could process the mass of sensory inputs bombarding him Colonel Richardson also noticed something was terribly amiss. "What the hell is going on here?" she asked, voice now raised with obvious tension.

"I don't know, Colonel. At first I was afraid of a systems malfunction, but it looks like the aircraft was deliberately placed in a slip to rapidly lose altitude. Systems malfunctions don't execute a precise maneuver like a forward slip. If I had to guess, I would say it looks like somebody else is controlling the aircraft. The bird is rapidly losing altitude and at the moment I have no control."

Both Adam Johnson and Trae Collins were standing several feet behind Colonel Richardson and observing the mission's progress but otherwise staying quiet. At this point, however, Collins felt compelled to speak. "What's going on, Colonel?" he asked.

"I don't know. This looks deliberate. At the moment I have no answers."

295

"You know your window is closing, Colonel. We need answers fast."

She was angered at the use of the pronoun "your" and briefly thought about correcting him by saying "our", but quickly thought the better of it. She took a deep breath and tried to provide some leadership, which clearly wasn't coming from the men behind her. "That's not helpful, sir. Let us work the problem. You are seeing everything we are in real time."

Collins bristled a bit from the rebuke from a subordinate, but he knew she was right, so he decided not to press it. It wasn't the time or the circumstances. He quickly reflected on how lucky they were that Fitzpatrick wasn't in the room right now.

Richardson hit the button for the forensics lab and Agent Green. "Where are we, Amanda?"

"Nobody's on the phone right now and all I am getting is indecipherable chatter. I think they are very close to leaving, however. A couple of seconds ago we picked up sounds like car doors closing. I've got two people listening to the feed simultaneously," she said. "I'll alert you as soon as we have any indication at all that the van is on the move."

Undisclosed Location, Shanghai China

Flanking Lt. Xu on each side were two other LPA officers. To her left was the person responsible for maintaining communications with San Francisco Air Traffic Control. He was raised and educated in the United States, and his English was perfect with no hint of accent whatsoever. Since the drone was operating in a heavy commercial air traffic area, known as Class Bravo airspace, his job was to ensure the proper flight plans were filed and to maintain radio contact with local air traffic control as if he was the pilot. This would mask their true intent as long as possible. Of course, once Lt. Xu began the attack phase of their mission, that ruse would fail. That was part of the plan, actually. The Chinese wanted to make the last phase of this mission as visible as possible to the local authorities and population. To her right was another female officer who was monitoring the communications coming from the NDSA Spec Ops Center. She was able to hear every word spoken over Colonel Richardson's comms net.

"We are almost at 2,500 feet, sir," Lt. Xu announced.

"The Americans believe the terrorists are about to leave the warehouse," the officer to the right of Xu said.

"I'm picking up a communication now from air traffic control," the officer to the left of Xu reported. "They are attempting to make contact with the aircraft."

Air Traffic Control, San Francisco International Airport

"November three six eight one whiskey, San Francisco Approach. You have deviated from flight plan and are now in restricted airspace. Climb and maintain 5,000," the air traffic controller instructed.

Spec Ops Command Center, NDSA HQ

"Crap!" Richardson blurted out. "ATC is now engaged. Andrews, what's your control status?" she asked.

"I still have no control, Colonel. The aircraft is not responding to my commands, but it is clearly responding to commands from somewhere. I'm going to call ATC and report engine trouble. It will raise our visibility, but it might give us a couple more minutes before ATC decides to scramble F15s." Ever since the attacks of 9/11, emergency procedures called for local Air National Guard units to scramble jet fighter aircraft to intercept any civilian airplane that appeared as though it had the potential to be part of a terrorist attack.

297

"Do it," Richardson barked.

Andrews pressed a button on the top of his control stick to place his civilian aviation radios in transmit mode. "San Francisco Approach, Cessna eight one whiskey. We are experiencing engine problems but should be able to exit restricted airspace shortly." This was nonsense, he thought to himself, but it may at least buy a little time. He waited for a response from the tower. None was forthcoming. "San Francisco Tower, Cessna eight one whiskey. Do you copy? We are experiencing engine problems. Engine is still running but throttle is stuck at idle. We expect momentary resolution and will exit restricted airspace as soon as possible." Still no response. "Colonel, ATC is not acknowledging my transmissions. It would appear we have no communication capability as well. Diagnostics report everything is green."

Undisclosed Location, Shanghai China

The Commander smiled as he listened to the American's attempt to communicate with ATC. "Not a bad tactic to buy a couple of minutes. Lieutenant, send the same transmission to ATC and let's see what we get. This should get the American's hearts pumping," he said with what was now a discernible smile.

The officer to the left of the pilot pressed a button on his console and began speaking into the small boom microphone that was positioned directly in front of his mouth. "San Francisco Approach, this is Cessna three six eight one whiskey. We are experiencing some sort of engine trouble. The engine is still running but throttle is stuck in idle. We expect to have the problem resolved shortly and will exit restricted airspace as quickly as possible."

Air Traffic Control, San Francisco International Airport

"Eight one whiskey do you wish to declare an emergency?"

Undisclosed Location, Shanghai China

"Not at this time, not yet," the officer responded. "Engine is running, and we believe we figured out the throttle problem. We expect to be able to climb out momentarily."

Air Traffic Control, San Francisco International Airport

"Understood. Report as quickly as issue is resolved," the controller said.

Spec Ops Command Center, NDSA HQ

"Who the hell is that?" Richardson almost yelled the question. "Somebody is communicating with ATC on behalf of our bird," she said, almost shouting again, "and they just repeated exactly what we just transmitted to ATC!"

"We've obviously been hacked, Colonel!" Andrews said, almost shouting himself.

Richardson took a deep breath and regained her composure. She understood clearly that if she became rattled that would not bring out the best in her team. It would make matters worse. "Is it possible to get a fix on their location?" she asked.

"Negative, Colonel," said the systems analyst sitting next to Andrews. We started diagnostics as soon as we heard the transmission, but whoever is doing this is really creative. It appears that the signal is bouncing all over the place and we can't detect the point of origin. We should find them eventually, but I'm afraid not in time to do you any good."

"Andrews," Richardson barked, "are the weapons on that bird armed?"

"No, Ma'am," he answered. "Weapons indication still shows locked."

"Ok, let's try the kill switch on that bird. Option A," she said. The kill switch was a failsafe device on the drone that allowed the operator to disable it if there were mission-compromising malfunctions. It was a completely separated software routine on a separate logic board, and it was fire-walled from the rest of the aircraft systems to ensure it could not be compromised by other malfunctions. It provided two options. Option A was a simple command that would lock down the weapons systems, override the primary autopilot and all other control systems and cause the drone to return to its base. Option two actually resided on yet another independent and fire walled logic board and would detonate two separate magnesium explosive packages – one that surrounded all of the sensitive electronics and optics, and a second designed to destroy the aircraft itself. The magnesium burns at a temperature of over 5,000 degrees Fahrenheit and will burn under water as well. It would ensure all the hardware would be burned beyond recognition and make it impossible to extract any useful intelligence from the wreckage.

Richardson removed her key from the weapons board and inserted it in the abort panel. She then rotated the key 90 degrees to the right to arm the system and enable both options. "System armed. Execute Abort Option A," she commanded.

Andrews flipped a switch cover up on his panel and depressed a button that simply had a capital letter A on it. Everyone was staring intently at the aircraft's nose camera feed hoping to see the bird begin to execute a gentle bank that would be the first step in its return home. "Nothing, Colonel," Andrews reported. He reached forward and depressed the button a second time. "Nothing again. Abort Option A will not execute."

Richardson took a slow deep breath as she began to feel a cold chill and goose bumps. Who were these people, she thought to herself, and what were their intentions? "Execute Abort Option B," she commanded.

Andrews reached forward and flipped up a second switch cover that was next to the first. In doing so he exposed a second button that had a capital letter B on it. He depressed the button. Nothing happened. He depressed the button again. Again nothing. "Abort Option B has also failed, Colonel. It would appear that we are merely spectators right now."

"Mother of God!" NSA Director Adam Johnson whispered under his breath.

The momentary silence in the room was broken when Amanda Green's voice started speaking over the intercom. "Sparrow intel confirms the minivan has just left the warehouse and is en route to the bridge. We estimate only about 500 yards out at this point, but they are on the move."

"Mother of God!" Director Johnson said again, this time not in a whisper.

Chapter 30 – A Nasty Surprise

Undisclosed Location, Shanghai China

"They just attempted to execute both abort options, sir," Lt Xu announced. "Both options failed."

"I expected nothing less," the Commander replied. "We will now commence phase two," he continued. "Turn off the transponder, continue descent to 500 feet, level off and then go to 80% power," he ordered.

Lt. Xu reached up to her console and rotated the control button on the drone's transponder all the way to the left, shutting it off. In less than two minutes the bird was only 500 feet above the ground and beginning to draw some attention, though at this point not yet alarm.

"Transmission coming in from Air Traffic Control," the officer to the left reported. The Commander indulged again in a brief smile.

Air Traffic Control, San Francisco International Airport

"Cessna three six eight one whiskey, San Francisco Approach. We show your transponder just went dark and you are continuing to descend. Do you wish to declare an emergency?" the controller asked. There was no response. "Cessna three six eight one whiskey, do you copy?" The controller asked again. Still no response. "Cessna three six eight on whiskey, do you copy?" she asked a third time. Still no response.

At this point the air traffic controller pressed a button that connected her with the shift supervisor. "The Cessna I've been following is within about 10 miles of Golden Gate and is below 2,000 feet on our last read. Its transponder just went dark and it's not responding. The pilot has failed to answer 3 separate hails. I've got a bad feeling about this."

"Copy that and thanks. Let's not screw around. I'm notifying Fresno." With that, the shift supervisor depressed a button that linked her to the command center of the 144th Fighter Wing of the California Air National Guard. In less than 60 seconds a call went out to a pair of F15 Eagles that was practicing CAP, or combat air patrol maneuvers about 150 miles south of San Francisco just off the coast. The twin birds immediately turned north and went to afterburners which pushed them past supersonic to a speed of just over 1,500 miles per hour. Within less than 4 minutes they would eat up 100 miles of that distance and slow down to begin their intercept. It was not the first time the 144th had been scrambled to intercept a small plane that appeared to be a threat. It was usually some inexperienced pilot who either didn't know the rules or was lost, and the appearance of a pair of F15s off their wings was more than enough to make them very compliant, and quickly. Ever since 9/11 there were strict protocols, and if this particular airplane didn't follow their precise instructions, they would not hesitate to shoot it down.

Spec Ops Command Center, NDSA HQ

"Colonel, we confirm ATC has just contacted the 144th, and two airborne F15s have just been scrambled to intercept," Andrews announced. "Do we have any way to call off those planes?" he asked.

"No," Director Johnson interjected. "SecDef is not read into this program. Besides, given those birds were already airborne, I'm quite sure that by the time we place a phone call this will already be over."

How could this get any worse, Colonel Richardson thought to herself. She was about to find out.

Undisclosed Location, Shanghai China

"Let's commence phase three," the Commander said. "Turn the bird around and head back to the bridge. Take it down to 300 feet and rock the wings back and forth for show. How long to intercept with the F15s?"

Lt. Xu looked up at the radar screen on her console. "Between 4 to 5 minutes," she answered.

"What's the van's location?" the Commander asked.

The officer to the right of Xu replied, "Just approaching the entrance to the bridge. Reports are that traffic is unusually light for this time of day and their progress has been much faster than anticipated."

"Excellent," the Commander replied. "Arm the weapons systems. This should really quicken the pulse of our American friends."

Lt. Xu was the one to smile this time. She reached up to her console and touched an icon on the screen labeled "weapons hot". The Chinese regarded the physical switches used by the Americans, along with safety devices like covers that had to be flipped up to expose the switch, as anachronisms of a bygone era. The Chinese prided themselves in placing a much higher value on efficiency and simplicity.

Spec Ops Command Center, NDSA HQ

"Weapons just went hot, Colonel," Andrews announced, as everyone in the command center stared in horror as images of the Golden Gate Bridge from the drone's nose camera now filled the screen. "Aircraft is slowing down and beginning to circle the south side of the bridge." At that moment another image filled the screen, as the aircraft switched from the nose camera, or pilot view, to under the aircraft's nose, or target view. A large digital circle with cross hairs metered with hash marks appeared and began scanning the area underneath the aircraft. Within another few seconds the cross hairs acquired and focused on a grey minivan. Everyone in the room then heard a warbling

304

tone that signaled the drone's weapons system had locked onto the van as a target.

"Where are those F15's?" Richardson asked.

"Still about 2 minutes out, Colonel," Andrews responded.

"This thing is going to be long over in 2 minutes," she said, with a growing sense of nausea.

"The bird is now only 200 feet above the deck, Colonel, and it's rocking its wings again, probably to draw attention. I think we have to assume there are a lot of people with smart phones who are capturing the video now."

Richardson didn't respond. Through the target camera feed they could see the van begin to move. "What are these clowns up to?" Richardson asked. "If they intend to take out the van why aren't they firing?"

"One minute to intercept," Andrews announced.

Undisclosed Location, Shanghai China

"At present speed the van is about 15 seconds from the first support structure," Lt. Xu announced. "Ninety seconds to F15s' intercept."

"Standby to fire," the Commander ordered. The van sped up slightly as the traffic thinned, and within less than 10 seconds it was about 10 feet from the red columns that represented the southern support structure of the Golden Gate Bridge, or about 150 feet from where the brothers had been told to detonate the device. "Fire the weapon," the Commander said, in a voice that almost sounded bored.

"Weapon away," Xu responded, as she executed a sharp bank to the left to try and push the aircraft out of harm's way. The explosion was dramatic, but the design of the device focused the explosive force downward to maximize the damage to the bridge, and this resulted in the drone suffering only minor damage. Large chunks of steel and concrete fell into the Bay. The support structure seemed to hold, but the left column was canted at least 5 degrees to the right and had obviously suffered major structural damage. The scene was one of carnage. Numerous vehicles close to the van were burning, and many of them had actually fallen into the bay. The downward, instead of outward, force of the explosion however had also spared many lives. The terrorists had made a calculated decision to trade off fewer civilian casualties for greater damage to the bridge. It was not, of course, an act of mercy. It was simply a cold calculation that the catastrophic destruction of such an iconic symbol as the Golden Gate Bridge would have a much greater impact than civilian slaughter. There were still enough deaths to satisfy the terrorist's blood lust.

As the aircraft rolled out of its sharp bank, Lt. Xu descended to about 100 feet and flew the aircraft along the pier to ensure as many people as possible saw and photographed it. The drone incited large-scale panic as most people scrambled for cover. When it was about 100 yards from Pier 39 it made a sharp bank to the west and began to head toward open water. About this time the F15 Eagles arrived on station and began a hot pursuit. "The Eagles are painting the aircraft," Lt. Xu said. "We should expect them to fire momentarily."

"Execute phase four," the Commander responded.

With that order, Lt. Xu waited just a couple more seconds to buy a little extra distance, then pushed the drone's nose up, then down again into an arc and crashed it into the Bay. "Drone in the water, sir," she said.

"Well done, Lieutenant, very well done."

Chapter 31 – Mission Completed

Spec Ops Command Center, NDSA HQ

Everybody in the command center stood speechless for what seemed like an eternity. NDSA Director Collins silently thought to himself that this was the end. This organization was finished. He knew that within only minutes every news organization across the world would be streaming the video feed of the drone attack. In spite of the formidable air conditioning that seemed to be working overtime in the command center, he felt sweat drip down his forehead, and he could feel it running down the sides of his body from under his arms. They were running like faucets. Director Johnson looked at him and their eyes met but neither man said a word.

Lieutenant Colonel Richardson finally broke the silence. "Bring up ABC News and Fox News on monitors three and four," she ordered. "Let's see if network or cable news has picked any of this up yet." Both screens showed what appeared to be regular programming. Fox News was the first to cut away with their signature Fox News Alert banner. "Bring up the audio on screen four," Richardson said.

A sober looking anchor then filled the screen. "We bring you a Fox News Alert from San Francisco, California. Moments ago, the Golden Gate Bridge was the latest victim of a terrorist attack. We go to Frank Somerville with our local affiliate, KTVU, for details. Frank."

"Thank you. Moments ago, what appeared to be a small, civilian general aviation airplane fired what appeared to be a missile just short of the first support structure of the Golden Gate Bridge. The explosion appeared massive, and a portion of the bridge itself appears to have fallen into San Francisco Bay. The explosion also appears to have damaged the first support structure, or pillar, of the bridge, as you can see from this footage. Note that the left column appears to be tilted slightly to the right. Reports from the scene say that two U.S. military jets appeared to be closing in on the aircraft shortly after the attack as the aircraft turned to the west and crashed into the Bay."

"Did the military jets shoot the civilian airplane down?" asked the Fox News anchor.

"We don't know. We are literally just minutes after the attack, and details are still unfolding. I am told first responders are on their way, but they are having difficulty getting to the scene due to the heavy rush hour traffic. Just looking at the scene right now, I don't know how there can't be significant loss of life. Hold on, just a minute – my producer is giving me a report through my earpiece that the Coast Guard is en route to the bridge via helicopter and en route to the attacking aircraft's crash site with two Coast Guard cutters. Again, I have to emphasize that we are just minutes removed from the attack and details are very sketchy."

As the local Fox anchor was making his last report, the ABC News screen came alive as well. "We interrupt this program with a special report from San Francisco, California, which appears to be the site of a terrorist attack on the Golden Gate Bridge."

The White House Oval Office

The President of the United States, Sara Einhorn, and her Chief of Staff, William Fitzpatrick, sat in stunned silence as they watched the television screens. The silence was broken by the buzz of the Oval Office's intercom system. "Secretary Corsinni is on the line, Madam President." The two looked at each other as the President reached across the Resolute Desk and opened the line on the intercom. "Bill is with me, Tony."

"I assume the two of you are watching what is going on, Madam President?" SecDef asked.

"Unfortunately, yes."

"I just got word that about 3 minutes or so before the attack that the local air traffic controller called the California Air National Guard to ask for an intercept. The good news is we had two Eagles in the air about a hundred or so miles away, but the bad news is they couldn't get there in time. Although the civilian aircraft was acting a bit suspicious, nobody suspected anything like this," he said. "I've ordered them to stay on station and provide a CAP just in case this thing isn't over yet. We've also grounded all aircraft within a 500-mile radius of the city."

"What do you know about the airplane that committed the attack?" the President asked.

"Both the reports from the scene and some video that's being looked at appear to confirm it's a small civilian bird of some sort. High wing, so probably a Cessna. That's about all we know at this point."

"How could a plane that small fire such a destructive missile?" the President asked.

"Excellent question, Madam President. Frankly I don't see how it's remotely possible that an aircraft of that size could cause so much damage. That will be one of our most urgent lines of inquiry. I'm afraid at the moment, however, we are as much in the dark as everyone else. That should change within the next few hours, however, especially once the Coast Guard gets some of the wreckage out of the water."

"Let me know as soon as you have anything that's meaningful, anything at all. I'm obviously going to have to go in front of the American people in a few hours and I would prefer not to do so completely blind," the President said.

"Of course, Ma'am. At this point I am going to stand back and let the people on scene do their jobs. I'll call you as soon as I hear anything. I'm hopeful that the Coast Guard will find the aircraft quickly. Shouldn't be too hard given where it appears to have gone down."

"Great. As soon as possible, Tony." The President reached up, pushed a button on the intercom box and closed the line.

As soon as the call ended, the intercom on the desk buzzed again. It was the President's Secretary. "Madam President, Admiral Erby is in the outer office and is insisting on speaking to you. He says it is extremely urgent."

Fitzpatrick's face went flush as he heard the comment. "Somebody was going to have to clip that Admiral's wings," he thought to himself.

"Tell the Admiral I said to wait. I should be able to see him in a few minutes," the President said.

"He is extremely insistent, ma'am," she said with a stressful tone in her voice.

"Put me on speaker," the President responded. She waited a second, then continued to speak. "Tell Admiral Erby I appreciate his concerns, am well aware of what is going on right now, and I will see him in a few minutes. Under no circumstances is anyone to enter the Oval right now without my express permission." The phone went dead.

Undisclosed Location, Shanghai China

"Time to make a strategic retreat, Lt. Xu. Disengage the kill switch and return control of the aircraft to the Americans. It should give them time to deploy the self-destruct mechanism. I don't want their Coast Guard to recover the aircraft. Nothing to be gained by embarrassing our friends a little too much too soon," the Commander said with a modest smile. "Besides, continued uncertainty about the origin of the drone and all of the press speculation that will follow should prove far more destabilizing than too much direct attribution right now."

"Disengaging the command override sir," Lt Xu reported. "Control of the aircraft is now returned to the Americans."

Spec Ops Command Center, NDSA HQ

The Optics and Avionics of the aircraft were hardened to resist damage in all but a nose down crash into hard earth. As it lay on the bottom of San Francisco Bay, the nose camera continued to fill one of the monitors with an eerie and opaque scene of the Bay's seabed. "Andrews, are you still getting telemetry from the aircraft?" Colonel Richardson asked.

"Yes ma'am," the pilot replied. "It appears that the left wing was torn off when it hit the water, and the right wing is badly damaged, but the bird is otherwise in surprisingly good working condition. Telemetry also confirms that the remaining three missiles remain intact in the ordnance bay."

"I suppose it's too much to hope for that the self destruct mechanism will work now, but let's try it one more time," Richardson said.

"O.K., Colonel, but you are aware that I hit that button about 10 times during the attack run, right?" Andrews pointed out.

"Yes. Humor me. Do it."

Andrews reached across to the upward sloping portion of his console and depressed a button labeled "Option B". The flip up safety cover remained in the up position from his numerous previous attempts.

"Colonel, I'm getting telemetry that the command has been accepted this time!" Andrews almost shouted. "I think we have control of this thing again!"

Within a second or two there was a bright flash from the nose camera screen and the video feed went dead. Aligned along the fuselage of the aircraft were seven magnesium flares that were ignited and quickly began to incinerate the drone. Three flares in each wing began providing carnage to their hosts as well. The design was very purposeful, and the firing system for each was on an independent circuit to ensure if one failed the others would likely do their jobs. The self-destruct mechanism was not designed to just blow the aircraft up. This would likely leave too many articles of intact wreckage for a clever forensics lab to piece together. It was designed to incinerate the bird so completely that the only thing anyone could identify was maybe the type of metal used in its construction. And the largest flares entombed the outside of the avionics bay and the onboard optics. Both would be reduced to effectively nothing. When the Coast Guard arrived on site in a few minutes, there would be nothing they could do until the incineration had run its course.

Director Collins finally spoke up. "Well that's the only thing that's gone right since we all walked into this room."

Chapter 32 – An Unexpected Response, from an Unexpected Source

Palo Alto, California, Offices of PrinSafe

Charles Westbourne Reynolds III stared in disbelief at the television screen mounted on the wall in his office. The flood of adrenaline coursing through his veins had nurtured the second most base of human emotions, anger. The first was fear, but Reynolds was not a man often given to fear. "Those bloody morons," he whispered under his breath with a cold fury, "how could those idiots let this happen?" Each time one of the drones was airborne Reynolds' team at QuarkSpin followed its every move by capturing the aircraft's video feed in real time. QuarkSpin actually had a small control room that was a downsized version of the NDSA's SpecOps command center. Nobody at NDSA knew this, of course, although Fitzpatrick suspected it. But Fitzpatrick was a survivor, and survivors kept their mouths shut and didn't engage in potentially dangerous speculation.

Although Reynolds was angry, very angry, he was also a master of his emotions. "Think with your brain, not with your glands," he would often tell himself, especially at times like this. He knew applying one's intellect and working a problem in a cold, analytical way always maximized chances of survival. Anger was satisfying but otherwise largely a useless emotion. He wouldn't give into it. He knew this disaster would kill the domestic drone program. Fitzpatrick would never allow NDSA to use one again. He didn't care. The drone itself wasn't even his idea; it was Fitzpatrick's. Sparrow was the real prize, and that was still safe. But the Chief of Staff insisted on the development of the drones as a covert way to proactively deal with the threats the Sparrow revealed. Reynolds had pushed for a team of special operators as an alternative to take out the threats, but Fitzpatrick thought that too risky and too flagrant a violation of the U.S. Constitution compared to the drone. Reynolds argued that was a distinction without a difference, but in the end he conceded for the sake of expedience.

This had to be a hack, he thought to himself, but by whom, and what was their objective? And who would have the capability? A ring of the phone on his desk interrupted his train of thought. He shifted his focus from the television to his call director and saw that it was Dr. Emma Clark. He reached across and picked up the receiver.

"It was the Chinese," she said, without any introductions. "We knew it the second McLean lost control; it had to be a hack. It was clever and control was bounced all over the globe, but we traced the origin to a commercial building in Shanghai. Has to be Third Department; they are the only ones on that corner of the globe with the capability. We don't have any concrete intel on their objectives, but the chances of figuring that out just went way up now that we know who they are. I suspect it was to embarrass the Administration, maybe destabilize it in some way. I find it interesting they relinquished control just in time for Collins' people to activate the self-destruct device. We are still getting telemetry and I am confident the Coast Guard will find nothing but a little bit of molten metal on the bottom of the Bay. Certainly nothing that is going to give them any intel on origin or capabilities."

"Good," Reynolds replied. "This is obviously going to kill the domestic drone program, at least for a while," he continued, "but that was never important to us anyway. I've already given the order to sanitize the factory. Everything related to the drone program will be gone within 24 hours and we are pre-staging several of the Air Force T-41 trainers on the assembly line to look like higher power prototypes in case anyone comes sniffing around that factory, which I doubt."

"Good idea," Clark responded. "The T-41 is basically a military variant of the Cessna 172, correct?"

"Exactly. Do you still have a line of sight to the origin of the hack?" he asked.

"Yes. As a matter of fact we are in the process of refining it, bypassing some of their subterfuge and establishing a more direct link."

"Good," Reynolds replied. "Are we in a position to launch any sort of countermeasure?"

"Yes, absolutely. We have the full compliment at our disposal."

"Great. I don't want to overreact, though. Let's ping them and then shut them down for about 5 minutes. Damage something minor so they know we have the capability. That will send a message that we know who they are and that we are capable of responding."

"Got it. Do you want me to stand by until you clear it with the Administration?" she asked.

"No, do it," Reynolds said. "It's not just the Chinese I want to send a message to. The Chinese will obviously think it's the U.S. At the same time it should keep our friends in McLean distracted and worried that there is a third party somehow involved in this. They might even suspect DIA or CIA. They'll be much more likely to come to us for help in figuring it out instead of pointing fingers."

"Exactly," she responded. "And the irony is we have a lot more sophisticated countermeasure options than NDSA. I'll respond with something that's beyond their capabilities. That will certainly send McLean a message."

"Great," Reynolds said. "Go do it."

"Countermeasures will be complete in less than 10 minutes," Clark responded.

"I'm very glad you work for me, Emma."

"So am I, boss," she replied. "Neither the Chinese nor the American Government pay nearly as well," she said with a chuckle in her voice. "You get what you pay for."

Reynolds chuckled to himself at the comment. His ability to inject a laugh at a time such as this was a measure of his confidence in Clark, and his supreme confidence in himself. "Somehow, Emma, I suspect that is something you know as a matter of experience and not speculation," he said, again with a slight chuckle.

Clark did not respond.

"Let me know when you have confirmation of success," Reynolds said.

"You bet," she responded. "Countermeasures will be completed within 10 minutes, 9 minutes now, actually. We will need a little bit of time to assess the damage and their response. I'll call you within about half an hour."

"Good hunting, Emma."

"Thank you, sir."

Reynolds reached across his desk touched an icon on his call director and disconnected the call. He then moved his finger about three icons to the left and touched another. This one was going to be interesting. Time for a bit of acting. As much as he didn't like the risks that present circumstances presented, he had to admit that this was going to be fun. He loved playing people. And the call he just placed would connect him with people he could play very well.

317

Undisclosed Location, Shanghai China

Lieutenant Xu lifted a cup of tea from the 8 inches of flat space that served as a desk directly in front of her control console and lifted the top of the cup off with her left hand. Many of the more traditional Chinese teacups came with a fitted ceramic top that kept the liquid hot far longer than leaving the cup uncovered. She slowly lifted the cup to her mouth and started to take a sip. As she did so she was startled as the monitors on her console went blank and then glowed a sky-colored blue. Chatter began erupting around the room as numerous other soldiers started announcing similar system failures.

"Reboot your system then run diagnostics, Lieutenant," the Commander ordered.

"Already in the process of doing that, sir," Lt. Xu responded. "Unable to reboot. The system is completely locked, sir. Nothing is responding. Could this be a counterattack?"

At that precise moment the Commander was thinking exactly that. He was stunned. Not only stunned that the Americans had far more capability than he had assumed but even more stunned that the Americans had so quickly identified them as the source of the drone hack. And if they had such an impressive capability, he thought to himself, why on earth did they allow us to continue to control their aircraft? That just didn't make any sense at all.

Chapter 33 –- Angst

The White House Oval Office

Bill Fitzpatrick stood in the Oval office about five feet to the right of the President, who was sitting behind the Resolute desk. They both stared into a television screen watching coverage of the attack on the Golden Gate Bridge. His forehead was covered with beads of sweat, and he could feel a profuse amount of perspiration under his dress shirt, in spite of the strong flow of air conditioning in the room. The bright sunshine beaming into the Oval didn't help things, although the sensation of heat was more mental than physical as the sun's warmth hardly penetrated the thick, bulletproof glass. His heart was racing and almost in his throat. His knees felt week as he reflexively reached out a hand to steady himself on the back of the nearby chair. He felt dizzy. If only she had offered him a seat, he thought, but upon walking into the Oval her summons had been curt. She knew nothing about the NDSA op, of course, and that was by design. Shielding her, protecting her actually, from such details was understood as a prime directive by everyone read into the program. It's what gave her plausible deniability and enough degrees of separation to ensure her survival in the event of discovery. He had realized that if things ever went South, really South, he would play the role of fall guy, with the implicit promise of a Presidential pardon as his insurance policy. This mess was about as far South as one could get. To call it a worst-case scenario was a monumental understatement he thought. As he left the West Wing and headed down the hall, he had no idea that in the short time it would take to walk the distance to the Oval Office the President would already have received a phone call from Homeland Secretary informing her of an attack. Ironically, the networks had become aware of the attack shortly before the information had made its way to Homeland Secretary. It didn't have to work its way through as many layers of bureaucracy as in the private sector. It was being broadcast as breaking news by the time the President took the Secretary's call. She was obviously in no mood to demonstrate kindness or grace.

He felt his phone buzz in his pocket. He retrieved the device and saw that it was a call from Adam Johnson. He touched the green virtual button on the screen to accept the call then placed the phone to his ear and listened. "I assume you are watching the news feed," a familiar voice announced. "We've obviously been hacked. The team is working on identifying who it is. The only piece of good news I can report is we reestablished control in time to execute the self-destruct mechanism. The Coast Guard won't find anything useful. You can be sure, however, that DOD, DHS and the FBI will be evaluating every bit of video taken at the scene, to say nothing about almost every news agency in the country. I've ordered the operational arm of NDSA to stand down immediately."

"You can include the California State Police, the Governor, and every politician on the planet to that list!" Fitzpatrick barked into the phone. "I'm in the Oval with the President. I thought I came over here so the two of us could watch news feeds of another terrorist bomb prematurely detonating before any serious damage could be done to its target, and instead you hand me a shit storm! For Heaven's sake, video of that drone is all over the news! And there are close-ups, including footage of it actually appearing to fire ordnance into the support structure of the bridge! Whoever was controlling that thing even rocked the wings like it was greeting the crowd. Rocked the wings! Shut that organization down and find out who did this and do it quickly."

As the President stared into the television screen, Fitzpatrick turned and walked towards the side of the Oval Office to continue the conversation a bit more discretely. "And don't think in terms of protecting your job, Adam, think in terms of staying out of jail. I'm serious. If we can't contain this, then you can be certain you will be the first sheep thrown under the bus. I promise.

The President is apoplectic. Her plausible deniability is out the window. She connected the dots immediately. She's not stupid!" he almost yelled into the phone, before aborting the indiscretion. "I had my head removed the second I walked in here. If she could have gotten away with it, she probably would have had the Secret Service shoot me on the spot! I'm almost apoplectic myself." He touched the red icon to disconnect the call before Director Johnson had a chance to respond. Fitzpatrick looked up at the President and started to speak but was interrupted by another buzz on the Oval Office intercom.

"It's Westbourne Reynolds, Ma'am," her secretary announced. "He says it's extremely urgent."

"Tell him to wait," the President replied. President Einhorn then looked back at her Chief of Staff. "What was that phone call about? What did you just learn?" she snapped.

"It was Johnson with one small piece of good news. Evidently, they regained control of the aircraft in time to execute a built-in destruct mechanism. The Coast Guard isn't going to find anything. As a matter of fact, they won't be able to go near that thing until it's mostly burned up. Most of the drone was encased in some kind of magnesium flare device that burns crazy hot and continues to burn underwater. The underwater fire will be so bright that cameras won't be able to glean any useful images until it's too late," Fitzpatrick said. "Just like you Ma'am, they suspect it was a hack. They're trying to figure out who."

The President didn't respond. Instead she reached across her desk and pushed the button on her call director to open the intercom. She punched the button so hard the device actually moved a couple of inches. "Put Reynolds through," she said. "and tell Admiral Erby to continue to wait. If he gets grumpy again, tell him to go................" After a short pause, in spite

322

of a bright red face that betrayed her anger, she took a breath and didn't complete the expletive. "Tell him I should be able to see him in just a few minutes," she said, momentarily regaining her composure.

The moment she heard the line open, the President began to speak in a clipped tone. "I thought you employed a group of geniuses over there." She then raised her voice and almost started yelling, "What kind of crap control software gets hacked so completely that somebody actually takes control of that thing and turns it on us?" There was a long silent pause on the other end of the line as Reynolds just let her outburst hang in the air without responding. She took a deep breath to calm her temper, and as she did so, realized that attacking such a powerful ally only had a downside. "Ok, sorry, but to say we are all a little on edge now is an understatement. I appreciate what you have invested in this, Westy, but we're all a little busy here right now. What do you need?"

"I didn't call to ask for anything, Madam President. This is obviously tragic on a number of levels, and I'm not worried about our investment. I'm just calling to help. I agree the NDSA control systems were obviously hacked. The film I've seen of the aircraft clearly suggests someone was controlling it. Its actions were too deliberate to be a systems failure. I've got the best digital forensics team on the planet and I wanted to offer our help. As you acknowledged, we developed the control software. Nobody is in a better position to figure this out than the people at QuarkSpin. Let us help."

The President momentarily put Reynolds on hold without comment and looked at her Chief of Staff. "What do you think?" she asked Fitzpatrick.

"Reynolds is right, Ma'am. Nobody knows that system better than they do."

"What about the security concerns? I'm not crazy about giving them access to our intel regarding the terrorist threat we, no, you were trying to stop," the President responded, with an emphasis on the word you.

"Frankly at this point I wouldn't worry too much about that. The CEO of QuarkSpin and several of their systems engineers have the highest possible security clearance. And besides, most of this is 'off the books' anyway. We need answers ,and we need them quickly, and Reynolds' people are in the best position to deliver on that."

"O.K., but Westy doesn't have that clearance – no need to know. I don't want to give that arrogant SOB more leverage over me than he already has. I think we have to tell him that Clark has to report her findings directly to us, and we will tell him whatever we think we can." She realized it was a foolish statement before she even concluded it. There was no way his people wouldn't keep him briefed on every detail. "Alright, forget that last comment," she said.

The President reached up and punched the mute button a second time to disable it. "I think we have to agree you are right on this. We need answers quickly, Westy, very quickly. I have to go before the American people to speak about this before the end of the day. I can hear the talking heads right now – too sophisticated for Al' Qaeda or ISIS by themselves, must be state sponsored, act of war etc. and blah blah blah. We will shortly have multiple intelligence agencies looking into the attack. Other than the NDSA folks themselves and the oversight committee none of them is read into the Sparrow Program. Even though CIA, DIA, and NSA have all thrown everything they have at this, their assumption is going to be that this was a terrorist attack and not the hack of an "off the books" domestic anti-terrorist program. Without that context, which we are obviously not going to give them, I think they will be running down blind alleys. You've got anything you need from NDSA itself, but that's it. I can't risk disclosure."

"Understood and agreed. I'll have Emma contact Dr. Johnson as soon as we get off the phone. It will be best to have her do the digital forensics on-site in McLean. I can arrange to have a jet go wheels up with her team within the hour."

"Great, do it," the President responded. "I'll have Bill liaise with Dr. Johnson and make sure she gets what she needs. Sorry' but I've got to go. And again, I, no we, need answers quickly. I can't emphasize this enough."

"Understood, Madam President. Emma won't let you down."

The President punched the disconnect button to end the call, moving it even more this time. "Not let me down? Did you hear that?" she barked. "Now get out of here and go fix this mess. And on your way out tell Erby he has to reschedule."

Palo Alto, California, Offices of PrinSafe

Reynolds placed the receiver back into its cradle. The President was spot-on about the coming widespread speculation about state-sponsors being behind the events, he thought to himself. He had already concluded that. That realization was the main reason he cleansed the drone program. If there was ever to be credible evidence of two state-sponsored actors in this drama, China and the United States, it would present him with a terrible risk. Unacceptable. His team had already traced the hack to China. At some point he would have to reveal this to the President. Or would he? What could she do? Publicly accuse the Chinese? Not hardly. China would deny it. More importantly, if accused, China could easily ensure that highly incriminating evidence of a domestic drone program somehow made it into the public domain, and do it without attribution. No, she would keep her mouth shut about China. The greater risk was that one of the other agencies would figure it out. That would take time, however, and time was the progenitor of options.

He swiveled his chair around and looked outside. He could hear sirens in the far distance. No doubt first responders, he thought. Warm sunshine bathed the office. It felt good on his face, although the warmth was more imagined than real, given the UV coating on the windows. The common look at tragedy and see only tragedy, he thought to himself. The gifted look at tragedy and see opportunity. And it wasn't enough to stay just one step ahead. One wins by staying at least two or three steps ahead. So, let's think about those steps, he mused. Russia? Iran? North Korea? His mind was beginning to fill with the possibilities. As he leaned back in his chair, he was surprised to realize that a slight and almost imperceptible smile had just crept across his face. Maybe it wasn't going to be that bad of a day after all.

Chapter 34 – Connecting the Dots

Residence Inn, Northern Virginia

Joe Barber stood in the outer room of his two-room suite and stared at the television. There wasn't a single channel on the cable service that wasn't covering the attack on the West Coast. The most dramatic footage came from a tourist in a convertible that had just entered the bridge and was about 200 yards back of the explosion. CNN was playing it over and over. In the right-hand corner of the screen was a reporter who was droning on with mindless speculation about who was behind it. Barber's concentration was interrupted as he heard his cell phone ring from across the room. He walked over to pick it up all the while still looking at the TV screen. The accelerometer in the phone caused it to light up from the motion of lifting it off the desk, and he noticed it was a call from Marcus Day.

"Yeah," he simply said.

"Lauren has already done some quality analysis on that convertible driver's video. After enhancing the images she's come to three rather telling observations. First, the aircraft doesn't seem to have a pilot. There's a figure in the left-hand seat, but it has absolutely no animation. Must be a dummy of some sort. Second, this is no civilian Cessna. There is something very peculiar about the underside of the aircraft's nose. She's still evaluating that, but she said if she had to guess it looks like some sort of optics. Third, and most telling, the video of the attack itself clearly shows something being fired from underneath the fuselage. Nobody leaned out of a window to do this. And whatever was fired was propelled. We think it was some sort of missile. Long story short, Joe, this was no lone terrorist using a civilian aircraft to stage an attack. This bird was a highly specialized weapon, which leads us to the most troubling conclusion of all. This has to be state-sponsored; couldn't be some domestic militia type. It's way too sophisticated for that. This looks to me like some sort of domestic variant of a Predator, disguised to look like a general aviation airplane. And the other troubling point is what state sponsor would have the chutzpah to do this? Russia or China? That would be crazy. Iran or North Korea? OK, they're crazy enough but they don't have the capability to get something like that bird onto U.S. soil, which brings me to the most troubling theory of all. I don't even want to think this, let alone verbalize it, but what about it being brought to you courtesy of the U.S. Government?"

"But why would the U.S. Government stage an attack on the Golden Gate Bridge?" Barber asked. "That doesn't make any sense."

"Agreed," Day replied. "But let me point out another one of Lauren's conclusions that the networks haven't picked up on yet. We looked closely at the impact of whatever the aircraft fired on that minivan. Bottom line is there is no way a bird of that size could have launched something with enough firepower to cause that big of an explosion or that much damage. It clearly looks to us like a secondary explosion from within the van itself. If I had to venture a guess, I would say that van was an IED being driven by a terrorist cell. The aircraft's mission was to interdict. When the aircraft ordnance hit it, the IED exploded a bit earlier than the terrorists had planned. If it had happened 150 feet or so closer to that support structure, it would have done a whole lot more damage."

Barber remained silent for a few seconds as he processed what Day was saying. His blood began to run cold as conclusions started to come together, but still he wasn't convinced. "OK, but why would they have done it in a way that was so visible? And why use a drone to take it out? Why not scramble a couple of F16s? And why use aircraft in the first place? If they were aware of a pending attack why not just send an FBI SWAT team to round them up before they even got that van on the road? And why for Heaven's sake do it in such a visible way, take a victory lap for all to see, then crash the thing into the Bay?"

"I don't have good answers to those questions," Day replied. "Maybe something went terribly wrong with their plan. Maybe it was a rogue operator. Maybe somebody hacked them. I don't know. Problem is I can't think of any other remotely plausible conclusion other than the Feds."

Barber continued to hold the phone to his ear but remained silent as a thought raced through his head.

"You still there?" Day asked to break the silence.

"Yes," Barber responded.

"You know what this means Joe, right?"

"Yes," Barber replied, with a voice devoid of the considerable emotions that were welling up within him. "You just connected a whole lot of the dots, Marc, a whole lot of them."

"We've been focused on the wrong thing," Day continued. "Some sophisticated foreign terror cell did not perpetrate Michigan and Tyson's Corner. The patterns there are too similar to Golden Gate. They were courtesy of the United States Government. I can't think of anything else that supports the fact patterns."

"I can't believe that. I won't believe that," Barber said emphatically. "There are too many good people there to allow that to happen, at least something that egregious. Drones disguised as civilian airplanes? Absolutely no way! That kind of scale is breathtaking. Too many people at CIA would have to know about it. Somebody would have to have designed those things. Somebody had to build them. Somebody had to fly that thing and pull the trigger on that ordnance. How do you keep something like that a secret?"

"I agree that's the hard part. Maybe it's some kind of off the books group of nut jobs thinking they are doing God's work or something."

"I still find it hard to believe, but frankly I wouldn't put anything past this administration," Joe said.

"Neither would I," Day replied. "That likely means the attempt on you was courtesy of the same group of folks. Special Activities Division?" Day asked, referring to the paramilitary arm of the CIA.

"I would say contract of some sort," Barber responded, "except this wasn't some average rent-a-wet team op, it was highly sophisticated. The agent that killed Jen and likely killed Longstreet was engineered to be virtually impossible to detect and to make the deaths look like natural causes. That would have required a state-of-the-art lab."

"Bottom line is we can speculate all we want about this," Day continued, "but the only way we are going to get a real lead is to engage these people somehow. We need to find out who they are. I'm now all over your plan to use yourself as bait. We need to snag one of these assholes and interrogate him. I see no other way."

"I agree," Barber replied. "I'm going to talk to Benson again and at least tell him what we think. He may or may not put resources on it, but I want him to know. It's also clear now we need some help from a big gun. I'm going to contact Pegasus."

"I thought you might want to do that, and I agree."

"Give me a little time to put together a plan," Barber said. "I'll call you back in a couple of hours."

"Got it Joe. Given what I fear we are up against, I am going to deploy more protective assets in your general area, and that's not negotiable. Be safe." With that, the line went dead.

NDSA Digital Forensics Lab, a Few Minutes Later

Brian Falzone felt sweat trickle down the back of his neck in spite of the air conditioning, which seemed to be cranking at capacity. The call he was listening to went dead. He digitally rewound the recording of the conversation and listened to it again. His stomach churned as he heard the words a second time and considered their implication. He recalled how Jennings, in one of his fits of rage, vented about Barber being a threat to the organization and why nobody at ExComm could see it. Falzone had actually wondered what the word, existential, meant. When he looked it up, it confirmed his impression that Jennings was a paranoid nut job. But now he understood, and he was afraid that Jennings might actually be right. This guy had figured out way too many things. Not everything yet, but he had put together enough of the pieces that the entire picture would soon be clear. And once that happened, the existential threat comment would be no exaggeration. He knew he had to get this to Green and Jennings right away. He clicked on the audio file he had just created, selected the email option, and then hit send. He then reached across his desk to his call director and touched the icon for Special Agent Green's Office. She answered on the first ring.

"Yes, Brian?" Agent Green responded.

"Take a listen to the conversation I just sent you. Barber and Day have tied the San Francisco incident to both Michigan and Tyson's Corner. They no longer believe it was an act of terrorism perpetrated by a foreign agent. They are now operating on the theory all three were U.S. Government sponsored." He let those words hang in the air several seconds.

Amanda Green sat silently and contemplated what she had just heard. "I'll listen to it right now and call you back."

"There's one more thing. It confirms Barber intends to use himself as bait and abduct one of the team to interrogate. His security firm is now planning to station more agents in the area as backup."

She listened to the comments but didn't respond. After a long pregnant pause, Falzone said, "I've also sent the conversation to Agent Jennings. I think it's important you call him and have him listen right away. After you listen to it yourself I'm sure you will agree. I don't think an email from me will get his attention as quickly."

"OK, Brian, I'll listen to it right now then call Ryan. Call me as soon as you get anything else, especially any details related to their plans." The hair stood up on the back of her neck as she disconnected the call. "How had this thing unraveled so rapidly?" She asked. She knew the answers. Hubris, coupled with inexperience and a lack of strategic vision, all seasoned with a healthy dose of stupidity had led to the screw-ups. And with so many screw-ups discovery could only be a matter of time. She swallowed hard at the realization that she would get sucked into the interdiction of this Barber guy. All it would buy them was a little more time, she realized. And the effort to neutralize him could even fail. But they had to try. The NDSA and its minions had become like wounded animals backed into a corner. Survival instincts would triumph over logic and reason, let alone the law. More tragically they would completely obviate the principles the organization was supposed to stand for. Yet she knew she had no choice. They all had to try. What had she gotten herself into, she reflected as her stomach began to churn.

Chapter 35 – Another Player

CIA Headquarters, Langley Virginia, Director's Office

Dr. Margaret Shevchenko looked neither like a Margaret or a Shevchenko. She was the unlikely combination of a Russian Orthodox Ukrainian immigrant father and a Baptist African American mother; two people separated about as far from each other both culturally and geographically as one could image. Love always finds a way her parents would proudly tell her, and the stable home and nurturing nature of her upbringing was a large part of what made her so confident and comfortable in her own skin. Her father was trained in theoretical physics at the National University of Science and Technology in Moskva, Russia, and defected to the West during the late 80s as it was becoming evident that the Soviet Union was collapsing under its own weight. Her mother was an accomplished artist. Being the product of two gifted parents is what made her scary smart. Smart because, well, she was. Scary, because her appearance and ambiguous ethnicity often caused people to reflexively underestimate her. It was a reaction she had come to relish, and she had all but weaponized it. She was medium height and athletic looking from years of relentless training with a particular focus on Cross Fit. Men considered her attractive, although she was not pretty, per se. She graduated in the top 10% of her class at West Point and was selected for an off the books program to test promising and athletic female officers as potential Rangers. She excelled and outperformed many of her male colleagues. But policies were policies, and neither a Ranger billet nor the coveted Ranger uniform tab were awarded her, given the ban on women in combat. She swallowed her frustration and applied for Army's Ph.D. program, and studied Middle Eastern history at the University of Michigan and Oxford. When it became apparent the best she could hope for from the Army was a return to West Point as a professor, she resigned her commission and accepted a position from a very eager recruiter at the CIA, where she was promised both analytical work and direct support for the Special Activities Division. Once again, she excelled. Fifteen years later, and several close relationships with Presidents from both major political parties, she sat in the Director's chair.

Dr. Shevchenko sat in her office and watched the video of the attack on the Golden Gate Bridge, along with Jorge Bisongno, Deputy Director Intelligence and Analysis, and Gerhard Krause, Deputy Director National Clandestine Service. "I want you both to tell me we had nothing to do with this," she said with a stern but even tone.

"I'll admit this has our fingerprints all over it," replied Krause, "but absolutely not. Think of the scope of this. Who could have built that drone? Where, and by whom could it have been controlled? You can keep something like this off the books, but no way could it be done without the senior leadership team being aware. Also, this is obviously not the product of a terrorist cell. The sheer scope and complexity of it renders that conclusion impossible. Can't be a state actor either. Only a handful of countries would have the ability to develop such a thing and nobody could have possibly gotten it onto U.S. soil, undetected. I'm sure of that."

"I agree," Bisongno replied.

"Which leads me to the most troubling conclusion," Krause continued. "Somebody in Government, but not CIA is behind this. This has all the earmarks of a royal screw up by some overzealous B Team."

"Again, I agree," Bisongno replied. "And the only conclusion that fits the fact pattern of it being a U.S. government op and the way that thing behaved is a hack of some sort into the drone's control systems. Even a B Team is not going to be stupid enough to fly that drone in such an open and visible way. Hell, the thing actually rocked its wings like it was saying hello as it flew away from the scene."

Director Shevchenko carefully watched the body language of the two men for any hint of discomfort. She had become quite adept at reading people, and some of the staff at the Agency called her the human polygraph. To her considerable relief she saw nothing untoward in the way either man acted. "I'm thinking the same thing myself," Shevchenko responded. "The President has told all of us, CIA, DIA, NSA & the Joint Chiefs this is our highest priority. I've got to tell you though, during that conference call, my BS detector was ringing five alarms. I'm convinced the President knows something. And I don't trust that pompous ass Fitzpatrick any further than I can throw him."

"You could throw him quite a way, Maggie," Krause responded.

"OK, bad analogy," replied Shevchenko, "but if this is indeed a U.S. anti-terrorist op gone bad in the worst of ways, I've got to believe both the President and the Chief of Staff are up to their necks in it. If that's true, this is going to become interesting, very interesting. And it also will become potentially very dangerous for us."

"Agreed, Madam Director," Bisongno said, "very interesting and dangerous indeed."

"Nobody eats or sleeps until we know who is responsible for this," Shevchenko said. "Now get out of here and go find out."

Five minutes later

Shevchenko retrieved her personal cell phone and dialed a familiar number, albeit one she hadn't used in a while. After the second ring, a male voice answered. "How are you madam Director?" the voice responded. "I can imagine that you might be a bit busy at the moment."

"You might say," she replied. "I'm going to need your discrete services for a few days. How quickly can you get here from Rye?" she asked.

"I'm not in Rye, I'm actually in D.C. and I was actually about to call you," the male voice said. "I could be there in thirty minutes, but you might say I'm a bit busy myself right now. I suspect we have a mutual interest in current events at the moment."

His reference to a mutual interest really set off her alarm bells. What could that be? What could he know? This call might prove to be far more fruitful than she imagined, she thought to herself. "Let's meet in the Agency cafeteria," she said. "I don't want your visit to be part of the official Director's diary."

"Got it. I like it. Hide in plain sight and all that. See you soon."

With that, Director Shevchenko disconnected the call. How could he possibly be involved in this, she asked herself. This was about to become even more interesting than she had feared, and it was going to be a long thirty minutes.

Chapter 36 – Pushback

Lt. Col. Julia Richardson's Office, NDSA HQ

Colonel Richardson sat at her desk and couldn't believe what she was hearing. This guy was certifiably nuts, and this was not what she had signed up for. She grew increasingly angrier as Agent Jennings laid out his case. When Jennings finally paused for a second, she had to interject, and did so with almost a sense of cold fury. "Ryan, my gut reaction to this is you are 'going off the rails'. I am not about to sanction a hit on two U.S. citizens, both of them veterans with distinguished service records, based on some misguided notion of this institution's self-preservation. These guys are guilty of nothing more than being smart, and last time I looked that wasn't against the law. The concept of a contingency, and wow, isn't that an antiseptic term, was developed to address a domestic-based threat, not an inconvenience or certainly not our own incompetence. I don't think this conversation should even be taking place. I'm no lawyer, but I suspect you are breaking a number of conspiracy laws just suggesting this nonsense."

Jennings' back stiffened at her words. His own sense of fury was also growing. He took a deep breath and tried to speak in an even tone, and in his view, be the adult in the room. "This organization's operations, Julia, based on whatever is sanctioned, to use your word, is covered by a Presidential Finding. Anything authorized by ExComm is therefore, by definition, within the law. This boils down to a matter of simple arithmetic – two lives for many. Try and think for a minute about the terrorist attacks that won't be stopped if this organization folds or is even compromised in any way. Think about that. That's why the concept of a domestic contingency was contemplated. I am only trying to discuss the art of the possible here. You know as well as I do that our job is not to make the decision – our job is to present ExComm with options. They make the decisions. And we need to present them with our best assessment of the full range of options. And it's also important that we sit in front of ExComm with a united front and speak with one voice."

Richardson sat in stunned disbelief as Jennings finished his comments. "Perhaps you didn't hear me, Ryan. There is to be no further discussion of this bullshit in my presence, understood? I am not going to engage you or anybody else in a conversation about assassinating two American citizens, full stop. I am not going to walk into ExComm with this nonsense, and there will be no 'one voice' or 'united front', as you say. We, no make that you, need to focus on finding out how and by whom this organization was hacked.   That is our number one priority now, and until we have the answers Director Collins has ordered SpecOPs to stand down, which in my mind is clearly the right decision. Is there any part of this you don't understand?   Besides, you know as well as I do that the whole ExComm process has become far too political, especially with Fitzpatrick playing such a prominent role."

Jennings' back again stiffened at the comments. He locked eyes with Richardson and summoned his best authoritarian tone and said, "Be careful, Colonel, the walls have ears."

Richardson stood up and leered over Jennings. "If that is your idea of a veiled threat, Ryan, let me respond in kind. If you don't get out of my sight right now, I just may have to grab that pencil neck of yours and execute a contingency myself."

Jennings was caught off guard by the forcefulness of her response. In his entire adult life he had never been physically threatened by anyone, and it frankly scared him a bit. It was obvious that he was not going to get her support, so he concluded that continuing the argument would be pointless. He wasn't inclined to take the threat seriously, but he knew that continuing to escalate would only seal their relationship as adversaries, and that was counterproductive. Now was the time to de-escalate and execute a face-saving exit. He would deal with her and her uncooperative attitude in his own time. He smiled, adopted a softer tone, and took a deep breath to try and control his racing heartbeat as well as the small lump in his throat and said, "Animosity between us will not help resolve any of our present challenges, so I'll agree to disagree and drop it for the moment. Thanks for your time, Julia. I'll be in touch." With that, he simply stood up and walked out of her office. What he wasn't about to do, however, was drop the issue. He knew that both Barber and Day had to be dealt with, and quickly. Time to switch to plan B. As soon as he got back to his office he would place a phone call to a very important person and put plan B in motion. It was good to have friends in high places, he thought to himself. That friend, however, regarded him as a mere pawn, easily turned, and easily played. As Jennings continued to walk down the hall a cold chill overcame him. He had never confronted a military person who was so angry with him. She just might be able to do it, break his neck that is, he reflected as he walked back to his office. He suddenly felt very small.

Palo Alto, California, Offices of PrinSafe

Westy Reynolds listened attentively to the voice on the other end of his phone. "Look, bottom line is there is no way that anyone in that organization is going to agree to placing Barber and Day beyond salvage. Everybody is worried about their own skins right now, and recent events are only going to strengthen the voice of that Boy Scout Erby. My guy tried to float the idea informally through channels; he was not only shut down, the Commander of SpecOps apparently threatened to cut off his balls if he ever brought the topic up again. I got the impression the guy walked out of her office with his pants wet. You and I both know, however, that we need to eliminate this threat. These guys are smart, they are not relenting, and it's only a matter of time before they have the entire puzzle put together."

"What do you want to do?" Reynolds asked.

"I need access to specialized resources that can make this go away," the voice said. "Barber evidently plans to use himself as bait to abduct someone and interrogate him. I think these resources I am referring to can use this to their advantage. Set a trap. Whatever."

"Interesting," Reynolds responded. Emma Clark had provided the audio feed of all of the conversations to Reynolds before Agent Green even had taken the phone call from Falzone. Reynolds made it a point to always stay at least one or two steps ahead. "Within the hour someone will contact you with a phone number. You and I are not to discuss this again, is that clear? You should have your guy, as you call him, place the call. Do not call the number yourself. Understood?"

"I'm not an idiot, Westy," the voice replied.

"I know that, but people under stress make mistakes, and you are very much a man under stress right now. Just be careful."

"Don't worry about me," the voice replied. "I just want to get this problem fixed before this thing turns even uglier than it already is. I have a great deal to protect here, so careful is my middle name."

"Good, Bill," Reynolds replied. "I've got to run." And with that he reached across the desk to his call director and touched the icon that disconnected the call. "I'm really becoming worried about this guy," he said under his breath.

341

Chapter 37 – Laser Eyes

The lines in the C.I.A. cafeteria were long and moving slowly as people poured in for their lunchtime ritual. The large crowd in the food lines stood in sharp contrast to the cafeteria's seating area, which appeared about a third full. Bad habit, Barber reflected. People were no doubt taking their food back to their cubicles to keep working through lunch. Obviously, millennials were having a limited impact on the Agency culture. The unbridled ambition, however, that attracted young college graduates from elite schools to such a hyper-competitive environment like the CIA obviously transcended generations. And based on their choices of cuisine, if you could call it that, it didn't look like the average Agency employee was doing anything for Medicare's long-term viability either. He chuckled as he imagined the army of employees filling their trays with unhealthy choices only to stop by Whole Foods on the way home in prep for their dinners. Maybe it was a way to indulge themselves while out of sight of the judgmental view of their significant others. Besides, given their high-stress jobs, they probably figured they were entitled to a little mid-day indulgence. That's likely part of how they rationalized it, he thought. Everybody took it for a given that millennials had a strong sense of entitlement, right? This was just a micro-infidelity to their green, low carbon footprint and overall progressive lifestyle, so they told themselves. Whatever. Screw it, he thought, as he grabbed a bacon cheeseburger and a large pile of tater tots.

"Well, Maggie, I see the food here still sucks," Barber said as he took a bite of his cafeteria cheeseburger.

"What, you don't approve of the wine list?" she asked. "Come on, Joe, every meal can't be at Le Diplomate," Shevchenko replied with sarcasm. "Besides, where else can you get such exquisite tater tots?"

"Like, at every government cafeteria I've ever been to," Barber replied, returning the jocularity. "Somehow I suspect the food in the executive dining room here may be a bit nicer."

"Stop your grumbling," she retorted. "Your palate can survive an occasional plebeian experience. Besides, exec would be way too high profile. We're in the covert business, right? Look around – nobody cares. Hiding in plain sight, like you said."

"You're in the covert business, Maggie. I'm in the security business."

"Right, and I've got a bridge in Brooklyn I'd like you to look at," the Director retorted. She then casually laid a device on the table that looked like a cell phone.

"Somehow I suspect you're neither waiting for a call or planning to look at your Facebook page. Jamming device?" Barber asked.

"Among other things," the Director replied. "And I don't have a Facebook page. That would be something for DCIA, wouldn't it?" Barber just smiled.

"So what do you know about this Golden Gate fiasco, and what is your involvement in it?" she asked.

"You've got to learn to stop beating around the bush," Barber replied.

"Neither one of us has time for that. This incident is the major focus of every alphabet agency in this town. I'll be even more direct. I suspect it was somehow an inside job. I'll admit I have no evidence to back that up. It's just an instinct at this point. But nothing else seems to fit the fact pattern. So I was planning to ask for some off the books help from my favorite civilian, and then you mention a mutual interest. I need to know your involvement before this discussion goes any further. So what do you know and how are you connected to all of this?"

Joe could almost feel the temperature in the cafeteria rise a bit as her blue eyes started to bore holes in him with the question. It was like she was suddenly concentrating her intellect and focusing it into a death ray. He put down the cheeseburger figuring it was going to be a while before he could pick it up again. He picked up the glass of water and took a drink to wash down what he was chewing at the moment she fired her question at him. He found himself sitting a little more erect in the chair with his hands folded on the table as he prepared to answer the question. Not formal, or nervous, but more alert, serious and attentive. Amazing. And his change in posture wasn't a conscious decision. He did it reflexively, without even thinking. She had that affect on people. The woman had the ability to shift from friend to grand inquisitor without even stressing a single gear. It unnerved people, especially her opponents. No wonder half the seniors in the West Wing were scared to death of her. It also short-circuited the useless chatter that seemed to be the preamble to so many serious conversations and brought them immediately to point. Fear in the face of one's better had a way of doing that. It was a skill he greatly respected, and one he wished he had himself. Joe briefly cleared his throat after the drink of water and began to speak. "I have a friend whose wife and children were killed in that incident outside of Detroit and I promised I'd look into it for him."

"I'm sorry to hear that, Joe," she said with sincerity, as though she had momentarily flipped the safety for the death ray to the "on" position. The moderation of her alert status was only tonal; however, it was only evident in her voice. Her eyes continued to project the death ray as though a red dot from a laser gun sight continued to rest right between his eyes.

"Then there was the vehicle explosion in Tyson's corner," Barber continued.

"I thought that was the result of a gas tank that exploded," she interrupted. "That's what the press reported. It was, like, on page 17 of the Post."

"So they say. I decided to check it out, and found forensic evidence at both scenes that I am certain link the two. The story of a vehicle gas tank fire was a crock. Both were hit with some type of ordnance. I believe it was a missile of some sort, likely fired from a drone. The warhead appears to have been made out of titanium, with the explosive being some kind of Semtex. I had my lab look at the metal fragments. The bits of titanium I found at each site came from the same source. The Semtex traces had similar chemical signatures, although not conclusive. I have connections inside the Bureau, so I gave them a few pieces of the metals from both locations for their lab to look at as well, which then mysteriously disappeared. When was the last time you heard of the FBI losing evidence? And that's just the simple stuff. From here the story starts to get ugly. That reporter for the Post, Longstreet, was an acquaintance of mine. He had uncovered some suspicious forensic evidence at the Tyson's Corner site himself and was investigating the case. We compared notes. Then the guy winds up dead, by an all too convenient cardiac problem or something like that. There's no direct evidence of foul play, but I don't believe in coincidences."

"That's a pretty big leap," she snapped. "I am hearing nothing from you but speculation."

"Hang on, Madam Director. It's now about to get head-melting ugly," Joe said with a slightly raised voice as he leaned over the table towards her. "I am obviously on to something, because the bastards tried to kill me. Let me repeat that. They tried to KILL ME!" he said, with cold fury in his voice. He then looked suddenly sad as he continued. "But they killed my secretary by mistake. A healthy 20-something cross fitter, who looked like an Olympic athlete, dropped dead after taking two steps into my office as I sat there and

346

watched. We think she was the victim of some kind of highly engineered type of cyanide that is all but impossible to trace. I had my lab look at it. It was delivered in a FedEx envelope intended for me."

"Oh my, Joe, I am so sorry," she exclaimed, genuine now, with eyes that looked sympathetic.

"Thanks. Then this attack on the Golden Gate happens. All I can say is the MO looks very similar to Detroit and Tyson's Corner, and I am convinced the drone that went down in the bay is exactly the same variant used in the previous two attacks. Which brings me to the nastiest conclusion of all. No way a terrorist organization, domestic or foreign, could have had that kind of technology to deploy on U.S. soil. A nuke would have been easier to hide: impossible for a foreign government as well. Few have the capability, and even those who do could never get it into the country and make it operational without somebody noticing. Somebody such as you, for example. Which means it must be some sort of U.S. government Op. As much as it pains me to say that, I can't think of any other explanation that fits the fact pattern. Even some rogue government agency wouldn't be crazy enough to attack the Golden Gate Bridge, so I suspect there was some other government that was on to whatever this program is and hacked the systems; maybe to embarrass us, maybe to reveal the program, I don't know. But what I do know is there is a very short list of players with that kind of capability. I suspect it must have been either the Russians or the Chinese."

The Director sat silently with a return of the piercing eyes that were burning holes into Barber's face as she listened. Joe could almost feel the temperature in the room rise considerably now. He was always amazed at how the woman could cook an internal sense of rage and focus it entirely with her eyes. Her face wasn't even flushed. "You're telling me that elements of the United States Government, our government, deliberately and with malice aforethought actually assassinated two of its citizens for being nothing more than a little too clever?" she asked.

"Yes," Barber replied.

"Well, I can tell you that if I can confirm that to be true beyond a reasonable doubt I may have a little more work for you than I thought," she said. A chill now ran up Barber's spine as he momentarily speculated as to what that work might entail. He was pretty sure he knew. The temperature in the room suddenly went from very warm to very cold.

"OK, so you are already up to your neck in an investigation of this. What are your plans? What are your next steps?" she asked.

"I think it's better you don't know, Madam Director," Barber replied.

"Ok, so I take that to mean you are planning to arrange, shall we say, an informal interview with one of the responsible individuals?" she asked.

"No comment," he replied.

"Fine," she said, with a voice completely devoid of emotion. "Just make sure I get the results of that interview as soon as it happens. If making the arrangements, so to speak, turns out to be difficult or in any way troubling, you know what number to call."

Barber looked into her cold steel blue eyes and asked, "Why is it I suspect that phone call won't even be necessary now that I've become, shall we say, a person of interest?"

"Don't be ridiculous. Domestic surveillance by the Agency is against the law," she replied as she stood up and retrieved the device she had put on the table. "I expect to hear from you as soon as you have anything more. If what you think is true, no, make that if what WE think is true, I will not let it stand. Be careful." With that she gathered her tray and left.

Barber sat there for a few seconds as she walked away and reflected on the nature of some of the people he had run across in his career: the Teams, Agency work, and even a few bad asses he tangled with since starting Orion Bellicus. I'm glad we're on the same side. This woman is the only person who scares me, he thought, as he gathered his tray and began to walk away himself. Yes, I am VERY glad we are on the same side.

Chapter 38 - Bait

Residence Inn, Northern Virginia

Joe Barber walked back into his room after spending 30 minutes on one of the hotel's treadmills. Four miles in 31 minutes. Not bad, he thought to himself, although he would rather have done it in fewer than 30. He realized that maintaining the same level of conditioning he enjoyed in his 20s while part of the Teams, was unrealistic. But it was part of his wiring to give it everything he could. He took great satisfaction in knowing that if, not quite there, at his ripe old age he was still close. He then dropped to the floor and did 125 push-ups as fast as he could before dropping to the floor again to let his breathing recover. A hot shower and a change into non-descript street clothes completed the process, and he felt invigorated. He picked up his iPhone from the room's desk, touched the phone icon on the bottom row, then favorites, then Marcus Day's name on the list to place the call. Day answered on the first ring.

"Hi Joe. I have a couple of teams of two operators stationed about three miles from the hotel. They have the tracking software, obviously, and will maintain a fix on your location. They have instructions to stand back unless they get specific direction from me or if you activate the distress warning on your phone."

"Sounds, good," Joe replied. "I'm about to venture out right now. I'm going to find a Starbucks at least a few miles from the hotel then plant myself there for a few hours or so to see if I can pick up a tail. Best way to cast myself as bait."

"Good luck and be safe, my friend. We'll be watching you," Day replied.

"I suspect you won't be the only one," Barber said. "The DCI has taken a personal interest in this and my welfare as well. Try and stay out of each other's way."

"Roger that," Day replied. With that the phone went dead.

Northern Virginia, several miles away

The Washington D.C. area and the suburbs of Northern Virginia were home to a large number of people who did various types of work for the government. Many of them worked for the endless number of U.S. Federal Agencies that toiled through countless tasks, some important and some utterly useless. Many of them were employed by private companies that ran the gambit from lobbyist firms to think tanks to private contractors that provided all measure of personalized services, most of them perfectly legal and some, well, not so much. John Dent and Eric Reeds were business partners who maintained a highly specialized practice out of their respective homes in Alexandria. Both were former Army Special Forces, Delta to be exact, tier one, and in their late 30s. The type of service they provided didn't exactly lend itself to a business office, published phone numbers, letterhead and business cards. Potential clients always came via referrals and would contact them via an encrypted internet message board. A handful of highly select clients kept them on an annual retainer to ensure rapid availability. None of their clients knew them by name. They were simply referred to as "The Service". In turn, Dent and Reeds did not know the identity of any of their clients either, although in some cases they had their suspicions, which were more often than not correct. Sometimes the pair operated in the shadows of the law, but on occasion their actions took them completely outside of it. Missions came from several of the various alphabet soup agencies – CIA, NSA, even DIA where "plausible deniability" was essential. Much of their business came from private clients as well. And they operated internationally. Uncooperative Afghan warlords, foreign agents about to go

351

wobbly, as well as any number of other individuals who for whatever reasons disappointed their employers, or were deemed inconvenient, found themselves in the sights of Dent and Reeds. They were the best of the best – the top 10% of the top 1% of the combat soldiers. Each of them could still run a 5K in under 20 minutes, and Reeds could do it in fewer than 19. Both could put a 223 round in a target circle from 1000 yards as well as lethally take down a much larger man while barely breaking a sweat. Neither looked the part in their street clothes, which were deliberately loose fitting so as not to betray their superb conditioning despite both men being almost middle-aged. And Dent's personal grooming was sufficiently relaxed to make him blend seamlessly into any urban center. He sported a long beard that made him look more like a member of Duck Dynasty than a former elite combat veteran. In fact he appeared more goofy than threatening. Reeds maintained a more traditional look, with a high and tight brush cut. This gave them the flexibility as a team to meld into almost any environment. Both were hardened from the experience of multiple deployments in Iraq and Afghanistan, as well as a few other places that were off the books. Their services were expensive, but they always delivered the desired outcome. In almost six years of private contract work they had never failed a mission. Not even once.

John Dent sat in a recent model Ford Taurus and looked at the file on his laptop. The deployment message had come to him about fifteen minutes earlier along with the standard $500,000 deposit to a private bank account in the Caymans that helped verify its validity. His partner, Eric Reeds, sat next to him and quietly surveyed their surroundings. It was a simple wet job as they called it. The method and the tools were entirely their choice. Should be a cakewalk, except they both knew that a cakewalk never required their skill sets. The document on the laptop was the bio on the subject, and it included a fairly detailed account of his military background, including the subject's time in the SEALs. The Op carried a much higher than normal risk. They would have to get close to their target to accomplish the takedown. And they would

352

have to do so without alerting the target to their presence or their intent. The primary issue was not hitting the target. It was doing it in a manner that didn't bring attention to them or create too many witnesses. Shooting or knifing someone in public would certainly accomplish the mission objective. A lot of screaming civilians, however, created way too much risk of being spotted, especially given the extensive use of surveillance cameras in suburban Washington. They had decided that the most judicious approach would be to abduct the target first, transport him to a remote location, then send a .22 caliber bullet into the back of the head. Problem was they both knew the takedown would not be easy. This was no out of shape middle-aged man. They had a ten-year age advantage working in their favor, but Dent and Reeds were far too smart to indulge in a false sense of confidence. They knew Barber's background would make him a formidable adversary, and although his combat skills had likely atrophied, he would still be able to put up quite a fight. And who knows, he could get lucky. Fortunately, they knew where he would be. Their client evidently was able to track the subject's location in some manner, and they were told to standby and wait for intel. They would ID him, wait however long it took for the subject to decide to leave the Starbucks he was supposed to visit, then administer a quick acting sedative with a small pressurized dart to render him more cooperative. Brut force was not an option given the subject's background. It would also create too great a risk of being noticed. The last thing they wanted to deal with was somebody calling the police.

A message appeared on Dent's laptop. "Subject will be headed to Starbucks at 100 Union Street. Intel confirms subject plans to identify and abduct his tail."

"Look at this, partner," Dent said to Eric Reeds, as he turned his laptop towards him so Reeds could see the screen. "How the hell did they know that?"

"I could guess, but I really have no idea. I'll take the intel, though. So this guy is trying to make the hunter the hunted?" Reed asked.

"Evidently. The bio says he is aware of a previous failed attempt to take him down and is expecting a second. He's pretty pissed about it and wants to find out who's after him. So he's going to put himself out there as bait, try and ID one of us, then snatch and interrogate."

"Not a surprise, given his background. This is going to complicate things quite a bit; although we should still have the edge, given we know what the guy is up to. First, we need to stay out of his range. No way can he handle both of us, but we can't risk an altercation. It would blow our cover, he would then know our faces, and it would be game over. We won't get a second chance at this."

"Agreed," Dent replied. "Total failure. This guy can probably spot a tail a mile away. He's obviously betting on being better at his art than we are at ours. It's a good thing we know that up front."

"Absolutely," Reeds said. "So, I think hiding in the wide open is the smartest approach strategy. You should stay in the background. Let's run back by the room quickly and I'll change into the combat greens and grab the military laptop. I'll walk into Starbucks looking like an Army noncom. I'll sit there and pretend I am working on a PowerPoint. If he hasn't moved in an hour or so, you can walk in and check things out yourself, then leave and stay in the area. When he finally gets restless and starts to move, I'll message you and we can follow him out, hopefully towards his car."

"We should stay out of this guy's range until we deploy the dart," Dent replied. "Ideally, we can hit him just as he is getting into his car. That should give us the lowest possible profile. We can drag him to the passenger side then I'll drive to the takedown point and you can follow."

"Done," Dent said. "Problem of course is if things go south the subject is no ordinary mark and will likely try to engage. I'll stay in the background as an insurance policy until you have deployed the dart. If we get made, I've got the silenced LCP. I'll double tap him, then we calmly walk to the car, get out of Dodge and just leave him there."

"I don't like that John. Not a direct hit on the street. There's too much risk of disclosure," Reeds replied. "If we think we've been made, I think one of us needs to call an audible based on whatever circumstances we are dealing with, but no open hit on the street. Not in this area. I'd rather abort than run the risk of being identified."

"OK," Dent replied. "I guess you've got a point. Let's run through a Burger King or something and get a quick bite on the way back to the hotel. We can deploy the minute we see him start to move."

"Sounds good; gotta love GPS tracking!"

* * * * *

Residence Inn, Northern Virginia

Barber walked over to his backpack and pulled out the Glock 19 and a couple of extra loaded magazines. He was more a fan of the Sig, but had to concede that it was a bit too fat and the Glock was easier to conceal, especially if he wanted the extra firepower of a double stack mag. The Sig P226, of course, would be safely tucked into his backpack, just in case. He slipped the Glock into a sticky holster and inserted it inside the waist band of his blue jeans at the small of his back. He took out a Glock 42, the 380-caliber baby Glock as they called it, and strapped on an ankle holster. Redundancy was a good thing, he thought to himself. He slipped a loose fitting windbreaker over his tee shirt for extra concealment, and placed the two additional 9mm magazines in the pocket. "OK, let's go do this thing," he said to himself as he walked out the door and headed to the car.

Northern Virginia, several miles away

"Subject is on the move, partner," Dent said as he looked at the GPS tracking software on his iPhone. "We're about 2 miles now from the target Starbucks. Let's deploy to the area and wait. I'd suggest we give him about 30 minutes or so to get settled there before I walk in."

"Sounds like a plan."

Starbucks Coffee Shop, 100 Union Street, Alexandria Va

Barber walked into the Starbucks and did a quick and discrete scan of the interior. The ambiance was relatively dark, which he liked. He noticed a long table with room for about eight people towards the back. Just behind the table there was a large framed black and white picture of an Alexandria street scene at night with a number of shops with their inside lights glowing to give the photograph drama. To the side there were eight additional, smaller black and white photographs, obviously taken by a photographer who fancied himself or herself an artist. Three large lamps hung over the table and gave it just the right amount of illumination for whoever happened to be working there. Joe noticed two people presently sitting at the table on opposite ends each with their faces buried in their laptops. One was a young woman, probably a college student working on some assignment. The other was a middle-aged man, perhaps an author writing a novel of some sort, or just whiling away his evening hours in the hopes of a hook up. Joe walked up to the table, selected the middle chair against the wall with a great view of the rest of the interior, and set his laptop down without acknowledging either of the other two people at the table. Neither of them looked at him either, even for a brief glance. Useful sign, he thought, and immediately ruled out both of them as a potential tail. He walked up to the counter and ordered a venti

Sumatra, black, with a shot of espresso. It would be the first of several large cups of strong coffee he intended to down that evening. Good to be alert, he thought. He then walked back to the table, placed the steaming coffee next to his backpack and sat down. He unzipped the backpack and retrieved both his Macbook pro and an orange colored copy of the FT, or Financial Times of London. He opened the laptop, booted up Safari and opened the Drudge Report web page, then opened the newspaper, double folded it and started to pretend to read, all the while keeping at least one discrete eye on his surroundings as customers went about their business. Nobody seemed to be displaying behavior that would suggest "tail". After about an hour, and now working on his second caffeine fix, he noticed a soldier walk into the shop, purchase a coffee, then sit down at a table about 15 feet from him. The man wore the insignia of a First Sergeant. He seemed about the right age for the rank. The soldier pulled a military-style looking laptop out of a messenger bag, opened it up, and began to do whatever. Although Barber had quickly glanced at the guy as part of his almost instinctive threat assessment, the soldier had not made eye contact with Barber from the moment he walked into the coffee shop to the moment he began burying his face in his laptop. Barber's first instinct was to believe the guy was exactly what he appeared to be. He noticed the soldier had a 101st Airborne shoulder patch, and his prominent nametag on the right-hand side of the uniform read "GRAHAM". No harm in checking, he thought to himself. He fired up the Orion Bellicus encrypted message board and typed a message that asked Day to check the database for a First Sergeant named Graham from the 101st. Within about three minutes he was reading Day's reply. "No such animal. Only Graham with the 101st is a Light Colonel. Several non-coms named Graham in the Army, but only one First Sergeant, and he's black."

"My guy definitely isn't black," Joe typed.

"Must be a phony."

Joe's interest in the soldier suddenly soared. It was possible the database was wrong. The government wasn't exactly known for setting the bar for accurate record keeping, but Joe had operated on a simple principle his entire life, whether in the Teams, CIA, or running his business. There was no such thing as a coincidence. Admittedly that principle had been wrong a handful of times, but there also were a number of times where believing it had delivered success and even saved his life. He needed a closer look, so he sent Day another message asking him to call Barber's cell phone. In about ten seconds the ringer went off, and Barber got up from the table and walked to the front of the shop by the window to answer the phone, feigning a desire to carry on a conversation that would not disturb the two other people at his table. As he walked towards the front he passed directly to the side of the soldier sitting at his table. As he did so, the man didn't take his eyes off the screen of his laptop. If this guy was somebody after him, he was really good, Joe thought. As he passed the man he glanced down at the four o'clock position on the man's waist. Because the soldier was sitting erect and leaning forward a bit as he tapped away on his laptop's keyboard, the material of his uniform blouse was stretched slightly. This revealed an ever so slight bump just above belt level at about the 4 o'clock position on his waist. It was subtle enough that not a single other person in the coffee shop was likely to notice it, but Barber had a very well-trained and perceptive eye. The bump was the unmistakable print of an automatic pistol's handle. The man was armed. That was a dead giveaway. Soldiers were not armed in public. And even the ones who were allowed to carry weapons, like military police, would do so openly. Nobody in the military would carry an automatic handgun concealed inside their waistband, under their blouse. This guy was definitely a tango. OK, game on, Barber thought to himself.

After a couple of minutes pretending to be engaged in a phony phone call, Barber walked back to his table and sat down again. He opened the window with the encrypted message board and started typing another message to Day. "The man in uniform with the Erikson name plate is armed. He's carrying concealed under the uniform blouse. He's definitely not Army. I'll bet he's part of a wet team, which means he is after me. I'm going to watch him for a bit longer to see if he moves."

"Got it," came the typed reply. "I'm going to move our assets a bit closer just in case this clown tries something."

"Negative," Barber typed back. "I don't want to spook him. I think we can be pretty sure this guy isn't alone, and I suspect they are every bit as talented at spotting a tail as we are. They are handing me a prime opportunity here, and I don't want to blow it. Keep the assets back."

"OK, but I'm doing so under protest," Day typed back.

"I'm serious Marc. Keep them back. Pretty sure he doesn't know he's been made, so I've still got the advantage here." Barber then closed the laptop window and opened a word file that gave the impression he was writing some sort of article, or maybe even a book. There was a constant stream of customers in and out of the shop, none of which looked particularly suspicious. All the time the guy dressed as a soldier kept his eyes buried in his laptop. The guys avoidance of eye contact with anyone was so disciplined it began to appear unnatural to Joe. Then something odd happened. A large man with a flowing grey beard, who looked like a refugee from a Duck Dynasty episode, walked in the door, stood a few feet away from the counter and looked at the boards on the wall as if trying to decide what to order. At about that time the guy dressed as a soldier leaned back in his chair, stretched his arms, and looked around. Joe then noticed he made eye contact with the Duck Dynasty guy. It was brief, but maybe just a nanosecond longer than casual brief. More like intentionally brief, and why make eye contact at all? There was no change in his facial expressions to suggest recognition, but once again Joe didn't believe in coincidences. That must be number two, he thought. He wouldn't alert Day to his intention to start to move. Day could be a mother hen sometimes, and Barber was convinced if he alerted him that Day would move the assets closer, maybe even too close, despite Joe's admonition not to. He was being handed a prime opportunity here and had no intention of blowing it. Day of course was tracking Barber on GPS and would see him start to move, but at least by not saying anything, he would delay Day's reaction by a couple of minutes which could give him time to make a move.

Barber closed his laptop and slid it into the backpack, slung it over his shoulder, stood up and started to walk out. As he did so he intentionally bumped into the Duck Dynasty guy and said, "Excuse me." The unexpected move obviously caught the guy off-guard, and drove an almost involuntary reaction where he and the soldier made eye contact again, this time in a more obvious manner. The soldier's eyes definitely flashed recognition, something the guy probably knew and instantly regretted, but it was the sort of thing that sudden, unexpected moves were designed to flesh out — a failure of tradecraft. Dent and Reeds both independently and simultaneously came to the same conclusion that there was a high probability they had just been made. Both men were professionals, however, and would not allow the slip up to throw them off their game. They wouldn't make the same mistake twice.

Barber walked out of the coffee shop and across the street and looked in the storefront window. He could easily see the Starbucks in the window's reflection, and saw the soldier walk out first and start down the street headed toward where Joe's car was parked. Just a few seconds later, beard-man walked out, crossed the street, and started walking in the same direction only a bit slower. This is the set up, Joe thought to himself. Both men were now wearing what appeared to be Apple ear-buds, but Joe assumed they were likely comms. After staring into the store window a few more seconds, Joe began to walk down the street towards his car as well. At this point, the guy dressed as a soldier was about 50 feet in front of him, and beard-man had slowed his pace and looked into enough windows that he was now about 10 feet to Joe's rear.

"Subject is now about 40 feet behind you," Dent said into the microphone hanging from his right ear bud. "Pretty sure at least you've been made, probably me as well, but I think there's still a chance I'm clear. I suspect he's trying to position himself to grab you. That little incident in the coffee shop seems to have thrown both us and him off of our respective 'A plans'. I suspect the subject is right now trying to figure out what audible he wants to call."

"There's no way I am going to be able to discretely deploy the sedative with him on the alert. And there are too many people still on the street for you just to pop him," Reeds said. "So, forget that. Bad idea."

"Agreed," Dent replied. "I've got a novel idea. For plan B, how about you just ask him nicely to come for a ride with us. I'll flash the laser sight on his head which should make him more cooperative."

"Interesting. He certainly won't be expecting that. Not subtle."

"Do it," Dent said.

As Barber continued to walk in the direction of his car and toward the soldier, he noticed that the guy had stopped walking and was looking into a storefront window. Odd, he thought. The distance between the two men slowly started to close. When Barber was only about 15 feet away, Reeds backed up, turned towards Barber and made direct eye contact with him. "Good evening, Mr. Barber. Hope you enjoyed your coffee tonight."

Chapter 39 – A Failure of Tradecraft

Joe froze in his tracks, momentarily disoriented by the surprise engagement. Not only had the guy spoken to him, he had called him out by name. Obviously, any pretense of deception was being dropped. "My coffee was fine, thank you, and given you seem to know my name, you are obviously not who you appear to be. How may I be of service?" Barber asked, with subtle but distinct sarcasm in the question.

"You have no doubt noticed I am not alone tonight. My partner is the gentleman with the rather prominent beard standing about 15 feet behind you. I can assure you neither of us entertains any intention of harming you. We would simply like you to accompany us for a short ride so we can have a conversation with a little more privacy. You have come to the attention of our employer who is very interested in certain information he suspects you may have."

This guy is good, Barber thought to himself. He knew the part about them having no intention of hurting him was a crock. But they had made him and he was, at least for the moment, still breathing, which was good. Yeah, these guys were really good. "Well, you'll forgive me if I'm not in much of a talkative mood at the moment, and if your employer wishes to have a conversation with me, I suggest he simply give me a call. I suspect he has my number. I'd be happy to give it to you if you wish, otherwise gents I think we can all be on our separate ways." Barber's head was spinning. He realized he had dual objectives at the moment because he had lost the initiative. He had to save his skin, but this was the closest he had gotten to the actual people accountable for this mess, and he wasn't prepared to give up the chance to regain the upper hand and interrogate them. His internal threat radar and flight instincts were raging right now. To completely disengage and retreat, however, could blow an opportunity for him to find out who was after him and why. He stood there, eyes locked with the man in the First Sergeant's uniform, waiting for the next move.

"Well we thought you might feel that way, so my colleague will now provide a quick demonstration of our resolve. If you could be so kind as to turn around and face him, so you can simply better see, of course." Barber slowly turned around, not exactly knowing what to expect. His internal threat radar ratcheted up to maximum signal strength. He noticed the man's right hand appeared to be inside an over-the-shoulder camera bag, with a bright yellow NIKON logo on the front. He then noticed a red dot appear in the middle of his chest. "You may turn around again and face me, my friend," the soldier said. "And to be clear, if you are wearing body armor of some sort, which we assume a man of your background no doubt is, the next time that red dot appears it won't be on center mass, it will be on your forehead. I can assure you that my colleague is an Olympic-caliber shot, if you will forgive the pun. Let me say again that taking such action is the last thing we wish to do and will be totally unnecessary if you will simply cooperate. All we would like is a little conversation. I promise not to take too much of your time."

He was had, and royally pissed at himself for being outflanked. Round one to the bad guys. Reeds once again began to speak, using a tone again as if they were great friends. "Now, Mr. Barber, my colleague is going to close the gap between the two of you by about 5 feet. Not enough to become a threat, but enough to be easily heard. He will provide you with your next instructions. If you could kindly turn and face him again. And I would be ever so grateful if you could do so slowly. Sudden moves make us very nervous, especially from a man with your background and training. As I am sure you have assumed, I am armed as well. Only as a precaution, of course. Once again let me assure you we mean no harm. We wish to stay out of your range as much as you desire the same."

Bullshit, Joe thought to himself. But he had to hand it to them. These guys knew how to keep someone off guard. He began to slowly turn towards beard-man, all the while with a growing concern that he was running out of options. As Barber completed his turn, he locked eyes with Dent and Dent smiled. Reeds slowly retrieved from his right pocket a device that looked like a small flashlight, raised his hand and aimed it at the back of Barber's neck. A red dot appeared at the desired point of entry, at which point he pushed a button. An almost silent but nevertheless powerful burst of compressed air propelled a small dart into the base of Joe Barber's neck. At the moment the dart entered his skin, the force of impact injected a small dose of Etorphine hydrochloride and Tubocurarine, a powerful combination of a fast-acting sedative and a neuromuscular blocking agent. The problem with using these drugs, of course, was the dosage. Too much would kill a man, and too little might not deliver the necessary effect. The dart had been dosed based on Barber's weight. The intent was to immobilize him for the first few seconds before he passed out, which would make it easier to get him into the vehicle. Allowing him to collapse on the spot created too much risk of inviting unwanted attention. This had to be low profile, and Barber becoming wobbly could be explained to any inquisitive bystanders as him just having a bit too much to drink. Joe felt the prick of the dart as it entered the back of his neck. The sensation itself was momentarily disorienting. By the time he realized what had happened, a second or two later, his body was rapidly becoming numb and refusing to answer his commands. Damn, he thought to himself. Mistake number two, and his last conscious thought was the fury he felt about being caught off guard. Dent and Reeds quickly walked up to him and each grabbed an arm and walked him to the car just a few feet away. They opened the back door and slid him onto the seat as his body was quickly becoming limp. Round two to the bad guys.

The dosage seemed to be perfect. Seemed to be, that is. What they hadn't accounted for was the 30 milligrams of Adderall XR Joe had popped right before he entered the Starbucks, or the three large cups of black coffee he had downed, each fortified with a shot of espresso. Round three was going to be interesting.

Chapter 40 – Rising Confusion

NDSA HQ, a Few Minutes Later

Ed Rodgers' back went straight as he yanked off his headphones and threw them on his desk. With one fluid motion, he then pushed his chair back slightly and spun it to the right to face Brian Falzone, who was sitting next to him. "Shit," he yelled as he knocked over a large cup of coke with the inelegant moves. The arc of the headphones in their downward flight towards the large cup caused it to spin slightly as its side hit the table, ejecting a large portion of the cup's contents not only all over Rodgers' shirt but also on Falzone's pants.

"Hey!" Falzone barked. "What's with you?"

"Sorry! You're not going to believe this, but I think Barber was just abducted by someone," he said, astonishingly.

"What?" Falzone replied.

"Seriously, man!" Rodgers exclaimed. "Listen to this," as he quickly cropped a copy of the conversation to where Barber had been confronted, then with two clicks of his computer mouse he highlighted it and emailed it to his partner.

"Whoa!" Falzone exclaimed, as he immediately listened to the conversation. "You need to get this to Green, like 30 seconds ago!"

"Already on it," Rodgers responded, just as he clicked send a second time, this time to his boss. "I'm calling Agent Green right now as well. Keep listening to this channel while I do. I don't want us to miss anything." With that Rodgers pushed the button that connected him directly to Agent Green's office. He was relieved to hear her pick up on the second ring. "Agent

Green, you've got to listen to the file I just emailed you. It sounds like Barber was just abducted by two men outside the Starbucks in Alexandria as he was walking to his car. Do we have an op in progress right now?" He asked, regretting the question the moment it came out of his mouth.

"Ops are above your pay grade, Ed. But I can tell you, at least this time, the answer to that is absolutely not. We are under strict instructions to monitor, but not engage. Hold on while I listen to this. I'm putting you on hold."

Green felt a chill as she listened to the conversation. She knew if there was an op, she likely would be aware of it and would have been directed to follow the conversations from the field as part of ongoing support for Colonel Richardson. She highlighted the file herself and emailed it to Jennings, then reached across her desk and touched the icon on her call director to connect her with his office. "Just emailed you a phone conversation. Listen to it now. I'd like to know if there's an op going on to abduct Barber, and if so why I wasn't aware of it," she said, with an accusing tone in her voice."

"Hang on a second," Jennings replied, as he clicked on the file and listened. "I'll be damned," he said. "I don't know anything about this. But I can assure you I am about to find out. Hold tight, and I'll be back to you shortly." Jennings then highlighted the file and emailed it to Colonel Richardson. He then quickly bolted out of his chair, blew past his secretary and almost ran towards Richardson's office.

When he arrived, he threw open her office door and almost slammed it behind him. Richardson, momentarily stunned by the dramatic entry, was on the phone, but looked up and asked, "What's going on?"

"Hang up now, Julia!" Jennings shouted. Richardson told whoever she was talking to she'd have to call him back, disconnected the call then looked up at Jennings again. "Settle down, Ryan, there had better be a very good reason for this drama."

"You bet there is," Jennings said. "Are you running an op right now on Barber, and if so, who approved it and why wasn't I, or anybody on my team in the loop?" he asked.

"Slow down," she almost barked. "I don't know what you are talking about. What Op?"

"I just emailed you an audio file the lab recorded from Sparrow less than ten minutes ago. Listen to it now."

With a puzzled look on her face, she turned towards her laptop, tapped a couple of keys, and a conversation began playing from the speaker sitting on her desk. They both stood there and listened to the portion of the conversation that occurred on the side street next to the Starbucks in Alexandria. "Somebody must have gone off the reservation. I don't know anything about this, Ryan, and no, we are not running an op of any kind." She then thought, "I probably would have refused that order anyway."

"My team is now tracking them via GPS, and they appear to be in a vehicle headed west," he said.

"Well, they couldn't very well head east, now could they?" she asked.

"Sarcasm noted and not appreciated," he replied.

"Sorry," she said. "Any intel on their intentions?"

"Nothing," Jennings said. "But I doubt it's good."

"Agreed. We need to go see Director Collins on this right away. I'm going to ask that we call an emergency ExComm meeting."

Within minutes they had briefed the Director. "I don't want to take the time to get ExComm together, I'll brief the members via phone in a few minutes. Can you get your people in the field quickly enough to intervene?" he asked.

"I don't know," Richardson replied, "but I'm on it and I'll certainly try."

"Good," the Director responded. "If you get there in time, sedate Barber and get him back here along with his abductors. We'll figure out what to do with him later, but I want those abductors conscious for questioning. Maybe this will be the break we need to figure out who the other players are in all of this mess."

In less than 3 minutes Richardson was back in the Command Center and watching as they continued to track Barber's movement real time via GPS. She confirmed there were assets in place close enough to give them at least a chance to interdict. But it was going to be close, real close. And the assets were green – just a few months with the organization. Also, they worked for Jennings, not her. What a mess, she thought. You can't make this stuff up.

Chapter 41 – Primal

In a Vehicle Somewhere West of Alexandria

Barber was sitting in the back seat on the driver's side of the Taurus with his head resting against the A-pillar, eyes closed and mouth wide open. Reeds sat in the passenger side of the front seat and periodically glanced back at him to ensure he remained unconscious. About 25 minutes down the road, Barber slowly began to experience a sense of motion as he gradually started to regain his faculties. The Adderall and the caffeine had shortened the impact of the drugs. As the fog in his head began to lift, he recalled the conversations with the two men outside of Starbucks and then slowly began to regain appreciation of the threat that confronted him. As he sat there he kept his eyes closed and his mouth open so Dent and Reeds would remain unaware that the sleeping dog was coming back to life. As the ride progressed, Barber noticed the ambient noise from the surroundings began to fade. Not nearly as much traffic, he concluded, so they must be progressing towards a more rural area. He could no longer detect any of the normal sounds associated with a city or even a suburb. The intent of his captors was now becoming all too obvious. Drive him to some remote area, execution style shooting of an unconscious man, no doubt with a bullet to the back of the head, likely with a small caliber handgun like a .22. Then deposit the body somewhere it would take days to discover. His hands were behind him trapped between his body and the back of the seat. He could feel his wrists tightly bound with a zip-tie of some sort. At the moment, his hands were useless as a weapon. But he always had a backup plan. It was a last-ditch defensive maneuver he had learned at the Farm. It was too brutal even the Teams, but highly effective. Nobody could even begin to contemplate using it unless it was their last hope. He had never used it before. He had never even practiced it, except on a dummy. It was personally revolting. But this was life or death.

371

It required a modest knowledge of human anatomy. He had certainly studied that. As Barber began thinking through the plan he started flexing the muscles throughout his body as a way to warm them up and improve blood flow. Isometric flexing also would quicken his recovery from the after effects of whatever drugs were administered. As he did so, he became much more optimistic about the outcome of round three. He knew that optimism and self-confidence were key elements of success in any encounter. The best way to lose a fight before it even began was to concede defeat upfront. He was not about to do that.

Barber could feel the vehicle slow down. It then made a turn onto a road that felt much rougher. They must be getting close to wherever they intended to do their deed. After a few more minutes the Taurus gradually came to a stop. He heard Reeds speak to Dent and say, "I'm going to take a quick walk and scout out a proper place. There's a creek about 20 yards into the woods and it's about 4 feet deep. We'll tie the pair of 50-pound dumb bells to him and drop him there. That should buy us at least a week before anyone discovers him. If we are lucky he may be eaten by then as well, which will add a few more days to the authorities figuring out his identity. Probably have to use dental records after that."

"Sounds like a plan, Partner. I'll drag him a few feet into the woods before I pop him. Should make it harder to see the blood splatter from the road."

"Good. I'll be back in a few minutes." With that, Barber heard the passenger-side car door open and Reeds get out. There was a distinct sound of brush crunching as Reeds began walking into the woods. A few seconds later, the driver's side door opened. "This is it," Barber thought to himself. He heard Dent get out of the car, and within a second or two Joe's door opened. Eyes still closed, he sensed Dent's entry into the vehicle and felt a hand slide under his right armpit as Dent obviously was about to extract Barber from the car.

NDSA HQ, Real Time

Ed Rodgers shot vertical right out of his chair as he grabbed his phone and this time hit the button to connect him to Green's cell. She answered on the first ring. "Getting a real time conversation again," he barked, this time with a controlled voice. "Sounds like they are about to pop him and drop him in a creek. GPS shows our guys are still at least 20 minutes out."

"Richardson!" Rodgers could hear Green yell through the phone as she tried to get the Lt. Colonel's attention. "Just intercepted a conversation that they are likely just minutes from executing Barber. We are too late?"

In a Vehicle Now Stopped Somewhere West of Alexandria

In movies or novels, catastrophic blood loss from the neck area is often associated with damage to the jugular vein. In truth, however, the carotid arteries of the neck are far more vulnerable, with the outer carotid lying closer to the surface at the base of the neck and close to the Adams apple. Sever one of those, and it's absolute game over. As Dent began to pull on Barber to lift him out of the car, Joe subtly slung one of his feet out of the car onto the road to provide more leverage. This was now Joe's point of maximum advantage. Dent's perception of threat was low, due to Joe's apparent unconsciousness. He didn't even notice the move. Pulling Joe out of the vehicle was a process that required both hands, so Dent's 9mm remained inside the waist band, or IWB holster and the .22 intended for the deed itself remained inside his jacket pocket. As Dent inserted his right hand under Joe's left armpit and began to pull, it happened. Barber became an animal. With all the force he could muster he uncoiled his body with an upward thrust towards Dent, propelling his mass with the leg he had swept out of the car. Dent's head collided with the upper door frame of the vehicle with a violent force from the upper thrust, temporarily stunning him and adding a few extra milliseconds to Barber's advantage. As part of the same fluid motion, Barber opened his mouth wide and with the aid of the upward thrust forced as much of the lower right-hand side of the base of Dent's neck into his mouth. He then bit down as hard as he could and twisted his head viciously to accent the move with a primal tearing motion worthy of an attack by a wild animal. He had to hold down the bile rapidly rising in his throat in response to the coppery taste of blood that was overwhelming his senses. A massive chunk of Dent's flesh, along with a piece of his severed carotid artery left Dent's body and was hurled towards the road as Joe reopened his mouth and flung his head to the side to release the prize. Dent tried to scream but nothing audible came out, just an horrific gurgling sound. He was dead before he hit the ground, although the heart took several more seconds to get the message as blood from his neck continued to squirt like a fountain and stain the ground. The scene was horrific. The arterial spray looked like someone was squirting blood out of a garden hose, and even though Joe completed his motion by pushing Dent to the side with his shoulder, he couldn't help but be soaked by a good portion of the blood. Barber's face looked like something out of a Hannibal Lecter movie. He kicked Dent's lifeless body over and noticed a knife clipped to his blue jeans pocket. He retrieved the knife with his hands, which were still zip tied behind his back, opened it, then cut off the tie. He then retrieved Dent's 9mm from its holster and began to take a walk into the woods. Round three to the good guys.

NSDA HQ, A Few Minutes Later

Amanda Green and Ryan Jennings both stood a few feet behind Colonel Richardson and listened intently to the chatter in their Bose noise cancelling headphones. Everyone heard the conversation between Dent and Reeds and the intentions of the two men towards Barber were now crystal clear. They planned to kill him and dump his body in a stream. There were sounds of car doors opening and closing, then the distinct sounds of leaves or brush crunching under someone's feet, likely as one of the assailants started walking into the woods to find the ideal spot for the execution. A second car door then opened, and the feed coming from Sparrow sounded like some kind of altercation. Why an altercation? Barber was presumably unconscious. If it was between Dent and Reeds, it was odd there were no voices accompanying it. The background audio delivered by Sparrow then became just noise. They continued to listen intently for several more minutes, expecting to hear gunfire as Dent made good on his threat, but things remained quiet for what seemed like an eternity. Then there was a rustling of leaves and something like the sound of small tree branches breaking. A gunshot rang out, followed by total silence again.

"What was all that?" Jennings asked.

"Computer analysis of that noise is inconclusive," Richardson said. "If I had to guess I would say there was some kind of altercation. Maybe Barber managed somehow to overpower the assailant who stayed with him at the vehicle."

"That seems highly improbable given what we heard up to that point," Green said.

"Agreed," Richardson said. "GPS confirms our agents are about two minutes from the site." She then pressed a button attached to the headphone cord and spoke directly with the two agents in the field. "Let me repeat rules of engagement, gentlemen. This is a mission to arrest and transport. You are to identify yourselves as Federal Agents and inform anyone on the scene that your intent is to take them in to protective custody. Under no circumstances are you to use deadly force. Let me repeat, under no circumstances are you to use deadly force. If you are fired upon, you are to disengage and retreat to a safe distance. If pursued, you are to exfil the area immediately. Are these rules of engagement clear?" she asked.

"Clear," the first agent replied.

"Clear," the second agent replied. "We just arrived on location", the second agent continued. "We see the car. No sign of …. oh my God," he said with a startled voice. "One man down. Blood everywhere. Nasty wound at the base of his neck. Subject is not Barber. No sign of Barber or the other man."

"Gunshot wound?" Richardson asked.

"No," the agent replied. "It's horrific. Looks like part of the guys throat has been literally ripped out. Almost like a bobcat attack, or maybe even a small bear."

"Barber must have taken him out in that altercation we heard," Jennings said.

"I don't see how a man could create a wound like that," the agent replied, "unless his killer was about to use an improvised weapon on him to make it look like an animal attack and Barber somehow got his hands on it."

"Figuring out the murder weapon is not the priority at the moment," Richardson said. "Do not pursue subject into the woods. Do not stand in the open. Retreat to your vehicle and take cover behind the doors and wait."

"Roger that," the first agent replied.

Both men returned to their car, opened the side doors and positioned themselves just behind the doors in a manner that gave them a fairly clear view of the other vehicle. Their car was positioned far enough from the other vehicle so that it wouldn't be immediately seen the moment either of the remaining men emerged from the woods. Both agents peered through their night vision binoculars as they crouched and waited. They didn't have to wait very long.

"I hear the crunching of brush," the first agent whispered into his mike. "Somebody is definitely walking towards the vehicle from the woods. Subject has just emerged. It's Barber. He seems to be alone. No sign of the other man."

"That gunshot must have been Barber taking out his other abductor," Jennings said over the comm net.

Close Proximity to the Vehicle Stopped Somewhere West of Alexandria

Joe emerged from the woods and began to walk towards the vehicle. Time to get out of Dodge, he thought, before anyone stumbled onto the bloody scene. He knew his ride should be fairly close, as Day would be following his moves via GPS. A backup team likely would have been sent immediately after it was clear Barber had been abducted. He was not happy he had to shoot the other guy, but he knew he had no choice. And after his encounter with Dent squeezing a trigger almost seemed benign by comparison. Reeds had obviously heard someone coming and had become suspicious. When Joe found him he couldn't get close enough to the guy to

378

physically take him down before Reeds raised his gun to fire. There was no choice but to shoot first. Unfortunately, dead men make lousy interrogation subjects, he thought. The beam of a strong flashlight aimed directly at his eyes suddenly interrupted Joe's thoughts.

"Federal Agents," a voice called out. "Drop your weapon."

Joe turned around and spotted the government-looking sedan with both front doors open. Well, I guess I'm not going to buy a lottery ticket today with this luck, he thought. He tossed the pistol about five feet or so in front of him, and then raised his hands. He took comfort in the fact he still had Reeds' Glock in his right jacket pocket. "Federal Agents from what agency? Let me see your credentials," Joe said.

Both men slowly stood out from behind the open car doors, and with guns continuing to point at Joe, withdrew something from their pockets. Each flashed a gold-colored shield that was impossible for Joe to read. His immediate thought was these guys were likely phonies, but he knew that killing a couple of Federal Agents would bring pandemonium on him and his company. He had to be sure before he acted. "What Federal Agency?" he asked again.

"There'll be time enough for proper introductions in a few minutes," one of the men said. "For the moment, my partner and I would appreciate it if you would please remove your jacket and toss it in front of you as well."

Both men appeared a bit nervous to Joe. This was good, he thought to himself. First, because it meant these guys were unlikely to be another wet team after him. Pros wouldn't be nervous, and besides, they would have already shot him by this point. Second, if they were not pros, they should be easy to take down if he could only close the distance between himself and the two men. There also was something very suspect about the way they displayed their creds and their refusal to identify their Agency. Even the creds themselves were suspect. They were shields emblazoned with the moniker Federal Agent, but the shield didn't say which agency. The right-hand side of the shield wallet was illegible from this distance and no help. Also, they weren't wearing windbreakers. If they were FBI, they would be wearing the standard field windbreakers. The same thing would be true if they worked for somebody like Secret Service or even NCIS. No windbreakers. And agents were trained to announce their affiliation when confronting a suspect. Something was very much out of sorts. It then occurred to him that these guys may be well worth interrogating. Maybe the night would not be a waste after all.

One of the agents spoke up again. "Now, sir," he said with more of a command, but with a voice that still betrayed a lack of confidence to Joe's well-trained ear. "We've been instructed to take you into protective custody and ask a few questions. My guess is the scene here would suggest protective custody would be a pretty good idea right about now."

"Not so sure about that, gents. As you can see I'm still standing, and this dude isn't," Barber retorted.

"You were lucky tonight, Mr. Barber. I'm not so sure I would want to count on that luck holding. Besides, it's not a request. You are under arrest."

Barber slowly removed his jacket and tossed it in front of him as instructed. As he did so he said, "I gotta tell you, you're the second pair of guys who asked me to go for a ride tonight and answer a few questions. Didn't go so well for the first two."

"Are you threatening Federal Agents, sir?" one of them asked, again with clear nervousness in his voice.

"Not at all," Barber replied. "I'm just trying to explain my natural skepticism at the moment."

"Now my partner and I are going to slowly approach, and he will cuff you while I cover."

Rookie mistake, Barber thought. Whoever these clowns worked for, their training, or maybe their discipline, was woefully inadequate. The second man should always stay back to cover so he or she is out of reach of the subject. This could put both men within his range. He would take them down with non-lethal force. Then they would be the ones going for that drive to answer a few questions. Maybe his luck was improving.

Richardson spoke into the comms net. "One of you stay back!" she almost shouted. "Don't allow him to get within range of both of you! This guy is ex-special forces!"

It was too late. Whether the two of them didn't hear what she said, or they were so amped up at what they were about to do that it didn't matter. Both men eased around the car doors and started to walk. Barber stood there with his hands still up in the air as both agents slowly approached. Richardson was now holding her breath. Jennings let out a "you dumb bastards" as neither man acknowledged Richardson's admonition. As they closed to about three feet, the first agent stopped walking. The second continued to walk and pulled a pair of conventional handcuffs out of his pocket. As he got another foot closer, he told Barber to turn around. Barber smiled and started to turn, but as he did so he executed a swift roundhouse kick to the man's midsection. A knockout punch has three essential elements. The first is surprise. Barber accomplished this one in spades. Possession of a handgun can give a lesser man a false sense of security that relaxes his defenses just enough. The second is accuracy. Extensive training, to say nothing of his field experience, gifted Barber with an extraordinary ability to land a blow exactly where he wanted. The third was power. This one he would hold back a bit. His intention was to temporarily stun to gain the upper hand, not to kill or maim. That would not go well if they really turned out to be Federal Agents.

As the first agent began to fall to the ground, the second agent was momentarily disoriented while trying to process what just happened. A moment's hesitation was exactly what Joe needed. Before the agent holding the gun could refocus, Joe swung his left hand in a downward arc towards the gun, which pushed the weapon towards the left and pointed it to the ground. Barber then swung his right arm with a cupped hand violently against the man's ear, twisting his shoulders to amplify the force of the impact. The force of the blow and the compression of air from the cupped hand burst the agent's eardrum, creating a lightning bolt of intense pain. This gave Barber the milliseconds he needed to re-cock his arm and swing again, this time with the base of his palm. He struck the man's temple with the hard boney part of the hand where the thumb is attached. The man immediately fell to the ground unconscious. Before either man could get back into the fight, Barber had their hands behind their backs secured with plastic zip-ties.

Time to figure out who these guys were. He retrieved the creds of the unconscious agent out of the guy's pocket and opened the wallet-styled container for a closer look. WTF, he thought to himself. National Security Agency? Why the hell would the National Security Agency be interested in him. Then it hit him like a ton of bricks. The NSA must be the agency behind all of this. This evening was not lost after all. Interrogating these two gents was going to be very illuminating.

NDSA HQ, Real Time

"I don't like the sound of this," Colonel Richardson said. "Agents, SITREP, do you have suspects in custody?"

No answer.

"Colonel, I suspect the kerfuffle you heard was Barber overpowering both of our people," Amanda Green replied, with resignation.

"Agents, I said report. Report NOW!" the Colonel barked into the microphone.

Still silence.

"Well that's a fine kettle of fish, Special Agent Jennings," Richardson said in a highly sarcastic tone as she pronounced the title Special Agent.

"They were up against a former special forces operator," he replied. "We knew this could happen."

"What I know is we were trying to arrest a former special forces operator and two trained killers, and you send Bert and Ernie," she barked in reply. "So much for overruling my tactical judgment."

Jennings just stood there and didn't reply.

"Moron," she whispered under her breath. The comm. net remained open, however, and everyone heard the remark.

Chapter 43 – An Existential Threat

Close Proximity to the Vehicle Stopped Somewhere West of Alexandria

Barber retrieved his iPhone and placed a call to Day. Day answered on the first ring. "Backup is about 3 minutes out," Day said. "How are you? Do you need medical attention?"

"Details later, Marc. I'm fine, and I've got a couple of prizes here. Two Federal Agents from the NSA just tried to arrest me. Claimed they wanted to take me into protective custody. This all happened after a wet team made a second attempt on me, but both of those guys are dead now. I need a safe house prepped and ready with a chemical kit in 30 minutes so I can have a chat with our guests."

"Did you say NSA, as in National Security Agency?" Day asked.

"That's correct," Barber replied.

"Since when did the National Security Agency employ armed field agents? That doesn't make any sense."

"Agreed, partner. That's one of the things I intend to find out."

"They are obviously tracking your movements," Day said. "Most logical explanation is they are using the GPS on your phone, so get rid of it, and make sure you do the same with both of the agents' phones. We'll have another phone waiting for you at the safe house along with a jamming device. Go to location Uniform Mike Twelve. Got it? Uniform Mike Twelve."

"Got it," Joe replied. "And one more thing, Marc."

"What's that?" Day replied.

"I suggest you get rid of your phone as well."

"Way ahead of you, buddy. I've got a burn phone at the moment, and the vehicle is equipped with a jammer."

"My apologies for even the suggestion," Barber said, and with that all communications went dead. Before he pulled away, Barber injected both men with a dose of the drug Versed from the interrogation kit Day had provided. Nurses liked to call the drug "Milk of Amnesia". It would wipe their memory of most of what was going to transpire over the near term.

NDSA Headquarters

"Shit!" Jennings yelled out as they all listened to the conversation between Barber and Day. "Is there any way to track our two guys without their phones?" he asked.

"Not without their phones," Rodgers replied.

"What about their car?" Jennings shot back. "Don't we have a tracking device on the car?" he asked.

"No Sir," Rodgers replied.

"Why the hell not?" Jennings was almost shouting now.

"Settle down, Ryan." Colonel Richardson's words came over the comm net. She was now using her command voice and was displaying a much higher level of self-control than Jennings. "Vehicles used by my special ops are equipped with tracking devices, but we never envisioned using a Special Agent's vehicle in a tactical situation. That was your idea."

Jennings took a breath to try and regain his composure. He was not unaware that his present behavior was viewed as unsettling. "Ok, I get it," he responded. "So how do you suggest we get our guys back?" he asked.

"We may just have to let this play out a bit more. Look, Barber is pissed but he's also rational, and he has a lot at stake that's likely to restrain him. Taking out two guys who were obviously about to kill him is one thing. Murdering two Federal Agents is another thing entirely. No way he's going to do that."

"I'm more worried about him interrogating them," Jennings replied, regretting the words the minute they came out of his mouth. Everyone looked at him, and Colonel Richardson looked like she was about to leap across the table that separated them and grab him by the throat. His face flushed as he quickly tried to craft another comment that would limit the damage. "Obviously I didn't mean that the way it sounded. What I meant was we cannot allow Barber to interrogate these guys. It could unravel this entire organization. And besides, we all heard him ask for a chemical kit, Julia. Doesn't sound so harmless to me."

"He's probably just going to try and loosen their tongues a bit, or maybe try and scare them," Richardson said. "No way is he going to do anything harmful. Besides, given the way we compartmentalize things, these guys really don't know that much. All they know is that they were sent to serve a protection warrant for a person of interest whom we believed to be in danger. That's going to become quickly evident to Barber, and when it does, he is likely to just leave them someplace. We may even get some useful intelligence from them when they are recovered."

"Those two agents know they work for me. They know my name. They know about this building and they know at least some of the things that go on here. We're not THAT compartmentalized," Jennings replied.

"He's right," another voice announced over the comms net. It was the voice of Director Collins, who was following the communications network real-time from his office. "Find those two, before this organization is irreparably compromised. I'm gathering a meeting of ExComm within the hour. It's time to resurrect those contingencies. We need to cauterize this wound and stop its hemorrhaging."

Richardson's and Jennings' eyes met in response to the Director's comment. She could detect a faint but distinct smile on his face and noted how he held eye contact with her this time, which was not characteristic of their previous stare-downs. "The only contingency I'm going to contemplate," she thought to herself, "is the one against you, asshole."

Palo Alto, California, Offices of PrinSafe

Westy Reynolds sat at his desk and stared into the 10K report in front of him. He was deep into the minutia. It was how he always did business. Always know more than the guy sitting across from you, always. And always take the time and the effort to sweat the details. An outsized IQ, he realized, was of little help if you didn't use it to arm yourself better than the other guy. It was a principle he applied to everything he did. The ring of his phone momentarily disrupted his concentration. He pressed the button on the intercom to answer his secretary. "There's a Mr. Edwards on line one, sir. He asks that you call him on a secure line about his capital offer."

"Thanks," Reynolds said. With that he picked up the receiver connected to a scrambled Iridium satellite line and pressed 3 numbers which represented a coded speed dial line. The line was answered on the second ring. "What's up, Dennis?" he asked before the man on the other end could say anything.

"I have bad news," the caller replied. "Second attempt failed. Subject terminated both members of the team. The Service is down, permanently."

Reynolds pushed the red "end" button and disconnected the call. He already knew. Dr. Emma Clark had called him about 5 minutes ago and relayed the salient points of the encounter, which she had followed in real-time. Maybe it was time to exercise his stop loss, he thought to himself. It had been a great idea, but an idea that was implemented by incompetent fools.

Chapter 44 – The Inquisition

Orion Bellicose Safe House, Northern Virginia, Location Code 12 Uniform Mike

The room was unsettling. Almost "Silence of the Lambs" unsettling. Certainly scary enough to loosen the tongue of anyone who had never been held against their will. Joe stood in the dim light and looked at the two agents. It was a relatively small space in the interior of the safe house, measuring about 15 feet by 15 feet. Both men remained quiet and compliant. That was good, Barber thought. It signaled they were very green, and likely had never experienced anything like this before. It signaled they were clearly very frightened.

Each man was secured to a metal, folding chair with arms and legs securely duck-taped in place. Their mouths also were covered with duct tape, although that was arguably a redundant measure. Barber told them screaming would do them no good because nobody could hear them and screaming would only piss him off. Unbeknown to the two agents, the odors of human sweat, as well as the faint smell of urine and otherwise soiled clothing were being pumped into the room from vents positioned at the top of the walls. The noxious odors were intended to reinforce a subliminal message that this was a very unpleasant place and a place where unpleasant things were likely done. It worked. A series of sub-woofers fed a steady stream of infrasound, or sound waves below 20hz, throughout the space, which gave the specially designed floor a rather creepy vibration.

There was a folding table at the side of the room positioned to be clearly visible by the guests. Resting on the table were an electric drill and an electric chain saw. Joe picked up the drill and looked at it reflectively, almost admiringly. He then turned towards the men and pressed the trigger. It filled the room with its high-speed whine. The sound was reminiscent of the interrogation scene in the movie Marathon Man where Dustin Hoffman was about to have his un-anesthetized tooth drilled by the Nazi Dentist, and who was played with a superb menacing demeanor by Sir Laurence Olivier. Barber then lay down the drill and picked up the chain saw. Both men's eyes now looked like they were going to bulge out of their heads. As Barber pulled the tool's trigger he immediately filled the room with another sound, even more menacing. It was a sound that was not supposed to be heard indoors. Barber had no intention of using either tool to harm the men, but they didn't know that. He wanted to take their fear to a whole new level. The tactic worked.

One of the agents had his back positioned next to an open shower stall. It was one of those showers where the floor was only recessed about an inch. A loose hanging curtain served as the only barrier between the shower and the rest of the room. The shower curtain was drawn back about half way revealing a faint smell of bleach, as though someone had just scrubbed and sanitized the space, perhaps to clean up some ungodly act perpetrated on an earlier guest. Barber hoped the agent had seen the movie Scarface, especially one of the opening scenes where Tony Montana was witness to a particularly unpleasant interrogation conducted in a shower.

The second agent was positioned about seven feet away with his chair turned about 90 degrees from the first. This allowed the second agent a restricted view of his colleague but prevented a direct line of sight. It was a clear enough view to ensure he could see what was going on, but not clear enough to detect any sleight of hand. Barber wore a black balaclava, even though both men had already seen his face. It created a menacing look that added to the men's fear and confusion.

Joe tossed a couple of face towels into a plastic bucket and carried it to the shower stall. He then grabbed the handle of the removable showerhead, pulled it out of its holder, turned on the water and began to fill the bucket. As he did so, the eyes of the man positioned next to the shower morphed into terror as he realized what was about to happen. Barber was careful to maintain eye contact, in part to gauge the man's mental state, but also to continue the menacing appearance. As he noticed the agent's eyes, he almost felt a pang of guilt. He strongly suspected they were just a couple of pawns in the overall scheme of things. This made him even angrier with their bosses. All the better that this was going to end quickly, he reflected again. He had no desire to abuse these guys any more than necessary. But they were clearly in possession of information he had to have - information he had every intention of extracting.

Barber forcefully grabbed the back of the chair and slammed it down onto the floor of the shower stall, such that the man's face was now looking upward. The initial downward thrust was violent and stunned the agent. Barber was careful, however, to break the speed of the fall at the last minute to avoid serious injury. He didn't want to concuss the guy. The violence of his initial action masked the breaking move as the entire thing morphed into one fluid motion. The man was now attempting to scream through the duct tape, and Barber barked out an order to "shut up" as if he were a drill sergeant dressing down a new Marine recruit just stepping off the bus. A shove of Barber's toe into the man's ribcage reinforced the command. It was done with enough force to affirm unmistakable domination but, again not enough to injure. By this time, of course, the agent was incapable of discerning such subtle differences. All he felt was a foot, and it hurt. The man's screaming immediately stopped. Barber briefly looked over at the other agent whose eyes were now wide with fear as he strained to see what was going on.

Barber then turned back to the man in the shower stall and said, "We're going to have a little conversation, my friend. I am going to ask you several questions, and it is very important that you answer truthfully and completely. How unpleasant this is will depend entirely on you. I have no desire to be any more unpleasant than necessary. I'm in a bit of a hurry, as well, so you should expect me to rapidly escalate the intensity of our conversation if you are the slightest bit uncooperative." It was a time-honored tradition of successful interrogations: first create fear, then hope, and fear again. Punishment or reward represented a simple binary function. And all men, no matter how strong they were, had their breaking point. Joe suspected these two guys had breaking points considerably below average. He continued, "I'm going to remove the duct tape from your mouth now. It's hard for us to have a proper conversation with you wearing it. Before I do, I'll remind you again that nobody will be able to hear you scream, and if you do so it will just piss me off. Do we understand each other?" Barber asked. The man's eyes were still wide with fear and he seemed almost catatonic. "Answer me, my friend," Barber continued. "Simply shake your head yes if you understand and promise to be a good boy." The man shook his head yes. With that, Barber yanked off the duct tape, hard, intentionally causing the man pain. "I've not seen creds like yours before," Barber observed. "Your shield looks very official, although they are admittedly easy to forge. I wasn't aware that the National Security Agency deployed armed, credentialed agents in the field on U.S. soil. What part of the NSA do you work for, and who is your boss?" Barber asked.

"I'm a Federal Agent. That's all you need to know. You're facing a heap of trouble," the first agent said.

"Wrong answer," Barber retorted, and with that he placed a soaking wet towel over the man's face and began to slowly pour the bucket of water on it. The man started screaming, but as his lungs depleted their air, the sound ebbed into a muffled gurgle. Barber let the moment linger just a few seconds after the contents of the bucket were emptied, then pulled the towel off the man's face. The agent began gasping desperately to refill his lungs.

"Let's try this again," Barber said. "Who do you work for? Your department and boss's name, please."

The man on the floor was now crying, but to Barber's surprise he continued to resist. "I can't tell you that," the agent said with a sense of desperation. "Who are you and why are you doing this to us?" the agent asked.

"Wrong answer again, my friend," Barber said with a calm voice. "And I'll ask the questions if you don't mind. By the way, at the moment I'm not doing this to the two of you, as your question suggests, I'm doing it to you. Your friend over there is next if we don't get anywhere." With that, he draped the towel over the man's face and began pouring water from a refilled bucket. Same result. The man screamed desperately, then the screams softened to a sickening gurgle as his lungs depleted their air. Now it was time to stage the *coup de gras*. Barber leaned down over the man so as to block the other agent's line of sight and retrieved a small syringe from his pocket. He then quickly gave the man an injection of Ketamine before removing the towel from his face. The agent immediately went limp. Barber pulled the towel back so as to uncover the man's mouth and nose and let him breath, but remained crouched over the man for several more seconds before completely removing the towel from his face and tossing it aside. The effect was to appear as though he was continuing to hold the towel in place. Barber then stood up and lightly kicked the agent in the ribcage again and barked out the order "wake up". He jostled the man's side with his foot a few more times before bending down and slapping him in the face. All the time the terror on the other agent's face was becoming more pronounced as he strained to see what was going on. "Wake up, damn it!" Barber shouted now for affect. He then stood over the man, silent for a few seconds. "Damn," he said in a slightly softer tone. "Guess I must have left that towel on a few seconds too long. Your partner here didn't have a heart condition, did he? I didn't think of asking that before we started. But I usually don't give my guests a physical before these discussions." Barber then retrieved a cell phone from his pocket and pretended to place a call. "Hey, it's me," he said. "I'm going to need a clean up here. Looks like I lost one of them."

Barber waited a few seconds, and then glanced at the other agent. The man was whimpering now. He obviously had just wet himself. There was actually a puddle on the floor right beneath the chair. "OK, thanks," Barber pretended to say into the phone, which he then returned to his pocket. "Looks like I was just a little too enthusiastic with your friend, here. He's not going to tell anybody anything now. That means it's your turn." Barber had fully expected the first man to talk and was surprised when he resisted. The ruse, of course, designed to provide the necessary motivation to the second agent if Plan A failed. He suspected the second man was about to sing like a canary.

Barber walked around the first agent's limp body, still duct-taped to the chair and lying on the floor and approached the second agent. The man's eyes remained wide with fear as he grabbed the duck tape on the agent's mouth and ripped it off quickly for effect. Barber got right up into the man's face, and said with a menacing voice, "You and I are now going to have a conversation. As you can see, I now have little downside on what I ultimately decide to do with you, so I would suggest you cooperate. What happened to your friend was an accident. I didn't mean to kill him, and I have no desire to kill you. But understand this; I will do whatever is necessary to get the answers I want. How long that process lasts and how much at risk you are is entirely up to you. Do we understand each other?"

"Yes," the man said, almost crying.

"Good," Barber replied. "Now, I've never seen credentials like yours with no agency identification. Who do you work for?" Barber asked in a calm voice.

"National Security Agency. The Department of Special Activities," the man replied.

Barber backed away from the agent, just a bit, and with a confused look on his face asked, "Why the hell is the NSA interested in me? And exactly what is the Department of Special Activities?"

"Information at the NSA is highly compartmentalized. They don't give me a lot of details. All I know is you are a person of interest and somebody seems to think you have gotten too close to something or somebody. I don't know which."

"Why did the NSA put out a hit on me?" Barber barked, his calm voice morphing into something a bit more menacing.

"I don't know anything about a hit," the man said, "we don't do that sort of thing."

"Don't BS me!" Barber barked. "You two clowns were obviously the back up team sent to take me out after the first two guys failed."

"No!" the man yelled. Barber couldn't help but notice a real sense of sincerity in the agent's voice and was starting to believe that maybe the guy was telling the truth. "We were given orders to intercept whoever those guys were and to take you into protective custody!" the agent said with growing desperation.

"Bullshit!" Barber fired back. "You two clowns were sent to take me out!" Barber exclaimed again, but more probing now, trying to discern from the tone of the agent's answer if he was telling the truth.

"No!" the agent said, almost pleading. "I told you we don't do that sort of thing. I have never heard of anyone at NSA doing that sort of thing, even the Department of Special Activities."

Barber now stood up and looked down at the man. "What the hell, exactly, is the Department of Special Activities?" he asked, with a voice that was more incredulous than menacing.

As the agent sat in the chair looking up at Barber, he was overwhelmed with a sense of resignation. He had just disclosed the existence of the Department. From his perspective the options were pretty clear. Tell this guy what he wanted to know or likely be killed just like his partner. He knew whatever career he had, likely ended the moment the two of them were abducted, so the choice was easy. "It's the anti-terrorist arm of the NSA. It's totally off the books. Nobody outside of the Department, other than the director himself and I think a couple of high-ranking administration officials, know anything about it." OK, slow down he said to himself. Answer this guy's questions, but don't volunteer things.

Barber's head was spinning. Anti-terrorist arm? A lot more dots were starting to connect.

He was almost afraid of the answer to the question, "Does this Department of Special Activities deploy drones on U.S. soil?" Barber asked.

The agent looked pained. "Yes," he replied.

"Were those drones involved in the incident in Detroit?" Barber asked.

"Yes?" the agent replied.

Barber was reeling as he processed the answers. "Was the vehicle explosion in Tyson's Corner the result of a drone attack and not a fuel tank explosion?" Barber asked.

The agent looked down and started to almost whimper without answering.

"Answer my question!" Barber exclaimed. "Did our government deploy a domestic drone to attack the vehicle that exploded in Tyson's Corner?" he almost shouted.

"Yes!" the agent shouted back, and then began to sob.

Barber was furious. For a moment he almost lost control and attacked the guy but managed to regain control. He still got into the agent's face and started screaming at the man. "Why did you clowns murder a bunch of innocent people whose only crime was driving to a soccer game?" he yelled.

"It was a case of mistaken identity," the agent managed to get out through his sobs. "The NSA's threat detection computer screwed up and got it wrong. My God, I'm so sorry. This isn't what I signed up for."

Barber backed off a bit. He almost felt sorry for the guy, as it was becoming obvious he was closer to a victim than a perp. There were still a couple of pieces of information he would need, however.

"OK, if you weren't the backup team, how the hell did you know where I was?" Barber asked.

"We were tracking you," the agent answered, consciously stopping himself from saying more, although he was certain that Barber was not about to relent and would keep probing.

"How did you track me? My cell phone?" Barber asked.

"Yes," the agent replied.

"But how did you know I had been abducted?" Barber asked. "How did you know I wasn't just taking a drive in the country?"

"We could listen to your conversations," the agent said, with a sickening feeling that he was about to be compelled to confirm the Agency's darkest secret.

"But I never talked on my cell phone," Barber said, "and there was no way you could have any listening devices deployed in the field where we were, unless they were deployed in the car itself. If that was the case, I'm right back to believing those guys were working for you!" Barber barked. "Did you have a listening device deployed in the car?" Barber asked, with menace in his voice once again at full bloom.

"No," the agent said, almost pleading.

"Stop playing games!" Barber shouted as he grabbed the man's face with his right hand and squeezed it hard. "This isn't twenty questions! Tell me how you were able to listen to what was being said in that car!" he barked, as he violently snapped the man's head to the left as he released the squeeze.

"The Department developed a new technology. They call it the Sparrow. It's a nano-drone that implants itself into the back of the neck of its target. You were one of the targets. There's one in the back of your neck. I have no idea how many other targets there are, but the chatter is there are a lot. The drone turns any cell phone within a certain radius to a listening device and NSA can then monitor, whether the owner is talking on it or not. It doesn't even have to be turned on. We've been able to hear almost everything you've said for days now. It's what let us know those guys had you and planned to kill you. We heard everything that went on between you and those two thugs. Everything. My partner and I were trying to save your life, you dumb bastard, and you killed him!" the agent said, now sobbing again.

Barber now stood in front of the man in utter disbelief. His head was spinning. The agent had just told him things that made the scope of this whole mess far beyond anything he had expected. Barber knew that information was highly compartmentalized like the agent said. It was the way the alphabet agencies worked. He suspected that neither of these two guys would be able to tell him much more. But there was one more very important answer this guy could give him. He wanted a name. "Who do you work for?" Barber asked, once again with a calm voice. "Who's your boss?"

"Special Agent in Charge Ryan Jennings. He's the guy who runs the intelligence side of the Department. We were told our orders to take you into protective custody came directly from him."

Pay dirt, Barber thought. There was now one more interrogation he would have to do, and that should reveal the mother load. He couldn't wait to talk to Special Agent in Charge Ryan Jennings.

"So where do I find this guy, Jennings?" Barber asked.

"He spends most of his time in his cushy office at the Department's headquarters," the agent said.

"Could you please be so kind as to give me the address?" Barber asked.

The agent did as he was asked, right down to the floor and suite number of the building. Barber remained stunned at the revelations and was certain he had just scratched the surface. He walked over to the table at the side of the room where the pharmacy kit sat, opened the lid to the hard-shell Pelican case, and retrieved two syringes. He placed one of the syringes on the table next to the case and kept the other one in his hand as he walked back to the agent sitting in the chair.

"Well I guess this is it," the agent said. The sobbing had stopped, as though that part of him had been depleted. Replacing it was a voice of calm resignation. "I guess I never really expected you to let me live after what you did to my partner."

"Relax, my friend," Barber replied. "Your friend over there is actually fine. I just gave him a fast-acting sedative to make it look like I killed him. It had the desired effect on you, I am happy to say. And this," Barber said, as he held up the syringe to the light to inspect it and make sure it was clearly in the agent's line of sight, "is simply another dose of an amnesia drug. One for you, and one for your friend over there. A couple of my colleagues are going to pick you up and deliver you to a more familiar part of town. You won't even go to sleep on this, but when you become aware of your surroundings again, I suspect you will both be highly confused. Good news for me, of course, is you are likely to remember very little of what happened here, and whatever you do remember will not appear particularly credible."

"You bastard," the agent said, with anger that replaced the resignation.

"Well, I'd be happy to kill you if you prefer," Barber said, with a smile on his face as he injected the agent with the drug. "By the way, when you wake up and see your boss again, if you happen to remember my name, please tell him I am looking forward to the two of us having a little chat."

As Barber walked out of the room he was consumed with a singular thought. If not the U.S. Government, who was trying to kill him? He intended to find out.

401

Chapter 45 – Pegasus

It had been a brutal 24 hours, but at least at the moment he was back in his comfort zone. Joe pushed the throttles forward and the big King Air accelerated down the runway. As the airplane passed 110 knots, he applied a slight bit of back pressure to the control yoke and the bird leapt into the air for the short flight home. He felt like crap. His head was killing him. It was one of those headaches where you could actually hear your heart pounding from the sound of your pulse in your ears. The muffled hum of the aircraft's twin turbine engines, which normally was almost soothing, only added to his misery. He was able to take a shower at the safe house and clean up the remnants of the horrific act he had to commit to save his life. At least clean up on the outside, he reflected. No matter how vigorously he had brushed his teeth or how many gallons of mouthwash he seemed to have used, he couldn't rid himself of the coppery taste of Dent's blood. He had to admit his appearance no doubt greatly accelerated the loosening of the agent's tongue during the interrogation. The grizzly look of a man still covered with blood from tearing out a large chunk of another man's throat could do that. And make no mistake, Joe was very glad he was alive. But he was under no illusion of being spared a heavy emotional toll for his choice of methods. Showering wasn't optional, as he imagined the reactions he would have gotten if he had walked into the airport looking like he did from his interrogation of the two agents. Blood was not just on his clothes, but also on his face and on his MOUTH! It was revolting. He felt a profound chill course through his body as that act involuntarily flashed across his consciousness again. It took every bit of his considerable self-discipline to stay focused on the important task of being a pilot.

During the last 12 hours someone tried to kill him. His stomach churned as he kept replaying in his head the revelations of the past couple of hours. Things were moving in an unimaginably ugly direction. He had become concerned about the existence of a highly sophisticated terrorist cell operating on U.S. soil, one with capabilities heretofore not seen, or at least not admitted to by the authorities. He had become angry at the likely conclusion that the U.S. government was engaged in some kind of cover up. Anger couldn't even begin to describe his present state of mind. He was seething. His first suspicion certainly turned out to be correct. There was indeed a new and extraordinarily sophisticated terrorist cell operating on U.S. soil, but it had nothing to do with the usual suspects. It was the U.S. government itself. He still couldn't believe it.

Barber sat in the medical office of Orion Bellicus as a nurse injected a small amount of a numbing agent at the midpoint of the back of his neck. He then directed the beam of a powerful surgical styled light to the area and retrieved a small tool from a stainless steel tray that looked like a tiny spoon attached to the end of a thin stainless steel rod. It was the surgical tool used to remove skin cancers, and the nurse carefully started scooping small amounts of flesh and examining each extraction under a well-lit magnifying glass. After the third scoop, he uttered the words "got it", as Barber turned around and looked into the magnifying glass which now revealed a small grey object that appeared to be man-made and mechanical in nature. "So that must be what that guy referred to as the Sparrow," Barber said. "Let's get that thing down to Lauren. See what she can make of it."

"Guess I'm next," said Marcus Day, who was standing next to Barber as the device was removed from under his skin.

"Yeah," Barber replied, "and everyone in this building."

* * * * *

It was good to have friends in high places. Danny Goldman didn't look like much. He was five foot ten, of average build and average features.

His physical presence belied a remarkable capability that lay within, as well as a first-class mind. After graduation Magna from Princeton, he had accepted an OCS slot in the Navy with a direct ticket to SEAL training, or BUDS. This greatly disappointed his father, who had pushed him to take one of the many offers at investment banking and a career on Wall Street. But Danny wasn't motivated by money. He was motivated by challenge and meaning. As providence would have it, he wound up being a BUDS classmate of Joe Barber. The two had stood erect, at attention, in the same formation on graduation day as the BUDS OIC, or Officer in Charge, congratulated the young men on completion of the toughest training course the U.S. Military had to offer. It was often said by guests at BUDS graduation ceremonies, "These men can't be SEALS; they look so ordinary." And to all outward appearances, ordinary was the perfect word to describe Danny. He loved it. It gave him an enormous advantage of being able to hide in plain sight. It also assured that potential adversaries almost always underestimated him. He had spent over seven years in the Navy, including three deployments downrange as platoon OIC commanding the battle-hardened alpha warriors on missions. But as his stock-in-trade grew and he advanced in rank, the price was increasingly more staff assignments and further distance from the men. He couldn't help but envy his friend Joe Barber whose decision to pursue an enlisted track led to training as a sniper and the opportunity for deployments downrange long after Danny would be relegated to an office. So, Goldman decided to find another mountain to climb, and climb it he did. After leaving the Teams, Daniel Goldman joined the ranks of the Special Activities Division of the CIA, and once again enjoyed the privilege of commanding men in the field. The Division, called SAD, the Agency's paramilitary arm, was largely staffed with former special operators from the SEALs, Delta, and Force Recon. But that first-class mind once again put him on a management track, and he found himself being groomed for increasing responsibilities as history repeated itself. He had risen to Assistant Director, Operations, of the Division. As the AD, he had command responsibility for all the Division's ops, and was the master of the Agency's stable of alpha predators. It also gave him access to some of the most extraordinary intelligence capabilities on the planet. Goldman and Barber had been downrange several times together and had become great friends. The friendship had a special bond as Barber had pulled Goldman out of a hot spot during an op somewhere in Somalia. It was one of those missions that never happened, according to the books, but still left American blood on the ground and almost got both Barber and Goldman killed. As they were being exfilled from the LZ in a Blackhawk, Barber tried to lighten the mood by pretending to push Goldman out of the chopper's open side door. He loved to exploit Goldman's one abiding phobia. Almost nothing scared Daniel Goldman, but the guy was terrified of helicopters. Laughter was a highly effective way, however, at relieving the extraordinary stress of a mission, and both would always exploit it to its maximum advantage.

Joe and Danny crossed paths in the Teams much less often as Danny rose in the ranks, but they remained friends, if somewhat more distant ones. After Joe left the CIA and started his own business, both men made the effort to keep in contact both personally and professionally. Personal contact was usually restricted to the annual SEAL team reunions. A professional relationship blossomed, however, as certain parts of Orion Bellicus developed capabilities the CIA found very useful. Joe would, on occasion, find himself and his firm doing contract work for the Agency --always overseas and always off the books. Direct contact on a professional level between the two men was risky to both of them, so their contact was always very discrete. Goldman had given himself a code name for their correspondence. He referred to himself as Pegasus and would communicate with Barber via an encrypted internet message board to which only the two of them had access. Joe had never used Danny for personal reasons, but that was now about to change. If ever circumstances warranted it, Barber thought to himself, it was certainly what had transpired over the last 24 hours, and time was of the essence as Joe was certain whoever was after him would be quickly making another attempt.

Barber sat in his office and stared into his computer at the message board that was displayed across the screen. "Good to hear from you, my friend. What can we do for you?" the message read.

"I need anything you can dig up on somebody at NSA. The guy's name is Ryan Jennings, and I believe his title is Special Agent in Charge of the Department of Special Activities, whatever the hell that is. Also, anything you've got on whatever this Special Activities organization is. I've never heard of it," Barber said. He waited a minute or two then a response came back across the screen.

"We are logging into the Federal HR system right now. I should have something preliminary on Jennings in less than a minute or so."

Barber leaned back in his chair and massaged the bridge of his nose as he waited for a response. In less than 60 seconds Joe saw another message come across the screen. "We've got his records, at least what's available on the Government site and none of it is very remarkable. Lists his title as Special Agent, but nothing about Special Agent in Charge. Here's his home address and contact info – both a cell phone number and his .gov email address. Listed as single, never married, and no kids. Has an undergrad in public policy at Johns Hopkins and a JD from Georgetown Law. Clean record, at least as far as what's in the file." Joe stared at the screen, then began to type. "Anything on this Department of Special Activities?" He hit send, then sat there and waited again.

Once again his screen came to life with a response. "There's nothing about a Special Activities Division. It just refers to NSA and nothing more granular than that. I've heard rumors about some black op organization inside NSA but not much in the way of details. It's way outside of our remit."

"Understood," Joe typed. "It would be helpful if you could poke around and see if you can come up with anything else without raising suspicions, but the address and contact info are very helpful, thank you." Again, he hit send.

"Roger that," was the typed response after several seconds. Then it continued, "Why are you so interested?"

Joe sat at his desk and thought for a few seconds. How much should he reveal to Danny? It was a reasonable question, given the sensitive nature of the information he was seeking, but he didn't want to get Goldman more involved than was absolutely necessary. He began to type again. "Fair question. Let's just say that I have stumbled across some information that may prove inconvenient to the NSA. I have reason to believe they may have had pre-knowledge of several of the recent terrorist attacks – Michigan, Virginia, and Golden Gate, and tried to cover that fact up. Also, there have been two attempts on my life in the last few days, most recently last night. I don't know who's behind it but I believe this guy Jennings may have knowledge of same. I need to have a detailed conversation with him." He hit send. He had just revealed far more than the message suggested. Detailed conversation was code for an interrogation, and one that usually occurred after the subject was abducted.

It took almost two minutes, but a response finally started streaming over the message board again. "Got it. I'll see what I can find out." With that, Barber logged off, closed the internet browser, and shut down his laptop.

Chapter 46 – The Abduction

Flight Level 25, Beechcraft King Air, En Route to Northern Virginia

Barber and three other men sat in the King Air as it began a gradual descent towards Stafford Regional Airport. As Barber programmed the autopilot for the descent, he struggled to hold his anger in check and focus on the important task of getting the plane back on the ground. He was still seething, but knew he had to push it all out of his mind, at least for the moment. But it was hard. Two attempts on his life made it very hard to think about anything else. He was stunned at what he had learned from the agent whose tongue had become so highly lubricated after Joe had faked the accidental death of the agent's partner. Sure, the American people had clamored for a vigorous response to the attack on Disneyworld a couple of years ago. Bringing down a symbol of American capitalism like the World Trade Center was bad enough, but deliberately targeting families, children and such an iconic symbol of the American way of life had brought a real call to action. He got that, and if anyone understood the capacity of the Federal Government for overreach it was Joe. But of all organizations, why the NSA? What the hell was the NSA doing in the covert ops business? Their remit was signal intelligence, and they were superb at it; but if the current Administration had fallen so far off the rails as to actually start applying extra-legal military-style measures against the homeland, why use the NSA as the tool? It didn't make sense. And how do you cover up something like that? Why were there no rumors about it? And the very existence of such a thing seemed ripe for a reckless Edward Snowden – type disclosure. NSA had neither the inclination nor the skill set for covert ops. He wouldn't have been a bit surprised if the NSA had taken domestic surveillance to a whole new level. That sort of thing was certainly within their skill set, and there was plenty of precedence for it. The Sparrow thing, whatever the hell it was, was a prime example. But that was a whole different kettle of fish from actions that were nearly para-military in nature. It just didn't make sense. Or maybe, he thought, that was the very reason this new activity, whatever it was, found its home in the NSA. That was one of the several questions he looked forward to asking this Jennings character as soon as he got his hands on him.

In about 30 minutes the King Air started its turn to final for runway 33 at Stafford Regional. In less than two minutes it made gentle contact with the pavement, taxied off the active and towards the FBO, where a non-descript rental car was waiting for the four men.

On the Ground, Northern Virginia

Three of Orion's premier alphas accompanied Joe on this trip and would provide the muscle and security for the op — capture and interrogate. The plan was simple, as most successful plans were, but it had its challenges. First and foremost was how to lure the agent into a trap with little or no primary or collateral damage. Barber was royally pissed at the guy, but seriously injuring the man or any agents that might be on a protective detail was something they all agreed must be avoided. The aversion was driven more by professional ethics than by any fear of the legal consequences. Sure, almost everything they were about to do broke any number of laws. And some were serious; like kidnapping, assaulting a Federal Agent, and on and on. But Barber had acquired enough intelligence on whatever the NSA was doing to form three immutable conclusions — its actions were highly secret, highly illegal, and their disclosure would represent an undeniable threat not just to the NSA but to the Administration itself. Neither Jennings nor anyone on his team was about to go to the local police, let alone the FBI, for help. The second challenge was how to set the trap. They had debated something with a dramatic flair to throw Jennings off guard, like Barber calling his cell phone and demanding a meet. That idea was quickly dismissed as likely to put him on high alert. Once again, they settled on the simplest of solutions. They

411

would lay in wait for Jennings to return home that evening and abduct him there. The initial effort would be a "gentleman's abduction", as they called it. Two of the Orion operatives would be waiting for Jennings when he returned. Upon confronting him, the operators would simply tell him they were colleagues of Joe Barber and that Joe would simply like to talk to him. For obvious reasons, they would argue, it would have to be on neutral grounds. They would even suggest that it be outdoors, in a park, and that Jennings would be free to go when the conversation concluded. It was all a lie, of course. Barber and the fourth man would be waiting at the 12 Uniform Mike safe house where Barber intended to conduct the "conversation".

If Jennings demurred at the ruse, the two operators would then default to plan B - administer a sedative and deliver an unconscious Jennings to the interrogation site. The default, of course, could get a bit messy in terms of getting Jennings from his house to their car without being noticed, so they were very much hoping that Jennings would have a reasonable response to their request for a meeting.

Before the abduction it was important to sanitize the security systems at Jennings' home. They realized, given his job, it was likely he had a very sophisticated one. And it would not be enough just to disable it. The moment Jennings tried to disarm it and realized it wasn't working, he would know something was up and likely would not enter the place. It had to be disabled in a way that made it appear to function both to Jennings and the central monitoring station, including a phony video feed to the surveillance cameras so that everything appeared normal. Barber had once asked Dr. Cartwright, his Director of Forensics, how difficult it would be to hack into a home or corporate security system and disable it in a manner that wouldn't get noticed. She had just smiled and said, "If somebody can hack into the uranium enriching facility of a country halfway around the world and disable their centrifuges, how difficult do you think that would be?" He never again asked her the question "if", only "how long". The home security system would be disabled remotely from Orion Bellicus' digital forensics lab before the two operators even got there. Orion Bellicus would effectively become the central monitoring station, and Jennings would never be the wiser. The sanitizing of the residence would be completed when Barber's people arrived and placed portable signal jammers at several locations to block cell phone calls, and any signal intelligence coming from the Sparrow system. Joe was assuming that Jennings had the Sparrow implant as well.

* * * * *

It was 6:45 in the evening when Ryan Jennings walked into his office to close his briefcase and head home. It had been a very long day, and he was exhausted. Most of the day had been spent de-briefing the two agents who had failed to bring in Barber. Although Jennings was still angry about their failure, he had to admit to himself the two men were far outclassed by a man of Barber's background and capabilities. One thing was pretty clear – Barber's skills remained well-honed, in of spite his age. In truth, Jennings was just as anxious to find out who was behind the twin attempts on Barber's life as Barber was. Jennings certainly wished God's speed to whomever it was. Barber was a royal pain in the ass, and the sooner he was out of the picture the happier Jennings would be. Getting rid of the guy would make a lot of problems go away and free the entire organization to refocus on their primary mission. But his entire chain of command was getting very worried about who, or what organization, was carrying on some type of op in the background. They even suspected a connection to the Chinese who had hacked the drone over the Golden Gate. One thing was sure; somebody needed to clean up this mess quickly. Even Jennings was starting to worry about himself becoming collateral damage. If the Department of Special Activities was not able to get back on mission pretty quickly, the entire organization was likely to be thrown under the bus with fatal consequences.

413

Fatal consequences, that is, at least from a career standpoint. And maybe more, he thought to himself, as he was suddenly overcome with an abiding sense of dread.

It was a beautiful, warm summer evening as Jennings drove the 25-minute commute to his home. A hot sun burned through a near cloudless sky and kept the temperature in the high eighties along with the oppressive mid-Summer humidity so characteristic of coastal Virginia. Jennings had the air conditioning of his Ford Fusion blasting on max as an episode of "Yours Truly, Johnny Dollar" played on the satellite radio that was tuned to the Radio Classics station. Jennings loved listening to the classic radio dramas from the 40's and 50's and found them a good way to clear his mind of the stresses of the day. The awful northern Virginia traffic seemed even worse than normal, and his commute took 10 minutes longer than expected. At least there was an upside, he thought to himself, as the extra time allowed him to finish the episode of the drama he was listening to. He hit the garage door opener on the sun visor of his car, pulled into the garage, and after shutting off the vehicle, disarmed the alarm system from the app on his phone. He retrieved his briefcase from the back seat and walked through the door in the garage that led directly into the kitchen. Good night to throw a steak on the grill, he thought, as he placed his briefcase down, retrieved a bottle of red wine he had opened the night before, and poured himself a glass. As Jennings walked towards the door between the kitchen and the dining room, suddenly he had an odd sensation. It was as though he could feel somebody else in his house. He instinctively reached down and touched the bulge of his service Glock just inside his suit jacket but didn't draw the weapon. It was an irrational sensation, he quickly concluded, as the alarm system was clearly on when he went to disarm it. For the next couple of seconds, at least, he put the thought out of his mind. As he walked from the dining room into the family room with the intent of turning on the evening news, his stomach went to his throat as he saw two men standing there, both with pistols in their hands. He fought

414

the instinct to go for his weapon, quickly concluding he wouldn't even get it out of the holster before the two men shot him.

"Good evening, Agent Jennings," one of the men said. "First, let me assure you, we mean you absolutely no harm. Our weapons are drawn only as a precaution. You will notice that they are both pointed to the floor and not at you. You should take that as an expression of good faith. It would be a mistake to attempt to retrieve yours."

"Who the hell are you two, how did you get into my house and what do you want?" Jennings demanded with a mixture of both fear and anger in his voice. In all his time carrying a weapon as a Federal Agent, armed adversaries had never confronted him.

"Very reasonable questions, sir, and we will be happy to answer in a moment," one of the operators replied. "But first, I suggest it is in the interest of all of us that we de-escalate this from a confrontation to a conversation. We need to start that process by my partner here retrieving your service pistol. I will continue to keep my pistol drawn until he does so but will keep it aimed at the floor unless you give me a reason to do something different. Also, I'm not sure what kind of training you may have, but we are both former Delta with multiple deployments, and of course there are two of us. We would both very much appreciate it if you would allow my partner to disarm you without incident. Are we agreed on that?" he asked.

"Yes, we are agreed," Jennings said. With that, Jennings put his hands on top of his head and interlocked his fingers as a way to signal he did not intend to do anything foolish. One of the agents then walked over to him with gloved hands, retrieved Jennings' service Glock from its holster, ejected the magazine, worked the slide to eject the round that Jennings kept in the chamber, then removed the slide from the pistol's receiver, removed the

415

barrel and the spring and carefully placed the pieces on a coffee table that was sitting in front of a sofa.

"Great, that's better," the operator said.

"What do you want?" Jennings asked, this time with considerably more anger than fear, as it was becoming apparent the men intended no harm, at least for the moment. "Do you realize the maelstrom you have just gotten yourself into by threatening a Federal Agent?" he barked.

"Now, as you can clearly see, we do not intend to harm you; so there is no threat, Agent Jennings, only the potential for an act of self defense," the operator said with a smile. "And as for breaking certain laws, we are quite certain, and indeed have documented proof," he said, lying, "that you and your colleagues have broken quite a few yourselves. So for the time being let's just agree that you'll keep your little secret and we'll keep ours."

The comments had the desired effect, as Jennings swallowed hard and wondered just exactly what kind of evidence these two guys had. Jennings knew there was potentially a bounty of material that could be devastating if made public. And the threat seemed all the more real on the heels of his agents being interrogated. Jennings barked at the men again, not wanting to concede whatever little ground he had left. "What do you want?"

"We simply want to give you something you want. We work for Mr. Joseph Barber, whom we understand is a person of interest to you. We understand you have been wanting to have a conversation with him. Mr. Barber believes it would be of mutual benefit for the two of you to have that conversation. He also believes, for the benefit and safety of you both, that it needs to be on neutral grounds, and in a public place, and of course with you alone. The last point is the reason for the unfortunate drama here. It was the only way we could think of to arrange the meeting without the complication of your backup and whatever other obvious, considerable resources you may

416

have at your disposal. There is a public seating area in Georgetown just outside the restaurant Founding Fishers Farmers right by the water. He has asked us to escort you there. I assure you again, as I hope our actions here have indicated, that we mean you no harm. We will drive you there and introduce you to our boss, then the two of us will move out of earshot. When the conversation concludes, you are free to go and do whatever you wish with the information the two of you share. We will summon you an Uber to take you back home or anywhere you want when you are finished. Does this sound reasonable to you?" the operator asked.

Jennings stood there in disbelief. Everything about this confrontation seemed to reek of risk, but he had to admit to himself they had two points. First, he desperately wanted, needed, to talk to Barber; and although he would much rather have done so in an NDSA interrogation room it looked like he was being handed an opportunity he couldn't pass up. Second, at least for the moment, the men seemed sincere about not wanting to hurt him. If they did, or planned to abduct him, they could have done so without all of the upfront drama. Adding to his inclination to take their offer, of course, was the concern of what their actions might be if he decided not to cooperate. He seemed to have more upside than downside, so he decided to go for it. "OK," Jennings said, "let's go for a ride."

"Excellent," the operator responded. "Now there is just one more thing we need to do before we leave." Jennings got a knot in the pit of his stomach and began to think he had made a mistake. The operator noticed the worried look that just sprung all across his face. Jennings would make a lousy poker player, he thought to himself. "Not to worry, Agent Jennings. I simply need to tape this piece of wire mesh to the back of your neck before we leave," he said as he held up the mesh for Jennings to see. "We have become aware of your ingenious little communication device; I believe you call it the Sparrow. Is that correct? I am simply going to affix this to the back of your neck with a little bit of surgical tape. It will block any transmissions that device may be trying to send. I can assure you this is totally painless and non-invasive. I had to do this to Mr. Barber, actually, last night, before we got him back to our lab to remove the device and inspect it." The agent gave the words a few seconds to sink in. Jennings was horrified. Debriefing the two agents had caused Jennings and his bosses considerable concern. During their questioning by Barber, the agents had given up the existence of some sort of high-tech listening device. But these two operators had just mentioned it by name, seemed to know its function, knew exactly where it would implant itself in a subject, and claimed that the device on Barber had been removed and actually inspected. These were far more damaging revelations than Jennings' worst fears. It also meant he now had no choice but to cooperate and go to this meeting. He had to speak to Barber and try to find out whatever it was he had learned. It was essential. His mind raced back to an earlier ExComm conversation when there were so many skeptics about Barber being a genuine threat to the organization. Jennings now knew he was right.

With a sense of resignation, Jennings followed the two operators out the front door and the block and a half where their SUV was parked. One of the men opened the front passenger side door and invited Jennings to get in, careful to do it in a manner that didn't seem terribly threatening. "Best to set your house alarm, you never know who might try and break into a home in a neighborhood like this," the operator said under his breath, with a chuckle. Jennings retrieved the cell phone from his pocket, touched the app and entered the arming code. The operator in the back seat now leaned over the front console and said, "I'll take that, please, just for now, of course. We'll give it back as soon as you finish your conversation with our boss." Jennings reluctantly handed the phone to the man. The operator turned it off, and then placed it in a wire mesh case to prevent any signal from getting out or in.

For the first 15 minutes of the drive, Jennings was lost in his thoughts. His head remained spinning as he kept thinking through potential consequences of Barber going public with what he had learned. It was Edwin Snowden on steroids, he kept thinking to himself, maybe far worse. Snowden's revelations had been a carpet-bombing of documents that took enormous time and resources to sort through to find the more damning details. And to the average person, they really didn't seem to mean or matter very much. But this was different. It was surgical. And it was something that would make the vast majority of citizens really angry every time they picked up or started to use their ubiquitous cell phones. As the drive progressed, he began to have an unsettling feeling that all was not as it appeared to be. Initially it was the scenery, which his mind subconsciously processed as the drive proceeded. But something wasn't right. The scenery was becoming less familiar, and he was becoming increasingly convinced these two thugs were not taking him to where he expected. The growing cognitive dissonance finally forced his perceptions from the sensory regions of the thalamus and cortex to the amygdala, as he became increasingly aware of the unfamiliar nature of his surroundings. Jennings had gone from being concerned about what Barber could disclose to concern about where he was being taken. He glanced at the navigation system screen in the center of the dashboard, hoping the map would yield some clue. But the entertainment system controls were displayed instead of the map. He noticed at the top and just to the right of the screen's outside temperature reading, was the compass, which showed they were heading west. That was certainly not the direction to Georgetown, he told himself as his stomach once again rose to his throat.

The operator in the back noticed Jennings staring at the screen, as well as the frightened look on his face. "Where are you taking me?" Jennings asked with real fear in his voice now. "This isn't the way to Georgetown."

"Not to worry, Agent Jennings," the operator replied, "just taking an indirect route in case you had any kind of protective detail after last night. We'll be there in less than 15 minutes or so."

Jennings slowly moved his right hand and placed it next to the door handle. The driver noticed this as he instinctively looked in the side-view mirror for traffic as he prepared to change lanes. The driver then stared into the rear-view mirror until he made eye contact with the man in the back, then moved his eyes towards Jennings and back again. After this he slowly, almost imperceptibly, nodded his head, yes. As he did so, the man in the back retrieved a syringe from his pocket, removed the needle guard, and in a quick motion plunged the needle into Jennings' neck, depressed the plunger, injecting a fast-acting sedative. It would knock him out for only about 20 or 30 minutes, enough time to get Jennings into the seedy hotel room but not so long as to delay the interrogation. The plan had been to keep Jennings conscious as long as they could to reduce the risk of complications. They had succeeded. They were only about 5 minutes from the hotel now, where Barber and the third Orion Bellicus operator were waiting.

Chapter 47 – The "Conversation"

Orion Bellicus Safe House, Code Name 12 Uniform Mike

As Jennings awoke, the first thing he noticed was his arms and legs seemed to be immobilized. He had initially thought it was some kind of dream, but as he tugged on duck tape that held his wrists firmly in place, it hurt. The pain was the first clue that this was real. The next thing he noticed was he couldn't see anything. But as he gradually recovered consciousness and his senses spooled back up, he could feel some sort of cloth all over his face and realized he was wearing a hood. He struggled to remember the events that brought him to his present circumstances. As the fog of the sedative continued to lift, he remembered the men in his house, the car ride, and recalled there was something about the ride that had troubled him, but he couldn't remember what. Then suddenly he remembered Joe Barber and realized he had been abducted. His first reaction was anger, but as he violently tore at the restraints on his arms and barked out, "Where the hell am I," the anger was suddenly replaced by fear. He recalled that the meeting with Barber was supposed to be just a discussion. But this was obviously no mere discussion. It was clear that this was going to be an interrogation. And it certainly wasn't going to take place in some public place.

Barber sat in a chair opposite Jennings. He reached across, grabbed the top of the hood covering Jennings' head and gave it a hard yank. As the hood came flying off, Jennings shook his head in an effort to clear it and squinted as he tried to focus on the man sitting in front of him. The task was made difficult by the dilation of his eyes and the bright light aimed directly at his face. "Good evening, Special Agent Jennings. Allow me to introduce myself. My name is Joseph Barber. I understand you have been wishing to speak with me. Well, it's your lucky day, as the feeling is very mutual. By the way, I must also say that I have amassed a considerable amount of evidence over the last 72 hours showing that you actually have wished to do a great deal more than just speak with me."

Jennings' fear momentarily morphed back into anger, and he barked, "You have abducted and are holding a Federal Agent against his will. Do you realize how many laws you have broken?" Jennings said with a defiant scowl. "Do you have any idea of the shitstorm you are about to rain down on yourself?"

"You Feds must all have this playbook of scripted responses, because that's the second time in the last 48 hours I have heard almost exactly the same words. So let's dispense with a few preliminaries so we can move on to more productive endeavors. I'll concede that this little conversation here is, shall we say, somewhat extra-legal? But I'll remind you of the same thing I suggested to your colleagues when they attempted to abduct me. Whatever you are up to with your Department of Special Activities, it's also highly illegal, to say nothing about being politically toxic, even nuclear. You and I both know that you're not about to go the police, ask a judge for a warrant, or engage any other legitimate law enforcement organization in an effort to extract legal retribution. And by the way, I've given my lawyer a copy of both the recording and a complete transcript of my conversation with your two rookie agents with instructions to provide it to the Washington Post and the FBI should I suddenly go missing. So, don't bore me with idle threats," Barber warned. He then reached across the open space between the two of them and firmly grabbed Jennings jaw with his right hand and got right into the man's face. "You'll forgive my somewhat unfortunate mood at the moment, but I get a little grumpy when somebody tries to kill me, especially with the person I suspect was behind it. I also suspect you are behind the death of my secretary. That doesn't make me grumpy, it fills me with cold fury. So save your pathetic threats for someone who isn't in a position to end you right here and now. You and I are going to have this little conversation, and you are going to tell me everything I want to know. If you don't, I can assure you my colleagues and I are very skilled at making a clown like you completely vanish."

"I, we, had nothing to do with the attempts on your life!" Jennings cried out, his bravado replaced with panic as his fear returned in full bloom. "We have been trying to find out ourselves who was behind the attempt on your life."

Barber shoved Jennings' face backwards and snapped it to the right as he released his grip. "We'll get to me in a few minutes," Barber said. "First, we have some more basic business to discuss." His eyes locked with Jennings as he continued. "Listen carefully, because this is how this is going to work. I am going to start asking you some questions, and you are going to answer every one of them fully and honestly. If you are in the slightest way uncooperative, or I suspect you are lying, there are going to be consequences. Do we understand each other?"

Jennings stared at Barber and didn't answer.

"Do we understand each other, Special Agent in Charge Jennings?" Barber barked.

"Yes," Jennings replied, with a trembling voice.

"Good," Barber said. "Let's start with some preliminaries. Please tell me your name."

"You know my name, asshole," he responded, trying to summon his bravado.

"Now Agent Jennings, let's be polite. Yes, I know your name, but I want to hear it from your mouth. Your name is not exactly a state secret, so if you are uncooperative on this question I might as well have my colleague over there provide a little extra motivation."

"Ryan Jennings," he responded. "My name is Ryan Jennings."

"And who do you work for, Agent Jennings?"

"National Security Agency," he responded.

"What is your title, Agent Jennings?"

"Special Agent," Jennings responded again.

"Just Special Agent?"

"Special Agent in Charge."

"You're starting to piss me off again. Special Agent in charge of what? Complete answers, or I'll put my colleague to work."

"Special Agent in Charge, Intelligence."

"Very good. That wasn't so hard now, was it? Now, explain to me exactly what this Sparrow program is," Barber demanded.

"I don't know what you are talking about," Jennings replied, immediately regretting the answer, as he remembered Barber was already aware of the existence of Sparrow. He tried to recover by saying, "I mean, I can't tell you that! It's classified for national security reasons. But I can tell you it's an important part of the war on terror." He regretted that comment as well, the moment it came out of his mouth. It was a trite and scripted answer again and would no doubt do nothing but piss off Barber even more. He was right.

"Wrong answers, Agent Jennings. You greatly underestimate our resolve, as well as our patience. So, we obviously are going to need to provide you with additional motivation before continuing this discussion." With that, Barber looked towards one of his colleagues and nodded.

All three of the operators with Barber were wearing black balaclavas, in part to look menacing, but more importantly to protect their identity. Barber wanted to ensure he was the only one who could even remotely be exposed to any kind of legal jeopardy. It also was the reason he didn't refer to any of the operators by name, and why none of them talked. Jennings had seen the faces of two of the men, of course, at his home. But the chances of being able to render an accurate description were not particularly high given the trauma Jennings had experienced. On Barber's nod, one of the men walked up to Jennings with a piece of duct tape and a rag. He placed the rag in Jennings' mouth and secured it with the tape. He then taped down Jennings' left wrist even tighter. Jennings' eyes were now wide with fear. "I'm now going to give you a little taste of things to come if you refuse to cooperate." With that, the operator walked to Jennings' side and secured the tip of Jennings' left index finger with his hand. The operator then firmly grasped Jennings index finger between the first and second knuckles and started to bend back the finger until it started to cause considerable pain. He held the position for a few seconds as Jennings tried screaming through the rag in his mouth with no effect. The operator then sharply twisted Jennings' finger backwards until there was a sickening sound of a snap as the finger broke. Jennings' screams rocketed to a whole new level as the pain in his hand went white-hot. The screams had an awful muffle to them as his lungs struggled to recover enough air to make them audible. The operator then straightened the finger back causing another lightning bolt of searing pain; then stepped back as Jennings struggled again to scream. Barber continued to sit there quietly and let the pain do its work. One of the operators moved a small table next to Barber and placed two objects on it. The first was a meat cleaver. The second was an electric drill, fitted with a very small diameter drill bit. Barber picked up the drill and depressed the trigger. The sound of the drill echoed throughout the room. Barber then looked at Jennings and smiled. As he did so, he asked, "Have you ever seen the movie Marathon Man?" Jennings eyes seemed to almost pop out of his head as they exploded with fear. Barber smiled again and said, "Excellent. I can tell from your reaction that you have. I haven't decided yet exactly how I plan to use this – either an eye or a front tooth. I think a tooth. The eye arguably might be a bit scarier, but I have found the tooth to be far more painful. And starting with the tooth gives us an opportunity for a more gradual escalation." Jennings eyes welled with tears, and he couldn't speak. After about a minute, but what seemed to be a lifetime to Jennings, Barber finally spoke again. "This is just the beginning if you fail to cooperate. Now I suggest we continue our conversation, and this time with more candor please. Can we agree to that, Special Agent Jennings?" Barber asked. Of course, the threat of drilling a tooth was a ruse. It was an act, intended to loosen Jennings' tongue. Barber had never actually abused anyone like that. As far as the broken finger was concerned, it delivered maximum pain and motivation for minimum, and non-permanent damage. Barber had suffered a far greater break to a finger in his left hand while playing catch with his dad as a child. "Do we understand each other?" Barber asked, growing impatient with Jennings lack of response as the man just sat there sobbing as the pain continued to sear his hand. "I understand it may be a bit hard to talk right now, so just nod your head yes if you understand and agree that we can dispense with this unpleasantness." Jennings nodded his head yes. With the acknowledgement, Barber looked at the operator now standing a few feet from Jennings' chair. This time the operator retrieved a syringe from a bag and started to inject something into Jennings' finger. Jennings eyes went wide with fear again. "Relax," Barber said, "my colleague here is simply administering a numbing agent for the pain. In a few seconds you should feel fine again. When it takes effect, we can straighten out the break properly and splint it. After we conclude our little talk, that is." Barber looked at his operator and said. "Please remove the rag from his mouth.

Now, once again, Agent Jennings, explain to me exactly what this Sparrow program is."

Barber sat in stunned disbelief on the sheer extent and scope of what he was hearing. The fact that a government agency was illegally spying on its citizens, and even recording and retaining phone conversations, wasn't exactly a novel revelation. But the sheer magnitude of the program, its breadth and reach, was beyond anything even Barber could have imagined. The audacity was breathtaking. "How the hell did you get this through FISA?" Barber asked, referring to the Federal Intelligence Surveillance Court, charged with oversight of surveillance of supposedly foreign agents operating inside of the United States.

"We didn't run it through FISA," Jennings said, "it's strictly off the books, authorized by a Presidential Finding."

Barber was stunned again. He had a series of carefully scripted questions designed to methodically peel back the onion on the operation, but the more Jennings spoke the more Barber's sense of urgency was becoming overwhelming. He decided to short-circuit several of the next questions and go right for the gold. "Was your Department of Special Activities the organization that operated the drone over the Golden Gate Bridge?"

Jennings sat there and looked at Barber. He knew there was no way he was going to be able to avoid revealing the domestic drone program. The only question was how much pain he was willing to endure before giving it up. And what was the point of enduring the pain, he thought to himself. Thoughts of advancing his career were long gone. He knew now the program was likely over. Best case would be that Barber was bluffing about leaving information with his lawyer and that the powers that be would eliminate this guy before he could do any more damage. But that was unlikely. There was no way now the program wouldn't be shut down. Jennings was becoming increasingly convinced he could ultimately be in as much danger from his own organization as he was from Barber. Hell, at this point his best-case scenario was likely jail. So why suffer the pain? "Yes," he said in direct answer. "The Department has an Ops arm, and its main tool is a domestic drone program. The drone is designed to look like a civilian aircraft. Its mission is to take out a terrorist vehicle if more conventional methods are deemed untimely, impractical or too risky. Sparrow uncovered the Golden Gate plot, and a drone was mobilized to strike the terrorist's vehicle before it was detonated. We thought we could hit it at a spot that would limit the collateral damage."

Barber couldn't believe the stupidity of what he was hearing. Less collateral damage? What genius thought a deliberate air strike into crowded traffic created less risk for collateral damage than a SWAT raid, he thought to himself. Stay focused, Joe reminded himself, and fired back a simple and direct question. "What happened?"

"The system was obviously hacked," Jennings said. "We are investigating, but most signs point to the Chinese. They are the only ones who have that kind of sophisticated capability. Probably did it to embarrass the administration by revealing the program, although we will never know."

"What about the incident in Michigan?" Barber asked.

"First time the drone was used," Jennings replied.

"How many times in total?" Barber asked.

"Three."

"Don't piss me off with truncated answers, Jennings. Golden Gate was one, Michigan was one, what was the third?" he asked, fairly certain he already knew the answer.

"Tyson's Corner," Jennings responded, as he started to sob again. He struggled with the next words but managed to get them out. "It was a mistake, a false positive from the threat detection software. It was a drone strike that took out that Explorer and not a gas tank explosion as reported by the press. The men in that vehicle had been identified as persons of interest and kept using soccer terms to describe what sounded like a mall attack. It looked to be almost exactly the same M.O. as the cell in Michigan. My God, it was a tragedy," Jennings sobbed.

"But you covered it up and planted a false narrative blaming the manufacturer, correct?"

"Yes," Jennings replied. "We did it to protect the program. We were convinced the program would save lives."

A cold fury started to well up in Barber as he thought about Veronica Maxwell and her three children. "Well, it certainly didn't save the lives of that young mother and her three children in Michigan, did it?" Barber asked.

"No," Jennings replied. "That was a tragedy, but many more lives would have been lost if those terrorists had gotten to that mall. Their deaths were just plain bad luck that resulted from her making an unexpected turn at the worst possible time."

"So, you clowns wanted to kill me, and killed Eric Longstreet because we had gotten too close to the truth, right?" Barber asked with a controlled, but unmistakably menacing tone to his voice.

"No," Jennings said, with a pleading tone in his voice that almost made Barber believe the man was telling the truth. "Yes, you had gotten too close to the truth, and yes, that reporter from the Post had gotten too close to the truth as well, and yes there were contingency plans to protect the organization if anyone was getting too close to information that could reveal its existence, and yes, those contingency plans were even discussed. But the decision was no. Not to do it. The oversight process worked," Jennings said, immediately regretting the comment.

"Oversight process my ass," Barber scowled. "So, you are telling me a government agency, an arm of the National Security Agency, actually had contingency plans for the assassination of a United States citizen for no crime other than getting too close to the truth about what it was up to; and he motive was simply to protect the agency's ass? Is that what I am to understand?" Barber asked.

Jennings held his head down and looked at the floor for several seconds, then responded with a weak, "Yes."

"Say that again, Agent Jennings," Barber barked, "I didn't hear you the first time."

"Yes," Jennings responded, sobbing again. Barber looked towards the back of the room at the operator who was running the digital recording machine, and the man nodded his head yes, meaning they had clearly recorded everything Jennings had said.

"OK, I just have one more question," Barber said. "How did you find me? How did you get my contact information?" he asked.

"We had help from the FBI," Jennings responded.

Barber was suddenly enveloped with a cold chill. He thought about Benson. No way Don could be mixed up in this mess, he thought to himself. "Do you mean to tell me that the FBI is complicit in all of this?" Barber asked, afraid of what the answer would be.

"No, no," Jennings replied. "The Bureau is not read into the program. But one of their senior execs is a friend of William Fitzpatrick, and she looked you up and gave us the information." Once again Jennings regretted the words the moment they came out of his mouth. He had just revealed not only an F.B.I connection but a direct link to the White House. If he wasn't toast before, he certainly was now.

"Are you referring to William Fitzpatrick, the Chief of Staff to the President of the United States?" Barber asked, not believing the words that were coming out of Jennings' mouth.

"Yes," Jennings replied, with resignation in his voice.

"The Chief of Staff of the President of the United States is directly involved in all of this? Are you telling me the President is involved in this too?" Barber asked.

"No, no, we don't believe so, not the President, anyway. I mean, yes, Fitzpatrick. Well, no, not formally, but informally yes, Fitzpatrick is very involved. The whole program was Fitzpatrick's idea. People were demanding serious action after the Disney attack. The President was demanding action. Fitzpatrick came up with the idea. He had the President sign a secret finding with the "any necessary means" language but kept the President out of the details, or at least that's what we were led to believe. Fitzpatrick does not have a direct, ongoing role in the Department, but he still attends a lot of the Executive Committee meetings and puts his nose into a lot of the operational details. All of this was funded with a pool of black money from the NSA budget. Nobody beyond a handful of individuals who don't work for the department itself, is even aware of our existence. Not even within the NSA."

"So, who is this 'she' at the FBI who's a friend of Fitzpatrick?" Barber asked.

"Sandra McConnell, Executive Assistant Director for the Security Branch," Jennings replied.

Barber leaned back in his chair utterly aghast.

"Who do you report to, and who runs your Department?"

"I report to the Department Director, Dr. Trae Collins," Jennings replied. "An Executive Committee, that's what I was referring to a minute ago, supervises the Department. Collins is on it, as well as the Director of NSA, Dr. Adam Johnson, and the National Security Advisor, Admiral George Erby."

Barber couldn't believe it. "George Erby is part of this mess?" he asked.

"Yes," Jennings replied, "but at least from my chair he appears to be a highly reluctant participant and pretty conflicted about the whole thing. He's the guy who's usually arguing no, and he's given Fitzpatrick the 'what-for' a few times. He even threatened to go the President himself and resign."

A digital recording device had picked up the entire interrogation. Of course, there would be more than one version of it. An unabridged version would remain in the vault of Orion Bellicus headquarters. An edited version, where the finger incident and all explicit threats were removed, would be prepped within an hour. That version was Joe's "get out of jail free" card. A third version would digitally disguise Joe's voice as he asked Jennings the questions. Joe intended to share that version with Benson later that night.

Barber looked at Jennings and said, "OK, I think we are done here. As I am sure you are aware, everything that has been said in this room has been recorded. My team will craft a sanitized version that removes anything that could potentially place these gentlemen or myself in legal jeopardy. I think we can agree that it would be unwise for you or your organization to pursue any further action against me or any of my friends. If you do, I can assure you we know where to find you. At the moment I am inclined to believe that you were not behind the two attempts on my life. If I find out differently, I'll be in touch again."

Barber looked up towards his men and said, "Zip tie his hands, put a blindfold on him and drive him to about 3 blocks from his house and let him out." With those words, Jennings felt an overwhelming sense of relief that his life was not to end in this place on this night. But he remained very afraid of what was going to happen when he briefed his bosses on what Barber had said. **IF**, he briefed them, he thought to himself as the blindfold was placed over his eyes.

Chapter 48 – Stop Loss

FBI Headquarters, Washington, D.C., Early the Next Morning

Executive Assistant Director for Intelligence, Donald Benson, sat at his office desk and leaned back in his chair. He removed a pair of Apple ear buds he had used to listen to an audio file and threw them down, a bit more forcefully than he should have. To say he was angry would have been a monumental understatement. He was not a man normally given to outsized displays of emotion, especially anger, but what he was feeling right now approached rage. He was struggling to keep it in check. He had just listened to a copy of the sanitized conversation between Barber and Jennings. It was sent to him from an anonymous email account, encrypted and untraceable, but he knew the source. It was Joe. Barber had alerted him late last night to look for a "special delivery", as he called it. That's all Barber had said. And it had been sent to Benson's FBI email address, which ensured it resided on the FBI server. It thereby became property of the Bureau, and material evidence in what Benson knew would be a coming criminal investigation.

Benson picked up the ear buds and put them back on, then clicked on the audio file and began to listen to it again. Jennings voice was clear. At the beginning of the conversation he had identified himself as a Federal Agent and said he worked for the NSA. Barber's voice was digitally altered to mask it, but Benson knew who it was. Benson assumed the file was heavily edited. Nevertheless, the revelations had been shocking, almost beyond belief. The depth and breadth of what the file revealed took Benson's breath away. He listened again to a description of massive governmental electronic eavesdropping and the collection and analysis of personal conversations. Conversations between U.S. citizens without a foreign national even remotely involved. The NSA had no legal right to intercept those conversations and whoever was responsible for doing it had committed any number of felonies.

Benson regarded the details of the Sparrow Program itself one of the most shocking revelations of all. The notion that the government had created a miniature drone-like device that would physically implant itself in the neck of someone, a U.S. citizen, and without a FISA warrant, was so over the top it was almost difficult to comprehend. It wasn't just illegal; it was physically invasive. And the program appeared to lead all the way to the White House. Only marginally less troubling was the revelation that a senior executive of the FBI, Sandra McConnell, was somehow mixed up in all of it. That thought raced through his mind again. McConnell had provided this shadow organization with personal information on a U.S. citizen, Benson's friend Barber, evidently with full knowledge that this organization was contemplating taking him out. Assassinating him, a U.S. citizen, with the help of the FBI It was beyond the pale!

McConnell's connection to Fitzpatrick was no surprise to Don. It was one of the worst kept secrets that William Fitzpatrick and Sandra McConnell had been having an affair almost from the beginning of the present Administration. But this was no mere pillow talk, no mere concession to a lover's request. By Jennings' account, McConnell had actually attended several of the Executive Committee, or ExComm, meetings of the organization. She was actively involved. To so blatantly tarnish the integrity of the Bureau, to Benson, was the unpardonable sin. When he had completed listening to the audio file again, his first instinct was to storm down the hall and confront her. But he realized he needed take a breath and think and think first. This was not about confronting and punishing the actions of one person; this was the time to summon the best he could be to get to the bottom of all this in a disciplined, comprehensive and systematic way. It was the only way to take down this rogue organization. He decided the first step was to schedule a meeting with the FBI Director, the FBI's General Counsel, and the Attorney General, and he would meet with them all at the same time. It was a way to hedge his risk, because at this point he couldn't be certain who else might be involved. He also would schedule the meeting in the AG's office. That would make it difficult for either the Director or the General Counsel to turn the meeting down. As that thought floated through his head, it gave birth to another idea. He would also invite Dr. Johnson, the NSA director. It would be interesting to observe the Director's reaction. It might also prove useful in flushing out a few more rats.

Office of Jonathon Wellington, III, Attorney General of the United States (2 hours later)

Benson's decision to involve the AG in this mess was a good idea. Jon Wellington was in many ways an odd choice as Attorney General. On the one hand, he had impeccable credentials – Yale undergrad in philosophy, Harvard Law, including assistant editor of the Law Review, and a lucrative 15 years in private practice at Covington & Burlington, LLP, in the litigation division. Licensed to practice before the U.S. Supreme Court, his specialty was First Amendment cases, and he had prevailed in seven of the eight cases he argued before that august body. He then was appointed directly to the D.C. Circuit Court of Appeals, widely viewed as the second highest court in the land and a stepping-stone to The Supremes. But after five years as a judge, he longed to be an advocate again, so he returned to private practice with his former firm. It felt much more like home than the staid environment of the Federal Court. The first several cabinet picks of the President had suffered brutal confirmation hearings in a Republican-controlled Senate, so she decided to buy herself a much safer pick for AG in Wellington. On the other hand, the President and Wellington saw eye to eye on very few things and the guy could be a real pain in the ass. Wellington would be a safe nomination, however, and the Senate would be hard-pressed to stonewall. Once the guy was safely buried in the Justice Department, Wellington would no longer be able to constantly nip at the President's flanks. There was definitely something to that wise adage about keeping your enemies closer, the President reasoned. The President would soon regret the choice.

Five men sat in Wellington's office – AG Wellington himself, FBI Director Emit Fields, NSA Director Dr. Adam Johnson, the FBI's Inspector General and Benson. Benson pressed the touch pad on his laptop and began to play the audio file. The FBI Director had not been happy when Benson had respectfully declined to brief him on the purpose of the meeting. Wellington seemed to be a bit annoyed with the drama, but Benson commanded enormous respect at the Bureau and was widely regarded as the ultimate straight shooter. Wellington respected Benson and felt inclined to give him a wide berth and see what happened.

Benson was an astute observer. It was his "particular set of skills" that made him dangerous to potential adversaries. His success at the Bureau and rapid rise had been almost as much a result of his instincts and his ability to read people as it had been of his smarts. He noticed Johnson's body language as they all sat there and listened to the file. He was obviously uncomfortable, to the brink of appearing worried. But Benson knew there was uncomfortable based on shock and anger, and there was uncomfortable based on fear. Benson's instincts told him Johnson was displaying the latter. The Director and IG were clearly displaying the former. Wellington sat stone-faced, unable to read.

When the file had completed playing, all five men sat in silence for what seemed like an eternity. Johnson then noticed that the other four men were all staring at him. Wellington finally broke the silence. "What do you know about this, Adam? Is any of this true?"

Benson noticed that beads of sweat were beginning to appear on Johnson's forehead. Johnson swallowed so hard it was audible then finally began to speak. "Jon, you know I cannot discuss classified matters in this office. Justice is not read into the details of our most classified threat detection programs. What I can tell you is this – I am as shocked by what I just heard on that audio file as any of you, and you have my word that I am going to get to the bottom of it."

In his extensive litigation experience, Wellington had learned that there was nothing that could throw a potential adversary off guard quicker than the ability to remain calm and a master of one's emotions in circumstances that would ordinarily elicit exactly the opposite. It was a skill he had perfected to a high art. "Adam," he asked, with an even, almost prosecutorial tone, "have you ever had a conversation with Executive Assistant Director McConnell during which you asked, and or she provided, personal information on this Joseph Barber, or any other United States Citizen?"

"With respect, Jon, I'm not going to answer that. As I told you, I am going to get to the bottom of this, and you have my word on it. Now if you gentlemen will excuse me, I obviously have some very important work to do," he said, while rising from his chair and turning towards the door.

"OK, Adam, have it your way," Wellington responded. "But you should be aware that my next conversation is going to be with Fitzpatrick."

"I think that's a good idea," Johnson replied, now sweating heavily. "Let me know his reaction." With that NSA Director Adam Johnson walked out the door.

The Director of the FBI was the next to speak. "Well it doesn't take a Ph.D. in criminal justice or psychology to know that guy is as guilty as sin. Unfortunately, I think he just confirmed everything on that audio file."

"I agree," Wellington replied.

"And if you'll excuse me," the FBI Director said, "I'm going to head back to the office and have a conversation with Sandra."

"Hold off on that," Wellington responded. "I happen to know that Fitzpatrick has his calendar blocked for three hours this morning to work on some kind of special assignment from the President. I think I'd like to pay him a surprise visit and I'd like you to come along with me. Don, you come too, and bring your laptop."

Palo Alto, California, Offices of PrinSafe, a Few Hours Later

Reynolds' concentration was broken again for the third time in only an hour as he heard his office intercom buzz. He reached across his desk and pushed the button. "I thought I asked you to hold all of my calls," he said with a hint of irritation to his voice. He was not given to displays of anger or irritation with his inner circle, and immediately regretted the tone of his response. "Sorry, Patty," he said, referring to Patricia Compton, his secretary, or administrative assistant as they were now called. "It's been a crazy morning, and I'm struggling to get through this material."

"Yes sir, and sorry myself," she responded. "But it's Mr. Fitzpatrick on line one, and he says it's extremely urgent. He sounded upset."

"Thank you. I'll take the call." With that, he reached over and touched another icon on his call director to connect him with Fitzpatrick. Reynolds was really starting to get annoyed at how high maintenance Fitzpatrick was becoming, and he kept thinking about that stop loss provision he had made. "What's up, Bill?"

"It's over, Westy," Fitzpatrick said with a tone of resignation in his voice.

"What do you mean, it's over? What's over?" he asked, with growing irritation.

"Barber managed to get his hands on Jennings. The how is too involved for this conversation. Just suffice it to say Jennings sang like a canary. Barber knows everything. He knows about Sparrow, he knows about the domestic drone program, and he knows about me. Barber apparently interrogated him somehow, and I just had a surprise visit from the AG and the FBI Director. They played an audio file of the interrogation. Jennings revealed everything. Everything!!! It was all on a fucking audio file, Westy!" Fitzpatrick was shouting now.

"Calm down, Bill, we survive setbacks, and we prosper in the face of setbacks by keeping our wits about us. You need to get a grip on yourself."

"Get a grip on myself?" Fitzpatrick shouted again. "Did you not hear what I just said? Do you have any idea how bad this is all going to look? This is not just politically embarrassing – we are going to jail! Frankly my next call is going to be to a lawyer, and you should do the same."

"Calm down, Bill," Reynolds said again, this time in an almost fatherly voice. Of course, it was all for show. "We will survive this, and nobody is going to go to jail. First thing you need to do is concentrate on the tasks at hand. Do your job. Look normal. And for God's sake don't go and hire a lawyer, at least not yet. When that time comes, if it comes, and I don't believe it will, I'll make sure you have the best representation money can buy. Instead of calling a lawyer you need to do two things and do them right now. Reboot your emotions and go on the offensive. We have accomplished much together and will continue to do so. So, this is what I want you to do. Do you have that bottle of Opus One I sent you?"

"Yes, of course," Fitzpatrick answered.

"Good. As soon as you get home I want you to text me, and we are going to open our respective bottles and enjoy several glasses together and talk about how we cauterize this wound. So, go home, and go home early, and crack open that bottle of wine, and when you have a glass poured, facetime me. I'll be sitting in my study with same. Got it?"

"Yes, got it," he responded.

"Good, don't let me down here. We sink or swim together. I am going to get you through this, and you can take that to the bank."

"Thanks, Westy," Fitzpatrick said, somewhat calmer now. "Talk to you tonight."

"Sounds good," Reynolds replied, then leaned across his desk and disconnected the call.

The entire conversation, of course, was all for show. Reynolds was fed up with this weak link, and he knew now for certain that executing a stop loss was essential. Cut off the head of the snake. That, of course, would only be the first step.

Chapter 49 – More Stop Losses

Emergency Room, Inova Alexandria Hospital, Later that Evening

Ryan Jennings was consumed in the vice of abdominal pains like he had never experienced before. It had all started about six hours ago or about two hours after he had eaten a corned beef sandwich for dinner. Likely food poisoning, the ER doc had told him. The doctor told him it looked like a really nasty case, and he needed to take it seriously. During the last couple of hours, he felt like he had expelled every ounce of fluid in his body from both ends. Cramps and dry heaves continued to consume him with a vengeance. He laid there in a small room on a gurney with an IV line plugged into his arm to feed saline solution and broad-spectrum antibiotics into his veins. The doctor told him severe dehydration was a real risk, and they wanted to monitor his potassium levels to make sure he wasn't so depleted of the important mineral to put him at risk of cardiac arrhythmia. A small dose of dilaudid helped dull the pain, but he was still miserable. A television screen was mounted over his bed and tuned to the local ABC News affiliate. The "Breaking News" moniker had just flashed across the screen below a picture of Fitzpatrick, and a reporter began to speak.

"This just in. William Fitzpatrick, Chief of Staff and close confidant to President Sara Einhorn, was found dead in his Georgetown townhouse this evening. Cause of death at this time is unknown, although preliminary reports suggest there is no evidence of foul play. Additional details on this story will be shared as they are made available by the authorities. We are told the White House plans to make a statement in the morning."

Jennings suddenly felt a cold chill which made him momentarily forget his pain. This couldn't be a coincidence, he thought to himself. Even from what little the reporter had said, the circumstances seemed too similar

443

to the deaths of Eric Longstreet, the Washington Post Reporter, and the death of Barber's secretary. He remembered his thoughts about the likely existence of a "contingency" plan against him and was suddenly thankful he was safe in a hospital emergency room at the moment and not home in bed. Would he be next, he asked? He tried to focus and think through what he needed to do to keep himself out of harm's way, but the dilaudid was making it difficult to think. His thoughts were interrupted as two men walked into his room. They both claimed to be nurses, one of them with a syringe in his hand. Through the fog of the dilaudid he barely noticed they weren't wearing scrubs, and it didn't register. "Time for another dose of antibiotics," one of the men said. "This is Danny," he casually commented, referring to his partner. "We are about to go through shift change and I thought I would introduce you to your charge nurse for the rest of your stay in the ER. We are pretty sure you are going to be admitted for observation for a day or so, and they hope to have a room upstairs ready within a couple of hours." The other man smiled and patted Jennings on the shoulder in a reassuring manner.

Jennings' thoughts of Fitzpatrick slipped from his mind for the moment as the interruption allowed the haze of the dilaudid to take hold again. The man with the syringe carefully inspected the IV line, pulled off the needle guard and inserted the needle into a port just below the saline bag. As he did so, the second man, whom Jennings had noticed was unusually large, suddenly leaned down and pinned Jennings to the bed, immobilizing his arms and his torso. It then all happened very quickly. Between the man's weight and the dilaudid, Jennings was unable to move. The nurse with the syringe then pressed the plunger, much more quickly than would be called for by the routine administration of an antibiotic and injected the fluid into the IV line. As he did, he squeezed the saline bag to speed the flow of 120 mg of potassium chloride into Jennings vein. Jennings suddenly felt an almost unbearable, searing pain as the fluid felt like it was setting his body on fire from the inside. The bigger man continued to pin him down as Jennings

444

attempted to thrash, but shortly his movements stopped along with his heart. The men carefully rearranged the body, particularly the arms, to give Jennings the appearance of being asleep. The man who had administered the potassium chloride retrieved another syringe from his pocket, this one filled with saline, and flushed the port. The two men waited to ensure the hall was clear, then casually left the room and re-entered a room about 3 doors down, where their "father" was laying on a bed waiting for the results of an enzyme test after complaining about chest pains. It was all a ploy, of course, a way to position them for the night's work. After several more hours of waiting, the man and his two "sons" would be told it was a false alarm and sent home. And nobody would be the wiser. Hiding in plain sight was an extraordinarily effective strategy.

* * * * *

NDSA Headquarters, McLean, VA, About the Same Time

It was late at night as Collins, Johnson, and Erby sat alone around what was now a near empty conference table in the Room. There was a handful of analysts occupying their posts in the digital forensics lab, and an Air Force Major was the watch officer in Ops. A few Marines stood guard at various places on the space, but otherwise it was largely empty, much more than usual for this time of night. The orders from Johnson had been to stand down. Sparrow was shut off, and the three remaining domestic drones were in various stages of being disposed of with flights towards the ocean beyond the continental shelf, then a dive towards deep water and the triggering of their magnesium incineration devices. But there was another drone that nobody was aware of. A drone that actually didn't fall under the command of the NSA. A drone that essentially served as an insurance policy, and one that the owner had hoped would never have to be used, but its time had come. The owner, of course, was not prone to sentimentality about such things.

The Epic 1000 is an extraordinary aircraft: an ultra high-performance, single engine turbo prop capable of speeds in excess of 325 knots, a ceiling of over 35,000 feet and a useful load in excess of 1,100 pounds at full fuel. Its short take off and landing rolls allowed it to use many smaller, non-controlled airfields, a capability that was extraordinarily useful for the bird presently traveling at 300 knots towards McLean, VA. The bird had been painted black, to minimize its visibility, and the tail number had been painted over to conceal its identity. This particular aircraft had been fitted with four highly specialized customizations. First, it had a completely automated flight system allowing it to be flown remotely. In that sense, it was very much a drone. Second, its avionics included a custom-engineered and highly effective radar jamming device which would render it nearly invisible to any local air traffic control, as well as the onboard collision avoidance radars of more sophisticated private aircraft that happen to be sharing, unawares, its airspace this particular evening. Third, at several strategic places along the fuselage were a number of magnesium incineration devices that would ensure that the aircraft would be burned beyond any possible recognition if it crashed, or if the remote pilot decided it was in everybody's best interests to simply make it disappear. Finally, and most important to its mission, most of the interior had been removed and replaced with 500 one-pound blocks of Semtex, enough to easily take down a fairly large-sized building. Over 3,000 miles away an operator carefully monitored the aircraft's progress as it flew towards its intended destination. The event that was about to occur would appear to be yet another terrorist attack against a seemingly ordinary building with no strategic purpose. It would be subsequently revealed to be the Ops Center of a highly classified counter-terrorist effort run by the National Security Agency. A compliant, and insufficiently curious press working through the lens of their own bias, would no doubt spin the event as an act of revenge against Islam's demonstrable threat, the United States, and that was exactly what the planners hoped. But there would be no pilot on board who would shout Allah-u-Akbar as the aircraft hit the building. The reaction from the planners would more likely be a sigh of relief, and perhaps even a faint smile. The attack was not an event motivated by any religion – it was simply the cashing in on a carefully planned insurance policy. Or, as some preferred to call it, the exercise of yet another stop loss.

Erby stood up, looked at his two colleagues and said, "I'm done, gentlemen. As a matter of fact, I intend to go back to my office and dictate a statement of everything that has happened during the last week. How this all could have fallen off the rails so quickly I have no idea. But I know one thing, I will not be a part of this anymore. By the way, I also intend to engage the services of a lawyer, and I suggest both of you do the same. Good night." With that he walked out of the Room, out of the NDSA offices, towards the elevator and to his car in the basement garage. As he exited the elevator, he was struck with the pleasantness of the cool night air. It lifted his spirits slightly, but also created a sense of melancholy as he reflected on the likelihood that he would have precious few free evenings over the coming months to enjoy what remained of the summer. He was certain that all of his spare time for the indeterminate future would be spent with lawyers and putting his affairs in order. As he took the first few steps toward his car he thought he heard the faint sound of an airplane. Not a big passenger plane, but something smaller. It would be the last thing Admiral George Erby would ever hear.

Chapter 50 – Madam President

The Oval Office

A bright morning sun poured through the large, floor to ceiling windowpanes of bulletproof glass. Beams of light danced about the elegant room, casting shadows in some places and illuminating features in others. A bright reflection bounced from atop the Resolute desk, giving it an almost ethereal look. The unique shape of the room, as well as its stately furnishings, did much to reinforce the sense that this room was a special place, the seat of unimaginable power as well as abiding hope. What happened in this room changed people's lives, sometimes for the better, and sadly sometimes for the worse. No matter how cynical a person might be, however, simply entering this space could easily fill one with awe and wonder; awe and wonder, that is, until the lesser angels of one's nature and human fallibility brought back a sense of reality. For throughout the Nation's history it was all too often given to men and women to walk through those doors with troubling news, the darkest of secrets, and the most unpleasant of missions. At such times they would find themselves not overwhelmed with a sense of grandeur, but rather overcome with a sense of sadness, anger, or even disgust. Such a dark cloud was in full bloom as three men and one woman entered the Oval for the President's first meeting of the morning. President Einhorn stood up from the desk and with an extended right arm motioned them towards the sitting area. The President's Deputy Chief of Staff, Allison Belinda, was the first to sit down. With the untimely and as yet unexplained death of Bill Fitzpatrick, she was acting Chief of Staff; although she was not convinced it was a job she wanted. Much would depend on how things unfolded over the next 48 hours. Following her were two cabinet officers, Attorney General Jonathon Wellington and Allen Wellesly from Homeland Security. The Director of National Intelligence, David Ericson, completed the group. Each took a seat in proximity to the President that was in strict compliance with Oval Office protocol.

President Einhorn was the first to speak. "Terrible news last night, Al," she said, directing her comment to Allen Wellesly from DHS. "What do we know at this point about the building, why it was a target, and who was behind this?" she asked.

"We know very little, Madam President," responded Wellesly, "other than half of the fourth floor of the building was evidently home to some sort of a counter-terrorism op run by the NSA. Whoever planned the strike against the building must have been aware of that because it was that side of the fourth floor that the drone, aircraft, or whatever it was, hit.

"How do we know it was a Government anti-terrorism office?" the President asked. She would ordinarily be regarded as a pretty good poker player, but her faced betrayed a hint of nervousness.

"Well, there's the tape, ma'am," Wellington responded. "We'll get to that in a minute. But also, well, evidently there was a remote video recording system across the street that survived. The system is NSA owned, and we are guessing that it was installed by whomever occupied the fourth floor. The video feed picked up several license plates that we traced to Government-owned vehicles. And fortunately, we were able to tie some of the plates to specific individuals, or at least to agencies where the vehicles were assigned. The license plate data suggest that numerous Government employees, including a few senior ones, frequently visited the place or at least were in the area. Many of their jobs were counter-terrorism related. We also got hits on license plates assigned to the Marine Corp., several from the Navy, and at least two plates from the Air Force, many of which appeared at the facility almost daily. We are looking into that. Interestingly there is no facial recognition hits of any government employees actually entering the building, which is strange."

The President swallowed noticeably at the revelation of the recording system. Thoughts of Richard Nixon and his problem with recordings flashed through her mind.

"It appears," Wellington continued, "to be a pretty sophisticated effort as well. Early reports suggest virtually no trace of the weapon itself has been recovered. Our teams have recovered some trace evidence of magnesium fires, suggesting the device, or whatever it was, was equipped with something to incinerate it. Similar to what we found in the molten wreckage of the drone that went down in the Bay. Whoever was behind this obviously wanted to make sure it would be impossible to identify. The death toll at this point is believed to be 54, although that could change. The intensity of the fire is making it hard to identify bodies. Our forensics teams are collecting DNA samples and whatever else they can find to help with the process, but it's going to be slow and difficult. There is one thing we are fairly certain of. It appears that Director Johnson and Admiral Erby were in the building when it happened. They both are missing and presumed dead."

"How terribly sad," the President responded, trying to regain her composure.

"Madam President, there are a lot of questions that need to be answered here, not the least of which is exactly what went on in that building and who authorized it. As you are aware, a private citizen managed to question, I'll even say interrogate, Special Agent Ryan Jennings from NSA. You've been provided with a copy of the tape. I presume you've listened to it. We've done a preliminary digital forensics analysis of it, and so far we are unable to determine who is asking the questions. The questioner's voice is digitally altered, and whoever that was, seemed to go to considerable lengths to mask his identity. The answers, however, were clearly coming from Jennings. Our voice analysis confirmed that. And his vehicle plate is one that showed up routinely, almost daily, at the building, although he wasn't there last night. I am also sorry to say that Agent Jennings, in another of a long strain of uncomfortable coincidences, seemed to have met an untimely death in the last 24 hours as well."

"What happened to him?" the President asked, feigning surprise.

"All we know ma'am is he wound up dead in a local emergency room last night. He was taken there for some kind of food poisoning, but the ER staff doesn't see how that could be responsible for his death. They are doing an autopsy this morning. We'll let you know as soon as we get the report. Did you listen to the tape, ma'am?" he then asked.

"Yes, I've listened to the tape," the President responded with a clear and measured voice, carefully crafted to minimize any hint of unease. "I trust you are sparing no resources in investigating where that trail leads."

"That is correct, ma'am," the AG responded, with his own even voice, carefully crafted not to convey disrespect but leavened with a touch of skepticism. Wellington had a highly developed bullshit sensor, and the needle was presently burying itself on the right-hand side of the scale. His tone was intended to convey the message that he was indeed going to pursue this wherever, and to whomever, it led. "I'm sure you are also aware, then, that the tape also made reference to The Department of Special Activities, as it's apparently called, as being authorized by a Presidential Finding that was signed by you."

"Yes, that's absolutely correct," the President responded, "although I never knew what it was called. After the Disney attack I directed Bill to work within our intelligence community to put in place a state-of-the-art threat detection capability, as well as the ability to respond with sufficient dispatch to actually make a difference, all within the law, of course. Bill asked for, and I completely supported, an all-sufficient means clause in the Finding. He also argued on behalf of the intelligence professionals he worked with that there was a consensus on the need to keep it covert. That also made sense to me, so I agreed. We both agreed that this needed to be developed and managed by the professionals, and not second-guessed or micromanaged by the White House. The last thing we needed was a risk of someone tainting the process with political motives. That seemed to be the best way to develop a capability that was sustainable, and one that would survive beyond this administration. To ensure that, Bill insisted that nobody at or above cabinet level would be involved in any of the operational details. I wholly supported that concept at program inception, and I continue to support it today. Novel idea for politics – set the strategy, delegate, and let the smart people do their jobs."

An eerie, uncomfortable silence followed the President's comments as the four sat there and processed what the President had said. In both content and tone it was clearly a political statement carefully crafted to shield her from any major accountability or fallout. Of course, they all knew it wouldn't work. Being unaware of something was not exactly an effective defense for the captain of the ship. Einhorn, however, had one very important thing working in her favor. It would seem that almost everyone with direct knowledge of how involved the President had been was now dead. My, wasn't that convenient, Wellington thought. DNI Ericson finally broke the silence. "Madam President, with great respect, how is it that the Director of National Intelligence was not read into this program? One of the key findings of the 9/11 Commission was that lack of interagency cooperation served as a major contributing factor to threat detection failure. My job is to ensure that never happens again, yet I was totally unaware of this program. And I can assure you the National Counterterrorism Center knew nothing about the NDA's Department of Special Activities. It would seem obvious that the work of these two organizations greatly overlapped, at least on the intelligence gathering side. CIA was in the dark as well."

AG Wellington was the next to speak. "I am greatly concerned, ma'am, about the legal footing for the operations arm of this organization. Especially given it appears to have been operating on U.S. soil and targeting U.S. citizens who had zero connections to foreign nationals. Is there a legal opinion from White House Counsel on its Constitutionality? I know our office was not asked for, and never rendered, such an opinion. And, sorry, I have to ask, what was the legal theory behind NSA directing actions against U.S. citizens? That's the FBI's remit. It's hard to imagine any constitutional basis for that. All sufficient means language, in a Presidential Finding, would not be enough."

"I was assured of at least two lengthy legal briefs covering this," the President responded. "I, of course, would never have signed the finding without them. Bill suggested it wasn't necessary for me to read them, and I agreed. I'm not a lawyer, and I saw nothing I could constructively add. The fact that they existed is what was important. By the way, I assume you are sparing no effort in trying to determine who the other voice is on that audio file. Somehow, I can't imagine that Agent Jennings voluntarily agreed to that line of questioning, which means at the very least the person behind that other voice is likely guilty of kidnapping a Federal Agent and who knows what else." If President Einhorn was good at anything, she was good at turning questions around and going on the offensive.

That was rich, AG Wellington thought to himself. "Yes, Madam President, we are trying to identify the individual. The fact that Agent Jennings is dead is making that a bit difficult, as you might imagine. Fortunately, we believe that Assistant Director Sandra McConnell from the FBI may have some insight into that. She is being questioned as we speak." And she is alive at the moment, Wellington thought to himself.

"What was her role in all of this?" the President asked. "Given the covert nature of the organization's remit, I would have thought the FBI would not have been read into the program."

"I can assure you Madam President we were not," the FBI Director responded, with a hint of anger in his voice. "I knew absolutely nothing about it. Nothing. I am sure you are aware there was a close relationship between Ms. McConnell and Chief of Staff Fitzpatrick. It is also becoming pretty clear that Bill was much more involved in this organization than you were aware. I suspect it would be a pretty good working assumption that McConnell's involvement was connected to her relationship with him. I placed her on administrative leave first thing this morning and had her ushered out of her office after the questioning. Our digital forensics team is scrubbing her computers to see what she may have been up to. She will not be allowed back into the building or given access to her accounts until, and unless, she is completely cleared."

Even somebody with the discipline of Einhorn couldn't mask a troubled look at what the FBI Director had just said, and they all took notice. The President wanted this meeting over, and she took the initiative to bring it to a close. Summoning her command voice again, she said, "I'm preparing to release a public statement on the incident shortly and need to get back to work on it. We are not going to call this terrorism until we have more concrete evidence, although I will say we are ruling nothing out as yet. And we are not making any reference to the NSA until we better understand exactly what happened. Get to work on figuring this mess out. Let me know as soon as you have something," she almost barked. "I'd like a status report no later than 4 o'clock this afternoon, whatever you have at that point."

"Yes, Madam President," Allison Belinda, said, looking at the men in the room. The President then stood up and started walking towards the

Resolute Desk, signaling the meeting, and further discussions, were over. The
four senior Administration officials stood up on her cue and walked out.

Chapter 51 – Friends

Founders Fishers Bakers, Georgetown

Don Benson sat in the booth beside the window and took a long pull from his Arnold Palmer. He was an angry man, and not the least bit hungry. He knew his system well enough, however, to understand if he didn't force himself to eat something he would be next to worthless by mid-afternoon. It was one of the few downsides of his unusually high metabolism. He ordered a Caesar's chicken wrap and waited. Just as his food arrived, Joe Barber slid into the booth across from him. Joe was sporting a two-day growth of beard and a baseball cap, as well as a pair of aviator sunglasses, which didn't seem out of place given the bright sun shining through the window next to their table. The best tradecraft, he knew, was the simplest. Too obvious an effort to mask one's appearance would scream "look at me!" Yet small, subtle changes would easily throw off even an expert's ability to recognize a face.

"That was quite an audio file you produced," Benson said.

"Yeah, a veritable best seller on iTunes, I bet," Joe replied.

"I sure hope not!" Benson said. "But it's gotten a lot of people's attention, including the President's."

"How did she react to it?" Joe asked.

"I don't know yet. All I was told is that the AG, The Director, and the Acting Chief of Staff met with her this morning. Hopefully I'll get something later, but it's not exactly like I can ring up the AG and ask for a report on a meeting with the President."

"Have they figured out who I am yet?" Joe asked.

"No, but it's only a matter of time given they are talking to McConnell," Benson replied. "They've got her dead to rights, and I suspect that soon she will be singing loudly for a deal. I think her testimony, however, should only identify you as somebody NSA was after. I don't think there is any evidence, that I am aware of at least, that makes you the interrogator on that file."

"Who said I was the interrogator on that file?" Joe asked, with a smile.

"Don't bullshit me, pal, you and I both know perfectly well that was you."

"We most certainly do not," Joe replied, this time with a hint of seriousness in his voice. "And you would be well-served to remember that, Don, not for my sake but for yours. Stick strictly to the facts, as you always do. The Bureau may suspect it was me, but they will never be able to prove it. And in that lies our mutual safety."

"Are you taking any of this public?" Benson asked.

"I've already given a copy of the audio file to the Washington Post. It's the least I could do for Eric Longstreet," Joe said.

"I'm not surprised," Don said. "There's going to be a lot of collateral damage when the lid gets blown off this thing. It's hard to imagine the President surviving it. If ever there was a definition of an impeachable offense, this is it."

"She'll be lucky if this just ends in impeachment," Joe replied.

"Be careful, my friend. The walls have ears."

"I mean the woman should go to jail for the rest of her pathetic life. This rogue organization is not only responsible for who knows how many deaths, but it intentionally targeted lethal action against U.S. citizens. And worse yet, it didn't even do it to save lives. It did it as an act of self-preservation," Joe said.

"I know, and that's the sad truth about so much of what goes on in this town. People start out with good intentions but quickly lose sight of the real mission. I don't think there's a single part of our government that doesn't see self-preservation as a primary goal, although few would admit it. Fortunately, most seem to do at least a little good along the way."

"So how's this thing playing out at the moment?" Joe asked.

"I'll bet you dimes for dollars that the President is up to her eyeballs in this. She also probably thinks she has shrouded herself in some kind of cocoon of plausible deniability, but we'll be able to burn through that like a torch through cotton candy. Both the acting Chief of Staff and the AG seem to be playing along for the moment, but I'll bet they both believe Einhorn is as guilty as sin. Wellington will demand we get the remit on the investigation. He'll resign if we don't," Benson said.

"I hope you're right," Barber responded.

The President plans to brief the senior leadership of Congress this afternoon," Benson continued, "and there's no way they won't demand a special prosecutor once they get a whiff of what's really happened here. Your audio file is a bombshell. Einhorn can keep it from Congress for maybe a couple of weeks, tops, but once they start their hearings it's going to come out. I understand, off the record, that the AG has even suggested a plant question to ensure he gets a chance to reveal it."

"Somehow I suspect the senior leadership of Congress already may have the audio file, Don," Barber said again with a smile as he lifted his own Arnold Palmer and took a long pull.

"Seriously? Wow!" Benson said, then began rubbing his temples with a pained expression on his face. "I assume you don't want me to say anything to the AG about that?"

"Correct," Joe answered, "how would you tell him you knew?"

"There are visitor logs at the Bureau, Joe, and your name appears at least a couple of times of late. They will know we talked."

"Yes," Joe replied, "but there are no records of what we talked about. Besides, I had no knowledge of this mess when we met and was simply there to turn over what I thought could be evidence of a crime. You can reveal everything I said and nothing will point to, shall we say, more recent events."

"Point taken," Benson replied.

"And besides," Joe said, "I think it's better to let Congress set their trap. Of course, that's assuming that collection of clowns can keep their mouths shut long enough to spring the trap."

"I'll take the under on that, Joe," Benson responded, using a gambling phrase suggesting the collection of clowns could not keep their mouths shut. "Where do you go from here with all of this?"

"You know there's only so much I can tell you, Don, for both of our sakes. But I will say the following – I plan on finding out who was responsible for trying to take me out. If not the NSA, then who? I need to know the answer. I owe it to Longstreet, and I certainly owe it to Jennifer. I will work within the law. I'm an intelligence expert, remember? It's what I do."

"I understand," Benson replied. "Just remember, we will be running our own investigation too. You need to let us handle it, Joe." Benson didn't believe for a moment Joe would agree to that. And although he regarded

Barber as a consummate professional, he also didn't believe the guy would allow the finer points of the law to impede his search for the truth.

"I know that, Don, but you and I both know where your focus and resources are going to be directed. The Bureau is going to be going after the President on this, and other high value targets. The first order of business is going to be figuring out who gave birth to this rogue organization. The second will be its connection to those terrorist events. Somewhere way down the Fed's priority list, after everyone connected to it has already been fired, will be questions about actions directed against me, Longstreet, or who knows who else. I'm not going to wait that long."

"Understood," Benson replied. "But we also have that uncomfortable issue of who was asking the questions on that audio file. The fact that you scrubbed it won't keep us from running that to ground."

"I don't know what you're talking about, Don," Joe replied. "And that's the way things have to be. Our relationship has rendered some pretty big dividends for both of us over the years. We don't want to kill the goose that has laid so many golden eggs. Your investigation is going to show that I'm guilty of nothing more than being curious and good at connecting a lot of dots, to the chagrin of this rogue organization."

"And you'll stay within the law?" Benson asked.

"That's what I've told you," Joe replied. A very Clintonian answer, Benson thought to himself, but just smiled.

"I owe you an apology on all of this, Joe. Clearly, I was too much of a skeptic and should have trusted your instincts, especially after that forensics evidence went missing."

"You responded the only way you could. The Bureau deals in facts, not in instincts, no matter how talented the source. Besides, at least one of us has to be a Boy Scout," Barber said, smiling again. "If I turn up anything I believe could be useful to the Bureau I'll get it to you. Otherwise I think this should be our last meeting until this mess is sorted out."

"Agreed, be good."

"Always," Barber replied, as he slid out of the booth and walked away.

Chapter 52 – The Pet Cobra

Palo Alto, California, Offices of PrinSafe

Westy Reynolds walked into the conference room with the confidence and manner of a man who was thoroughly in control. The events of the last 72 hours would have greatly troubled many an ordinary man, but Reynolds was no ordinary man. Everything he did in business, and life, was meticulously planned, and every plan provided for multiple contingencies. He always stayed three steps ahead of every potential problem and, if faced with a Black Swan event, he improvised as only he could. He had accomplished much in his life, and he was convinced to an absolute moral certainty that there was nothing he could not do and no obstacle he could not overcome. To the weak, setbacks represented defeat. To the strong, the gifted, setbacks were only temporary detours along a road towards ever-greater heights. And Charles Westbourne Reynolds III was destined to achieve ever-greater heights. He was certain of it. He would not allow this setback, no matter how disappointing, to be anything other than that momentary detour.

A solitary woman sat at the long mahogany table as he entered the elegant conference room adjacent to his office. She was summoned there for the occasion, a briefing, face to face with the man himself. There were some matters that needed to be discussed in person and in a place that was as secure from electronic eavesdropping as any place on earth. Dr. Emma Clark, Chief Executive Officer of QuarkSpin, sat patiently, hands folded on the conference tabletop. There was nothing in front of her. No briefing books, no papers, no leather portfolio from which she could retrieve materials to present and discuss. The very existence of such things, whether in digital or written form, would have been reckless. It would have been a major point of failure in their security, vulnerable to disclosure from many potential mishaps, everything from a traffic stop to an accident. She carried everything she needed to know, and discuss, in her head.

As Reynolds passed through the door and closed it behind him, he entered an eight-digit code into a keypad next to the door handle. A medium sized touch pad lit up, signaling that the correct code had been entered and that the pad was ready to read a handprint. Reynolds placed his left hand on the pad and in precisely 3 seconds there was a faint buzz as a small lamp on the conference table switched from red to green, signaling the room was secure. He was the first to speak, and wasted no time getting to the point.

"So, the wound has been cauterized?" Reynolds asked.

"Yes," Dr. Clark answered. "If the aircraft is identified, and it won't be, it will be traced to a relative of a Saudi prince who remains a person of interest in the 911 investigation. It's a cold case in limbo due to lack of hard evidence and because no one in the last several administrations had the stomach to go after a member of the royal family without a case that was air-tight. If the FBI figures it out, which they won't, they will still have to run down that rabbit hole for years. And they'll encounter roadblocks from State, CIA, Defense, and no doubt any number of other governmental interests who need to protect the royal family from embarrassment. It will be a dead end."

"Good," Reynolds replied, "false records inculcated deep into the document history of State and the Agency."

"Exactly," she responded.

"Any principles left standing we need to be worried about?"

"We don't believe so. Not principals at least. We really got lucky on that front. There was an emergency ExComm meeting going on last night. They were all in the building at the moment of impact and to the best of our understanding there are no senior principles who survived."

"We do have an unfortunate loose end in Sandra McConnell. I underestimated the zipper risk," Reynolds said.

"Zipper risk?" Clark asked.

"Yes, Bill's inability to keep his pants zipped. He brought in McConnell on his own initiative. He trusted her, but his emotions clouded his judgment and he couldn't see the threat posed by bringing in an outsider, no matter how useful she might have been in a tactical sense, given her access to FBI information."

"It's handled, Westy. I don't leave loose ends," Clark retorted as coldly as a Mr. Spock.

"Seriously?" he asked, almost with astonishment. "Good. I won't ask."

"Don't," she responded.

"Collateral damage at the building?" Reynolds asked.

"Unavoidable, but the late hour minimized it. A few Marines, some low-level analyst types and that's it. We don't know who may have been about in the rest of the building, but it couldn't have been more than a few night security guards."

"Attribution risk?" he asked, without even a hint of regret at the loss of innocent life.

"Zero. The back doors we built into the systems of NDSA worked as planned and everything was cleansed about 2 minutes before the aircraft strike. There will be no digital forensics fingerprint and no attribution to anything. As to the physicals, the remaining operational drones have been moved to the secure site. We're completely clean."

"Good. Thanks. When more of this breaks in the news, I'm going to call the Minority Leader of the Senate and offer our help in the investigation. Should buy a bit of goodwill, and if he takes us up on it we'll get an inside track on where the investigation is going."

"Brilliant, Westy," said Dr. Clark, "we own him, don't we?"

"Yes," Reynolds answered, "when the guy was sinking in the last election we funded a good part of his election super PAC. It clearly bought him the 2 to 3 extra points he needed to skate by."

"Right. Exactly at the time he was railing against Citizens United. Love the irony."

"Well the guy may be a nebbish, but at least he's a useful one," Reynolds said, finding it difficult to restrain his smile.

"Love it, what do you want us to do about this Barber character?" she asked.

"Interesting question, Emma. As you know, Mr. Barber and I have a bit of a history. He's never figured that out, of course. My count is at two strikes on this guy now. I cannot abide the thought of a failure, a strike three."

"We still have real-time intel on him. I have a team deployed in DC on stand by. They are the best. All are former Russian Spetznaz. There won't be another mistake. By the way, two previous failures?" she asked, quizzically.

"Yes," Reynolds answered. "The first was a while ago. No need to dwell on it. Tell me your plan."

As she spoke, she looked at him with cold, emotionless eyes, contrasted by a slight smile. There was only one word to describe the look – lethal. It actually gave Reynolds a chill, something he rarely experienced. An image flashed through his head. It was as though he was sitting there

465

looking at a pet cobra. But this one wasn't in a cage. It was sitting right there in front of him. He also was certain of one additional thing. She already was thinking several steps ahead in formulating an Op plan. The cobra was plotting its strike. He was very happy she was his pet and that he was not her prey. As their discussion concluded and he stood up to leave, he felt an emotion he hadn't experienced since he was a child. Vulnerability. This woman was a force.

Chapter 53 – An Eventful Drive

FBI Headquarters, Washington D.C. (a few hours earlier)

To say it was the worst humiliation she had ever experienced would be an understatement. In point of fact, it was one of the few humiliations she had ever experienced. FBI Executive Assistant Director, Homeland Security, Sandra McConnell had just spent the last three and a half hours in what was essentially an interrogation room being grilled about her connection to the NSA's Department of Special Activities, as well as her relationship with the late William Fitzpatrick. To make things even worse, the Inspector General himself even pressed her on a number of areas of her personal life that she regarded as none of the Bureau's business. At the conclusion of the meeting, she was informed that she would not be allowed to return to her office until the investigation had been completed, and then only if she was cleared. The guy actually used those words. Her office would be extensively searched, and in the process any personal items would be packed up and sent to her residence. Then the ultimate humiliation for any law enforcement officer – she was asked to surrender her cred pack and her service sidearm, a Glock 43, along with her building pass. A member of the Bureau's armed security staff and a representative from HR then escorted her out of the building and to her car in the executive garage, parading her past her colleagues in what could only be described as a perp walk. It was called being placed on administrative leave. It felt more like being indicted for a felony. And to reinforce that impression, the Director concluded the meeting by suggesting it would be a very good idea if she retained defense counsel.

She remained silent as she walked with her escorts towards her Lexus GS F performance sedan parked in one of the prime spots reserved for the "top of the house" or "grown-ups" as executive management was sometimes called. But anger and resentment weren't her only emotions. She was genuinely frightened. As a lawyer, she knew full well the implications of her actions. As a former partner in the DC power law firm of Williams and Connelly, she had already settled on the name of the lawyer she would call as soon as she got to her car. The Bureau security officer had taken her FBI iPhone. Fortunately, she had the foresight to have one of her own in her vehicle's glove box.

They walked her right up to the driver's side door and waited for her to unlock and enter the vehicle. What did those two clowns think she was going to do, she thought to herself as she slipped into the driver's seat and secured the seat belt, run? They had even taken her briefcase. If the process of frog-marching a pariah out of the building was intended to impart a sense of humiliation and fear, it was working, she said to herself. She lit up the 467-horsepower engine and revved it a couple of times as if to flip her two escorts the bird. She slipped the transmission into reverse, then, as her final statement while on Bureau property, sped out of the executive garage at a speed that would have gotten most other employees in a great deal of trouble; and left a nice long set of skid marks in the process. Approaching the gated entry/exit about 25 feet outside of the garage itself, she slowed down to let the gate rise and then hit the accelerator to deliberately squeal the tires again as the powerful sedan rocketed towards the service drive. She knew perfectly well such a sign of aggression would accomplish nothing, but it made her feel better. And at this point, some cleansing from the ordeal she had just gone through was cathartic.

The Lexus, a 2016 model, was WiFi enabled. It was becoming a common feature of newer vehicles, especially the expensive ones. It allowed the driver to stream music and no doubt do a variety of other things that weren't particularly safe to do while driving. It also allowed the manufacturer to receive telemetry about how the vehicle was performing to, presumably, make it better.   The vehicle itself was essentially a computer, or more accurately a series of computers, on wheels. The various solid-state modules controlled everything from the engine to the transmission, to lane sensing, navigation, the entertainment system and everything in between.   In the hands of a skilled hacker, however, the WiFi capability also provided a back door to the vehicle's systems and even the ability to control it.

The first step was gaining access to the digital blueprints of the vehicle software itself. With that, the malware could be written. Then the specific targeted vehicle had to be identified.   This was accomplished by obtaining the vehicle's VIN, or vehicle identification number, akin to a serial number. This could be fairly easily accomplished by hacking into the records of the dealership from where the Lexus had been purchased. With the VIN in hand, the hacker then could direct malware code to the targeted vehicle and, if he or she was clever enough, make it do most anything. QuarkSpin, of course, only employed the brightest in their respective fields.

The Lexus sped down Pennsylvania Avenue as if to dare any member of the Capital Police to pull it over. None saw her, and therefore none did. But then an odd thing happened. After the initial burst of speed cleansed her anger a bit, she lightened her foot on the accelerator to slow down. But nothing happened. Several thousand miles away a programmer sat stooped over a desk staring into a laptop and sent a coded message to the vehicle's electronic control module. In spite of taking her foot off the gas, the powerful vehicle continued to accelerate. It reached 50, 60, 70, then 80 miles per hour. At about 85 miles an hour it made a sudden swerve to the right, an outcome also directed by the hacker thanks to the electronic assisted steering. The slight turn took it up over a curb, sent it airborne, then caused it to smash directly into a large concrete block protecting the front of the National Gallery of Art. As an insurance policy, the hacker also disabled the airbag sensors, so none deployed. As a result, Sandra McConnell was killed instantly, along with an unfortunate tourist who happened to be in the wrong spot at the wrong time and was struck by the fast-moving vehicle as it jumped the curb.

In the coming investigation conducted by the Department of Justice and the FBI, Sara McConnell's death would be regarded as yet another unexplainable coincidence. But there would be no evidence of foul play. The evidence would clearly show her Lexus experienced a stuck accelerator from a glitch in the engine control module, likely a software flaw. It would also show that multiple defective airbag sensors prevented their deployment. And although there were no recent field reports of similar incidents with other Lexus vehicles, the manufacturer had experienced related problems in the past and that bolstered the credibility of the preliminary conclusions. The manufacturer would face an inquisition from the National Highway Safety Administration about the safety defects and would ultimately be forced to recall over 40,000 vehicles.

As a finishing touch, the hacker had inculcated into McConnell's personal home computer browser history several fake online orders for depression medication, specifically Prozac and Zoloft, which would plant the seeds of doubt about the Executive Assistant Director's mental stability and vulnerability to suicide. This would be discovered during the investigation and would provide a convenient alternative path for the investigation, should there be any skepticism regarding the mechanical failures. It was a quality plan.

The hacker stared intently into his laptop screen and watched the progress of the vehicle via several of the street cameras deployed along Pennsylvania Ave. He had hacked into the traffic monitoring system as well. He quietly smiled to himself as he reflected on how almost anyone now was potentially vulnerable to this new weaponized software. Anyone, that is, driving a newer vehicle that was WiFi enabled. Not to worry, he thought to himself, as he reflected on the nature of potential future targets. The rich and famous, the one-percenters, and senior government officials don't drive clunkers. Jonathon Ayers then thought how unfortunate it was that his father didn't have access to this capability back in the day.

Chapter 54 – The Safe House

Four Seasons Hotel, 5 AM, the next morning

The coppery taste in his mouth overwhelmed his senses. The viscous life fluid spraying in his face had all but obliterated his vision, no matter how quickly he blinked to clear it. The weight of the man's body hurt Barber's neck badly as he violently twisted his head and endeavored to pull himself backwards. He knew he had struck an effective tactical blow at his assailant, but in the moment he had no idea of how effectively, and it was clear that the outcome of this engagement was still in doubt. The only thing certain was he was engaged in a battle for his life. He had to win. He summoned every ounce of his strength, because he knew that to let up even a little bit would mean death. As he squeezed his eyes tightly in the hope of expelling the noxious fluid and clearing his vision, he could feel his heart pounding like a roaring freight train from both the fear and exertion. He could actually hear his pulse. As he tried to open his eyes again, he was terrified by the unmistakable sensation that he was now on his back. If that was true, he knew the fight was over. He had lost. His thoughts went to Diana, his wife, and his father. Both of his arms flailed as he desperately tried to grab hold of something, anything that would give him more leverage. "I CANNOT end this way!" he shouted as he arched his back and continued to flail. As he managed to open his eyes and brought them into focus, he realized he was staring at – the ceiling – of his hotel room. He was in bed, dripping with sweat. It was the dream again. That horrific act had saved his life, but he was paying a high price.

CIA Safe House, Alexandria VA, two hours later

Gerhard Krause wasn't accustomed to attending meetings in a CIA safe house. As Director of the National Clandestine Service, he had become a "suit" and conducted most of his business from the 7th floor at Langley. But occasionally a task arose that required an extra measure of discretion. As a top Agency executive, he could easily delegate such things to his subordinates, but as a former SAD, or Special Activities Division operator himself, he actually enjoyed the occasional foray into the field. This was especially true when it involved meeting one of his former star employees.

Krause was the grandson of German immigrants. His paternal grandfather, Helmut Krause, was a protégé of Werner Von Braun and brought his young family to America as part of the wave of German rocket scientists who immigrated after World War II. Gerhard was destined to follow in the family's footsteps with a scholarship to study physics at MIT. But his experience in the college R.O.T.C. program revealed he was as gifted athletically as he was academically. After graduating from MIT, he put his Ph.D. studies on hold to complete his active duty requirements in the Army. It was a decision that would forever change his life. He graduated second in his Ranger class and qualified for First Special Forces Operational Detachment-Delta, the Army's Tier 1 Special Forces Unit. After several operations, commands and deployments, he was selected for the Army's graduate education program and completed an M.B.A. at the Wharton School with highest honors. It was that accomplishment that brought him to the attention of the Central Intelligence Agency. After several overtures and a lot of soul searching, Gerhard relented and agreed to join the Special Activities Division of the CIA, the Agency's paramilitary arm largely staffed by ex-special forces personnel. He quickly became a rising star and found himself in a succession of assignments that were designed to push him out of his comfort zone. He excelled in each one which ultimately led to his selection as Director of NCS, the number 3 post at CIA. Gerhard's father had been the chief engineer of N.A.S.A.'s shuttle propulsion systems office. He was initially disappointed in his son's decision not to pursue a Ph.D. in physics. The disappointment, however, dissipated, quickly.

Krause had commanded several SAD missions on his rise to the top of the service and had become somewhat of a mentor to Joe Barber during Joe's days in SAD. He was looking forward to seeing Joe again. But Barber's presence wasn't the primary reason he felt it necessary to attend this meeting in person. Indeed, Joe had been invited almost as an afterthought. Donald Benson, the Executive Assistant Director for Intelligence, FBI, had requested the meeting and Benson had specifically asked that Krause attend the meeting himself. Krause and Benson had become friends during each man's rise to the upper echelons of their respective organizations, but their friendship did not blind either man to the reality of appearances. Given recent events and the high profile of both their jobs, they could hardly visit each other's office. Such a meeting would be noticed by the press, who were now obsessed not only with the attack on the Golden Gate Bridge but also the attack on the building in McLean. Krause and Benson both knew that reports of a meeting between them had the potential to launch conspiracy theories. So the Alexandria safe house was selected as the venue that provided the most discretion and the best security.

Benson had been fairly brisk on the telephone simply saying, "We need to talk." Krause was seething with anger over the revelations of the last several days. CIA, of course, had no remit to investigate of domestic terrorism – that was the job of the FBI. But there could be license to look into the possibility of a Chinese connection to the Golden Gate Bridge attack, and he couldn't help but wonder if the attack on the NSA facility in McLean was perpetrated by the same forces. He hoped that Benson had asked for the meeting to propose they work together on that very theory.

Krause stood in the kitchen of the safe house and poured a cup of hot, black coffee into a non-descript mug. As he did so, he heard the front door open and knew it had to be either Benson or Barber, so he walked into the foyer to find out who it was. He saw Joe Barber standing there being frisked by his personal protection detail. As director of the NCS, two rather large bodyguards traveled with him everywhere he went. Krause knew the frisk was hardly necessary, but as a gesture of respect he allowed the two men to finish their task before walking up to Joe and extending his hand along with a broad smile. "Good to see you, my friend," Krause said, as the two men hugged without breaking the handshake. "Sorry about the formalities, but you know the drill," he said in reference to the frisk.

"No problem, boss," Barber replied. "Am I good gentlemen?" he asked of the two guards.

"Roger that," one of the guards answered with a complete stone face.

"Thanks," Joe replied, and lightly patted the man on the shoulder. He then turned to Krause and said, "Must be former Marines," then looked back at the men and said with a wink, "you guys need to crack a smile every once in a while, or I'm going to think you have no sense of humor."

"They don't, Joe," Krause replied, "and they both carry 10 mils, so I'd be careful if I were you."

"Roger that," Joe said with a chuckle. Neither of the guards seemed to move a muscle or in any way acknowledge the repartee. "I take it Don is not here yet."

"No," Krause said. "He just called and is about 10 minutes out. Come on in and have a seat. Coffee?"

"Yes, please," Joe responded.

"So, I have my theories on why Don wanted to meet here, but what I don't understand, no disrespect my friend, is why you were invited."

"None taken," Barber replied. "Can we talk off the record, in the clean room?" The clean room was a 15 by 20-foot room off the kitchen of the house that was lined with copper and electronic shielding and contained no recording devices. It also had a relatively new innovation from the NSA signet wizards – an electronic disabling device that would render permanently inoperative any electronics in the room not broadcasting the appropriate pass code. Krause emptied his pockets onto a small table just outside the room and Barber did the same. Krause also removed his Apple watch. Joe, sporting a Rolex Submariner, was not so bothered.

As the two men sat at the conference table, Joe began to summarize the history of his involvement. Krause sat there completely stone-faced as he listened. In spite of Krause's self-control, the revelations were truly astonishing – a secret government intelligence arm that had gone off the rails, the death of a prominent Washington Post reporter, the attempts on Barber's life, Joe's "extra-legal" abductions and interrogations. Gerhard now knew why Joe wanted this discussion in the clean room. "That's quite a story, how much of this does Don know?" Krause asked.

"Enough," Joe answered. "Problem is none of it's provable, at least not yet. I still don't know who was responsible for Eric's and Jennifer's deaths, or the other attempts on my life. I'm inclined to believe the people I talked to at this NSA Department of Special Activities were telling me the truth. Those guys are definitely dirty, but I don't believe they were directly behind the attack on me. As for some of the other recent events, I'm not so sure; but I can't prove anything yet."

"The people at the NSA you talked to, Joe?" with a special emphasis placed on the word 'talked'. "It sounds like it was a lot more than just talk."

"As far as I'm concerned all we did was talk. Nobody is any worse for the wear and there's absolutely no physical evidence I did anything else," Joe said.

"Guess I trained you well," Krause replied. "Of course, we don't do those things anymore."

"You did train me well, boss, but we're getting off point right now. The issue isn't what I did. The issue is if these clowns were actually telling me the truth, somebody else must be behind some of this. I think that's the most likely conclusion at this point, and my concern is that they are still out there."

"Don't you think the attack in McLean took them out?" Krause asked.

"I don't think so. Again, I think this rogue agency is behind a lot, but not all of it – certainly not behind the deaths of Jennifer and Longstreet, nor the attempts on me. I suspect the other players in this, whoever they are, are the ones behind the McLean attack. I don't believe for a moment that the Chinese would actually launch a drone strike against the US homeland. That's just plain stupid, and there are so many other things they could do to accomplish similar results without the risk of the extreme political blowback. But what if some Chinese intelligence organization became aware of a domestic attack drone program in the US? It seems entirely plausible to me that they might want to hack into it as a way to embarrass us. After all, why did that thing fly so low and in plain sight? It was like somebody wanted the world to see it. It puts us in a no-win situation. On the one hand, we can't blame the Chinese, even if we are certain. There would be an outcry for some kind of retaliation, to say nothing of forcing us, in the process, to reveal way too much about our intelligence capabilities and methods. On the other hand, if we don't blame somebody else, it's going to look like a domestic program and none of us can even imagine the political maelstrom that's going to bring. No, I think the Chinese stumbled onto something and tried to play the

477

opportunity. That's what they do. What they don't do is directly attack a US Government facility on US soil. There's got to be someone else involved, almost certainly domestic."

"What about some other arm of the Government that stumbled on it and is trying to clean house? Maybe the FBI? There's the issue of Executive Assistant Director McConnell; and the issue of the missing evidence you delivered certainly casts suspicion on the Bureau," Krause said.

"How did you know about that?" Barber asked. "Yeah, ok, never mind. McConnell was dirty, there's no doubt about that. But I can't believe the Bureau itself was implicated. If that was true Don would know it. And absolutely no way Don would be any part of it, I'd bet my life on that. Which means if it was true and Don had been aware of it he'd be one of the several much too convenient deaths we're trying to figure out. My instincts tell me the Administration itself is somehow connected to all of this. Don't ask me why I think that because I don't know."

Both men sat there and looked at each other for several seconds before Krause finally broke the silence. "You understand the problem with that theory, right?"

"Of course," Joe replied. "The Chief of Staff is dead. Natural causes, supposedly, but it looks very similar to Jennifer's and Longstreet's demise, and I don't believe in coincidences."

"Neither do I," Krause replied.

"Right. Which means we're talking about the highest level here," Barber observed.

"Say it," Krause responded.

"POTUS," Barber replied.

The conversation was interrupted by a knock on the door. A buzzer sounded to signal the room was no longer "clean", a door opened as Don Benson walked in. Benson was dressed in his normal FBI uniform, a dark navy-blue suit with the jacket buttoned and a starched, white French-cuffed shirt framing a light blue, striped tie. As he walked to the conference table he lightly patted Barber on the left shoulder, then reached across to shake hands with Krause, offering each man a "good morning."

"I trust my security detail didn't relieve you of your service pistol?" Krause said.

"No Federal Agent disarms an Executive Assistant Director of the Bureau," Benson replied, "unless, of course, said person is either being relieved or placed under arrest," he added, in an obvious reference to Director McConnell.

"Good," Krause replied. "I instructed them not to, just to avoid their potential embarrassment. So what's on your mind, Don? By the way, Joe and I had a chance to talk a bit before you arrived, and he brought me up to speed on why he's here. This whole affair seems to be getting uglier and more complicated every time I ask a question."

"I agree. And I'm afraid there are a lot more questions that need to be asked, the first of which I need to ask you. Did the CIA have knowledge of this rogue organization within NSA?"

"Right to the point, my friend," Krause replied without any hint of irritation. Benson had a reputation for being direct, and Krause respected that. It was an efficient way to conduct business. "No. It wasn't even remotely on our radar screen until the Golden Gate attack. That incident at least glances up against our remit given the suspicion of foreign authorship. The more we thought about it, the more we became convinced there had to be a domestic connection somehow, but we suspected terrorists, likely

479

foreign, given recent events; but we didn't rule out some domestic nutcases either. I have to say, though, it never occurred to us it could be our own government. What Joe just shared with me is breathtaking. The irony is we actually contacted McConnell and gave her our intel. We offered to look into the potential Chinese connection with our assets overseas, but we regarded anything domestic as strictly Bureau business. I was certainly not aware of what was going on over at Fort Meade or McLean, whatsoever, and was never read into anything even remotely connected to it. I intend to have a discussion with my senior leadership team when we are through here to make certain. I can also tell you I'm going to insist everyone take a polygraph, and I'm going to have the digital forensics office start with me. Having said that, I can say with almost a moral certainty, that I do not expect to find anything."

"Polygraphs are a great idea," Benson replied. "I'm going to take that back to Director Fields and suggest that he and I be the first two to be examined."

"By the way," Krause said, "we need to have this conversation with Welsh at DIA as well."

"Already on that, Gerhard," Benson responded. "He's my next visit, but I think there is virtually a zero probability they have anything to do with this, or any knowledge either. DIA couldn't be involved without the knowledge of the Joint Chiefs, and you can take it to the bank that none of them would have anything to do it. And if they became aware, they'd put an end to it or resign en masse; it's in their DNA."

"I agree," Krause replied, "but I was actually thinking of a different angle. They have assets in Asia who could be very helpful in ferreting out any potential Chinese involvement in Golden Gate."

"Good point," said Benson, "I'll actually approach him from that angle. And I agree with you that there can't be a connection there.

Unfortunately, this process of elimination keeps pointing us to the growing likelihood of an even more unsettling conclusion."

"Right," Krause agreed. "This Department of Special Activities had to have sponsorship up the chain. Which means," Krause continued, "that the evidence is increasingly pointing to the Administration."

"Right," Barber interjected, "and given Fitzpatrick was one of the casualties, that can only mean one thing. POTUS."

"Right," Krause responded. "POTUS. Joe and I had just reached consensus on that point when you walked in."

"But it can't be the entire picture," Barber replied. "One important part of this puzzle is the technology itself. And the hardware. We're looking at very sophisticated hardware and very sophisticated software. This stuff wasn't manufactured or written by NSA. Oh, they're smart enough, all right; but it's not what they do. There has to be some civilian contractor behind the drones, this Sparrow thing, and the software running it. Find out who that is and we crack the puzzle wide open."

"Yes, I think that makes sense," Krause said. "But how do we do that?"

Barber looked towards Benson. "Old fashioned detective work, gentlemen," Barber answered. "And I think it starts with looking into Fitzpatrick's and Einhorn's connection with contractors that could potentially have the wherewithal to develop something like this."

"These two are politicians, Joe, which means that's a very long list and no way to quickly narrow it down. Virtually every company that fits your description has contributed to the campaigns of both parties, and those who have given outsized donations have done it through super PACs, which means their names are anonymous."

"What about physical," Benson asked this time. "We've now got several of the Sparrow devices, thanks to Orion's forensics lab, but whoever built those things went to great effort to mask their origin. It's not exactly like they've got a company name or serial number on them. And the only drone material we've recovered is from the one that went down in San Francisco Bay, and it's just a melted heap of metal. We're looking at the metal's chemical composition but I'm not confident that's going to tell us much."

"DIA has to be studying the video of the Golden Gate attack. Maybe they've learned something from analyzing the video," Krause speculated.

"Thought of that, Gerhard, and it's one of the first questions I'm going to ask Welsh when I see him this afternoon." Benson replied. "But I'm not sure I'd count on much. I can't imagine whoever built the thing took less care to mask their identity on a drone."

"What about........," Barber's comment was interrupted mid-sentence when the three men in the room suddenly felt a vibration that seemed to be coming from the floor. The lights suddenly went out for several seconds, and then came back on. At the same time they heard the distinct whine of electric motors as 3-inch steel doors slid across the two entranceways to the room, sealing off entry from the outside.

"What the....," Joe started to say, then stopped as Krause started to speak over him.

"That's the emergency power supply coming on line," Krause said, referring to the resumption of lighting. "The vibration we just felt and that noise are coming from the steel doors that are sealing the entrance to this conference room." He then reached across the table and picked up a phone sitting in front of him and asked, "What's going on out there?" Krause's face remained expressionless as he waited several seconds for a response.

"What's happening?" Benson asked. "Gerhard, what are you hearing?"

"Nothing," Krause responded. "Nothing. There's nobody on the line. I think we're under attack."

Chapter 55 – The Attack

CIA. Safe House

"What?" Joe almost shouted.

"I said I think we are under attack. The room's been sealed, so we are safe, at least for the moment, but nobody's responding on the com net, which means they are likely all down."

"Who the hell would be brazen enough to attack a CIA safe house in the middle of a Virginia suburb in broad daylight?" Joe asked, definitely shouting now as he rose to his feet. "And what do you mean they are likely down?"

"I mean exactly what you think I mean. Down! Dead!" Krause answered, as he inserted a key into a console and rotated it, bringing several video screens online. All of the screens were void of images and displayed only snow.

"I'm thinking that's not good," Joe said as he stared into the snow.

Just outside the clean room

Two men walked through a hallway of the house carrying silenced Heckler & Koch MP5 machine guns. Three other men, also armed with MP5s, fanned out to clear the other rooms. A half dozen CIA. Special Activities Division Operators and Marines who provided security for the safe house lay dead on the floor. Just as the assault team leader rounded a corner and had the clean room door in sight, a shot rang out and hit the man behind him in the side of the throat. He could feel the man's warm, arterial spray on the back of his neck as blood pulsed out the wound. He knew instinctively his man was not only out of the fight but was likely dead. "Paren' ubit!" he shouted

484

into his throat mike in Russian, or "Man down!" "Yest' strelok vniz po koridoru za predelami chistoy komnaty, - there's a shooter down the hall just beyond the clean room door."

"Roger that," another member of the assault team responded. Just as he did, another shot rang out from somewhere towards the kitchen.

"We have a second active shooter," the team leader called out over his com net. "That shot was not silenced so it wasn't one of us."

"Yuri's down!" a voice replied. "We are three on two now. That is two as far as we know."

Another shot rang out.

"Anybody else hit?" the team leader asked.

"No," responded the operator who had just spoken. "But whoever that is has me pinned down."

"What's the status of the targets?" another man asked.

"It appears as though they are sealed in some kind of steel vault, although I can't get a closer look until we take out the shooter," replied the assault team leader. "We need to take those shooters out pronto! This is taking longer than it should, and I think we have to assume they got a signal out, so time is limited. Let's go infrared. I'm going to pop the smoke so I can get to the door and use the plasma torch."

"Roger that," said the two other operators who were still standing.

The team leader grabbed the strap of his over the shoulder backpack and spun it around to the front of his chest. He unzipped one of the pockets and retrieved a pair of infrared vision goggles. The infrared goggles would capture the heat signature of any person masked by smoke and provide good target contrast against a cooler background; whereas traditional night vision goggles, which magnified ambient light, would be worthless in this environment. He placed the goggles over his eyes and tightened the strap. He reached around to the other side of the backpack and unzipped another pouch and retrieved two British-manufactured Enola Gaye wire pull smoke grenades. Ex Russian Spetsnaz freelancers apparently purchased their ordnance wherever they could get it. He removed the caps from each, exposing the ignition wires. He then grabbed the ring at the end of the wire attached to one of the devices and pulled it sharply away from the body of the grenade itself. As the device began to hiss, and smoke poured out of the top, he carefully rolled it towards the clean room door. He then repeated the process with the second grenade and smoke began to quickly fill the hallway. He reached up on the right-hand side of the goggles and flipped the switch, and everything in the hallway immediately became visible. "Lay down some suppressing fire to cover me," he said as he started to crawl down the hallway on his hands and knees towards the door. A second operator was crouched about 2 yards behind the team leader. The operator began spraying 9mm rounds down the hall on the command. As he did so, the team leader crawled along the floor through the smoke. Once at the clean room door, he retrieved a small plasma torch out of his backpack and lit it, flipped up his infrared goggles, then placed the flame just to the left side of the door handle and began cutting the steel.

Inside the clean room

"Look at that, guys," Barber said pointing to the door handle. Just to the right of it the steel began to glow red. "They must be using a cutting touch of some sort."

"It must be plasma," Krause said. "That steel is over an inch thick."

"How long before they breach that door?" Benson asked.

"Hard to say," Krause replied.   "There are two spring loaded steel rods that are pushed into holes at both the top and the bottom of the door to secure it. A wedge is pushed forward between two cams to push the rods into place.   If they cut the rods it won't accomplish anything, because at a minimum, gravity will keep the bottom rod in its hole and the door can't be moved. If they cut the spring, or cut out a section of the wedge, the cams will spring back down and the rods will automatically retract, freeing the door."

"Can you tell what they are doing?" Joe asked.

"Not yet," Krause responded. "When they make a turn in that cut we'll know. If it turns away from the handle, it's likely they don't know anything about the locking mechanism and we will have bought a bit more time. If they turn towards our left, then bring the cut upwards, they know the lock design and we'll have less than three minutes before they breach the door and are inside the room."

"Did we get a distress signal out?" Benson asked, looking at Krause.

"I don't know, but I don't think so. It looks to me like everything was taken off line before the attack. But there's a backup. This facility constantly broadcasts an all-clear signal that's read by Langley. If our systems go down, the all-clear is interrupted, and Langley will read that as distress. That's the good news. The bad news is because this is a tier one safe house with heavy security to begin with, backup is not pre-positioned. It will take at least 30 minutes to get a backup team here."

"Looks to me like this thing is going to be over in less than 10 minutes," Benson replied.

All three men stared at the cut in the door as it was now about an inch below the door handle. The cut then began a turn to the left.

"I would say less than 5," Barber observed.

Just outside the clean room

As the team leader continued to cut through the steel, the sound of another gunshot rang out. This one definitely had a much different, more sinister sound to it. It definitely wasn't a 9 mm. But the sound was distinctive. The members of the assault team who were still alive recognized it immediately. It was a Weatherby 300 magnum. At the instant of the gunshot, the assault team leader's head exploded in a spray of skull fragments, brain matter and blood all over the side of the clean room door and the hallway floor just in front of the area he was working.

The man behind him immediately went flat to the floor and quickly scurried backwards towards the corner, removing himself from the field of fire. "Vassili is down!" he shouted. "I repeat, Vassili is down! That last round was a head-shot. Mission abort immediately!"

Inside the clean room

"What was that?" Benson asked, as all three men heard a loud bang from inside the house.

"That was no 9 mil," Krause responded.

"Sounds like a 300-magnum round," Joe said. The three men continued to stare at the cut being made in the steel door that now ominously turned upwards, confirming their fears that whoever was trying to get into the room knew the design of the locking mechanism. Then they noticed the red glow started to fade.

"They're no longer cutting!" Benson shouted.

"Right," Joe said. "I would say he likely dropped the torch and is down. Which means the cavalry arrived."

"I thought we were looking at a 30-minute minimum before we'd have backup," Benson said.

"They're not SAD," Krause replied. "Joe, what's going on here?" he asked.

"Let's just say I have a pretty good life insurance policy."

Outside the clean room

Marcus Day continued to peer through the infrared scope of his sniper rifle and survey the scene. As he did so, he heard one of the Orion tactical operators over his own com net. "We now have eyes on two other men. They are each carrying silenced MP5s so they must be the last remaining members of the assault team."   "You mean absent that guy sitting in the black Escalade waiting for them?" Day asked.

"Well technically, yes, but we've now got a man with eyes on him as well. Should we take them out?"

"What are the two tangos doing?" Day asked.

"Both seem to be crawling backwards right now towards the front of the house. I'd say they are probably about to exfil."

"Then negative on the engagement," Day replied. "Do not engage unless they engage. Our job was to stop the bad guys from killing the good guys, to protect Joe. It wasn't to kill all of the bad guys – just to neutralize their mission. We've done that. We need to pull back now before SAD arrives. Let's remain staged just in case there's a second wave, although I seriously doubt whoever tried to pull this off has anyone else in the area or they'd already be in the building."

"You wanna grab one of these guys, boss? Take him back and interrogate?" another operator asked.

"Negative," Day replied again. "Yes, if we could have gotten hands on the team leader, but that's a moot point now. The other guys aren't going to know anything about who sent them or why. It's not the way their business works."

"Roger that," the man replied.

"OK, I want everyone to get out of Dodge, pronto. Let's pull back to the staging location and wait until we know the targets have been retrieved by the Feds."

"Our intel suggests they were not able to get a distress call out. The assault team jammed all of the communications just before the strike, and the jamming devices appear to still be on."

"I know," Day replied. "But I suspect they have some kind of backup method. Just in case they don't, as soon as we can get a few hundred yards away I'm going to make a phone call. No worries; they'll be rescued. Now let's get out of here."

"Got it."

Back inside the clean room

"It seems to have gotten quiet out there," Benson observed.

"I suspect they are either down, have left, or some combination of both," Krause replied.

"Don, give me your service weapon," Barber said.

Benson looked at him with a puzzled and obviously uncomfortable expression. "Why do you want that?" he asked.

"Because we are not out of the woods until we see friendly faces, and I'm a lot more skilled in using that thing than you are, my friend. We need to sit tight for the moment, but at some point that door is going to open and we don't know who is going to come through it. I am the best equipped among the three of us to assess and react," Barber replied.

"He's right, Don," Krause agreed.

Benson withdrew his Glock from the inside the waistband holster that was positioned at about 4 o'clock on his right hip and handed it to Barber.

"10 mil," Barber observed as he took the pistol. "Gotta love the FBI. Do you have any extra clips?" he asked.

"No, Joe. I'm not a field agent. I'm an AD. ADs don't carry extra clips," Benson replied.

"Right. Ok. Is there one in the pipe?" Joe asked.

"Yes," Benson said.

"Good man. Now let's line up to the side of the door so we don't present a pretty target for whoever walks in. Me first."

Chapter 56 – The Consequence of Failure

Palo Alto, California, Offices of PrinSafe

A bright late afternoon California sun beamed through the two floor-to- ceiling office windows. It bathed the large, ornate desk sitting in the corner and cast long shadows throughout the richly appointed workspace. Westy Reynolds sat quietly reading the daily risk report, which detailed the VaR, or value at risk, of the numerous and varied positions held by the firm's flagship investment arm. It was a report that informed him what his maximum overnight loss could be from unexpected market moves, to what statisticians called a 99 percent confidence level, or in other words there was a 99% probability that his loss would not be worse than the report. Devouring the report was part of his afternoon routine. His concentration was broken, however, by another annoying ring from that damn phone. It seemed in the last several weeks that phone brought him almost exclusively bad news, and he was developing a Pavlovian aversion to it. He reached across the desk and pressed the intercom button. "James Osborne on line 3, sir," came the report from his administrative assistant. Osborne was an Executive Vice President of the Holding Company, CWR LLC, and in charge of the organization's global security. It was a remit that included managing the security personnel and, on occasion, certain tasks that were, in the terms of the trade "outsourced".

"Thanks, put him through," Reynolds replied, then waited.

"Mission failure, Westy," Osborne said. "Our contractor was proceeding according to plan then another team showed up and engaged."

"CIA?" Reynolds asked.

"I don't think so. We assumed the facility had some kind of failsafe threat warning device, but CIA couldn't possibly have arrived before we

492

would have finished. I don't have a read on who the other force was as yet, but my educated guess is it was a team from Orion Bellicus. They employ SpecOps as well. And not outsourced – their operators are actually on their payroll. We've even recruited a few folks from them in the past."

"So, none of the targets are down?" Reynolds asked.

"That's correct," Osborne replied. "Our team was engaged and neutralized before we could cut through the security door."

"Survivors?" Reynolds asked.

"Our team, two. They got out safely and fortunately they managed to extract the team leader and the other two operators who were down. They should be in the jet and in the air within 30 minutes."

"Good," Reynolds replied. "I don't like leaving loose ends, but I think it's time to cut our losses."

"You want us to stand W down, boss?" Osborne asked.

"Yes. Another attempt would present way too much risk. Besides, I suspect the Feds will assume it's the same foreign government that was behind the McLean attack."

"Agreed," Osborne replied. "I want you to know I've made a command decision," he continued. "This is the highest profile and riskiest covert mission we've ever attempted. Attribution would be catastrophic, and I don't like loose ends either. The mission brief calls for a diversion to Miami and 7-day stand-down before the contractor's team returns to Europe. The flight to Miami will take their Gulfstream over the Atlantic. I pre-positioned a number of the weaponized Hawk variants on the aircraft. They will take out everyone on board once the plane is off the South Carolina Coast. That includes the pilot. Emma's people will reprogram the autopilot to then turn the aircraft east and dump remaining fuel after about 90 minutes of flight time. Just before the turn East, she will also activate onboard countermeasures to mask the aircraft's new flight path and location. It should run out of gas and hit the water well off the continental shelf and be unrecoverable in deep water. The contractor registered the aircraft to an Argentine company and it will depart a private airfield with the transponder turned off per normal procedures. It won't be missed. This will erase any evidence of the mission. Our agent will be pissed, but we'll buy him a new jet. I know that's not an inconsequential expenditure, even for us, but we need to consider the cost of the jet an insurance premium for preserving our ongoing viability. I'll remind W that it preserves his as well. I don't think I'll get much pushback. As for the people in the aircraft, their loss is regrettable but necessary."

"Well done, Jim," Reynolds replied. "W will undoubtedly insist on standing down for a bit as well to let the heat subside. Problem is that leaves us with a very dangerous loose end."

"I believe a more subtle and discrete effort presents the best risk/reward trade-off at the moment," Osborne continued. "I've already contacted a freelancer and given her the contract. Best solo asset in the business."

"Good," Reynolds said. "When can she deliver?"

"Soon. I've stressed the time-sensitive nature of our objective."

"Great," Reynolds replied again. "How will W respond to us using another supplier?"

"His pride will be hurt a little, and he'll complain, but he failed. Besides he's already been paid. He's a professional. We've been too lucrative a client for him to let his pride get in the way of potential future business. He'll be fine."

"Agreed. Let me know when it's done."

"Of course, boss," Osborne replied.

Somewhere in Washington D.C.

Barber felt his phone vibrate. He stopped walking, dug his hand deep into his pants pocket, retrieved the phone and looked at the screen. It simply read "Private Number". He touched the green icon to connect the call and listened.

"It's Margaret, Joe."

"Hello Maggie."

"Hello. Forensics has completed their work. We've identified the team leader and have a 99% confidence level in the name of the man he works for. I am having a briefing book delivered to your office within the next two hours. Your eyes only."

"I'm still in D.C. Marc plans to handle this. I'm a bit too hot a commodity right now."

"Agreed," she replied. "Since you are still in town I'll amend the authorization to Marc as well. I want the name of his client. Use any necessary means."

"Of course, Maggie," he replied. "But you realize the likelihood of getting that name is very low."

"I know that."

"So, what's our secondary objective, other than scaring the guy?"

"Terminate his business," she replied. "With extreme prejudice."

"With pleasure," Barber replied. He disconnected the call, placed his phone back into his pocket, and began to walk towards his car.

Chapter 57 – A Deadly Dance

Geneva

He turned heads as he walked through the lobby of the Mandarin Oriental. He was the kind of man who was noticed, and for several reasons. First, he cut a very imposing figure. He was about six foot seven, which meant he towered over everyone else in the room. Second, at somewhere north of 250 pounds he projected such a mass as to appear to have his own gravity field. Third was his manner of dress. He was wearing an Italian silk suit, obviously made to order, and a Hermes silk tie that must have cost more than most of the hotel staff made in a week. Cuff links were diamond incrusted gold. His wristwatch was a Patek, understated in its presentation but still with a retail cost north of $50,000. It didn't have to be gaudy. This was Geneva. Everyone knew. And then there was the way his clothes fit. The suit was tailored so expertly that it appeared almost to be sprayed on which emphasized an almost unnerving perception that the man had the strength of an NFL linebacker and the physique of a bodybuilder. And he had strikingly good looks, almost pretty, if any such specimen could be described with that term. But his most striking attribute and often the most useful was the one he was born with. He was black. Nobody knew what to make of him. This was Geneva.

He walked through the lobby with an air of confidence that broadcast the impression he owned the place. It was an understated but very clear countenance of a man serenely in control. As he continued through the lobby towards his intended destination he passed a family on his right. There were two parents and a little 5-year old blond-haired girl. The parents looked wary, the girl looked curious. The father gently placed his hand on the girl's shoulder as if to hold her in place and keep her from getting any closer to the giant stranger. The girl was smiling at the giant as he looked down at her. He was amused. French, he thought to himself, but then he heard the father say something to the girl, inaudible, but clearly in German. She made the slightest twist of her body to pull her shoulder away from her father's hand, a child's defiance, and looked again at the giant and smiled as their eyes met. He smiled back and said, "Wie geht es dir an diesem schönen Morgen, meine kleine Prinzessin?" or "How are you this fine morning, my little Princess?" in an almost flawless Bavarian accent. The little girl's eyes brightened, and she giggled. The mother turned towards the stranger and was now smiling as well. Her face appeared slightly flushed, and her upper body now leaned subconsciously ever so slightly forward. The Father had initially looked startled when the man had addressed his daughter in flawless German, but as he shifted his focus from the stranger to his wife his look morphed from startled to annoyed.

The man continued through the lobby and past the family with a confident gait towards the entrance of the hotel's signature Indian restaurant, Rasio by Vineet. He was greeted by the Maitre d, who confirmed his reservation, then ushered him to a table for two where a waiter carefully removed the exquisitely folded napkin from his place setting, flattened it and placed it on his lap. He ordered a Manhattan, straight up, with an upgrade to Michter's Celebration Sour Mash. He then picked up the menu, perused it with modest curiosity, and waited. Marcus Day didn't have to wait long, and he was ready for the role he was about to play.

A shorter, but still stately tall northern European man in his early sixties with a full head of pure white hair, perfectly coiffed, was ushered to Day's table by the Maitre d. He was dressed as impressively as Day, in Seville Row, double breasted, navy, broad chalk stripes with a perfectly folded handkerchief in the breast pocket. Not a pocket puff, mind you, but a perfectly squared cut of silk with fine stitch lines visible, more appropriate for a dignified gentleman of his age. Between the two of them, the cost of their suits alone would cover the purchase of a decent American sedan.

Day stood up and they shook hands. It was not the greeting of two friends, or even of two business colleagues. It was polite but perfunctory. Neither man smiled and there was no small talk. It was the careful dance of two alpha males. They lingered in direct eye contact for a second or two longer than normal. Their corneal contest was not a display of bravado or aggression but a contest of who could convey the greatest serenity. Bravado was for lesser men, the unsure or insecure. At this level of alpha, the winner was not the person who best conveyed what they could do to the other; the winner was the person who conveyed confidence in what he knew the other could not do to him. This was no mere contest between two hyenas fighting over a scrap of meat. It was the confident dance of two apex predators.

Both men sat down and the older man ordered a glass of 2007 Screaming Eagle Cabernet. The wine retailed for over $3,500 per bottle if you were lucky enough to get it. The restaurant actually sold it by the glass. The place was dimly lit to impart the right atmosphere, one elegant enough to justify the menu's prices. Actually, the menu didn't list prices. It was considered impolite. And if you had to ask, so they say. After all, this was Geneva. And it was quiet. At the table to their left was a couple enjoying what appeared to be an intimate dinner. To the right and in front of Day, and to the older man's back was a longer table where eight people were seated. They were all men and appeared to be engaged in a business discussion of some sort. The conversations were muted, however, and individual words were indiscernible. A perfect environment, Day thought.

The waiter brought the men their drinks. The older man lifted up the glass of wine and performed the obligatory assessment ritual. Deeming it worthy, he took a sip then held it in his mouth for several seconds before

499

swallowing it. He was known in the business as simply "The Wolf". "What is it you want?" he asked, not wanting to waste time and getting right to the point.

"Why did you agree to meet me?" Day replied. "I'm surprised."

"I am most curious to find out who gave you my name," the older man responded. "And besides, I enjoy going to the zoo. Or shall I say doing field work in cultural anthropology."

His comments were clearly double entendres with thinly veiled racial overtones. He was trying to rattle Day. He knew that even a small flash of adrenal anger would throw a man off his game. It didn't work.

"I need to know who engaged your services," Day continued. "Your men killed two Marines and three CIA Special Activities Division operators in that little show of yours back in the States. I will give you a pass on that if you give me the name of the person who engaged you for that mission."

"And if I don't?" asked the older man.

"I won't insult your intelligence by answering a question to which you already know the answer."

"Well, you know I wouldn't be in business very long if I gave up my customers. And besides, you know that's not the way the business works. I am engaged through an intermediary. I have no idea who the actual customer is. And let's not forget that you neutralized several of my assets. I would say we're even."

Marc Day knew the older man's comment about working through an intermediary was a credible comeback. It was credible, that is, for a garden-variety purveyor of wet work. Day knew the elderly predator sitting across from him managed an elite service comprised of former special forces

500

operators from Spetnaz, Israeli Shayetet, British SAS and, much to his consternation, even former Tier One Navy SEALs. These were no ordinary soldiers of fortune. The Wolf would charge tens of millions of dollars for engagements and had a fifty million dollar minimum for any mission on United States soil. He knew his customers. It was a very short list, and one that usually resulted in repeat business. The comment about "being even" angered Day, but he quickly compartmentalized it. Indulging even legitimate emotions right now would only be counterproductive, and he knew it.

"I suggest we not waste each other's time," Day responded. "You have a well-deserved reputation for superb due-diligence, and we both know that you not only know who your customer is, you know him well and have likely been engaged by him several times in the past. There is no way you would take an assignment on U.S. soil without an intimate knowledge of the person requesting your services. As I said, I simply need to know his name. No need to give up any additional information. I can take care of the rest myself."

"How did you know my identity and how to contact me?" he asked.

"As to your identity, it actually wasn't that hard," Day answered. "Prosperity has made you and your employees a little sloppy. We collected a DNA sample from the operator in Virginia who appeared to be the team leader. He actually left quite a bit of DNA at the scene of your botched mission. The natural consequences of my putting a 300-caliber magnum round through the back of his head. Turns out he appears prominently in Interpol database. Russian. He was a former Spetsnaz officer named Vasilli Alexandrovich. Bounced around Eastern Europe, the Middle East and South Africa until you recruited him. We found his laptop at a hotel in Georgetown. The guy had actually made a screen print of the encrypted message board he used to communicate with you, and left it in a messenger bag on the hotel room bed. From there let's just say the puzzle was pretty easy to put together."

The Wolf sat stone-faced and didn't say a word. He picked up the glass of wine, swirled it a couple of times, took a sip then carefully placed it back on the table. He pulled a cell phone out of his pocket, touched the screen a handful of times and returned it to its resting place. He then looked up at Day with cold eyes, his expression still unchanged since before Day started talking, and said, "You realize, of course, that you are not going to leave this building alive. As a matter of fact, point certain even, you were dead the moment you walked through the lobby door."

Day returned the expressionless gaze, then picked up his Manhattan, took a sip without breaking eye contact then asked, "Whatever in the world makes you think that?"

"I just texted my personal security service. They are in the hotel. You won't be able to discern them from any of the patrons. You, on the other hand, are somewhat, shall we say, conspicuous. If I were you I would probably leave now. Who knows, you may still have time to escape before they spot you."

"I'm afraid your assistants are not presently in a position to be of much help to you," Day replied.

"And why is that?" the Wolf asked.

"Because they are both dead," Day answered.

"Rubbish," the Wolf responded, breaking discipline and projecting annoyance for the first time.

Day retrieved his cell phone, opened the photo app and slid it across the desk towards the older man. The Wolf didn't pick it up, he just looked down at the picture that was displayed on the screen. It showed a woman lying on the ground with her eyes closed. There was no blood, no bullet holes or other evidence of trauma. Wolf was momentarily confused but then realized what likely happened and then asked, "So you broke her neck? Pity."

Day didn't respond.

"I assume her partner met a similar fate?" the older man asked.

"Swipe the phone screen to your right to display the next picture," Day instructed. The older man didn't move, and the two men continued to lock eyes. Day slowly reached his hand across the table, placed his index finger on the iPhone screen and swiped right himself. Another picture appeared, this time of a man with eyes closed and a similar look of death emanating from his face and also lacking any visible evidence of gunshot or other trauma. The older man's eyes remained locked with Day's for several seconds, then briefly glanced down at the photo and quickly returned his glare to Day, betraying no emotion. Day with an ever so slight smile, reached his hand across the table a third time and swiped the screen again, displaying a picture of a third man, eyes closed in a death sleep and his head pointed in a direction clearly not intended by nature. "It would appear as though you were not entirely honest with me about the size of your security detail," Day said.

Even a man of extraordinary discipline cannot hold back nature's adrenaline surge indefinitely, especially when presented with unmistakable exigent circumstances. The older man's eyes blinked involuntarily several times. His face quickly became flushed and several beads of sweat appeared on his forehead. Day could actually see the breast of his slimly tailored double-breasted suit move in and out as his reparation quickened. His right hand trembled slightly. At this point, all were involuntary responses, beyond his control. His primary plan was gone. His backup plan was also gone. He was alone in the presence of an exitential threat. For the first time in as long as he could remember, the Wolf was unsure of his next move. He improvised, quickly trying to regain the high ground of being the hunter. "So, it would appear that you might live at least a few more hours. I wouldn't make a lot of long-term plans, however. As I said, you are fairly easy to mark. I can assure you that you will not learn the name of my client."

"I know," Day responded. "At least not from you." Day picked up the half-consumed Manhattan and downed the rest of the drink. "But let's at least try and end this conversation amicably, shall we? I've lost my appetite. I am sure you have as well. Allow me to walk you back to the lobby."

"Walk me back to the lobby?" the older man asked, puzzled. "Whatever would be the point of that? You may simply consider yourself free to go," he said declaratively in an effort to maintain a front that he still held the upper hand and the ability to grant Day freedom or otherwise.

"As you well know, there is only one corridor out of this restaurant back to the lobby. If I keep you within a foot of me as we walk it together, any of your assets I may have missed will be reluctant to attack for fear of injuring you. Let's just call it an insurance policy."

"Ah, I see," the Wolf said, now having fully regained his imperious voice. "Very well, if you insist."

"I insist," Day responded. With that, the two men rose from the table, walked out of the restaurant without saying a word to the Maitre d, and began walking towards the lobby. As they did so, Day cupped a hand on the older man's elbow to keep him in close proximity. It was all for show.

A fishing knife is a simple, elegant and highly effective tool. It has a small, thin, yet fairly long blade that is razor sharp. Most blades have a slightly upward curve ending in an incredibly sharp point. Perfect for penetrating the tough scales of game fish like Northern Pike, Muskie, or Bass, and perfect for filleting them. In skilled hands it also can be quite effective in filleting a man. As for its penetrating power against human skin, its thin profile and incredibly sharp point make it much more like a flat hypodermic needle than a knife. And it is exceptionally easy to conceal, inside a jacket sleeve, for example.

Day and The Wolf turned the corner outside the restaurant entrance and progressed about twenty feet down the corridor. Day kept the older man on his right. He then turned towards him and stretched his head as if he was looking at something or someone just to the side and behind them. As he did so, The Wolf responded in a predictable and all too involuntary manner – he looked in the same direction himself and momentarily took his attention away from the large man standing next to him. There was nothing behind them, of course, and just a split-second glance away was all Day needed. He deftly moved his left hand just inside his right jacket sleeve and withdrew the fishing knife in one fluid motion. The Wolf noticed Day's move and turned back to look, but it was too late. Before the older man could even process what was happening, Day used the tip of the knife to flip open the left flap of the man's suit coat, then, with his hand now fully underneath the flap, plunged the blade all the way to the hilt at a slightly outward angle just to the right of center mass of the abdominal cavity. He then swept the knife cleanly from right to left inside the abdominal cavity itself in a pivotal motion that didn't widen the entry wound. As the leading edge of the blade swept through the older man's gut, it met little resistance, found its target, and severed the abdominal aorta. At that point, though still breathing, the Wolf was essentially dead. Day then withdrew the knife and pulled the suit coat flap over the wound to mask it. The older man was bleeding, but the small size of the wound kept it from being too visible. Day had timed the move so the two of them were adjacent to a sofa sitting on the side wall of the corridor. He placed his powerful arm around the older man's waist and moved him over to the sofa, propping him upright in the corner, wrapped one of the man's arms around the body to hold the suit coat flap that was covering the wound, in place. He removed a paper towel from his breast pocket, wiped the knife clean, returned it to the sheath under his sleeve, then tossed the soiled paper towel into the nearby trash bin. Day then resumed his walk down the hall, at a normal pace, and continued into the hotel lobby, out the door, and down the street.

Chapter 58 – The Unresolved Loose End

Somewhere in Washington DC, about two hours later

It was another one of those oppressive summer days in the Nation's Capital. Temperature and humidity were in the high 90s with absolutely no breeze. The mere act of walking could have a person dripping with sweat inside of two minutes. The city was crawling with tourists, who for the most part at least could dress for the weather, but the reality was there was little relief to be had other than being indoors in strong air conditioning. It was a good day to be visiting the Smithsonian, and all of its museums were packed with long lines to get in. People on official business had it better, for the most part, but at times also had it much worse. The fact that they were on official business meant they spent at least a decent part of their day indoors and cool. Problem was the army of lawyers, lobbyists and Government employees who made up the city's professional class also had to spend a good part of their day getting from one place to another, from one building to another, with distances usually too short to warrant a cab or an Uber but long enough to make the process of walking in the summer heat miserable. And most of them had to dress in suits, which in this heat and humidity felt like being dressed in plastic bags.

Joe Barber was walking up 15th Street just north of Constitution Avenue. He was wearing a pair of stone-colored cotton dress pants and a long sleeve white dress shirt, cuffs rolled up, open collar, with a navy blazer flung over his left shoulder. He had foregone an undershirt that morning which meant no extra layer of insulation against the heat. As a result, the back of his dress shirt was soaked with perspiration. Sweat covered his forehead and matted his hair. He looked perfectly in place with the rest of DC's motley crowd on a hot, late summer afternoon. He retrieved his cell phone from his

507

right pocket without breaking stride, unlocked the screen, opened his contact list and touched a number which, although not often called, was very familiar. A female voice answered with a simple and neutral-sounding, "hello".

"I just talked to Marc," Barber said. "It's done. As we expected, no meaningful information was exchanged," he continued, in a reference to the Wolf's refusal to give up the name of his client, "but he won't be a bother anymore."

"Understood," the female voice replied, "and as I expected. We've been trying for years to connect him with his client list and have always come up cold. All of our background intel points to him being a lone wolf, if you will pardon the pun, with no designated successor. The snake only had one head. Now that he's no longer a threat I'm afraid I can't continue to devote assets to it, and I don't believe we'd be successful even if I did. I'm sorry about that, Joe."

"I understand," Barber replied, "and agree. I plan to keep looking, because whoever the client is, he or she remains out there."

"I realize that," the female voice replied. "But Joe….."

"What?"

"Be careful. I know I don't have to say it, but I believe you remain a loose end to whomever this is, and that you are still in mortal danger. They are going to try again."

"I'm counting on it," Barber replied. "The more often they try, the higher the probability of a mistake. And I've taken out the A-team."

"You've taken out the A plus team. There are still plenty of A-teams out there if a single civilian is the target. They won't be inclined to go after anyone from the Government again. That would entail too much risk now.

But they will go after you and continue doing so until they succeed. No offense, but with everyone focusing on this mess as the top priority nobody is going to divert resources to protecting a civilian. And no offense again, but you're not the young Turk you used to be, and whoever is behind all this is not the only one capable of making a mistake."

"No offense taken and point taken," Barber replied. "Not to worry. Thank you for your help, Maggie. We'll talk again soon."

"I'm counting on it, be careful out there," Dr. Margaret Shevchenko said.

Barber touched the screen of his iPhone to end the call, placed it back in his pocket and continued his walk. "Man, this heat," he mumbled to himself as he passed a pair of teenagers in cargo shorts and sweat-soaked t-shirts that celebrated a couple of rock bands Barber never heard of. "Whew!" he thought. "Hygiene dudes, hygiene!"

Palo Alto, California, Offices of PrinSafe

Westy Reynolds sat the non-descript North Face backpack on his desk and started to pack it with the homework for the evening. The reading material for the night included about a dozen 10K financial statements of companies in his crosshairs, a copy of Foreign Affairs magazine, as well as the reports that measured his overnight risk from the investment positions he held in numerous global financial markets. He far preferred the backpack to some high-end leather or metal brief case, although he could easily afford anything he wanted. The backpack tended to downplay the importance of what was inside, but that wasn't the only reason he preferred it. It made him feel young, more hip. He knew the one thing his enormous wealth could not purchase was perpetual youth, so he compensated for the passage of time any way he could. With the backpack slung across his shoulder, he could almost fantasize himself a student. Almost, that is, until he walked past the randomly placed mirror, glanced at himself and was reminded of his actual age. He was a fan of the TV program, Billions, and even came into the office one day sporting a high-end pair of denims and one of those $2,000 plus hoodies. Then he caught his secretary smiling, snickering actually, under her breath. Ok a bridge too far, he thought. Enormous wealth couldn't protect you from looking like an idiot if you acted like one.

As he shoved the last report for the evening in the backpack, James Osborne walked into Reynolds' office, breathing hard, and closed the door.

"What's up with you?" Reynolds asked. "Why the heaving chest, Jim?"

"I just heard from Geneva, Westy, W is down. Murdered. Somebody gutted the guy at the Mandarin Oriental."

Several seconds passed as neither man said a word. Reynolds then sat down in his desk chair and blew air out of his mouth in an exaggerated manner with puffed cheeks. He then rubbed his forehead with his right hand before making eye contact again with Osborne. "Well, that sucks," he said.

"It certainly does," Osborne replied.

"Do we know by whom?" Reynolds asked.

"No," Osborne answered. "He certainly had a lot of enemies. Government?"

"I doubt it, at least not this soon," Reynolds replied. "I don't put it past our Feds to do this sort of thing, but there's no way they could have acted this quickly. NDSA is essentially completely down right now, so they are out of the question. Any other agency would need time to figure it out, develop and vet a plan, and put assets in place to do it."

"Agreed," Osborne replied.

"Maybe unrelated to recent events?" Reynolds speculated. "Maybe some European Government, or even the Russians, made him and his takedown was in the works for a while."

Osborne didn't respond. "I know," Reynolds said, "too much of a coincidence."

"You know my worst fear, boss?"

"Barber, somehow?" Reynolds asked.

"Yes."

"He runs a corporate intelligence and security service," Reynolds continued. "He's been inconveniently good at connecting a lot of dots, and his capabilities are obviously a lot better than we assumed, but he does defense. He doesn't do offense. And he certainly doesn't do wet work."

"Agree with all your points, boss. But I don't like coincidences. I don't DO coincidences."

"Neither do I," Reynolds said. "Is your asset in place yet?"

"She's close."

"Tell her we will double her fee if she completes the job within 24 hours."

"We don't exactly know where Barber is right now, boss."

"OK," Reynolds replied. "Make it 48 hours."

"He owns a plane," Osborne said.

"OK, make it 72 hours, but this guy has to be taken out in no more than 3 days or I fear our risk of disclosure starts to climb exponentially."

"Done," Osborne agreed, then turned and started to walk out of Reynolds' office.

"Jim," Reynolds said as Osborne placed his hand on the office door and turned the handle to open it. Osborne paused and looked back at his boss.

"Tell her we'll triple the fee."

Chapter 59 -- Emilee

Cross Fit Gym, Fredericksburg, VA, present time

At five feet five inches tall, she did not possess the stature that would strike an imposing figure; she was an imposing figure nevertheless. She weighed a solid 133 pounds. Hanging from the chin-up bar in her gym shorts and sports bra made it abundantly evident that it was 133 pounds of mostly muscle. But she didn't possess the physique of a body builder. Her arms and legs appeared dense with striking definition, but they would not be considered large for her frame. In spite of their normal proportions, her limbs looked powerful, very powerful, almost like the mechanical arms in a junkyard that could lift and crush steel. And they framed a torso of washboard abs. As she completed her 17th chin-up and pulled her head above the bar, the muscles in her shoulders and back displayed an impressive show of force and definition, like a series of thick bands popping and twisting underneath her skin. They were large enough to broadcast undeniable strength, but they were not large, per se. They were just there, but really there. Seventeen pull-ups would be considered an impressive feat for any athlete, even a Cross Fit enthusiast like her, but she was doing it with twenty pounds of weight chained to her waist. And she wasn't done.

She had blond hair, almost white with a slight hue of yellow that betrayed her Nordic lineage, along with a pleasant face and green eyes. She would be considered attractive but not beautiful. In her street clothes she looked almost ordinary, her muscular frame hidden under layers of clothes. She preferred to dress that way in all but the hottest summer months. Masking her athleticism caused people to underestimate her. She found that useful.

Emelie Magnesson was 32 years old and had been an athlete her entire life. Her sport of choice while growing up in her native Sweden was field hockey. She loved the close quarters combat of the game. She loved its reliance on strength for the scrum and peak conditioning. She took up Cross Fit as a way to acquire both and soon became a hooked, full-on endorphin junky. She was good at the game but not great. She would stumble across her greatness in another field of endeavor, almost by accident.

Four years ago, she had been discharged from her service with the Swedish Army. In Sweden, all military billets were open to women, including combat ones. She had displayed so much talent during unarmed combat training that she was promoted directly to Sergeant and made an instructor. Some of her larger male students would instinctively underestimate her and even go easy on her when told to attack during a training session. It was a decision they would always regret. She could easily put down a much larger man, and she loved doing it. She found her true calling, however, the moment she picked up a rifle. She entered sniper training and could put a tight pattern in a target at 1,800 yards, something few of her peers could replicate. She left the Army under somewhat questionable circumstances, however, after a diagnosis of antisocial personality disorder. It was considered borderline, but clearly something about her brain wasn't wired correctly. Problem was she enjoyed putting down larger men and looked for opportunities to do it never showing the slightest hint of remorse. Officers were her favorite target, and that complicated things. The Army decided it wasn't a great trait for a sniper, so she was given a medical discharge. It was not voluntary, and initially she had been angry about it. They had given her a choice. The straw that broke the camel's back was that training incident with the newly minted Lieutenant where three guys had to pull her off him. Arrest and a formal disciplinary hearing, then criminal charges, beckoned at the end of that road. Or she could take a voluntary separation, files sealed, then submit to psychiatric counseling and get on with her life. She opted for the latter. She loved what she did, but she found military discipline tedious and was fed up with saluting men and women she regarded as her inferiors. It was presented to her as a separation under mutually agreeable circumstances and she accepted. She went to a few of the psychiatry sessions for show then quietly disappeared. She had a plan. The premature discharge would open the door to a whole new career path for her, one that was much more lucrative, and one that would take her to the United States.

She tended to avoid serious relationships. Anything serious would present too many "professional" challenges. Of course, she didn't live the life of a monk either. No surprise, her periodic entanglements had a habit of not ending well for the men who tried to cross her path. There was that time, for example, she had gone on a date with a football player from the Washington Redskins, a second-string defensive lineman who weighed about 275 pounds. He was a superb athlete who regarded himself, not without considerable justification, as a "pretty boy". It was a combination that gave him an ego even bigger than his body mass. As they walked together into a local Georgetown parking garage after dinner, he decided it was a good time to test his luck and get a bit aggressive with a come-on. Bad decision! She politely turned down his advance. Her demure only emboldened him. He tried a second time. Now she was becoming angry, not frightened, just really pissed off. She drew energy from the emotion, almost like an endorphin high. She uttered an obscenity, then turned and started to walk away. She was done. Easy enough to grab an Uber in this part of town, she thought, as she started to confidently walk towards the garage exit. Her entire demeanor telegraphed a sense that she didn't even regard the guy as a threat, and that really angered him. She needed to be taught a lesson. No woman could resist the pretty boy, he thought. No woman was going to say no to the pretty boy. He caught up with her and grabbed her elbow, then tried to turn her around. He was smiling. He was going to enjoy this he told himself. He wasn't trying to hurt her, but he intended to telegraph something himself – physical dominance and an unwillingness to take no for an answer. Another bad decision. He hadn't grasped his deteriorating reality; he was about to become prey. He emerged from the experience with a permanent limp and as a result, unemployed. He was actually lucky. She had only been playing with him. If he had actually tried to hurt her, he likely wouldn't have emerged from the incident at all. The guy had no idea what she was capable of. He had been playing with a pit viper.

She let go of the chinning bar and dropped to the gym floor after pull up number 22. As she did so, she heard a loud clang about 10 feet away as a heavy barbell was racked after some body-builder type completed a set of heavy bench presses. She reflexively looked in the direction of the noise and noticed the guy's spotter had his eyes on her and not his training partner. The spotter was quite a specimen himself, but as her reflexive look morphed into a glare, he immediately turned away. She had that effect on people. She was a person not to be trifled with. The aura radiated from her.

Her attention shifted as she heard her cell phone chirp inside her gym bag, indicating an incoming text message. She unzipped the bag, retrieved the phone and looked at the message displayed on the still-locked screen. It simply read: "Interested in dinner tonight?" It wasn't an invitation to dinner. It was a coded text telling her to check the encrypted Internet message board she used to communicate with her clients. Adding the word "tonight?" to the end of the text meant she needed to do it quickly.

Impatient clients annoyed her, but they were occupational hazards. Her work required careful planning, rehearsal, and picking the perfect time and place to deliver her commitment. It couldn't be rushed. The process was equal parts flawless execution and risk management. She had to do it right the first time, every time. There were seldom second chances in her line of work. And it was essential that she walk away from every successful assignment with absolutely no chance of attribution. Anything less and the consequences would be catastrophic.

She showered at a deliberate but unhurried pace, not allowing the urgent nature of the text message to alter her stride or compromise her professional discipline. She dressed back into her street clothes, still unhurried, and walked calmly out of the gym into the parking lot. The hot midsummer Virginia sun felt good on her face as she walked towards her car. The sky above her was a clear azure blue, although she could see dark clouds to the West. The humidity was in the high 80s and the forecasters were predicting thunderstorms later that evening. The modest breeze felt good and caused her to momentarily forget the annoying client. She pressed the button on the key fob of her one-year old Lexus LS sedan and heard the vehicle chirp to betray its location. She enjoyed the car, its luxury and every one of its 416 horsepower. She could have easily afforded an exotic Italian sports car but she liked how the Lexus broadcast her success in a way that didn't beg too many questions. That was professionally useful.

She lived on Washington Avenue in the historic district of Fredericksburg, Virginia. It was reasonably close to the Nation's capital which was beneficial for her work yet still provided a decent amount of breathing room from the congestion and high security of Washington, DC. Central Virginia was also more rural and gun friendly, which provided a number of professional advantages.

At the conclusion of a fifteen-minute drive, she pulled the Lexus into her driveway, got out of the vehicle and walked towards her front door. Just before entering the house key into the lock she pushed the button on the Lexus' key fob which produced another chirp to confirm the vehicle was successfully locked. She walked into the house, dropped her gym bag on the foyer floor and then proceeded directly into the study just to the right of the entrance. She clicked on the light, then sat down at an elegant but

517

understated six-foot-long desk she had purchased from Restoration Hardware. She opened her laptop and logged into the encrypted message board. There was a simple, three phrase message waiting for her. It read "Sierra Charlie. Essential that you complete delivery within 72 hours. Normal commission tripled." A flash of irritation welled up in her. Sierra Charlie was military code for the letters SC which meant "situation critical". More likely a client's unwarranted panic than something truly critical, she thought. She started typing her response. "Delivery guarantee remains consistent with original agreement of one week. Expedited delivery entirely at my discretion. Best efforts only." She clicked send, then moved the curser to another icon representing the target package and clicked again. A document opened. It contained the name, address and other background information on her target, along with several pictures. The target himself was a middle-aged man, reasonably fit. He ran a security business of some sort. She was never given a reason for her assignments. She could care less about whatever it was this guy did to warrant her attention. It wasn't important. She clicked on the next picture which displayed the image of an expensive looking twin-engine airplane. She noticed the tail number of the aircraft was clearly visible. Very useful, she thought. She could access the FAA flight plan website to see if the target had any near-term travel plans. She quickly memorized the tail number, opened a new tab, logged on to the FAA website and entered the aircraft's identifier. After several seconds another document was opened. Pay dirt! How could she be this lucky, she thought. The FAA website revealed the aircraft had just completed a flight yesterday from Michigan. A new flight plan was filed for tomorrow morning. The aircraft was to be flown to Rye, New York where the target lived. But that wasn't the best part. The plane had landed yesterday and was to leave tomorrow morning from Stafford, Virginia. Stafford was just a short drive from Fredericksburg, right up the I-95 corridor. And the pilot was the target himself. That request for accelerated timing was now starting to be reasonable. And the triple commission was now looking very likely. She sat there staring at the screen not believing her luck, then logged off all the open pages and closed the laptop.

She rose from the desk, walked out of the study towards the back of the house and into the family room. On the wall opposite the outside picture window sat a large gun safe. Gun safes were not exactly a rare item in central Virginia and hiding one in plain site was part of her tradecraft. She spun the combination dial back and forth several times to unlock it, turned a stainless-steel handle and opened the right hand door. She pulled a Steyr SSG 69 Austrian sniper rifle from a display mount and examined it. It was chambered for NATO 7.62 X 51mm rounds, essentially much like the .308 Winchester hunting round and was crazy accurate. Atop it sat a Leupold VX-2 snipe scope. She examined the weapon, almost lovingly, placed it back in the safe and prepared to lock it. "You and I will play together again very soon, my little girl," she said to the rifle as she took one last look before closing the safe door and spinning the dial.

She was looking forward to the job. She loved her work. She found it peaceful. And this assignment was close to home. She'd be back in Fredericksburg in time for lunch.

Chapter 60 – Target Acquisition

Stafford Regional Airport, the next morning

The morning sun glistened off the skin of the majestic looking Beechcraft King Air C90 as it sat on the ramp just outside the small but modern looking terminal building. A fuel truck sat next to it as an attendant filled the starboard wing tank with jet fuel for the twin-turbine engines that would power the bird back to its home in Rye, New York. Joe Barber stood in the terminal building, cell phone to his ear, and carefully listened to a weather briefing from Lockheed-Martin's Flight Services. After getting the detailed weather report for his flight path, he then verbally filed an IFR flight plan for the short trip home. A quick stop in the men's room before departure was an essential part of his flight prep, he always joked to himself. It was important to keep one tank full and one tank empty. He had learned early in his flight training that nothing could compromise one's attention to detail on a short-final approach to landing like a painfully full bladder. After the quick stop, he returned to the service counter to sign the credit card bill for his fuel, then with his flight pack slung over his left shoulder and his duffle in his right hand, he proceeded towards the door and braced himself for the hot Virginia morning sun and high humidity.

About 400 yards away, just inside a tree line, Emilee Magnesson lay in a prone position wearing a digital camouflage coverall underneath a full ghillie suit. The ghillie suit was a standard part of the tradecraft for a military sniper and rendered her all but invisible in the overgrown weeds and brush. Her Austrian Steyr sniper rifle lay on the ground next to her, supported by a bipod and fully masked by its own cover. She looked through the scope and gently moved the rifle back and forth to survey the target area. The aircraft filled a good portion of her field of vision through the powerful scope. The Bird was

521

parked parallel to the terminal door with its port, or left-hand side, facing her. That was good, because just to the rear of the left wing was the location of the airplane's door. That meant that the target would have to walk right into her field of fire to enter it. Perfect. Also, at a distance of only 400 yards, give or take a little, it wouldn't be a particularly difficult shot for someone of her capabilities. She would aim for center mass. Headshots were how Hollywood liked to portray this sort of thing, but in the real world no sniper would choose a small target over a larger one if they had a choice. And the round she was firing would bore a hole through the target's chest so large that chances of surviving it were essentially zero. The round would also easily pierce any protective body armor the target might be wearing, although the chance of Joe Barber wearing a bulletproof vest as he walked from the terminal to the airplane was essentially zero as well. The only contingency that might require a headshot would be if he somehow managed to get into the aircraft before she could fire. That would require her to shoot him through the window. It would be a much more difficult shot, but at this distance she knew she could do it. That contingency was very unlikely unless that fuel truck or a person got in the way.

Barber turned slightly sideways and used his right shoulder to push the terminal door open. He instantly missed the cool of the building's air conditioning system as the morning heat and humidity assaulted his face and engulfed him as he proceeded out the door and onto the ramp. He said "good morning" to the ramp attendant as the young woman was re-coiling the fueling hose back onto its reel on the side of the truck. He walked around the tail of the aircraft towards the open door, tossed his duffle in and set his flight bag on the ground. He would need access to the bag to retrieve his walk-around checklists. Doing a thorough walk around the bird to "make sure all the big pieces are still hanging on," as pilots like to joke and say, was an important part of the pre-flight prep.

Emilee's pulse quickened slightly as the target walked into her view. It was a natural physiological response and something her training would allow her to easily dissipate. This was the point where she needed to crawl into the zone, that place where she bathed herself in complete calm and became one with the rifle. Slow down the heart, sense the cadence of its beat, and slowly take up slack on the trigger in prep for that final step that would be completed between heartbeats. She closed her eyes momentarily, took a cleansing breath, and descended quickly towards that place.

Barber bent over, unzipped the top of his flight bag, and retrieved a laminated card that displayed the necessary checklist. He took off his sunglasses, folded them closed, then hooked one of the ear pieces over the second button of his golf shirt as a resting place until the walk around was complete. He lifted the checklist up to review it and kept it in his hand as a reference as he began to examine the aircraft to ensure it was in good shape to fly. Even though pilots did the exact same series of tasks thousands of times, they always read every item on the list as each individual task was completed and did so every time they flew. Missing something on a checklist was a common cause behind fatal crashes, even for experienced pilots.

The target was now standing erect with his back towards her. She had no problem shooting the target in the back. Picking the exact moment and precise profile for the shot had nothing to do with honor. It had everything to do with efficiency and probability of success. She was now fully in her zone. The target was stationary and at the optimum spot in her cross hairs. She was perfectly in tune with her heartbeat and one with her rifle. She knew that a good shot meant the muted bark of the rifle would almost come as a surprise to her. She started to increase pressure on the trigger.

Chapter 61 – Man Down

The Stafford County, Virginia deputy sheriff's patrol car slowly pulled up behind the late model car that was parked on the side of the unpaved road. The deputy sheriff had noticed a cloud of dust rising from the road while he was on a routine patrol near the airport and decided to drive up and take a look. The road provided access to the airport's light beacon tower. The tower flashed a bright blinking light after dusk that pilots used to locate the airport at night. He wasn't alarmed, but thought it unusual that somebody would be up there this early in the morning. He was particularly suspicious that some kids might be up to mischief and trying to vandalize the beacon.

As he stopped behind the parked vehicle, he put his patrol car in park, reached for the radio and called in the license plate. It was a rental car, owned by Budget. That meant it certainly wasn't kids, but the information made the circumstances even more unusual. Who in the world would drive a rental car up here, and for what purpose, he wondered. He concluded the only way to find out was to get out of the patrol car and go for a walk.

"What the.......?" A voice called out from what sounded like several feet behind Emilee as she was about a nanosecond from completing the trigger pull. "Lady, you can't hunt here!" a man's voice barked with authority. "Stafford County Sheriff's office. I'm going to need you to step away from that firearm and show me some identification."

She let go of the weapon and turned her head around to take a look at the officer. Once turned around, she sat up and pulled back the hood of her ghillie suit to uncover her head, then said, "I'm sorry officer," in a meek voice.

"Ma'am you are on airport property which means you have broken a whole bunch of laws by bringing that firearm up here. Please stand up and show me some identification."

"Of course," she said. "I'm so sorry, officer. I didn't know. My driver's license is in the zippered pocket on my right hip here." She slowly moved her hand downward, unzipped the pocket, then slipped her hand inside.

Something about the scene just didn't set well with the deputy. He looked down at the rifle. It looked expensive and the scope even more so. He looked up at the girl. Why in the world would she go to the trouble of camouflaging herself in a ghillie suit, he wondered. He then looked back at the rifle and noted the direction to which it was pointed. It was pointed towards the airport. Then it all clicked. The pieces came together, and he realized what the scene actually meant. His brain sent a signal to his mouth to yell, "Stop!" as he slowly processed a potential threat from her hand movement. His hand started to move towards his service revolver, snapped tightly in the holster on his hip. He was too late. In a flash Emilee pulled a silenced Glock 19 out of the zippered pocket, and before the deputy could even process what was happening she put two rounds in his chest and one in his forehead. He was dead before he hit the ground. She suddenly became aware of the sound of roaring engines. She turned to look. The King Air, and her target, were lifting off the runway and rapidly climbing. It now looked like she wasn't going to get that performance bonus after all.

Chapter 62 – When It's Not Your Time to Die

Aboard the King Air, real time

Barber looked at the aircraft's vertical speed indicator to confirm the bird had achieved a positive rate of climb. He then reached up and lifted a lever on the flight deck to retract the landing gear. As he did so, he felt the slightest shudder, then heard an alarm go off indicating there was a problem with the left, or port engine. Looking at the engine's performance gauges, he noticed a dramatic drop in oil pressure, which signaled what was likely a catastrophic failure. He noticed smoke starting to pour out of the nacelle, the aluminum cladding that covered the engine, and the shudder became much worse.

Emergency procedures started to flash through his mind. Altitude and airspeed, he thought, the two most important things to have in an emergency. He was screwed on the altitude thing – he was just a few hundred feet off the ground after takeoff. But speed. At this moment in time speed meant survival. He looked at his indicated airspeed gauge and was momentarily relieved to confirm the plane had accelerated beyond the minimum control speed, or VMC, for continued flight with thrust from the remaining engine. That meant he could continue his climb, albeit at a much slower rate, turn the plane back into the airport's traffic pattern and land. The relief was short-lived, however, as the right side of the plane's windshield suddenly blew out, with the force of the wind spraying shards of plexiglass back into the cockpit. His first thought was he had suffered a bird strike. It would certainly explain the engine failure, but it shouldn't have damaged the windshield that badly. And the windshield shouldn't have blown out. It should have blown in, or more likely the bird should have just bounced up

527

the windshield's slant and not dislodged the windshield at all. He then noticed a hole in the headrest of the right-hand seat. Holy crap, he thought. It looked like a bullet hole. Somebody was shooting at the plane!

The combination of a dead engine and severe aerodynamic drag from the missing right windshield were now causing a rapid loss of airspeed. He was at the moment of truth when a pilot realizes his airplane is about to quit flying. The danger was all the more real because it happened shortly after takeoff and he was only 600 feet off the ground. The more altitude between an airplane and the ground, the more time and flexibility a pilot has to deal with the emergency. Barber now had precious little of either.

Things started to unfold before him in slow motion. Emergency procedures, he said to himself again. He immediately started looking for a place to land. Then things got worse. The left engine was now on fire. Not a good thing to happen with full fuel tanks, he thought. Pilots liked to say there was only one time you had too much gas, and that was when the airplane was on fire. He struggled to fly the plane as the controls became more sluggish and was now worried the bullet might have damaged some of the control surfaces. He muscled the control yoke to the left to aim for a cornfield. It was the only landing site he could see that offered a reasonable chance of survival. The airplane barely changed direction. He then realized the lone right engine was compounding his problem by creating a torque-induced proclivity to turn to the right. But to his right was Interstate 95 and a lot of early morning commuter traffic. Trying to set the plane down there would be catastrophic and would likely result in much loss of life. He pulled back the throttle for the right engine, bringing it to idle and eliminating its thrust. The loss of thrust would cause him to descend more quickly but would also reduce the torque that was working against his attempt to turn towards a safer crash area. It worked. Unfortunately, as he feared, he had traded one problem for another. A stand of trees was between him and the cornfield, and he had to get past them, over them, to get to the field. His speed continued to slow and his rate of descent increased. It was going to be very close.

As he approached the stand of trees he pulled back on the control yoke to increase the airplane's lift and slow the descent. Problem was that bled off airspeed as well, and he now was dangerously close to the stall speed of the airplane. If the airspeed fell below the stall speed the wings would suddenly lose their lift and the bird would literally fall out of whatever sky he had left. As he started to cross the trees, he guessed he was no more than 10 feet above the tallest ones. Three quarters of the way across, he felt the undercarriage of the King Air start scraping branches, but he kept moving forward. He must have just grazed the tops, he thought, but he knew that friction from the encounter would still cost him more precious airspeed. As he passed the last of the trees, with the open cornfield ahead, he was still about 100 feet off the ground. He pushed the control yoke forward to try and capture a little more speed and avoid a stall. A drop from 100 feet would most certainly be fatal. If the crash didn't kill him, the resulting fireball certainly would. The stall warning alarm was ringing throughout the cockpit as he passed through 30, then 20, then 10 feet off the ground. He pulled back hard on the sluggish controls to keep from hitting the ground nose first and tumbling into a catastrophic breakup. It worked, and the nose started to rise.

He felt the tail hit the ground. The airplane then was assaulted by hundreds of mature cornstalks as it started sliding on its belly through the field at over 70 knots. Chunks of corn stalk and cobs were flying through the open side of the cockpit and ricocheting around the interior like shrapnel, assaulting his body and face. The plane was bouncing violently as it slid across the field. The energy of each bounce was being transmitted through the bottom of the seat and painfully up his spine. The violent deceleration threw the upper half of his body forward. His entire chest felt like it exploded as the shoulder harness brought his body's forward momentum to a sudden stop. The harness prevented him from slamming his head into the flight deck but didn't stop it from a violent forward snap that hurt like hell as his brain collided suddenly with the inside front of his skull. A leaf from one of the stalks, dried and hardened by the sun, sliced through the side of his right cheek as if it were a surgeon's scalpel. Then suddenly everything was quite. Everything was still. He was no longer moving. There was no fire, at least not yet. He hurt all over, but he was alive. Somehow, he had survived. It must not be my day to die, he thought. He slowly lifted his throbbing head and looked around the inside of the cabin. His vision was graying out, but he could still see. He noticed again the bullet hole in the headrest of the seat next to him.

Now even more than ever, he had a score to settle. Then everything went black.

Chapter 63 – The Protégé

Offices of PrinSafe, Palo Alto, 48 hours later

Westy Reynolds was really feeling his oats. He had just concluded a meeting with an Oligarch who owned a third of Russia's natural gas reserves. Reynolds had pitched a natural gas pipeline project that would connect a new field in the Crimea to points west. Both men emerged from the meeting with a sense of being the winner. The Russian was sitting on a secret. The Crimean discovery was believed to have the potential of being one of the biggest natural gas fields ever discovered. They had to keep that fact close to the vest, however, or the price of natural gas futures would plummet before the new capacity came online and generated revenue. There was also something very delicious about American capital financing an infrastructure project in their newly annexed province. Reynolds was fully aware of the field's potential, however, thanks to a secret CIA report he had gotten from his paid informant inside the Agency. As soon as he secured the pipeline contract, he planned to start quietly shorting natural gas futures, then arrange an untraceable leak of the discovery news.

Dr. Emma Clark walked into his office and found her boss in an exceptionally good mood. It was in sharp contrast to the previous day, when she had to deliver the news that a third attempt to take out Joe Barber had failed. Reynolds was apoplectic about the screw up and let loose a volcanic tirade, demanding to know how an asset could be so stupid as to shoot at an airplane on takeoff instead of following the guy to his home in Rye and quietly completing the job the next day. The sniper's stunt was going to bring down a storm of federal agents from FBI and Homeland to investigate, and that was exposure nobody needed. Reynolds' anger was justified, but his obsession about Barber was becoming a real problem. He couldn't let go, and he was starting to take unacceptable risks. He had actually ordered Clark to find another asset to take out Barber in what would be a fourth attempt, and then to cover their tracks, eliminate the asset who screwed up. She had tried to convince him otherwise, arguing that there was no way Barber was ever going to connect the dots back to them unless they continued dropping breadcrumbs with repeated assassination attempts. He had exploded at that comment. He was becoming reckless, and she was greatly concerned that his recklessness was going to bleed into other areas of the business. What made Reynolds so formidable was the combination of his extraordinary intelligence coupled with his equally extraordinary discipline and self-control. He was losing the latter.

But Reynolds had another blind spot. He had made Emma Clark the firm's continuity plan; his designated successor. He knew her capabilities. What he misjudged was the extent of her ambitions. He thought he fed it well, or at least sufficiently. Her compensation was second only to his, and she ran the crown jewel of the darker side of his empire, QuarkSpin. She was the "go to" person for any difficult task that required the dark arts and great discretion, and she answered that call with ruthless efficiency. She was a trusted advisor on all of the most important strategic decisions of the firm. He regarded her as his protégé. But there is another name for protégé, and it's called second fiddle. Like so many gifted protégés, Dr. Clark had become impatient with her mentor. Every great mentor had the same fatal flaw. They didn't know when to let go. They always held on too long, created great impatience in those waiting in the wings, and worse, started making mistakes. In most of the business world it usually resulted in eventually being shown the door. In the world of Charles Westbourne Reynolds, III the endgame was seldom that benign.

As she walked further into his office, she proffered a Starbucks coffee carrier with two cups in it. Reynolds lifted the cup closest to him, said "Thank you," and sat down at the large conference table. She extracted the other cup and sat down as well. They began discussing how they would finish vetting the Crimean project before wiring the initial funding. Reynolds continued his upbeat mood and was particularly enthusiastic about the profit potential from selling short natural gas futures. An hour and a half later the meeting concluded, and she stood up to leave. Both coffee cups were now empty. She proffered the coffee carrier again and suggested he slip his empty cup in it next to hers, so that she could throw them both away. He did so. She walked out of his office holding the carrier with the empty cups as far from her body as she could without creating suspicion. Just outside the door, she deposited the debris into the trash container. The container was emptied every afternoon, and the contents would be long gone and untraceable by the time anyone figured out what had happened. She returned to the building, went to the ladies' room and washed her hands thoroughly for about 15 minutes. She then proceeded back to her guest office in the building to get some additional work done. No point in returning to the QuarkSpin offices until later in the day, she thought. After all, she had another meeting with Reynolds in about two hours.

Stanford Medical Center

It was an extraordinarily unpleasant death. His first symptoms were acute stomach cramps, diarrhea and vomiting. Exhaustive testing failed to yield a diagnosis, at least initially. The illness progressed to severe kidney and liver damage. They suspected a virulent strain of cancer, but the speed of onset was puzzling, especially for a man who just a short time ago had been so healthy. Then his hair began to fall out. An extraordinarily wealthy man like Reynolds, of course, had access to the very best of medical resources. Not that it would change the outcome, but it could help solve the mystery. A nuclear medicine specialist from Stanford Medical Center was asked to consult, and he suspected acute radiation syndrome; but the normal testing

533

kept returning negative results. Finally, blood and urine samples were sent to Los Alamos Labs for testing, using a highly specialized process called gamma spectroscopy. Initially those results were negative, until a very skilled set of eyes noticed a slight gamma ray spike at an energy of about 803 kilo-electron volts, barely visible above the background. As luck would have it, the specialist was from Great Britain and was the same person who had investigated the mysterious death of the Russian spy, Alexander Litvinenko. Litvinenko had shown exactly the same symptoms as Reynolds. The culprit was Polonium 210, a radiation agent that after being ingested, cooked a person's insides. Reynolds remained lucid enough to be told what happened. He died believing his recent Russian business partners had fed him the radioactive agent to silence him about the natural gas field discovery. He never knew it was his protégé and heir apparent, Dr. Emma Clark, who had engineered his brutal, brilliant and perfectly timed demise.

Chapter 64 – A Change of Profession

Historic District, Fredericksburg VA, Two Weeks Later

Emilee Magnesson pulled up in front of her home and placed her Lexus sedan in park. She sat in the vehicle a few extra seconds for no particular reason. She was exhausted, physically and emotionally. The client had been very clear in the communication she had read on the encrypted, internet message board. They had pulled the contract on her recent target. She had not only lost the performance bonus, she had lost any payment whatsoever. There had been no reasons given. It was just a brief message that the "engagement", as they had called it, was terminated. She didn't need an explanation. She had screwed up, and she knew it. Shooting down an airplane taking off from an airport, even a smaller, local airport, to say nothing of the collateral damage of a dead deputy sheriff, created a statewide manhunt and was a prominent story on several national evening news cycles. She was going to have to lay low for quite some time, then likely leave the country to escape this one. There was plenty of work to be done in Europe, she told herself, especially Eastern Europe, although the lifestyle would not be so pleasant. She would miss Virginia, but at this point she was quite happy not to be rotting in some jail.

She finally exited the car, and with gym bag in hand, pushed the key fob to elicit the familiar chirp confirming the vehicle was safely locked. She walked up to the door, disarmed the alarm system, unlocked the door, opened it, and walked inside. Her first order of business was to step into her study and fire up the laptop to look for messages, not that she expected any. After checking the message board, her email, and several news websites, she got up and walked through the kitchen towards her family room.

As she passed into the kitchen she noticed something in her peripheral vision. The family room seemed very dark. Odd, she thought. She didn't remember closing the drapes that morning. As her brain started processing a number of sensory inputs, she became overwhelmed with a sense of foreboding. Goose bumps erupted over both her arms, and the hair on the back of her neck stood up, driven by some sixth sense that something was terribly out of place. Then she noticed him. A man was sitting in the burgundy leather Churchill chair in the corner of the family room, just to her right. He was wearing a Washington Nationals baseball cap and mirrored aviator style sunglasses. He was also holding what she could see was a Glock 19 pistol with a long cylindrical suppressor emanating from the barrel.

"Please take a seat on the sofa," the man said in a calm and quiet voice.

Her mind was racing. She was angry with herself again. She wasn't armed, and the nearest weapon was in a gun safe on the kitchen counter about seven feet from where she stood. Anger wasn't a productive emotion in her present predicament, she reminded herself, and so she put it out of her mind. Every synapse in her brain was now working overtime to try and find a way to neutralize the threat, but at the moment she knew she had no choice but to comply. At least that would buy her a little more time. She walked over to the sofa, positioned across and at a slight angle to the man, sat down, then asked, "Who are you, and what do you want?"

"What I want first is to introduce myself," he said. "I understand you've been looking for me. My name is Joseph Michael Barber."

She swallowed hard at hearing his name. She immediately realized his identity combined with the silenced Glock meant this was not going to end well for her. Think, she told herself.

"What do you want?" she asked, hoping to buy a little more time to figure out what to do before he made a move that would likely end her.

"I don't suppose you'd be willing to buy me a new airplane, would you?" he asked.

She didn't respond.

"Didn't think so," he said. "So how about this," he continued, "let's take a little walk into the kitchen and have you sit down in that chair." He pointed to the chair with the Glock's suppressor. It had a cushioned seat and back and two wooden arms. "Turn the chair towards me and have a seat, please. Do it slowly. I'll admit I'm still a bit sore from your little stunt a couple of weeks ago so I'm not going to risk an altercation. If you make any sudden moves and I will double-tap you in the head. Are we clear on that point?"

"Yes," she responded.

"Good," Barber replied. "This would not be a good time to test my veracity."

What was this guy up to, she wondered, as she walked towards the chair, turned it around and sat. Things were taking on the appearance of an interrogation, but at least she was still breathing, she thought. "You know I have no idea who my client is. And you also know that's not the way this business works. Our clients never give us their names. It would be reckless for them."

Barber didn't respond. He walked behind her and placed the Glock at the back of her head. "We are going to do a little preparation. If you make any sudden moves I will put a round in the back of your skull. I am sure you are a very skilled operator in spite of your recent screw up at Stafford airport. I assure you I am even better, and I have a pretty compelling motive right now to do exactly what I just threatened, so don't try my patience. Your best chance for survival is to do exactly as I say. Do we understand each other?" he asked.

"Yes," she answered, with no further comment.

"Good," he replied. He pulled a roll of duct take out of his jacket pocket. He tore off two strips of it and instructed her to tightly tape both ankles to the chair. She complied. He then tore another long strip and laid the adhesive up over her right forearm. "I'd like you to take that strip and tape your right forearm to the chair's arm. Do it tightly please. I'll be watching."

She complied. He tore off another strip, and momentarily let it dangle from his fingertip as he placed the Glock firmly at the base of her skull, forcing her head forward a bit. "Now I am going to tape your left forearm myself. Any sudden moves and this exercise will quickly end in a less pleasant manner. Believe it or not, if you behave you may actually survive this." He carefully affixed her left forearm to the chair. He then pulled off a third strip of duct tape, much longer this time. Before she even realized what was happening, in a swift move he threw the tape over her head, yanked her upper torso backwards with it and affixed her snugly to the chair. She was now completely immobilized. He took a final small strip of tape and placed it over her mouth. As he continued to stand behind her, she heard two clinks as he laid two items on the kitchen's granite countertop. It then sounded like he plugged something into the electrical outlet just under the counter. She couldn't see the items. They were a pair of pruning shears and a soldering iron.

Barber placed the Glock back into the shoulder holster under his jacket. He then pulled a smaller automatic pistol out, a .22 caliber which was also equipped with a suppressor. While still standing behind her, in a quick motion, he reached out, placed the muzzle of the .22 against the top of her wrist, and fired a shot. She screamed out in pain, but the tape over her mouth muffled the sound.

"I could kill you if you prefer," he said, as he grabbed the back of the chair and lowered her to the ground. "But there's been way too much killing, so instead I'm going to suggest a change of profession." Barber retrieved the pair of pruning shears with his right hand and held her right index finger tightly in his left hand. She was screaming again and thrashing back and forth in the chair in an effort to release herself from his grip but to no avail. He then snipped off her index finger at its base like it was a small branch he needed to prune. He repeated the exercise on her middle finger. Retrieving the soldering iron, which was now glowing red hot, he cauterized both of the wounds. Muffled sounds of an animal's agony emanated from her taped mouth as the red-hot soldering iron burned flesh to stop the bleeding. He set the soldering iron back on the counter and unplugged it. "All over now," he said, almost with the voice of a doctor who had just treated a painful injury in the emergency room. He pulled the chair back into an upright position. She was sobbing. He tossed a bottle of pills in her lap and said, "That's 10 days worth of penicillin. It's not exactly like you are going to go to the local emergency room, is it? At least you're not going to be killing anyone anymore." Her career as a sniper was over.

Barber pulled out a pocketknife and cut loose the tape on her left arm. "Unless you want to give me one more chance to put a bullet into your head, I suggest you sit there quietly for about 5 minutes before freeing yourself." With that, he gathered his things and walked out.

Epilogue

Offices of PrinSafe, Palo Alto, One Week Later

Dr. Emma Clark sat in the relative spartan guest office she was accustomed to using during her visits to PrinSafe's headquarters. It had been several weeks now since she had assumed the Chief Executive position as provided in the Last Will and Testament of Charles Westbourne Reynolds, III. She thought it would be bad form to take over Reynolds' office so shortly after his demise.

The front page of the New York Times was laid out on her desk and she was fascinated as she read the lead story, displayed on the paper's right-hand column above the fold:

White House vows ruthless investigation of "Deep State" factions allegedly behind Federal Response to recent terrorist events

The Einhorn Administration promised a thorough and relentless investigation of the forces behind the botched, extra-legal Federal response to the high-profile terrorist events over the last several weeks. The scope of the investigation is said to include the attacks in Detroit, Tyson's Corner, Virginia, San Francisco, and the mysterious Federal Government offices in McLean Virginia. Unnamed sources confirmed the growing consensus among Administration insiders that a cohort of senior Federal officials, potentially including those at the Cabinet and sub-Cabinet level, are behind recent events. It is also believed that those responsible worked directly with other state-sponsored intelligence agencies without the Administration's permission or knowledge. President Einhorn has promised that no stone will be unturned in an effort to bring those responsible to justice. In what is believed to be a related development, the Secretary of Homeland Security, the Attorney

541

General and the Director of the FBI were fired this morning and placed under arrest in what was described as a house cleaning. Their whereabouts are presently unknown. When asked for clarification of the summary dismissals, the White House issued a "no comment". Members of the Republican minority leadership of Congress have demanded an immediate investigation of the dismissals and have demanded transparency regarding the location and status of the individuals in question. During a special news conference, The Speaker of the House promised an investigation would be forthcoming, but advised they planned to wait until the Administration concluded its preliminary review so as not to impede that process. This is an unfolding story, so please check www.nytimes.com for real-time updates throughout the day.

Perfect, Clark thought. Fake news stories would be fed into Facebook and Twitter throughout the coming days to bolster the story, all courtesy of QuarkSpin's digital forensics lab. There was much work to be done. She was going to build something even better from the ashes of this disaster. She reflected on her mentor's saying, that "The ashes of today's defeat yield the DNA for tomorrow's greatest victory for those smart enough and committed enough to see the opportunity and pursue it." She would miss Westy, but not very much.

Her thoughts were interrupted by a buzz from the intercom. "Yes," she said.

"Dr. Clark, the President of the United States is on the phone."

The End

(For now………)

Soli Deo Gloria

Made in the USA
Columbia, SC
10 December 2020